24

Avi Burra

Casanostra Creations

To Monika and Ishan, who inspire my best actions

PrOLOGUe

There was nothing. Not silence, but the *pressure* of it – a thick, suffocating blanket. A darkness so absolute it felt solid, pressing against his eyelids from the inside out.

And then, the sound.

It began not in his ears, but in the marrow of his bones: a low hum that vibrated up his legs, his spine. The hum clarified into a whisper, a million voices breathing a single, impossible harmony. A billion. The sound swelled, climbing from a conspiratorial murmur to a physical blow that flattened all thought, a crescendo that hammered at him for a single, infinite second before collapsing into nothing once more.

The void that returned was worse. An icy dread uncoiled at the base of Oliver's spine, slithering upwards until a high-frequency whine ignited behind his eyes, the feeling of his own thoughts vibrating apart.

"Help! Somebody, please help me! Maren, where are you?" The yell was raw and useless, swallowed by the void before it left his lips.

A voice, distant and serene, echoed in perfect German. *"Und jetzt bist du fast bereit, die wahre Bedeutung zu verstehen."*

"Maren? Is that you?" The name was a desperate guess, a splinter of familiarity in this ocean of wrongness. "How are you even speaking? I didn't come here with you!" Oliver screamed, the sound thin and reedy.

"Bist du bereit oder bist du es nicht, die wahre Bedeutung zu verstehen?"

"Maren, please! Help me! I don't understand what you're saying. I don't speak German," he pleaded, the words tumbling out, clumsy with panic.

"Mein Liebling, du bist fast bereit. Deine Zeit ist gekommen."

"How do I get out of here? I'm trying to do what you taught me, but it's not working!" His control was splintering, the edges of his sanity fraying into the darkness.

"Das ist alles, was ich dir sagen kann. Du bist jetzt frei."

With that, her voice dissolved, leaving a silence more complex than before. It had a texture now, a lattice of imperceptible echoes. Oliver could almost feel the gaps between the words she hadn't said, a resonance left behind. A hum. *Of voices?* Impossible.

"Battluuuu, I'm still here!"

The sing-song voice cut through the void like a child's drawing, bright and impossibly cheerful. It was the voice from before Maren spoke.

"Wait, how did you know that's my ..." Oliver choked on the question. His brain, a drowning man, grasped for the driftwood of logic. *Of course the voice knew. It's in my head. A figment. It's me.* The thought was a momentary comfort, a solid piece of ground in the abyss. But then, a crack spiderwebbed through it. *If this is my imagination, why can't I imagine a door? An exit?* The terror wasn't of the voice. It was of the crumbling certainty that *he* was the one in control of his own mind.

Goddamnit.

"Where am I?" he howled.

"Batlooo, you are exactly where you need to be, you already are. You are everything you need to be, you already are. You are exactly how you ought to be, you already are," the voice echoed, its cadence a maddening, gentle rhythm.

"What? That means nothing. Why can't I see you?" Oliver demanded.

"Well, of course you can. You're just choosing not to right now, you silly goose."

"Choosing? I want to see you! It's insane, hearing your voice from everywhere at once while seeing nothing!"

"Ah, Battolo, maybe that's it. You are too attached to the thought of seeing me. Let go, and I will appear to you," the voice instructed.

Oliver surrendered. A wave of exhaustion washed over him. "This is obviously a dream," he said, the words heavy and slow. "I just need to wait for it to end."

The voice replied:

"Dream dreamy dreams of a different hue,
That take you to lands that nobody knew,
That take you to lands of uncertain terrain –
Twenty-four dreams in the magic timechain"

"Please, just stop," Oliver groaned, the nonsense rubbing against his frayed nerves like sandpaper. "Stop saying things that don't make sense. It's bad enough I don't know how to get out of here ..." A raw sound of pure frustration ripped from his throat.

"Oh yes, Battloo, that's exactly how you will find the answer. I'm so glad you're getting there." The voice turned pensive. "But I fear today is not that day. I was so happy to see you again after all this time, but it appears you'll be ready the next time we see each other."

This new layer of confusion felt like another turn of a screw. "All this time? What are you talking about? I've never seen you – you're a made-up character."

The voice seemed to brighten. "The good news is, the next time won't be too far away! Okay, Battloooo, you are ready to leave now." With those last words, the voice began to thin, stretching and fading like smoke.

Panic seized him again. "Wait!" Oliver yelled into the receding presence. "You really are the Nose Smiter, aren't you?"

STAGE 1: DISBELIEF

CHAPTER 1. VIOLIN

Oliver Battolo stared at the stage, but the stage wasn't really there. Instead, a blurry space where a man's mouth moved produced a low, meaningless drone that vibrated behind his eyes. The air, thick with the cloying sweetness of overripe lilies, felt heavy in his lungs, as if he were breathing water. He was separate from it all, encased in an unmoored, silent bubble of disbelief.

A sharp whisper pricked the bubble's surface. "I can't believe *he's* speaking next. Your dad never liked him." His mother's voice, a familiar irritant, felt alien. He watched her face contort into an expression of mild disgust as the next speaker, a short man swimming in a poorly fitted suit, approached the microphone.

Oliver tried to shrug, but the signal from his brain to his shoulders got lost in the fog. The room tilted gently, a slow, nauseating spin.

The man cleared his throat, a dry rasp amplified into a cannon shot in the dead air. "I first met Nate over twenty years ago on my first day at work at WilcoxRe. I remember being very nervous …"

The voice faded. *Nate.* The name was a punch in the gut. Oliver's mind tore away from him. It fled back three weeks, to the crackle of a phone call and his dad's laughter – a sound so real and vibrant it made this muffled room feel like a dream. *We'll fire up the grill,* he'd said. Oliver could almost smell the charcoal, feel the phantom warmth of a sun that was supposed to be shining today. Instead, he was here, listening to a stranger reduce his father – his brilliant, complicated, fiercely alive father – to a series of clumsy anecdotes. The absurdity of it built a pressure in his chest. This wasn't a nightmare. A nightmare had texture, it had fear. This was just … blank. A page erased. An impossibility that he was, impossibly, living inside.

"Oliver … Oliver … Oliver!"

His mother's whisper was louder now, urgent. The sound was a slap, shattering the memory and yanking him back into the stale, lily-scented air. He snapped his head toward her, the motion feeling sluggish and disconnected.

"Are you sure you don't want to speak today?" she asked.

"No, Mom. I told you, I can't." The words felt heavy in his mouth. The thought of standing, of walking to that stage, felt like trying to lift a car. "There's no way I can find the words. I don't think I can even get up from this seat."

"Please, sweetheart. It would have meant a lot to your dad," she persisted.

A low, grating hum of irritation started deep in his gut. "Mom, please," he said through a clenched jaw. "I'm begging you, I can't do it. Please stop asking me." He finally folded, burying his face in his hands, pressing his palms into his eyes to block out the light, the sounds, everything.

After the service, Oliver stood outside, performing the grim pantomime of shaking hands. The faces and condolences blurred into one another – a stream of hushed tones and averted eyes. Then, a familiar face, Maren, a woman slightly older than his mother. She didn't offer a clumsy phrase. Instead, she came up to him and gently brushed the side of his face with the palm of her hand, a simple, grounding touch.

"Oh, hi Maren," Oliver said, the name emerging from the fog. "I'm sorry I couldn't speak to you earlier. Things are a bit mad right now."

"Don't worry about it," Maren said, her lilting Bavarian accent a soft melody in the dissonant afternoon. "I'm about to leave but wanted to let you know that we need to meet soon. There's something your dad wanted me to give you."

A flicker of genuine curiosity cut through the numbness. "What is it?"

"Now's not the right time. Why don't you come to my studio one evening this week?" Maren replied.

"How about tomorrow at six p.m.?" Oliver asked, a strange sense of purpose solidifying within him, even if he wasn't sure where it was leading.

"That works. 39 Carmine, between Bleecker and Bedford. Remember?"

"Sure, I'll be there." Oliver watched her leave, then turned to the next guest, his social mask sliding back into place.

When the last guest had finally departed, his mom walked over. "What did Maren have to say?"

"Nothing much, Mom. Just the usual condolences," Oliver said, the lie coming easily. He didn't have the energy for the truth.

"Well, at least I know your father wasn't sleeping with her," she said haughtily.

A spike of heat shot through Oliver's chest, momentarily burning away the fog. "Mom, how can you say something like that *today*? Aren't you even a little sad?"

She seemed to register the tactlessness of her comment. "I'm sorry, sweetheart. I know he was a good father to you. But I had to close my heart to him after everything else that happened."

Her apology felt thin, practiced. "You weren't able to prove a thing in twenty years," he said, his voice a cold and flat wall of ice. "Please, Mom. I just can't have this conversation right now."

Still dazed, but now with a shard of anger lodged in his chest, Oliver walked off toward the parking lot. Six years ago, their divorce had felt like the end of the world, a seismic event that threw his life off its axis. It had taken him years, and his dad's steady hand, to find his footing again.

But this … this was different. A void. A complete system failure. It had been over a week, and the tears he thought should come were lodged somewhere deep inside, a frozen dam he couldn't break. None of this made sense. It simply couldn't.

730459 (April 4)

The click of the laptop closing was a sound of finality. For eight hours, Oliver had found refuge in the clean logic of code, a world of defined problems and elegant solutions. Now, that refuge was gone. The low hum of the office returned, a sound that suddenly felt hollow and alien. With a sigh that carried the weight of the entire empty evening ahead, he picked up his satchel and started for the door.

"Leaving early today?"

The voice was soft, cutting through the ambient noise. Hope was curled on a beanbag chair near the exit, her beaten-up MacBook Pro looking ancient against the office's sleek minimalism. She looked up at him, and for the first time all day, Oliver felt like he was actually being seen.

"Hey, Hope. Yeah," he managed, the words feeling clumsy. "Heading out to meet a friend in the Village."

She gave him a kind, knowing look that made his shoulders ache. "I know what you're going through," she said gently. "You know you don't have to come in for a while, right? Work gives us two weeks of bereavement time."

"I know," Oliver replied, the confession feeling heavy. "But I need to take my mind off … everything. Being here, it's a distraction. It's easier."

"You're going to have to process it at some point …" Hope began, then immediately caught herself. A flush of red crept up her neck, and her gaze dropped to her keyboard. "I'm so sorry, that wasn't for me to say."

A flicker of irritation sparked in him, but it was extinguished just as quickly by a wave of exhaustion. She was trying. In a world that felt muted and distant, her clumsy empathy was a rare point of warmth. "It's all good," he said. The effort to pull the muscles of his face into a smile felt strange, like working a machine he hadn't used in years. "I know what you're saying. Right now, this just feels easier."

He appreciated the genuine concern in her eyes, a small island of humanity in the sterile sea of his workday.

"Okay," she said softly. "I'll see you tomorrow then."

"Bye Hope."

He walked past her and into the elevator. As the doors slid shut, his reflection in the polished steel looked like a stranger's. The short ride down was a descent back into the chaos. He stepped out onto Mercer Street, and the city hit him like a physical force. The afternoon was a riot of noise and motion – the impatient honk of a taxi, the chatter of a dozen conversations he didn't care about, the hurried footsteps of people with places to be. The chilly spring air did nothing to touch the cold, dense knot in his stomach. He was just an object moving through a current, a ghost navigating a world that was suddenly too loud, too bright, too relentlessly alive.

The ten-block walk to Carmine Street felt like crossing a continent. Each step was a conscious effort, his feet heavy on the pavement. He kept his eyes down, the faces of the crowd a meaningless blur. He was walking toward a mystery, a final, cryptic breadcrumb left by his father, and the absurdity of it all felt immense. He, a man of logic and code, was about to visit a "Spiritual Healer."

He arrived at the address and found the buzzer board. His eyes scanned the list of names until they landed on the one Maren had told him.

Maren Dehnert, Spiritual Healer - 4C

The words floated off the metal plate, a signpost to a world he didn't believe in but now had no choice but to enter.

The buzz from the intercom was harsh and immediate. Oliver pushed the heavy door open and began the climb. Four flights. Each step was a deliberate act of will, pulling his leaden legs up one after another. By the time he reached 4C, his heart was pounding – less from exertion and more from the anxious dread of what lay behind the door.

Maren opened it before he could knock. She lived in a sprawling loft, and the first thing that hit him was the smell – a heady cloud of sandalwood incense trying, but failing, to mask a damp, dusty scent beneath. A fragile violin melody drifted from somewhere inside, accompanied by the manufactured trickle of a water fountain.

The space was exactly what his cynical mind had conjured: a spiritual buffet. Buddha statues sat placidly next to Native American dreamcatchers; Eastern European trinkets were scattered among polished crystals. It felt less like a sacred space and more like a carefully curated performance of one.

"Oliver, I'm so glad you're here," Maren said, her smile warm but her eyes intensely analytical. She guided him into the "healing studio" and gestured to a comfortable-looking armchair. As he sank into it, she sat across from him, her posture perfect.

Maren was a tall, striking woman who wore her mid-fifties like a costume, the age underneath betrayed only by the faintest lines around her eyes. A longtime family friend, she had always orbited closer to his dad's world than his mom's, a fact that now felt significant. He remembered the family lore about her meticulous lifestyle – the diets, the routines – that seemed to hold the years at bay. It all felt like another part of the act.

A hazy memory surfaced, less a memory and more the ghost of one. He was thirteen, sullen and struggling to focus at school, brought here as a last resort. He remembered the strange scent and the low music, but the session itself was a blank. All he knew was that in the following months, the fog in his brain had seemed to lift. Maybe it had worked. Or maybe he'd just grown up. Who knew? The past felt as unreliable as the present.

They sat in a silence made heavier by the relentless trickling of the fountain.

"Would you like some water?" she finally asked.

"Sure, I can get it." He started to stand. "That's the dispenser over there, right?"

"Ah, ah, ah …" Maren raised a hand, a gentle but firm command. "Let me get it for you." She moved with a practiced grace to the kitchen counter, removing the lid from a large glass jar and pouring a glass.

"This is special, blessed water," she said, handing it to him with a mysterious air. "It's good for you to have in these times."

Blessed by whom? Oliver thought, but the energy to argue was a luxury he didn't have. He took a sip. It was water, a few degrees warmer than from the tap. He couldn't taste any discernible blessing.

He put the glass down, the need for a straight answer in this crooked room suddenly urgent. "So, what did you want to tell me about Dad?"

"Oliver, you are so impatient. We'll get there. First …"

"Okay Maren, I'll be back later tonight …" a voice called out from the hallway, interrupting her. A young woman, vibrant and alive in a way that felt jarring in the quiet studio, stepped through the doorway. "Oh, sorry," she said, her eyes landing on Oliver. "I didn't realize he was here already. Hi, I'm Daniela." She extended a hand.

"Oliver, this is my student, Daniela," Maren explained. "She's just heading out to her yoga lesson."

After a few awkward pleasantries, Maren walked Daniela to the front door. Just before closing it, she leaned in and gave Daniela a soft, lingering kiss on the lips.

Oliver felt a prickle of awkwardness crawl up his neck. He shifted in the armchair, the fabric suddenly feeling coarse against his skin, and found himself fascinated by a loose thread on the armrest – anything to avoid looking when Maren returned.

"So, Daniela is your …?" he trailed off, unsure of the correct, polite term for what he'd just seen.

"Oh, she's just a friend who's staying with me for a few months," Maren replied, dismissing the entire moment with a wave of her hand. "I'm training her."

"Ah." The sound was noncommittal, but his mind said otherwise. *Not convinced.*

"Okay," Maren said, her gaze steady and pointed. "So tell me, have you cried yet?"

The question was so unexpected, so clinically direct, that it startled him. "I'm sorry?"

"You need to feel it. Everything that's happened." Maren widened her eyes, gesturing with her hands as if physically pulling an emotion out of the air. "You have to feel it to let it go."

"I don't …" Oliver started, but the words died in his throat. He had no idea where this was going.

"Sweetie, you're blocking it out," she said, her voice softening slightly but losing none of its intensity. "You need to feel the anger, the sadness. You need to feel … how do you say it in English? The great injustice of the universe."

Oliver was taken aback. For the past week, he had navigated a minefield of sheepish condolences and whispered apologies. People had tiptoed around his grief as if it were a sleeping animal. He'd wished he could just say, "I accept your apology," to every "I'm so sorry," just to end the awkwardness. Maren's bluntness, by contrast, was almost refreshing.

"Maren, I think I'm still in shock," he replied, the words feeling true and inadequate at the same time. "I'm not sure my brain has processed what's happened."

"Okay," she nodded, a look of absolute certainty on her face. "Maybe we'll get you there."

They fell into silence again, the only sounds the thin violin melody and the relentless trickle of the fountain. To fill the space, Oliver latched onto the music. "What is this playing?"

"It's Russian folk music. They use a special kind of violin that makes it sound almost magical." A distant, wistful look came into her eyes. "In fact, it *is* magic. One day I will tell you the story of how the Russian folk people saved my life when I was a girl."

"Wait, what?" Oliver asked, surprised again.

"Oh yes. I was very, very sick. The doctors said it was too late." She smiled faintly. "But the Russian folks, they made me okay. That is a story for another time. Today, we talk about your father, yes?"

The mention of his father brought back the urgency. "Yes," Oliver said, leaning forward slightly. "So tell me then."

Maren inhaled sharply, gathering her thoughts. "Oliver, I don't need to tell you this, but your father was a great man. An expert in mathematics and computers, yes? You know this. To the world, he worked for a big company doing insurance and finance. To you, he was a good father."

Oliver gave a slight, noncommittal shrug. He wasn't sure why Maren was giving him this preamble, but he chalked it up to her unique brand of psychic eccentricity. He remembered his dad always being there, a steady presence, his patience endless when it came to math homework. He remembered his dad teaching him to code when he was nine, planting a seed that would grow into his entire career. But he also remembered the paradox that had puzzled him for years – this brilliant man, so passionate about complex systems, spending his life at WilcoxRe, a mid-tier reinsurance company where he never rose past upper middle management. It was a piece of his father he'd never understood.

Maren continued, her voice lowering. "He also did things I don't fully understand. Things he didn't explain. "

"What kind of things?" Oliver asked, the intrigue pulling him in deeper.

"He didn't say, and out of respect, I didn't push. But a few months ago, he did say a day like this might come." Maren's expression turned grim. "And that if it did, I would have to teach you something."

"Okay, I'm lost. This is making no sense," Oliver said, the fog of confusion thickening.

Maren smiled gently. "Why don't you have some more water? Then sit back and close your eyes."

"Maren, what are you talking about?" He took a defiant sip of water, the lukewarm liquid doing nothing to calm him. "You're speaking in riddles, and now you're trying to do your spiritual healing stuff on me?" His voice rose, sharp with frustration.

Maren sensed the fraying edge of his composure and switched her voice into a soothing balm. "Hon, it's going to be okay. Your dad planned for this. He wanted you to understand what he did. I'm going to teach you a method he asked me to teach you, in case he wasn't around anymore."

The implication hit Oliver like a physical blow. "Wait … he knew he was going to die?"

"Everyone knows they're going to die at some point, no?" Maren gave him a soft, philosophical smile that felt entirely out of place. "Knowing about our mortality is what makes us human."

"Maren, please. You're making this very difficult for me …" A hot pressure built behind his eyes, the first hint of tears he'd felt in over a week.

"Sweetie, just listen," she said, her voice a lifeline. "In all my years doing this work, I discovered a method I call 'time projection.' I can guide people back to past events in their minds, to see and hear and feel everything as if it were happening right now."

The absurdity of it was a shock of cold water. "Wait, like time travel?"

"In a way," she conceded. "But it is time travel inside your mind. A deep meditation that allows you to go anywhere you want in your past. Usually, people go to the places where they need to learn something, or resolve something."

A wild, impossible hope surged in Oliver's chest. "So I can go back into the past and talk to my dad?" The question came out as a raw plea.

Maren's expression softened with pity. "Oh no. Only the special masters of this method can interact. For most people, they go only as observers. You see what you need to see, remember what you need to remember. That is what helps you find resolution, find peace."

"And Dad knew how to do this?" Oliver asked, the words tight as he struggled with the implications.

"Yes. I taught him many years ago."

Oliver's logical mind found its footing, seizing on the flaw. "So why didn't *you* go back? Why didn't you go into the past to find out what he wanted to tell me? To learn about all these 'strange things' you think he was involved in?" He leaned back, crossing his arms, wrestling with the bizarre, maddening proposition she had laid before him.

Maren answered with a serene, infuriatingly patient smile that didn't reach her eyes. "It is not possible for most people to go into someone else's past. Only the rare, special masters can, as I said. And I don't know if there are strange things about your father – just things I don't fully understand," she responded.

That was it. The calm, mystical pronouncements, the riddles, the complete refusal to give him a straight answer – it was all too much. The fraying thread of Oliver's patience, stretched taut for an hour, finally snapped. A sharp hiss of air escaped his lungs.

He stood up so abruptly that his calves hit the base of the armchair, sending it screeching a few inches across the wooden floor. The ugly sound scraped against his raw nerves.

"Maren, this is ridiculous," he said, his voice tight and clipped. "I'm sorry. I know you help people, but I came here for an answer, not a fairy tale." He gestured around the room, at the statues and trinkets that now seemed to mock him. "If you expect me to believe this crazy stuff about time travel, then you've misjudged me. I'm not in a mental state to take this as a joke right now."

His grief was a real, heavy thing. To have it met with Maren's new-age parlor tricks was an insult. He had to get out.

He grabbed his satchel from the floor, the motion jerky and angry. He turned and stormed toward the front door, desperate to escape the cloying incense and the ghostly music. He needed the solid, logical reality of the city streets again.

As the door clicked shut behind him, he heard the faint, lingering sound of Maren letting out a long, weary sigh.

730601 (April 5)

Logic had warred with desperation all night. The logical part of Oliver's mind replayed his angry departure, cementing the conviction that Maren was a charlatan peddling nonsense. But the desperate part, the part that had no other leads and no other connection to his father's final wishes, kept replaying her words: *I have to teach you something.*

Desperation won.

The walk back through the SoHo foot traffic was a walk of surrender. The four flights of stairs at 39 Carmine felt like a climb of humility. Maren was waiting at the open door, as if she'd known he would return.

"Sorry again about yesterday," Oliver said, the words tasting like embarrassment. "I guess I'm not quite myself these days."

"Of course, hon." Her smile held no judgment, only a warm, unconditional welcome that disarmed him completely. "I'm happy you called. Happy you wanted to come back." She led him in. The same incense, the same strange violin music, but today Oliver chose to ignore them. He sat in the armchair, a willing, if still deeply skeptical, participant.

"Is Daniela here?" he asked, looking around for the friendly, normal face.

"No, she's gone for a massage and then maybe dinner with her boyfriend," Maren replied.

"Her boy ... wait, but yesterday I saw ..." Oliver began, the image of the kiss still fresh.

Maren laughed, a gentle, knowing sound. "You have a lot of questions. But today, I will help you find some other answers, yes?"

She brought him a glass of water from the same jar. "Blessed water. It's good for you."

Yesterday, he had scoffed. Today, he shrugged and took two large sips. It was an act of concession, a silent pact with the absurd. *Fine,* he thought. *Let's see your magic trick.* "So, what about this projection thing you were telling me about?"

"I think the best way is for you to experience it," Maren responded, her expression serene.

She asked him to sit back and close his eyes. "First, we need to see which symbol means truth for you. Hold up both your hands, palms facing upwards. Good. Don't keep your muscles tight. Just listen, and repeat my words in your mind: *'Higher consciousness, show me a sign for the truth.'*"

Oliver felt a wave of foolishness wash over him, but he did as she asked, his mind a running commentary of cynicism. *Higher consciousness. Right.*

And then it happened. A faint tingle, like a low electric current, ran down his arms. Slowly, without any command from him, his arms began to swivel outwards to his sides. The movement was smooth, deliberate, and utterly alien. His shoulders were slightly outstretched, elbows pressed against his waist, palms still facing up. He was a spectator in his own body.

"Maren, what's happening?" Panic seized his throat, his heart beginning to hammer against his ribs. "My arms are moving on their own!" A tremor started in his shoulders.

"It's okay, hon," Maren's voice was a calm anchor in his rising panic. She placed a hand softly on his trembling shoulder. "Your unconscious mind is moving them. We call it autokinesis. Just let go and follow me. You're safe."

His rational brain scrambled for an explanation, for anything solid. "Did you drug the water? This is so weird," he asked, the accusation born of pure terror.

"I told you, the water is blessed. There are no drugs. Relax, Oliver. Everything is okay."

He took a deep, shuddering breath and sank deeper into the chair, surrendering to the strangeness. His arms remained in their outstretched position, humming with a faint energy.

"Higher consciousness," Maren continued calmly, "Show me a sign for the truth."

Instantly, his left arm felt as if it had been filled with lead. A dense, alien weight pulled it downward in a slow, inexorable arc until it rested on his lap.

"We'll try it again to be sure," Maren said. As if on cue, his left arm floated back to its original position. She repeated the command, and again, the left arm dropped, heavy and decisive. "Now we try the opposite. *Higher consciousness, show me a sign for what is false.*"

This time, the right arm became the anchor, performing the mirror image of the downward motion. They tried it once more, with the same result.

"Good," Maren said, her voice full of quiet satisfaction. "So now we know. Your unconscious mind uses the left side for truth and the right side for what is false. Now we are ready. Say this in your mind: *Do I have permission to go back to what Dad has to show me today?*"

Oliver formed the question in his mind, his heart lodged in his throat.

His left arm dropped downwards almost immediately, landing with a soft but decisive finality.

"Look at that, Oliver! You are so ready for this," Maren encouraged, her voice bright with discovery. "Okay. Now that we know you can go there, imagine a peaceful, calm place in your mind. When you are there, let me know what you see."

Oliver wrestled with the darkness behind his eyes, a void that felt active and resistant. For several seconds, there was only the sound of his own breathing. Then he spoke, his voice sounding distant. "I see … an occasional flicker. A plume of green and purple, intensifying."

"Wonderful," Maren murmured, her voice a soft guide in the darkness. "Go on. What else do you see, Oliver?"

"The plumes are intertwining now, like asymmetric helices of smoke. They're … clearing." As he spoke, a profound relaxation spread through his limbs, his voice deepening, losing its anxious edge.

He concentrated, letting the images coalesce. "And now … the helices have opened up. I'm in a meadow at night. The grass is long, uncut, shimmering as the wind moves through it. There's a bright golden moon, and the light feels … heavy, almost liquid. I see short hills in the far distance, but mostly just a vast expanse of grass." A deep, calm breath filled his lungs, his heart rate slowing to a steady, peaceful rhythm.

"That sounds like a beautiful place," Maren said. "Find a direction. Ask yourself, which way is right for you? Let the signs guide you. Remember, the question must be answerable with 'true' or 'false.'"

Oliver formed the thought: *Should I move towards the hills?* His left arm dropped, a silent, heavy affirmation. He took a step, and the meadow began to move under him. His brisk walk became an effortless run, and the run a furious, exhilarating sprint, his feet barely touching the ground. A dim light on the nearest hill grew brighter, pulling him forward.

Then he noticed he wasn't alone. Running alongside him, their powerful bodies keeping pace with his unnatural speed, was a pack of lions. He had no fear, only a sense of deep, dream-like wonder. He ran closest to the largest lion, its mane a river of shadow in the moonlight and noticed a small, dark symbol on its muscular back – a tattoo, stark and black against its golden fur. Oliver drew closer, matching its impossible speed.

"Is that an old key?" he mumbled.

As the thought formed, the lions vanished like smoke on the wind. He was at the hill, standing before the light. Not a fire, but an entrance – a dark mouth leading into a cave, or a tunnel.

He stepped inside. It was a tunnel, impossibly long, stretching into an unseen distance. He walked, and just as before, his pace accelerated without his command, each step lengthening until he was no longer walking but flying, hurtling through the subterranean darkness. The journey was a nauseating, exhilarating blur – straight, then arcing left, then right, then rocketing upwards before plunging deep into the earth, finally stabilizing into a high-speed, sinusoidal meander.

"Maren, I think I'm trapped," he heard his own voice say, strained and small. "There's no end to this."

"Have you tried looking around you?" Maren questioned from a world away.

Oliver forced his gaze sideways, upwards. The tunnel walls were a streaking blur of rock. And then he saw it – a shape approaching in the blur, solidifying into a door. He willed himself to slow, and the impossible physics of the place obeyed. He drifted to a gentle stop, his feet landing silently on the stone floor before it.

"Should I go in?"

"Only if it feels right," Maren whispered.

He pushed, but the heavy wood didn't move. A faint, familiar music seeped from beneath it. He noticed a knob and a keyhole.

"It's locked," he said. "I don't have a key."

"Did you try turning the handle?"

He turned the knob. It clicked. He pushed, and the door swung open into darkness, the music growing louder. He followed the sound through one room and into another, this one lit with a faint, pulsing purple light. The light was so thick he felt he could run his fingers through it – an ethereal, impressionist haze. A man sat playing a violin, the source of the melancholic Russian folk song from Maren's studio.

The man stopped playing as Oliver entered. He looked at Oliver without surprise, then quietly reached into his pocket, pulled out an old cast-iron key, and held it out. It was identical to the tattoo on the lion's back. Oliver took it, his fingers brushing the man's, a fleeting touch of cold reality. The violinist immediately returned to his playing. Oliver waited, but nothing else happened. He turned and walked out of the room, and as he stepped through the door, the world snapped silently.

He was back in the meadow.

But now, it was daytime.

"Maren, what was the point of that?" Oliver asked, bewildered. "I went through all that just to get a key, and now I'm back where I began?"

"Maybe the key is for something else," Maren's voice soothed. "Look around."

Oliver scanned the sunlit landscape. Behind him stood a structure that hadn't been there before: a small cottage with a sandstone roof, ivory walls, and a solid wooden door. On the door was a large, rustic, cast-iron lock. Instinctively, he raised the key. It slid into the lock with a perfect, satisfying click, and the mechanism snapped open. He pushed the door and stepped into a dimly lit room.

The air was stale, motionless. The room felt like a museum of a life that was never lived, stuck in the 1950s. An armchair that looked exactly like his dad's favorite one sat in a corner. Across from it was a mahogany table bearing a transistor radio and a boxy cathode-ray TV. The radio was playing the same Russian violin music, a slow, ponderous loop of sorrow. On the arm of the chair sat a modern TV remote – a shock of the familiar. He picked it up. The telltale wear around the power and volume buttons was unmistakable. It was his dad's.

A powerful intuition told him to turn on the TV. First, he tried to silence the radio, fumbling with the old knob until it clicked into the OFF position. The violin didn't stop. The music was in the room itself. Giving up, Oliver pointed the remote at the TV and pressed the power button.

A few seconds of gray static hissed from the screen, then it flickered to life. And his breath caught in his throat.

It was his dad. The chiseled, handsome face, looking directly at him. He was alone in a room awash in that same purple light. His expression was calm, serious.

"Oliver, listen to me," the tinny, electronic voice said. "There are twenty-four words, and you need to find them."

A sound caught in Oliver's throat – a raw mix of a gasp and a sob. "Dad? Dad, is that you?" The burning behind his eyes was unbearable.

"Oliver, listen to me," his father's image repeated, the exact same intonation, a perfect, heartbreaking loop. "There are twenty-four words, and you need to find them."

"What words?" Oliver pleaded, tears now freely tracking down his cheeks. "Dad, tell me! How do I find them?"

"This is how," Nate's image replied, the voice flat and unchanging. "Doing what you're doing right now. One word at a time."

The screen glitched, collapsing into a single white point before vanishing. The TV was dead. He pressed the power button again and again, frantically, but it was useless. Suddenly, the room began to unravel. The walls grew thin, the furniture dissolving like sugar in water, the whole scene violently tearing apart around him.

Then, a cold shock. He was back in the meadow. This time, it was pitch dark. No moon, no stars. Just an absolute, silent blackness.

And in that silence, he knew. The music. The man. The journey. A single word crystallized in the void of his mind, a perfect note of certainty.

Violin.

"Maren, what do I do now?" he asked, his voice shaking.

"Do you feel you need more answers?" she asked from the world outside.

"Yes. So many more." *Twenty-three more,* he thought. He paused, the chaos of the experience settling into a strange new shape. "But for now ... for right now, I feel like I know one answer. And I'm satisfied." An odd sense of resolution settled over him, a single solid point in a universe of nonsense.

"Then you are done for today," Maren's voice, no longer a whisper, pulled him back into the room. "Take three deep breaths, releasing slowly. Then, open your eyes."

Oliver obeyed. The first breath was a gasp, his lungs suddenly remembering their function. With the second, he felt the heavy, solid weight of his own body in the armchair. With the third, the world returned. The scent of sandalwood, the soft light, the ever-present trickling of the fountain. He opened his eyes and noticed a coolness on his face. He brought a hand to his cheek and his fingers came away wet.

"Was I crying?" he asked, his voice thick with confusion.

"Yes," Maren smiled, a gentle, knowing expression. "Continuously for the last few minutes."

He had no memory of it, yet the physical proof was undeniable. The grief he couldn't consciously access had found its own way out. He pushed the thought away, focusing on the one solid thing he'd brought back with him. "Maren, my dad ... on the TV ... he said something about twenty-four words. That I need to find one at a time. Do you know what he meant?"

Maren simply shook her head. "I told you, Oliver. Your dad was doing things I didn't understand."

"And I feel like I know – with absolute certainty – that *violin* is one of those words," Oliver said, the conviction feeling alien and yet unshakeable in his gut.

"You can ask yourself," Maren suggested. "The way I showed you."

He closed his eyes again, sinking into the unmistakable darkness, a space that no longer felt empty but charged with potential. The tumult of the last hour warred in his mind – the lions, the key, his father's face – but he pushed it all aside, focusing on the task. The dancing plumes of color gave way to a quiet void. *"Higher consciousness,"* he thought, the words echoing in the silence of his own mind, *"Can you confirm that 'violin' one of the words Dad wanted me to know?"*

His left hand dropped. A heavy, silent, and immediate answer. He tried it again. Same result. He slowly brought himself back to the room and opened his eyes. "I believe it is."

A short, disbelieving laugh escaped him. "Here's what I don't fully understand …" he began, the massive understatement of the century hanging in the air. "You said this projection thing can take you back to specific memories or past events, right?"

Maren nodded.

"Well, I'm pretty sure what I just saw wasn't my memory. And it damn well wasn't a real event. My dad was in a purple room talking to me through a TV from the 1950s." Oliver ran a hand through his hair, trying to assemble the impossible pieces. "It's hard to believe that actually happened."

Maren arched her head upwards and closed her eyes, as if listening to something far away. "It is true that our minds can add fantasy to memories when projecting," she said softly. "However, it is very rare to go into places or events that did not happen at all. The only other people I have seen this with … they had …" She paused. "I'm not sure of the English word … ah, yes. Synesthesia."

"Synesthesia?" The word was a faint echo in his memory, a half-forgotten definition.

"Yes. When people transpose their senses. Sometimes they can taste colors or hear shapes," Maren explained.

The echo solidified into a memory – a magazine article on psychedelic rock he'd read in college, musicians describing how guitar solos would explode into color behind their eyes. "Oh, right. I've heard of that," he said. "So you're saying people with synesthesia can create whole new events when they do this?"

"It is very rare. In twenty, maybe thirty years, I have only seen it two or three times." She looked at him intently. "Do you know if you are synesthetic?"

"I've never thought about it," he said, a strange new uncertainty creeping in. "I mean, sometimes when I listen to music I really like and close my eyes, I see shapes and colors dancing. I thought everyone did that."

"Yes," Maren said, her voice gentle but the implication immense. "That could be a sign. Pay attention to your senses in the next few days. See what you notice."

Oliver felt a fresh wave of disorientation. Not only was the world outside of him not what it seemed, but now the world inside him began to blur around the edges.

"So what do I do now?" he asked, feeling adrift. "There are twenty-three more words."

"Come back for a few more sessions," Maren replied. "I will teach you how to project on your own."

He gathered his satchel, the distinct weight a small comfort. As he headed for the door, one last shard of skepticism, the final defense of his rational mind, surfaced. He paused and turned back. "Maren … are you sure there wasn't anything in the water?"

"I promise you, hon," she replied, her smile unwavering. "The blessed water is only to get you started. Once your mind is ready, you can do this by yourself."

Oliver shrugged, unconvinced but also out of options. He made his way out of the building and down to the West 4th station, the single word *violin* echoing in his mind like a tuning fork struck in a silent, empty universe.

CHAPTER 2. TODDLER

O'Connell's on Spring and Mercer was a performance of an Irish pub, and a convincing one, at least for the lazy observer. The sign was carved in the right font, the walls were adorned with a curated assortment of artifacts – including, for good measure, a Scottish kilt and bagpipes – and the solid wood bar smelled perfectly of years of spilled lager and Guinness. It was a comfortable fiction.

The man who would become The Hoegaarden waited impatiently at the bar until his eyes finally locked with the bartender's.

"Hi Aisling," he said to the stern-looking woman.

"Hey there. The usual today?" Aisling asked.

"Yes, the usual Hoegaarden for me, and I'll get a Żywiec and a Lagunitas as well. His tab." He pointed to a young man sitting at a table near the bar. Aisling's stern expression softened as she glanced at him. She nodded and turned to the taps.

"Dude, why order a Lagunitas here when it's free at the office?" The Hoegaarden asked as he set the beers down, passing the Żywiec to the tab-holder, Oliver.

The Lagunitas brushed off the comment with a sip. "Forget the beer. Did you guys hear Chris Anderson is coming to the office on Monday? Tomer's meeting with him. I think he's sniffing around for our next round."

"That's huge," The Hoegaarden gushed, leaning forward with an almost devout intensity. "Anderson's one of the best out there. He gets it. He makes the whole idea of Web3 so simple. It's about taking back the internet from the kings – Google, Amazon, all of them. 'Read. Write. Own.' It's a revolution, man."

"Totally," The Lagunitas agreed. "This is not about hype. He's focused on the tech – on how it actually empowers people."

They prattled on, their voices a feverish hum of acronyms and future-tense promises. But Oliver, The Żywiec, wasn't really listening. The sounds of their enthusiasm, the clinking of glasses, the drone of the Liverpool rerun on the TV – it all faded into a dull, distant roar. His attention was snagged by something else entirely.

Hanging behind the bar was a large, framed painting he'd glanced at before but never truly seen. It depicted a cherub-like little boy with a floral wreath on his head, standing in a garden next to an apple tree. Painted in a Renaissance style, it radiated a feeling of such primal innocence and quiet hope that it felt like a tear in the fabric of the rowdy, cynical pub. It was a world away from their talk of digital revolutions.

He was vaguely aware of the subject of their conversation. Web3. The promised third age of the internet. The first was just reading things online. The second, where they lived now, was about a handful of digital fiefdoms – Google, Facebook, Amazon – who owned all the land and let you live on it, as long as you gave them everything you had. Web3 was the promise of giving the land back to the people.

"Hey man, you doing okay?" The Hoegaarden's voice broke through his reverie.

Oliver sighed, a heavy, weary sound and brought his gaze back from the painting. "I'm okay, dude," he said, looking at the half-empty glass in his hand. The beer tasted like ash. "Not sure it was the best idea to get a drink this soon after my dad's passing. I thought it would take my mind off things, but I don't think it's helping. Sorry, didn't mean to be a party pooper."

"Of course, man. We get it," The Lagunitas reached over and patted his shoulder.

A flush of embarrassment rose in Oliver's cheeks. He hated making the conversation about himself, about the grief that felt too big and too real for a place like this. He quickly course-corrected. "I'll finish this and head out. But yeah, Anderson … what are we trying to raise? A hundred, hundred-fifty mil?"

"Something like that," The Hoegaarden shrugged.

"Chump change for them," Oliver mused. He took a sip, the beer doing nothing to wash the bad taste from his mouth. Then, a thought that had been bothering him for weeks finally surfaced, sharp and insistent. "Hey, can I ask you guys something, though? This Web3 dream is about giving people back their own data, right? Handing them the keys to their own digital lives?"

They both nodded.

"But with all this private blockchain stuff we're building for corporations … aren't we just building a fancy new castle and telling everyone we'll hold onto the keys for them? How is that any different?"

The Hoegaarden and The Lagunitas exchanged a look that Oliver knew well. It was the "Here we go again" look.

"It's a process, man. Crawl, walk, run," The Hoegaarden said, choosing his words carefully. "You can't just throw people into the deep end. We're giving them training wheels. Once they get a feel for it, they'll be ready to ride the bike themselves. The *true* Web3 route."

Oliver wasn't convinced. He thought of the public networks like Ethereum, messy and chaotic as they were. They felt like a public park – open to everyone. What they were building for their clients felt like a private country club. A slightly bigger walled garden, perhaps, but one with the same illusion of freedom.

The Hoegaarden slammed his glass on the table for emphasis. "Dude, big companies are never going to touch the public stuff. Think of the privacy issues, the legal headaches. Their lawyers would have a field day."

The Lagunitas chimed in, leaning back. "That said, the public chains – Ethereum, Solana, all that – that's the future for regular people. I just wish we did more of that." He took a long, ponderous sip. "Speaking of which, did I tell you guys? I dumped my punk for an ape last month."

Oliver watched them, the words barely registering. *JPEGs,* he thought. *They were talking about trading JPEGs of cartoon animals for the price of a suburban house.*

"Really? Which punk did you have?" The Hoegaarden leaned in, his voice hushed with the reverence of a collector.

"8843. Mohawk and beard. Sold it for sixty ETH and got a floor ape." The Lagunitas chuckled and raised his glass in an imaginary toast. "And the craziest part? Yuga Labs bought the whole collection a few days later. Man, cartoon JPEGs are the future!"

"So you're holding the ape?"

"For now. I got the ApeCoin drop, and there's a virtual land sale coming up for their metaverse. It's going to be epic."

The words floated in the air, abstract and weightless. Oliver couldn't let it go. "Help me understand," he interjected, his voice feeling strangely loud in the bubble of their excitement. "How is virtual land rare? It's code. You can make as much as you want. What stops them from creating an infinite amount?"

The Hoegaarden reclined with a smirk, the kind reserved for explaining a self-evident truth to a child. "Dude, you've got to stop falling for 'normie' talking points." The word was a smug dismissal, the tribal password of the newly converted. "It's all about *relative* scarcity. Digital neighborhoods. If I buy a plot next to some famous collector's plot, I'm set. That shit's going to the moon."

"I'm sorry, that makes zero sense," Oliver said, a mild irritation sharpening his tone. "The company, Yuga Labs, can just create new plots next to anyone, whenever they want. Who decides which anonymous collector is famous next week?"

"The market does," The Hoegaarden said with a dismissive snort. "Welcome to capitalism."

"Okay, but that just means you're trusting a company not to dilute the supply," Oliver pressed.

"Of course I trust them! Why would they blow up their own brand?" The Hoegaarden looked genuinely surprised that a concept so obvious was being challenged.

"Doesn't sound very decentralized to me."

The Lagunitas sighed, a sound of weary pity. "Dude, you've got to get with the program. The metaverse is going to be everything. You're going to miss out if you're stuck in that old Web2 mindset."

The words landed, and something inside Oliver gave way. The annoyance he'd been feeling curdled into a bone-deep exhaustion. He felt the full weight of the last two weeks settle on him, a heavy shroud of grief that made their conversation feel like a frantic, meaningless dance. His skepticism about work, a quiet hum in the back of his mind for months, was suddenly roaring.

He remembered the recruiter at the campus event a year ago, selling him the promise of a revolution. He'd bought it completely. He, a specialist in distributed systems, would build the new internet. But the reality had been a series of dead ends. The "Spirit of Web3" had somehow translated into building toy applications on private networks for corporate clients who, after the novelty wore off, would inevitably walk away, citing a "Lack of stakeholder buy-in." It was a game, a performance of innovation.

And the money. The promise of a windfall that had lured so many of his friends. He saw the ghost of his own bad bets: the NFTs he bought at the peak, now unsellable JPEGs sitting in a digital wallet; the "yield farms" that promised impossible returns but were just cleverly disguised Ponzi schemes, draining newcomers like him to pay off the early birds. He'd wanted to believe in a truly decentralized finance, but all he'd found was a new flavor of the same old greed.

He was done. Spent. He pushed his chair back.

"All right guys, I'm out," he said, the decision feeling less like a choice and more like a physical necessity. "Going to head home to chill for a bit."

"You sure, dude?" The Lagunitas asked. "It looked like you were just getting into it."

Getting out of it, Oliver thought. "Yeah, I'm sure. I'll see you guys Monday. Maybe we'll bump into Anderson." He picked up his satchel from the floor, suddenly grateful for the familiar texture of its strap on his shoulder.

"See you, Oliver. Enjoy the weekend," they both chorused, already turning back to their conversation, their revolution.

****

The click of the lock behind him was a sound of deep relief. Oliver got off the 2 train at 96th and Broadway and walked the few blocks to his apartment on Riverside Drive, the chilly April night air feeling sharp and clean after the stale warmth of the pub. His fourth-floor walk-up studio was barely 700 square feet, but tonight it felt like a sanctuary. He found the cold half of his morning bagel on the counter and sat at his desk to finish it, the silence of the apartment a welcome blanket.

He chewed slowly, deliberately. Maren's word echoed in his mind: *synesthesia*. He closed his eyes, paying attention for the first time not to the taste, but to the *shape* of the food. It was immediate and vivid. The "everything seasoning" was a chaotic tumble of sharp, pink rhomboids across his tongue. The scallion cream cheese was a series of deep lavender spheres, rolling gently in their wake. As he swallowed, the shapes dissolved into misty spires of color. The world inside his mouth had its own secret geometry. It was a strange and unsettling discovery – another piece of his reality that wasn't as solid as he'd thought.

He finished the bagel and lay on his bed, eyes closed. The quiet was no longer a comfort. In the absence of external noise, the cacophony of the day rushed in: the feverish hype of his colleagues, the hollow feeling of his own skepticism, the persistent, aching void left by his father. He hadn't had a real drink in over two weeks, terrified it would drag him into a darkness he couldn't escape. The single Żywiec at O'Connell's had only sharpened the edges of his solitude.

It was Maren's voice he heard in his head, calm and certain. Calling her felt like a surrender, an admission that the logical world he clung to had no answers for him. She picked up after a few rings, her voice warm, even as she was preparing for bed. He could hear Daniela singing softly in the background.

"Maren," he said, switching the phone to speaker and placing it beside him. "Can you lead me into that space again? I feel like I'm ready to go back."

He tried. With her guidance whispering from the phone, he sought the peaceful meadow, but his mind was a frantic storm of racing thoughts. The harder he tried to find calm, the more elusive it became.

"Hon," Maren's voice cut through the static. "Are you feeling any tension or anxiety that's blocking you?"

Oliver let out a breath he didn't realize he'd been holding. "Yes," he admitted, the word a heavy stone. "I feel angry. I'm angry at Dad for leaving. I'm angry at Mom for … being Mom. I'm angry at the people I work with for talking nonsense."

"Good," she said, not with sympathy, but with the satisfaction of a doctor who has found the source of the pain. "We will need to unblock those feelings. Tell me, where in your body do you feel this anger? I want you to invite it in, give it your full attention. Then tell me where it settles."

Oliver inhaled, and instead of pushing the anger away, he let it wash over him. It was an unpleasant orange heat that flooded his system before coalescing, concentrating into a dense, cold knot of energy in his solar plexus. He described it to her.

"Good," Maren said again. "Now, does this feeling have a form? Is it an object?"

"Yes," Oliver replied, surprised that the answer was so clear.

"Is it hard, or soft? Dark, or light? Heavy?"

"It's heavy," he said, the image shockingly specific. "And it's dark. It looks like a chicken, curled up in a tight ball." A small, absurd smile touched his lips.

Maren laughed gently on the other end of the line. "You have a great imagination. So, I want you to speak to this chicken. Thank it for revealing itself, and ask it what it would like to do."

He felt ridiculous, but he was so far past the shore of logic that he didn't care. He focused on the dense weight inside him. "It says it's there to protect me," he reported, his voice hushed. "But it would prefer to uncurl and be free."

"Then allow it, Oliver," Maren whispered. "Thank it for its service, for carrying that burden for you. But tell it that it doesn't need to anymore. It is free."

He did as she instructed, and he felt a subtle shift inside him. The curled-up shape began to loosen. Gently, it uncurled its body, and then, with a movement he felt more than saw, it jumped out. A sudden, shocking lightness in his solar plexus, a cool void where the dense weight had been. The shape walked away slowly.

"I want to follow it, Maren," his voice was soft now, his body humming with a strange new energy. "I want to see where it's going."

"Then do," she whispered.

The creature walked along a narrow path through vegetation so dense it was like moving through a green tunnel. As it moved, it changed. Its neck elongated, its beak flattened. It was a duck now, waddling with purpose through a thick wood that sloped steadily uphill. It finally broke through the trees into a clearing – a beautiful rose garden, impossibly blooming atop a high mountain.

And there, it transformed again. The duck's form stretched and swelled, its feathers becoming brilliant red scales. It was a dragon, magnificent and ancient, and it stood beside him, high above the world. The surrounding view was staggering, a tapestry of valleys and rivers stretching to the horizon. The dragon spread its considerable wings, caught a thermal current Oliver couldn't feel, and took off, soaring into the vast, open sky.

He watched it go, a feeling of profound awe washing over him. "I want to fly with it," he murmured. "It looks so beautiful."

"You should," Maren's voice was a distant echo. "But first, feel what is inside your body again. Is the anger still there? Is it still heavy and dark?"

He checked. The space in his solar plexus was no longer a cold void. It was light. It was warm. It was filled with a tingling, electric hum. "No," he responded, a sense of wonder in his voice. "The anger is gone. I feel … relief." It was a readiness for anything.

"Good," Maren said, her voice clear and pointed. "Now go fly."

Oliver pushed off from the mountaintop, and the air caught him. Gravity didn't win; he flew. The ground beneath him was a patchwork of farmland, houses, and clusters of trees that looked like tiny pieces of broccoli. A strange, uplifting sensation swelled in his chest – a warm, electric hum that felt thick and encompassing. It was the feeling of pure potential, the emotion he imagined a coiled spring would feel an instant before its release.

Soon, the red dragon disappeared into the distant horizon, a final, fading spark of his released anger. He felt no urge to follow. Instead, some new intuition guided him downwards, swooping toward a village nestled in the valley below. He landed with impossible softness on a quiet, pebbled road.

A wooden sign was posted beside him. Carved into it was the village name: *Bryce's Second.* The font was an elegant, slightly archaic script that tugged at his memory. *O'Connell's*, he realized with a start. *It's the same font as the sign at the pub.* A strange thread was being woven, connecting this dreamscape to the real world. The town itself looked ancient, as if plucked from the 1600s.

He walked toward a house with a crooked wooden fence. On the lawn, next to an apple tree, a little boy of no more than two was playing. As Oliver's footsteps crunched on the pebbles, the boy turned. He was wearing a floral wreath. A perfect, living replica of the painting. The boy wasn't a cherub; he was just a child, but the sense of primal innocence was the same. He looked at Oliver without fear, then pointed a small finger toward the front door of the house, a silent, clear instruction. Oliver obeyed.

He stepped across the threshold, and the world shifted. The 1600s vanished. The air, the light, the very smell of the place changed. He was in a house from the late 1990s, and the familiarity of it landed with a heavy force inside his gut. The scent of old wood and his mother's potpourri, the specific worn texture of the runner in the hallway … it all came rushing back in a tidal wave of lost memory. This was the first house he had ever lived in, the one in Connecticut.

Grasping at the ghost-like geography of a place he hadn't seen in over twenty years, he made his way up the small flight of stairs to his childhood bedroom. The door creaked open on a perfectly preserved diorama of his own past: toys strewn across the floor, the faded dinosaur-print curtains, the storage boxes tucked neatly under the bed. The room felt airless, a moment frozen in time.

The storage boxes. The thought was a quiet command. He slid one out. Stuffed toys and old clothes, smelling of cedar and time. He slid out the next. More of the same, but at the very bottom, a photo album with a worn, navy-blue cover.

He opened it. The plastic pages crinkled as he flipped through them. Family photos, moments he barely remembered: Oliver as a baby, his parents young and smiling, before he was born. Then, midway through, his fingers stopped. His breath caught in his chest.

He froze.

There, in the middle of the album, was the painting. Except it wasn't a painting. It was a photograph. A photograph of a child wearing a floral wreath, standing next to an apple tree. It was identical to the scene at O'Connell's, identical to the boy he'd just seen on the lawn, except for one, world-shattering detail.

The child was him.

With trembling hands, he slid the photo out from under its protective plastic sleeve. The glossy paper felt cool and real. He flipped it over. On the back, written in his dad's neat, authoritative cursive, were seven words.

Oliver as The Toddler, March 10, 2000

His dad's grammar had always been impeccable. The odd phrasing – *as The Toddler* – snagged in his mind, but the thought was overwhelmed by a deeper feeling. A profound sense of completion, as if a missing piece of his soul had just clicked into place. He slowly let the projection fade, not with a jarring snap, but like a gentle surfacing from a deep, quiet pool.

He opened his eyes. Tears had been streaming down his cheeks again, soaking the pillow beneath his head. They weren't tears of sadness, but of a vast, unnamable emotion – a mix of awe and connection and the painful, beautiful shock of understanding. He thanked Maren and hung up.

He didn't feel sleepy. He felt wired, alive with a strange new energy. He got up and walked over to his computer. On the floor by the desk, his wallet lay open, knocked over at some point. Oliver had a specific slot for everything. He noticed immediately that the one for his Amex was empty.

And then he remembered. The tab at O'Connell's. He'd forgotten to close it.

731130 (April 9)

Aisling McGinty moved through the late morning quiet of the pub with a practiced, powerful grace. She lifted two inverted chairs off a table, her movements fluid, almost a dance. Years of hoisting kegs and wrestling with rowdy drunks had given her a formidable strength, and the morning ritual of setting the dining area was a mindless, comforting rhythm she could perform in her sleep. She walked into the kitchen and pushed the service door open, the cold, drizzly SoHo air that rushed in felt no different from the Belfast mornings of her youth, when she helped her father set up for lunch.

"I got the kegs," a high-pitched, shaky voice said. The delivery kid looked like a gust of wind would knock him over. Aisling just pointed him toward the storage room. He scurried off as if she'd pointed a gun at him. Good. Fear was efficient.

She was a formidable woman. She had to be. Decades of running a pub in downtown Manhattan had sculpted her, stripping away every ounce of weakness until only statuesque efficiency remained. Her stern, piercing eyes – narrowed into a squint that could curdle cheap whiskey – were a shield forged in the fires of a bad marriage to an abusive drunk, of raising kids alone, of building a business from nothing in a city that was genuinely unsafe. She'd developed a deep and abiding skepticism for humanity as a result, but there was a chink in that armor. She had a soft corner for what she saw as genuineness, perhaps because it was so damn rare.

A handful of her regulars fell into that category. The tech kids from the startup down the street, for instance. For all their talk of nonsense she didn't understand, they were mostly good lads. One of them knocked on the locked front door now.

"We're closed. Open at noon," Aisling called out, but a warm half-smile touched her lips against her will.

"Sorry Aisling, I left my card here yesterday. Can I pick it up?" a young man's voice came from the other side.

"Ah, it was you then. Nick, right?" she asked, walking to the door.

"No, Nick's my friend. I'm Oliver."

"Right, right. I always mix you two up." She unlocked the door. Oliver followed her in, looking a bit lost, the way young men do when they're carrying something heavy you can't see. She retrieved his Amex from the register.

"We closed it out with a twenty percent tip. Standard policy," she said, giving him a small, genuine smile.

"Of course," he said, taking the card. He paused. "Hey Aisling … what is that painting behind the bar?" He pointed to the image of the boy in the wreath.

This old thing, she thought. "Oh, that was painted by my grandfather, more than fifty years ago. A small-time painter back in Ireland. He only made three major paintings, sold the first and third. This was the second. No one ever bought it, so it stayed in the family," she explained, the story as worn and familiar as the bar top.

"What was his name?"

"John."

"Just John?" he asked, an eyebrow raised.

Aisling laughed. "Jonathan Bryce."

Oliver went still for a moment, a flicker of something unreadable in his eyes. "So, this is Bryce's second?"

"Guess you could say that," she shrugged.

"What's the name of the painting?"

"Don't remember." She turned, squinting at the corners of the canvas. Not finding a name, she let out a small sigh of effort and lifted the large, surprisingly heavy three-by-three-foot canvas off its hook. The back was dusty. "Ah, here it is," she said, reading the faded script. "It's called *The Toddler*. Painted on August 15, 1971."

She turned back to hang it, but stopped. Oliver was staring at her, his face pale, his expression one of pure, unadulterated shock.

"You okay, Oliver?" she asked, her voice sharpened by a genuine flicker of concern.

He seemed to snap out of a trance. "Oh, sorry. It just … reminded me of something. It's a beautiful painting." He recovered quickly. "Who bought the other two?"

"Dunno, really. If you're interested, I can ask my mum. She might remember what happened to her dad's stuff," Aisling offered, her curiosity piqued by the boy's strange reaction.

"Oh, that's fine. I'm sure I can find it online. If not, I might check in again. Anyway, thanks for my card, Aisling. Appreciate it!" He waved and was gone.

"No worries, see you around," Aisling responded to the empty doorway. She hung the painting back on its hook, giving the little boy in the wreath a curious glance. Just another strange story in a city full of them. She picked up a dusting cloth and got back to work.

★★★★

Oliver walked out of O'Connell's, and the cool drizzle on his face did nothing to quell the fire in his mind. His heart was hammering against his ribs, not with anxiety, but with a new, urgent rhythm. *Bryce's Second. The Toddler.* The connections were too perfect, too impossible to be a coincidence. He was certain he had it. He had his father's second word.

The city felt loud and chaotic around him. He needed a quiet space, a moment of sanctuary to know for sure. He ducked into the nook of a building on the street corner, the stone cool against his back. He rested his head against the wall and closed his eyes, shutting out the frantic energy of SoHo. He took a few deep, ragged breaths, trying to find the calm place Maren had described.

He raised his hands, the gesture now feeling like a strange and secret prayer. He focused, pushing past the racing thoughts, and sent the question into the quiet darkness of his own mind.

"Is 'toddler' the second word?"

He held his breath. For a second, nothing happened. Then, he felt it – the alien weight descending upon his left arm. It dropped, a heavy, solid, irrefutable answer. He tried again, just to be sure. It dropped again.

A giddy, disbelieving smile spread across his face. It was real. None of it – the meadow, the lions, the photograph – had been just a dream. It was a map, and he was following it. Possessing the proof, a tangible link to his father that felt more real than any memory, he opened his eyes and brought his arms back to his side.

He wasn't alone.

A little girl, no older than six, stood a few feet away, staring at him with wide, unblinking eyes, her mouth a perfect 'O' of astonishment. She had clearly seen the whole strange ritual.

For a moment, the cosmic significance of his discovery evaporated, replaced by the mundane reality of being a strange man moving his arms by himself in an alley. A sheepish, embarrassed grin broke across his face. He gave the little girl a helpless shrug and continued his walk to the train station, the secret word burning like a hot coal in his mind.

CHAPTER 3. ALLEY

731401 (April 11)

"Ah, I knew I'd find you here bright and early, Mr. Battolo."

The voice was a blast of manufactured cheer, an Oxbridge accent so crisp it crackled in the quiet office air. It jolted Oliver out of the dull, protective stupor he'd been using to shield himself from the morning.

"Good morning, Mr. Wright," Oliver replied, his own voice sounding flat and distant. A knot of anxiety tightened in his stomach. A visit from his manager's boss this early on a Monday was never a good sign.

"Right, Oliver, you're on deck for the meeting with Chris Anderson at 10:30," Ian Wright said, already pacing. "Sri had a family emergency. Won't be in. I need you to run the Phoenix demo."

"The ..." Oliver's mind went blank. The words were just sounds.

"Yes, the Phoenix demo," Wright barked, his cheerfulness fraying into impatience. "Mortgage-backed securities. Alice, Bob, Charlie. That one. We need to show Chris we're positioned to tackle large-scale enterprise use cases."

As he spoke, Oliver felt the unmistakable pull of Ian's personality. The man was a character from a bygone era, a smooth-talking Englishman, a sales leader who could cast a hypnotic spell over a room. Oliver had watched him do it a dozen times, awestruck and slightly terrified. But there was another side to him – an overbearing, dismissive streak that made Oliver feel small, that made him want to either meekly concur or simply cower.

"Ian, I don't …" he started, the sinking feeling in his gut turning cold. He was being thrown into the hot seat with no preparation.

"Oh, nonsense, you'll be fine," Wright interrupted, flashing a withering faux scowl. "Simple demo. Ten minutes. Get another coffee, old boy. You look sleepy," he chuckled, then turned on an elegantly shod Italian heel and was gone.

Oliver stared at the empty space where his boss had been, his heart pounding. Chris Anderson. A titan in the venture capital world. And he, Oliver, had one hour to resurrect a demo he hadn't touched in months.

He scrambled, pulling up files, his mind a frantic blur. This was his job, his absurd role as a "solutions architect." It was the company's term for a software developer with just enough social skills to be put in front of a client. He was a coder tasked with playing salesman, a role he'd always shadowed his senior colleague, Sri, in. But this was different. This was an investor demo in front of an industry heavyweight. The pressure felt immense, and yet, underneath it all, a part of his mind remained strangely distant, watching the panic unfold as if it were happening to someone else.

"Always good to be back in Silicon Alley," Anderson said, rolling into the conference room an hour later, with an easy confidence.

"Silicon Alley?" Ian asked, all charm.

"Yes, our name for this strip in SoHo," Anderson replied.

"Ah, very clever," Ian beamed. "Chris, you know Tomer, our CEO. And this is Oliver, one of our bright young engineers. He'll be demoing a solution we built for Freddie Mac."

The next ninety minutes were a performance, conducted by Ian Wright. The playbook was always the same: *Tell them what you're going to tell them. Tell them. And then tell them what you told them.* Oliver played his part on autopilot. He clicked the right buttons, said the right words, the script he'd frantically rehearsed coming out of his mouth. He was aware of a slight tremor in his hand, a nervous stutter that crept into his voice once or twice, but Anderson, to his credit, sensed his unease and directed most of the technical questions to Ian and Tomer, who deflected them with practiced ease.

As the meeting wrapped up, Anderson turned to him. "Thanks for the demo. I liked how you framed the comment around asset ownership. That's right up my alley, you know. Right up my alley."

The word hit Oliver with a strange resonance. *Alley.* It seemed to detach from the sentence and hang in the air, glowing with a significance he couldn't name. *Could that be one of Dad's words?* The thought was a bizarre, intuitive jolt. He pushed it away. The first two words had come from the projections. This was just a coincidence.

"Good job today," Ian said, walking him back to his desk after seeing Anderson out. "Looks like he liked what he saw."

"Do you think he'll invest?" Oliver asked, his voice still shaky.

"That's the hope. He's a huge champion of the Web3 vision – user data, asset ownership, all that. Any product pushing that dream is a good candidate for him."

A familiar unease surfaced in Oliver, the same skepticism that had soured the conversation at the pub. "The solution we showed him was on a private blockchain, though," he said, thinking aloud. "The network operator has the final say on who owns what. I'm surprised he didn't push back on the lack of decentralization."

Ian chuckled, the smooth, dismissive sound of a salesman handling an engineer's pesky logic. "See, that's the engineer in you talking, Oliver. We're not selling the short-term implementation. We're selling the *dream.* The paradigm shift. He gets it. These private platforms will eventually become public utilities. He knows that." Ian flashed an immaculately white smile. "Anyway, nice work, old chap. Cheerio!"

Ian turned and walked back to his office, leaving Oliver standing by his desk. He was glad the demo had gone smoothly, but he felt a familiar, hollow ache. He was having trouble squaring the circle, trying to reconcile the revolutionary dream they were selling with the compromised, centralized reality they were actually building.

731437 (April 11)

The two-to-three p.m. hour at the Bluebird Café was a symphony of chaos –
the hiss of the espresso machine, the clatter of ceramic, a dozen conversations
competing for air. Oliver felt a wave of relief as he secured a small table on the
tiny patio, a pocket of relative calm. He set down his macchiato, the rich scent
of coffee a small, grounding comfort. Just as he sat, he saw Hope and Nick at
the counter. They spotted him and made their way outside.

"Thought we'd find you here," Hope said, her smile kind. "I heard you were
in the room with Anderson. How'd it go?"

Oliver shrugged, the motion feeling heavy. "It was fine. Wright thinks he's
going to bite."

"Is he like he is on Twitter?" Nick asked, pulling up a chair.

"Hard to tell," Oliver replied, swirling the foam in his cup. "His Twitter is
all about empowering the user, but in the room, he seemed pretty keen on our
strategy of … institutional capture."

"Whoa!" Nick interjected, almost defensively. "Institutional capture? It's
'land-and-expand,' man. That's what Wright calls it. We get in the door with
the big players, make a splash, and then the benefits trickle down to everyone
they work with."

"Does that trickle-down actually work, though?" Oliver pushed back gently, the question feeling less like an argument and more like a genuine inquiry.

"Sure, we're seeing it already," Nick insisted. "Look at the Freddie deal … I
mean, Phoenix." He grimaced at his own slip-up; client names were forbidden
in public. "They're going to bring in their entire ecosystem. Agents, vendors,
everyone."

Oliver took a sip of his macchiato. The bitter coffee matched his mood. "I
don't think so. I was in a couple of meetings with their operations people. They
liked the demo, but they're trying to put the kibosh on the whole thing."

"Why?" Nick looked genuinely surprised.

"Scaling, throughput," Oliver explained with a sigh. He hesitated, contemplating how much of his growing disillusionment he really wanted to
share. He decided to press on. "And honestly, I'm seeing a pattern. There's

a huge disconnect between the 'innovation teams' we sell to and the actual business units who have to use this stuff. The innovation guys have a budget for cool-looking science experiments. But the moment it needs to become a real, working product, it hits a wall of friction."

Nick, however, was unfazed, his certainty a shield against Oliver's doubt. "I wouldn't worry. Web3 is inevitable. They'll all have to fold eventually. Besides, Wright says the execs at Phoenix want to move forward. The pressure will come from the top down. The operations teams will fall in line."

Oliver wished he could borrow some of that certainty. For him, the last few weeks had been a slow, painful erosion of it. The solid ground of his career was turning to sand beneath his feet. He looked at Nick's bright, confident face and felt the chasm between their realities widen. There was no point in arguing with faith. He was too tired. He gave a small shrug and let it go.

Sensing the shift, Nick changed the subject. "Hey, I know it's a few weeks away, but we're getting some friends together for Memorial Day weekend. My wife's parents are out of town until June, and they have this massive place upstate. We're inviting four or five people. Would love for you and Hope to be there."

The offer was a sudden clearing in a cloudy day. "That's awesome. Whereabouts?" Oliver asked.

"Near a small town called Andes, in the Catskills. Maybe a two-and-a-half-hour drive," Nick said, his enthusiasm returning. "Her folks bought about ten acres and built a house a couple of years ago. It's pretty sick. We'll fire up the grill; the weather should be great."

"What's the closest Metro North station?" Oliver asked, the thought of escaping the city, the office, the grief-soaked apartment, suddenly feeling like a desperate need.

"There is none. It's a drive. But Becky and I can pick you up if you need a ride."

The relief was palpable. "That's great, dude. I'd love to visit," Oliver said, a genuine excitement cutting through the fog for the first time in days. "I haven't been to the Catskills in years. It'll be a welcome change. Thanks for the invite."

"You'll love it," Nick said, standing up. "Right, we're heading back." He and Hope turned to walk out of the café, leaving Oliver alone with his macchiato and the small, bright promise of a weekend in the mountains.

731888 (April 14)

"I think you're getting the hang of this, Oliver," Maren said as he settled into the now-familiar armchair. The warmth in her voice was a comfort. "Maybe after this one, you'll be fine doing this on your own."

"Are you sure?" The question came out laced with an anxiety he couldn't hide. "I've only done this twice. I don't think I could do it without you guiding me." The thought of navigating that internal abyss alone was terrifying.

"Yes, but you know the basic rules now," she said, her tone reassuring. "First, make sure no strong emotions are blocking you. If they are, resolve them, the way I showed you. Then you continue. If you're ever lost, use the autokinesis to guide you. And once you find what you came for – that feeling of resolution – you will know it's time to come back. It really is that simple."

"Can we at least do a few more sessions together?" he pleaded, feeling like a child asking for the training wheels to be left on.

Maren laughed softly. "Hon, if we continue for too long, I'll have to start charging you. Someone has to pay the bills." She winked, softening the words. "Okay. Let's try today, and maybe one more after. I feel you are ready."

He closed his eyes, and the world of the studio dissolved. It did not snap or shatter, but gently washed away, replaced by a scene that coalesced out of the darkness. He found himself standing in an O'Connell's that was both vivid and deeply strange. The room was bathed in a sepia tint, as if he were standing inside an old, brittle photograph. A heavy, expectant silence echoed in the high-ceilinged room. He was at the bar, his gaze fixed on Bryce's painting of *The Toddler*.

"This again?" he thought. *"I thought I'd already found what I needed here."*

Then, a thread of sound began to weave through the silence. It was Aisling's voice, distant and urgent, followed by that of an older woman. The whispers seemed to emanate from the very walls, ghosts of a conversation already passed.

"Why didn't you tell me it was valuable? We can't leave it hanging in the bar. I'm moving it to the storage room for safekeeping."

"I thought you knew. There's something special in the myrtle wreath. I remember Daideó telling me."

"Mum, no one told me. What's in the wreath – the flowery thing on the boy's head?"

"That's it. I couldn't understand when he told me. Some computer people found a pattern in there and got really excited. One of them even bought his next painting. A Hungarian lad, if I remember correctly."

The voices faded, leaving Oliver alone in the sepia silence with the new clues hanging in the air. *A pattern in the wreath. Computer people.* He leaned closer to the painting, his analytical mind kicking into gear for the first time in this strange new world.

He could see it now. The wreath was a logical, recursive structure made of deep purple and white flowers and what he now knew were myrtle leaves. He traced the pattern with his eyes. Each leaf had a small, irregular lump at its stalk. Two of these leaf-stalk units were attached to each white flower. The white flowers, in turn, had their own lumps at their stalks. And two white flower units were attached to each purple flower. The petals on the flowers themselves bore faint outlines that mimicked the shape of the lumps. It was a repeating, self-referential design.

The intricate pattern sparked a flicker of recognition deep in his mind, the academic ghost of a lecture hall, a half-remembered algorithm from a textbook. He couldn't quite place it, but for the first time, he felt a sense of advantage. This wasn't magic or spiritualism. This was a system. And systems were something he understood.

His gaze snagged on a green notepad lying on the bar counter, the kind waiters use. A single sentence was scrawled on it: *It is writ round the right corner of 56 Franklin.*

Franklin Street? In TriBeCa? The clue was so concrete, so direct. He checked it with the method Maren had taught him, and his left hand dropped in affirmation. A surge of confidence went through him. For the first time, he tried to direct the projection himself. He focused on the address, willing the sepia-toned pub to dissolve, to be replaced by a downtown street.

Instead, the world fractured and reassembled with a jarring lurch. He was no longer in the ghostly pub. He was standing outside the sterile, glass-walled conference room at BlockWaves, staring at his own back. It was the meeting with Chris Anderson from a few days ago.

"Maren, this is an actual event from my past," Oliver said out loud, his voice laced with the frustration of a pilot whose plane won't answer the controls. "This happened a few days ago."

"Wonderful," Maren's voice whispered from the real world. "I'm glad you are having a normal projection experience, too."

"But I can't do anything," he protested. "I'm just an observer, completely detached."

"Yes. That is how it is supposed to be," Maren explained gently. "You have been having special, magical experiences until now. For a change, you are having a normal one."

Resigned, Oliver watched the scene play out. It was deeply unnerving to see himself as a silent, nervous figure going through the motions of the demo. *God, my voice sounds terrible,* he thought, cringing at the hesitant pitch, the constant 'umms' and 'ers.' *Why can't I sound more confident?* As his past self spoke, his observer's gaze drifted, freed from the anxiety of the moment. It was drawn to a small detail he couldn't possibly have noticed at the time. Anderson's leather satchel was on the floor, and on it was a small metal label with a name engraved: *Cortlandt.* The word seemed to lift off the plate, glowing with the same strange significance as the pattern in the wreath. His subconscious filed it away.

The conference room dissolved without warning, and the world shifted again. He was now walking down a real, sunlit street. Franklin Street. He saw the numbers: 52, 54, 56. The instruction from the notepad echoed in his mind: *It is writ round the right corner.* He turned right.

The street became a narrow canyon, choked with construction scaffolding. The walkway underneath was filthy, the walls a canvas of lazy, looping graffiti. *Writ,* he thought. *Writing.* This had to be it. He scanned the childish scrawl on the first wall. The words were barely legible: *There is no Cortlandt.* An arrow pointed up and to the right.

The name hit him with the force of a physical connection. *Cortlandt.* The satchel. The graffiti. But why "No Cortlandt?" Was "Cortlandt" not the word, then? What did it mean?

He was stumped. He closed his eyes and tried the test again. *"Can I find what I'm looking for here?"* His left arm dropped. The answer was here. He just had to see it. He looked back at the graffiti, this time focusing on the arrow. It pointed up and to the right, into the gloomy cage of scaffolding. He followed its direction with his eyes, and then he saw it: a sliver of a green and white street sign, mostly hidden by a metal pole. The visible letters read: *Cortlandt al.*

A cascade of connections fired in his brain.

There is no Cortlandt. A command. A subtraction. Take *Cortlandt* away from *Cortlandt al.* What's left?

al.

al?

Alley!

The memory of Anderson's voice: *That's right up my alley … right up my alley.* It wasn't a coincidence. It was a signpost, a breadcrumb he hadn't even known he was following. It was the third word. A giddy, triumphant laugh bubbled up in his chest.

Autokinesis? he asked himself, needing the final, physical proof.

His left arm fell, heavy and sure.

Yes.

"Well, how do you feel about it?" Maren asked as his eyes fluttered open, the sepia world of the projection dissolving back into the warm colors of her studio.

He felt a live wire of adrenaline buzzing under his skin. "I believe I found the third word, Maren," he said, the certainty in his own voice surprising him. "Do you know what these words could mean?"

"Maybe they will make a sentence that your father wanted you to know," Maren suggested.

"I've got *violin*, *toddler*, and now *alley*," he mused, his mind racing. "A toddler playing a violin in an alley? What about the filler words, the 'a's and 'the's? How am I supposed to find those?" He scratched his head, the practical problems of the puzzle already asserting themselves.

"You have to trust that your father knew what he was doing," Maren said gently. "He led you to three words. You knew them when you found them. Just trust the process."

****

Back in his apartment later that night, the adrenaline had faded, leaving a hollow, ringing silence. He walked to the small bar cart and his eyes fell on the bottle of Lagavulin 16, a gift from his dad for his last birthday. He'd never been a huge fan of the aggressive peat of Islay malts, but his dad had been trying to gently educate his palate.

Tonight felt different. He was no longer just numbly surviving. He had solved something. He had connected with something. He felt, for the first time in weeks, ready for a real drink.

He pulled the bottle from the shelf, the heavy glass cool in his hand. He poured a measure into a glass and added the tiniest splash of water, just as his dad had taught him. The first sip was a soft explosion of smoky peat, a taste that was so intrinsically his father's that it felt like a memory on his tongue. It gave way to a gentle warmth in the back of his throat, followed by a sweet, subtly spicy caress. He closed his eyes. If the last seven-and-a-half minutes of Steven Wilson's song *The Watchmaker* had been a liquid, this is what it would taste like. *Dad might have been onto something,* he thought with a ghost of a smile.

He sank into his chair, taking another sip. And that's when the dam broke.

The scotch dissolved the barriers that had been holding the feelings back. A tidal wave of confusion, anger, and a sorrow so profound it felt like a physical weight crashed over him. The intellectual puzzle of the last two weeks, the surreal projections, the strange clues – they had all been a distraction, a fantastic game to keep his mind from the simple, brutal truth.

How could any of this be possible? The question was a frantic scream in the silence of his mind. *Dad is gone forever! Who do I turn to for advice? Where does all this love I have for him go?*

The confusion curdled into a hot, searing anger. *How did he know he was going to die? Why leave these cryptic, insane clues? Why not just a simple note? A farewell?*

His mind raced, lashing out. *How is this woo-woo time-projection stuff even real? Is Maren just taking advantage of me? Drugging the water? What could she possibly want? I have nothing.* The hundred thousand in WilcoxRe stock felt like pocket change in a universe that had gone mad.

The anger found its true target, the only one it could.

How could you have fucking known this was going to happen, Dad?

The thought was a betrayal, a sacrilege, and it felt horribly, liberatingly true.

"Fuck!" The word was a torn, ragged sound in the quiet apartment. "I hate you. I fucking hate you! How could you do this to me?" The rage was a fire, burning away the numbness, the confusion, everything. But underneath the ash of that fire was the raw, unbearable grief. The anger collapsed, leaving only the sound of a boy's desperate plea.

"Please," he whispered, the word breaking. "Please, I'm begging you, come back. I'll do anything. Please …"

He slid from the chair to the floor, his body wracked with sobs he could no longer contain.

A lone bottle of sixteen-year-old Lagavulin stood stoically on the table, its amber liquid staring down at the writhing, inconsolable young man on the floor in front of it. This wasn't the first time it had induced such catharsis in men, and it certainly wouldn't be the last.

732032 (April 15)

"Four o'clock on a Friday, you're here a little earlier than usual …" Aisling's voice was warm as she saw Oliver approaching the bar.

He offered a weak smile, but his eyes were fixed on the wall behind her. A cold lurch in his stomach. The spot where *The Toddler* had hung just a few days ago was now occupied by a cheap, generic print of fruit in a bowl. The painting – his clue, his connection – was gone.

"Oh hey," he fumbled, the words feeling thick in his dry mouth. "Yeah, I wasn't going to get a drink. Just stopping by to … check on something."

Aisling laughed, wiping down the bar. "Around here? People either drink or watch soccer. I make sure of the drinking part. There's nothing else to check."

Oliver's smile felt like a mask. "Aisling, the painting of the boy we were looking at. What happened to it?"

"Oh, that?" Her expression brightened. "Funniest thing. I got curious after you asked, so I spoke to my mum. Turns out it's likely a pretty valuable piece. All these years, she thought it was safely packed away."

"She doesn't come to the pub?" Oliver asked, his mind racing, trying to keep his voice steady.

"Not really. She's got her own local out in Forest Hills."

"So where is it now?" he pressed, a knot of dread tightening in his chest.

"We moved it into storage," Aisling replied, oblivious to the impact of her words. "Going to connect with some art folks, see if we can sell it."

The memory of the projection hit him – the disembodied whispers in the sepia-toned pub. He was hearing the conversation for the second time, and the paranormal déjà vu made the floor feel unstable beneath his feet.

"How come it was never sold if it's so valuable?" he asked, the question a desperate attempt to keep the conversation going, to gather more pieces.

"Mum was saying it almost sold a few times – back in the 70s, the 90s, then about ten years ago. All the deals kept falling through last minute."

He needed another way in. A lie formed on his lips, born of pure urgency. "Can I talk to your mother about your grandad? I looked him up a couple of days ago … he seems like a fascinating painter. I'd love to learn more."

Aisling looked genuinely surprised. "There's stuff on the internet about my grandad?"

Oliver nodded, not looking her in the eyes.

"Sure. I can see if she wants to meet," she mused. "Maybe at Finnegan's. She's usually there on weekends."

"Finnegan's?" The name was unfamiliar.

"Her local in Queens," Aisling clarified.

"Ah. Yes, that would be great," Oliver said, relief washing over him. He had a new lead. "I can meet her tomorrow or the day after, if she's okay with it."

He thanked her and turned to leave, his mind a chaotic whirl. He took a few moments on the sidewalk to digest what had just happened, the drizzly afternoon air feeling cold against his flushed skin.

It wasn't just a dream. The projection, the sepia-toned pub, the ghostly whispers of Aisling and her mother – he had witnessed a real event. An event that had happened in his absence, in someone else's life. He had seen a piece of the immediate past, and now, stepping back into the flow of time, he had watched it become the present.

This wasn't what Maren had told him. This wasn't observing his *own* past for a fresh perspective. This wasn't a magical dreamland where he flew with lions. This was something else. This was a crack in the wall of reality itself. A terrifying, exhilarating power that followed no rules he understood. *What exactly is happening to me?* The question echoed in the sudden, unnerving silence of his own mind.

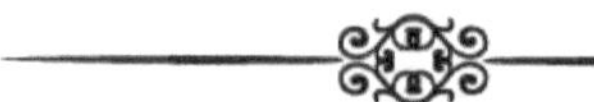

732159 (April 16)

Oliver never enjoyed leaving Manhattan. To him, the other boroughs felt like photocopies of the real thing – a little faded, a little wrong. They called themselves New York, but they lacked the vertical certainty, the relentless energy that was the city's signature. Queens was a prime example: a sprawling uncertainty of short houses under a too-big sky, with street names that followed a logic he couldn't decipher. In downtown Manhattan, a non-standard street name was a charming quirk of history; here, it just felt like a nuisance.

Finnegan's was a quiet Irish pub on Austin Street, tucked away as if it didn't want to be found. He had to descend a half-flight of stairs to a worn-out entrance, stepping down from the street into another time. The air inside was thick with the scent of old wood and spilled beer, cozy and authentically worn in a way O'Connell's never was. A handful of regulars populated the bar, their quiet camaraderie making Oliver feel like the immediate and obvious outsider he was.

He scanned the dim room for Aisling's mother. At the far end of the bar, holding court with the bartender, was an older lady in her mid-seventies, a tall glass of what looked like seltzer beside her. It had to be her.

He approached with a rehearsed casualness that he didn't feel. "Hi, are you Shannon?"

The woman's animated story trailed off mid-sentence. She turned slowly, her eyes taking a moment to focus, to place the unfamiliar young man who had just materialized in her Saturday afternoon world. "I'm Oliver," he said, his voice softer than he'd intended. "Aisling said she'd spoken to you about meeting today."

"Aisling?" she asked, the name floating in the air as if she'd never heard it.

"Your daughter, Aisling," Oliver clarified, a knot of worry forming. "You are Shannon McGinty, right?"

A flicker of recognition. "Oh, *Aisling*. Yes, yes." She finally locked onto him. "She did say someone interested in the painting wanted to meet." Her voice grew conspiratorial. "I've got to tell you though, we've had a lot of bidders. The price is going up." As she spoke, a waft of vodka fumes hit him – the seltzer was clearly just a mixer.

"Bidders? Oh, I don't think you understand." A nervous laugh escaped him. "I don't want to buy it. I just wanted to learn more about your father, Jonathan Bryce."

Shannon squinted, her gaze suddenly sharp, analytical. "What sort of work do you do?"

"What sort ... I don't ..." Oliver stammered, thrown off by the abrupt change in direction.

"Yeah, where do you work? What kind of work?" she repeated, her focus unwavering.

"I'm a developer. At a company called BlockWaves," he replied.

"Oh." Her face fell. "Aisling never said you were in real estate."

"No, no," Oliver chuckled, relieved to be on what he thought was solid ground. "I'm a software developer. A computer programmer."

Shannon's eyes widened, a slow smile spreading across her face as if she'd just solved a puzzle. "So you *are* the guy then! You want to buy the painting."

"I think there's been a miscommunication," he said, his own confusion mounting. "I'm not looking to buy it. I just want to find out more about your father's work. There wasn't much online."

She didn't look convinced. Her eyes narrowed, and she pointed a crooked, surprisingly steady finger at him, circling it in the air near his face. "You're a computer programmer, but you don't want to buy the painting?"

"That's right," he responded, taking a small, involuntary step back from her finger. "I want to learn more about it. And your father."

"Then how come," she asked, her voice dropping to a pointed, accusatory hush, "all those *other* computer programmers wanted to buy it back then?"

The words landed with the force of a revelation. *Other computer programmers.* It wasn't just his dad. It was a group. A tribe. Oliver's mind raced, trying to recalibrate. He was in over his head. He needed to change the dynamic, to regain some control. A memory of Ian Wright's sales training surfaced from the depths of his corporate life: *Empathetic distraction.* It felt absurdly out of place, but it was all he had.

He took a deep breath, shifted his tone, and smiled warmly. "Shannon," he said, trying to project an effortless calm. "Can I get you a drink? I see your glass is running a little low."

It's a tall glass of vodka with a splash of club soda," Shannon said. "But Mike here's got me covered, you don't need to worry." She winked at the bartender, who nodded and walked away to fix her drink.

Oliver decided a direct, honest approach was his only move. "Look, Shannon, I would really appreciate it if you could answer a few questions about Jonathan Bryce. I can't afford to buy any paintings right now, but I would love to learn more about his art. Could you indulge that for a few minutes?"

The arrival of the fresh, sweating glass seemed to focus her mind. She took a slow sip, her eyes clearing a little. "Okay, feller," she said, making direct, friendly eye contact for the first time. "What would you like to know?"

Oliver leaned in. "Tell me about him. As a painter."

"My dad?" A fond, distant smile touched her lips. "He wasn't a 'painter,' not really. Not at first. He did odd jobs all over Belfast. Painting was just …

something he did. A hobby. Said it quieted the noise in his head. Then some of his pals at the pub told him he should take it seriously."

"And that's when he made *The Toddler*?" Oliver asked.

"Lord, no. The first one was just a wee pastoral scene. Sheep on a hill, you know the type. Sold it for enough to keep us fed for a few months," she chuckled. "No, *The Toddler* ... that one took him two years. Agonized over it. And then, nobody wanted to buy it." She took another sip of her drink. "Not until the American showed up in the mid-70s. A 'computer guy,' he was. Ralph. Said he was fascinated by the pattern in the wreath."

Ralph. A computer guy, Oliver thought, the words lighting up in his mind like a neon sign.

"Dad, sensing he had a live one, asked for a ridiculous price," Shannon continued, shaking her head at the memory. "Scared him off. So, *The Toddler* stayed on the wall."

"Aisling said there was a third painting," Oliver prompted gently.

"The third one ..." Her eyes went unfocused for a moment, searching the past. "Lord, what was it called now? Something about a clock ... *It Is Time*, that's it. A strange one, that. All chaos and a rowdy pub, not like the others. Ralph saw it, but it wasn't for him. It sat around for ages." She paused. "Then, years later, after we'd moved here, one of Ralph's friends bought it. A Hungarian fella ... George, I think his name was."

George. The Hungarian. The second name clicked into place, and Oliver's heart began to beat faster. He tried to keep his expression neutral. "Why did you move to the U.S.?"

The light in Shannon's eyes dimmed. "That's ... a different story," she said, her voice heavy. "My husband, Eamonn. Aisling's father. He owned a small pub in Belfast. Got himself deep in debt." She stared into her glass. "Took his own life. Mid-80s."

She said it so simply, the weight of the tragedy immense in the quiet of the bar. "After that ... there was nothing left for us there. So, the whole family – me, the kids, Dad – we came here to Queens. To start again."

Oliver listened, the pieces of his own father's immigrant story echoing in hers. He felt a desperate urge to ask more about Ralph and George, about the "computer people," but he could see Shannon was drifting, the vodka and the painful memories pulling her into a haze.

"My dad, he never made another big one after the third," she murmured, her voice growing softer. "Just sketches, book covers, comics. Said the voices got too loud sometimes. But those computer people … they kept in touch with him. Right up to the end."

Voices, Oliver thought, another chilling connection. He felt a profound sense of both discovery and frustration. He had names, leads, a pattern of interest from a mysterious group his father was clearly a part of. But he could feel Shannon slipping away. Her memories were getting hazier, her story dissolving back into the past.

He thanked her profusely and offered again to pay for her drink. The bartender, Mike, just waved him away with a kind, knowing look. Oliver left Finnegan's and stepped back out into the Queens afternoon, his mind reeling. The wreath, Ralph, George, the voices … and his dad, staging a photograph of a painting that was somehow at the center of it all. He had to ask his mom. He had to know if that photo, that memory, was even real.

732311 (April 17)

It *was* real.

The realization hit Oliver with the force of a physical blow, making him sink back onto the sofa in his mother's Maplewood house. For an hour, he had been digging through the musty confines of a storage closet, the air thick with the scent of mothballs and aging paper. Then he'd found it. The album from his projection. His heart had hammered against his ribs as he opened it, and there they were – all the photos, in the exact same order. And in the middle, the one that made the air leave his lungs.

The photo of him as a child, wearing a floral wreath, standing by an apple tree. It *was* the photo. A tangible, physical bridge between his inner world and this one. He turned it over. His dad's neat, authoritative cursive was a painful, all-too-recognizable sight. *Oliver as The Toddler, March 10, 2000.*

"Mom, I don't remember this photo. Do you?" he yelled out, his voice strained.

His mother walked in from the kitchen, wiping her hands on a towel. She took the photo and stared at it, her brow furrowed. After a few moments, a flicker of recognition crossed her face. "Oh, I remember this now. Vaguely. This was back in Connecticut. Your dad dressed you up as some character from a play or something." She handed it back. "You probably don't remember because you were so young. What's the date? Yeah, you weren't even two."

"Are you sure it was a character from a play?" Oliver asked, the casualness of her memory a stark contrast to the storm in his mind.

"Oh, I can't remember. A play, a movie … something your dad was into," she replied with a shrug, her tone dismissing it as one of her ex-husband's trivial pursuits.

"Did Dad ever mention an artist called Jonathan Bryce?"

"Hmm, the name rings a bell. Why?"

"I think this photo is a copy of a painting by Bryce," Oliver said, gently probing. "I saw the painting in SoHo. And I found out a lot of computer scientists were interested in his work. Do you know if Dad was one of them?"

"So that must be it, then," she said, as if solving a minor household puzzle. "No, I don't know anything about computer scientists and this Bryce fellow. Your dad was hardly a computer scientist, dear. He joined WilcoxRe before you were born. He was a programmer in the 90s, sure, but he started running one of their modeling teams almost twenty years ago."

"But he studied CS at Princeton," Oliver countered, a familiar note of defensiveness for his father creeping into his voice.

"I guess," his mom conceded with another shrug. "But he got into reinsurance just a few years after that. I never really thought of him as a computer scientist."

Oliver fell silent, the old, persistent ache of the paradox of his father's life returning. A man with a mind built for things like information theory, who had spent decades in a corporate job that seemed to bore him to his core. What had happened on that path between Princeton and WilcoxRe?

He decided to try one more door. "Mom, do you know if Dad ever worked on secret codes or puzzles?"

His mother's posture changed. It was a subtle shift, but one he knew intimately. Her shoulders tensed, her easygoing expression sharpened into one of wary suspicion. "What do you mean?" she asked, her eyebrow raised.

"Did he ever talk about secret words? Hidden behind complex clues that make up a sentence with a deeper meaning?"

The air in the room grew cold. "I'm not sure I understand," she said, but her eyes told a different story. "Why are you asking about secret words? Is this something you found out about him?" Her voice began to climb, the old panic creeping in. "Tell me, Oliver! Don't you hide anything from me!"

He saw it then – the conversation spiraling down the same dark, well-worn path it always did. He had made a mistake. The word "secret" in this house did not mean "puzzle"; it meant "infidelity." He was watching her mind race, connecting his innocent question to her years of suspicion, the wound from their divorce tearing open anew. He realized it was pointless. He could never tell her about the twenty-four words, about this quest. And he certainly couldn't mention Maren, a name that was gasoline on the fire of his mother's long-held beliefs. He had to retreat. He had to lie.

The lie felt clumsy and sour in his mouth, but he forced a casual tone. "Oh no, Mom, it's nothing to do with Dad, really. I've been looking into word puzzles to take my mind off things. Was wondering if he had anything on the subject. It's a lot of fun. You should try it."

His mom searched his face for a moment, a flicker of disbelief in her eyes, but then seemed to decide that the lie was a more pleasant alternative than the truth she feared. She let it go. "Well," she said, her voice brightening, "I'm glad you changed your mind and decided to spend Easter with me. I feel like I barely see you anymore these days."

"I know, Mom. Work's been tough, and after ... the news, I just needed some time alone," Oliver replied.

"I know it's been hard, baby. You know I'm always here for you if you need to talk."

Oliver nodded politely, the gesture a hollow pantomime. *The last person I would talk to*, he thought, a bitter taste in his mouth. He knew, with a certainty that ached, why he didn't visit. He blamed her – her anxiety, her relentless, untrusting nature – for the fracture of their family. He was certain his dad had never cheated, and that certainty made her suspicion feel like a constant, low-grade poison. The only reason he was here today, sitting in this quiet suburban house, was for the photo album. He had what he came for.

He flipped through the album one last time, ready to put it away. On the final page, a photo he hadn't seen before caught his eye. It was his dad, younger, maybe ten years ago, sitting in a pub that looked European. He was laughing, a full-throated, unguarded laugh, sharing a beer with another man. The image was a punch to the gut – a glimpse of a happiness he hadn't witnessed.

"Who's this person Dad's with?"

His mom leaned over. "Oh, that's from his trip to Budapest. I think that's his friend, Gyorgy. Don't you remember him? He visited us once, and then Dad went to see him. You must have been about twelve at the time."

Oliver didn't remember the man, but the name hit him like a lightning strike. *Gyorgy. A Hungarian friend.* Shannon's voice echoed in his mind: *a Hungarian man called George.* It had to be him.

"Did you ever meet Gyorgy?" he asked, his voice tight with the effort of staying calm.

"Yes, when he was in New York. A nice guy, but socially awkward." Her expression began to shift, the usual storm clouds gathering. "I never fully trusted him, though. That's around the time your dad started acting so strange, so secretive." She leaned in, her voice dropping to a conspiratorial whisper. "I think Gyorgy knew the women he was sleeping with."

And that was it. A switch flipped inside Oliver. The carefully constructed dam of patience and polite detachment he maintained around his mother finally burst. A dense, searingly hot wave of rage pulsed through his body, starting in his gut and exploding in his head. It was the culmination of weeks of grief, years of frustration, and a lifetime of defending his father's memory against these baseless attacks. He couldn't stop himself. The words ripped from his throat, raw and loud in the quiet house.

"Shut up! Just shut the fuck up! How dare you say that about him? He never cheated on you, and you're the only one who thinks he did!"

The sound of his own voice and the ugliness of the words shocked them both into a heavy, ringing silence. There was nothing more to be said, nothing that could fix what had just been broken open. Unwilling to create any more unpleasantness, and unable to stay in the same room with her for another second, Oliver put the album down, turned, and walked out without another word.

CHAPTER 4. SHOULDER

"I know, I know. I'm definitely leaving early today," Oliver chuckled as he walked up to Hope's beanbag chair on his way to the exit.

"Mr. Battolo, I'm not your timekeeper," Hope retorted, tilting her head and batting her eyelids playfully. "You're free to come and go as you please."

For the first time in what felt like an eternity, a genuine, uncomplicated smile touched Oliver's lips. He remembered how much he enjoyed this – the easy, playful current that ran between them. A spark of the person he used to be. He'd be lying if he said he wasn't attracted to her, but the thought was immediately followed by a wave of caution. The company policy on inter-office dalliances was ambiguous at best, and the last thing he needed was a trip to HR. Still, she always went out of her way to be kind, and the flirting – if that's what it was – was a welcome glimmer of light in his otherwise gray world.

"I'm meeting one of my dad's colleagues in midtown," he explained. "He asked if I could meet him before five. Hey, are you planning on being at Nick's place upstate for Memorial Day?"

Hope laughed. "That's over a month away. Hard to plan that far ahead. I most likely will, though. You're going, right?"

"I'll be there," Oliver said, the thought of the mountains a tangible relief. "Looking forward to the break."

"Okay, if you're going for sure, I'll make it happen." She gave him a grin that was decidedly mischievous. "A weekend in the mountains with the dangerous Mr. Battolo sounds like fun."

"You know I'm one of the most boring people around, right?" he chuckled again.

"That's what you think, Oliver," she said, her smile lingering. "But I see your true potential."

After a few more pleasantries, Oliver waved goodbye and headed out towards the 6 train, a lightness in his step he hadn't felt for weeks.

A short while later, at the WilcoxRe office, he was greeted with a cheerful boom, shattering the quiet of his mind. "Oliver, how are you holding up there, tiger!"

Oliver cringed. *Eddie Garcia.* The man was a walking archetype of the American middle manager, from his ill-fitted polyester suit to the phantom image of the 90s minivan Oliver knew he still drove. Eddie considered himself a dear friend of the family; a feeling, Oliver knew, that had never been fully reciprocated. His dad, Nate, had taken a younger Eddie under his wing at WilcoxRe twenty years ago, a gesture of professional kindness that Eddie, in his infinite lack of self-awareness, had interpreted as a pact of eternal kinship.

"I'm okay, Mr. Garcia," Oliver offered, bracing himself. "I guess you're never really prepared for something like this."

"I'm still getting over my disbelief, chief, let me tell you." Eddie shook his head, a gesture of profound, theatrical sorrow. *Chief. Tiger. Big guy.* Eddie's vocabulary of endearments was a small, irritating universe unto itself. "I mean, Nate Battolo, give me a goddam break – one of my best buds! How crazy is that, you know what I'm saying?" He jabbed an animated thumb across the office hallway toward Nate's old, empty room. "Feels like just yesterday he was right there. You know, it was so sudden. One minute he's here, next he's at the offsite in Bermuda, and then …" Eddie clapped his hands together, the sound sharp and startling. "Boom! We get the news about the accident. Boom! Just like that, you know what I'm talking about?"

Oliver had feared this, the conversational vortex that was Eddie Garcia. He braced himself, trying to steer the runaway train onto the one track that mattered. "Has there been any further news? About the specifics of the accident?"

Eddie took a comically deep breath, puffing out his chest as if preparing for a grand oration, and stared out the thirty-fourth-floor window for a dramatic moment. "You know, we just got more details, and that's why I called you. I wanted to tell your mom, Diane, but who knows what she wants to hear. I tried talking to her at the memorial – you know, just to check if my speech was okay, that sort of thing – and she just brushed me off. Changed the subject to the kids' summer plans. The divorce hit her hard, you know what I mean, tiger?" He leaned in conspiratorially. "Nate never told me much about why it went south. Kinda a man's man, you know? Never one for personal stuff, and I respect that. A solid professional. I don't know how his models teams are going to keep up now, you know what I'm saying?"

He paused, but it was the brief, tactical pause of a marathon speaker catching his breath, not an actual opening. Oliver waited, trapped.

"It's hard enough with the markets turning," Eddie continued, his hands beginning to conduct an invisible orchestra of economic doom. "And Powell's talking about a seventy-five-point hike … our models need to be sharp as a goddam sushi knife. And Nate, he had a sixth sense for this stuff. Macro, micro, you name it."

A fond, faraway look entered Eddie's eyes. "I'll tell you something funny, big guy. Back in '08, '09, when QE was just starting, your dad and I were with a client. The client and I, we thought, 'Okay, a year of this, tops.' Bernanke will taper, the repo market will cool off, that sorta stuff." He chuckled. "Your dad just shook his head. 'No way, Jose,' he said. 'Once this money printing starts, it doesn't unwind easy. The market's going to get hooked on cheap liquidity.' He called it 'the everything bubble.' Said it would go on for ten, fifteen years and spur a bull market like we've never seen." A wave of pride, sharp and painful, washed over Oliver. This was his father – the man who saw the code underneath the world.

"We laughed so hard at him," Eddie said, his voice cracking slightly. "Poor son of a bitch. May his soul rest in peace." He wiped at the corner of his eye. "And look what happened? He was goddamn right. Every step of the way."

The anecdote hung in the air, a small, perfect monument to his father's brilliance. Oliver saw his opening in the emotional pause and seized it. "Mr. Garcia … so, the news? About the accident?"

"Oh, yeah, yeah!" Eddie snapped back to the present. "Sometimes I think I'll talk my own head off. So, here's the deal, champ. It wasn't a weather thing, like we first thought." He leaned forward again. "They finished dinner onshore, at a place on the wharf in Hamilton. Company rented the whole joint out. Best seafood in Bermuda, let me tell you. I can't believe I got the flu two days before the trip – a real blessing in disguise, maybe, because if I hadn't, I would have been on that boat with your dad, you know what I'm saying, big guy?"

Oliver stared back blankly, the phrase "blessing in disguise" landing with a thud in his stomach.

Eddie didn't notice. "Anyway," he went on, "They get on the yacht for the afterparty around nine. Supposed to be a two-hour cruise." He began tracing a map in the air with a thick finger. "Sail past the South Channel, turn, stop by a place called Daniel's Head, then back. Simple. But apparently, somewhere past the South Channel, the visibility got bad. Not a storm, but you know, no stars, hazy. And they were the only boat out there. So they missed the turn, just drifted for a while, never saw Daniel's Head. Then … they hit something. A reef, a volcanic rock, something like that."

Eddie paused, taking a breath, but it was only to switch tracks. "Did you know that the whole of Bermuda was created from volcanic rock?" he asked, suddenly a geologist. "It's not a real island like in the Caribbean. Birds flying between Africa and North America dropped seeds on it, and that's how you get the vegetation. Wild, huh?"

Volcanic rock? Oliver's mind screamed. *Birds?* He was suffocating with impatience, but he remained silent, a hostage to the narrative.

"Anyway, chief," Eddie continued, oblivious, "The yacht hit the reef hard. Knocked a couple of people right off the deck into the water. Your dad … and another junior actuary. Julian, I think his name is. Nice kid."

The words hit Oliver with the force of a physical impact. The distant hum of the office disappeared. All he could hear was the roar of the ocean in his mind, all he could see was the violent, tumultuous image of his father falling into the black water.

"There was chaos," Eddie went on, his hands waving to paint the scene. "It was one of those big fancy yachts, a hundred people rolling all over the place. The engine died. It took the coast guard twenty minutes to get there, and it wasn't for another hour that they did a headcount and realized your dad was missing. An hour, can you believe it? Julian, he got lucky. Didn't get dinged up too bad and managed to swim back. He was back in the office a few days later, a bit shaken, but crunching those numbers again. Yeah, good kid."

Eddie paused for a sip of water. The detail of the hour – his father in the water, alone, while a party devolved into chaos – was a shard of glass in Oliver's mind. He saw his opening and drove his question into the silence like a nail.

"When did the Coast Guard begin searching for my dad?" His voice was tight, controlled, desperate for a single hard fact in the swirling horror.

Eddie put his water down and thumbed through a few stapled pages. "So, the report," he said, suddenly official, "Says they arrived at 10:13 p.m. local time. By the time they figured out your dad was the only one missing, it was 10:44. They launched the search right after that. Helicopter, floodlights, the whole nine yards. Searched until almost one a.m. and then again the next morning."

He looked up from the papers, his expression turning grim. "When his body didn't float up after three or four days, they declared him dead." Eddie shook his head. "Who knows what really happened to him? Maybe he's still down there, stuck in a shipwreck, slowly turning into a skeleton. Or maybe …" he shrugged, his tone casual and utterly brutal, "… maybe he was eaten by sharks."

A wave of nausea washed over Oliver. His imagination, now his enemy, supplied the horrific images with perfect, sickening clarity.

"What a way to go, you know what I mean?" Eddie's voice cracked. "For a guy so smart to perish like that … it breaks my heart, tiger. It really does." Tears welled in the corners of his eyes, and he wiped them away with the back of his hand. "I loved him like a brother. I really did."

Oliver just sat there, frozen, the cold, hard facts of the report colliding with the monstrous images Eddie had so carelessly conjured in his mind.

His gaze fell on the report still sitting on Eddie's desk. It was a death certificate in bureaucratic prose. His eyes caught a few, stark words.

Location: Grimsby's Shoulder, 3 miles off the coast … Description: Nathan Battolo … declared dead after search teams were unable to recover his body …

Grimsby's Shoulder. The name was an obscure, alien piece of geography that would now be a part of his own internal map forever. He couldn't read any more. A wave of sickness washed over him, and he had to physically look away, focusing on a spot on the wall to keep the room from spinning.

He saw Eddie compose himself, wiping the last of the moisture from his eyes, his expression shifting as he geared up for another soliloquy. Oliver couldn't take any more. He had to change the subject, had to pull the conversation out of the abyss.

"I really appreciate you sharing this with me, Mr. Garcia," he interjected, his voice tight but polite. "I have another question, if you don't mind. I was going through my dad's old photos and saw one of him in Budapest about ten years ago with someone named Gyorgy. Do you know anything about him, or that trip?"

The new topic seemed to reset Eddie. He craned his neck back, staring at the ceiling as if it were a projection screen for his memories, mumbling the name softly. "Gyorgy … Gyorgy … Yeah, I remember that trip. Back in 2010. We were dealing with a large Hungarian account. A few of us went out there."

A distant, wistful look softened his features. "You've got to see Budapest to believe it, kiddo. What an incredible city. The architecture is like something out of a magazine." He launched into a classic tangent, a well-worn story about brutalist buildings and the surprising beauty of Hungarian women. Oliver listened with a coiled impatience, waiting for the one piece of information that mattered.

"Did you meet someone called Gyorgy on that trip?" Oliver asked, his voice almost desperate, cutting through Eddie's reverie. "I believe he was a friend of my dad's."

Eddie blinked, pulled back from his memories. "You know, now that I think about it, your dad did leave us a couple of nights to go meet a friend. The rest of the team … man, we had some wild nights out. We were still in our forties, most of us. But yeah, I don't remember Nate being there for the real parties. Said he had to meet a friend and left before things got started. Could have been this … Gay-orgy guy you're talking about. What kind of a name is that, anyway?"

Before Oliver could respond, Eddie was off again. "It's a strange language, Hungarian. Not Indo-European like German or Romanian. It's Uralic, like Finnish and Estonian. What a world, right, kiddo?" He smiled, proud of the trivia. "It was probably your dad who told me all that. He had a real knack for languages, you know what I mean? Grew up speaking four of them, spoke English with that fancy mid-Atlantic accent like an old newsreader."

This much Oliver knew. Eddie was right. His dad had been a collector of languages, a skill Oliver had always admired and been slightly mystified by. He had picked up German, French, and Spanish with an ease that seemed unnatural. Oliver remembered being in a tapas bar with him once in New York; his dad had spoken Spanish so fluently, with such a perfect Castilian lilt, that the bartender had asked him which part of Spain he was from. It was just another facet of the brilliant, complex man who was now just a description on a piece of paper.

"What a guy, you know what I'm talking about?" Eddie continued, his energy unabated. "So well-read, a keen understanding of everything. I once told him he was good enough to be CEO, and you won't believe what he told me, tiger. He said, 'Egg …'" Eddie paused his own story. "He used to call me Egg, you know that? My middle name is Gabriel, for my father. Eduardo Gabriel Garcia. E.G.G. Your dad came up with that. What a clown. My own father … bless his soul, fought in Vietnam. Oh, the stories he told me, tiger. You wouldn't believe …"

Oliver nodded along, a polite hostage. He had to let the conversational river meander through its usual tributaries – Eddie's nickname, Eddie's father, the Vietnam War – before it would ever return to the main channel: his own dad.

"Anyway, back to your dad," Eddie said, finally reorienting himself. "He said, 'Egg, that's a lot of unnecessary operations work. I'm happy where I am because I can do what I want. I have spare time to do other stuff, and everyone leaves me alone.'" Eddie threw his hands up in theatrical disbelief. "Can you believe this guy? Smarter than the CEO – I'll give you that in writing right now – and he chose not to move up because he wanted time for 'other stuff.' I swear to God, I never understood it."

The words hit Oliver with a jolt of cognitive dissonance. *Spare time?* The dad he remembered was always neck-deep in work, bringing it home, his mind often distant and occupied even at the dinner table. The man Eddie was describing was a stranger, someone who had actively engineered a life with secret, empty spaces in it.

"Do you know what the other stuff was?" Oliver asked, his voice sharp with a new, intense curiosity.

"Nah, he never told me," Eddie said with a shrug. "I asked a few times, but he'd just brush it off. Seemed like puzzles or math. But one time, a few years back, I came up behind him at his desk. He was writing code. The screen was full of it, green lines scrolling, you know, like in *The Matrix*. He jumped when he saw me, slammed the laptop shut like he'd been caught with contraband. When I asked what he was hiding, he just laughed it off, said he was playing with some C++ for fun."

Eddie shook his head again. "Your father was a bright guy, kiddo. Got interested in stuff normal folks like me wouldn't touch with a ten-foot pole. Puzzles and code as a *hobby*? Gimme a break. But that was your old man. Whaddayagonnado?"

Oliver felt a series of quiet clicks in his mind. *Puzzles. Secret code. A hidden life.* He had gotten what he came for, and more. He knew that to stay any longer would be to invite an endless chain of more anecdotes. He stood up, forcing a grateful smile. "Thanks, Eddie. I really appreciate this." He politely ended the conversation, extracting himself from the conversational quicksand.

As he walked out of the WilcoxRe building and onto the crowded sidewalk of 54th Street, the city noise felt miles away. He was left with a hollow, gaping ache. The new clues about his father's life were just pieces of a puzzle he couldn't solve, and the story of his father's death was a nightmare he couldn't escape.

It would be impossible to find full closure, he knew that. But a body … a recovered body would have been something concrete. A fact. A grave. It would have been an endpoint, a final, terrible punctuation mark.

This was different. This was an absence. A void. His father hadn't been given an ending, just a disappearance declared by a bureaucrat on a foreign island. There was no finality, no peace, just a story that stopped mid-sentence, leaving him unfairly, indefinitely, open-ended.

732900 (April 21)

Oliver's macchiato had just found a home at a small table on the Bluebird Café's patio when he saw her. Through the glass, a familiar face was at the counter, paying for a smoothie before turning to scan the crowded room for a seat. It was Maren's student, Daniela.

Without thinking, on an impulse that felt foreign after weeks of deliberate, heavy movements, Oliver waved and called out, "Daniela! Over here." The couple at the next table startled, but he barely noticed.

She was an attractive woman, around his age, with an indefinable heritage that had intrigued him when they first met. There was the slightest of accents in her speech, a musical lilt he'd guessed might be Mediterranean. Her gaze followed the sound of her name and locked onto his. It took a moment for her expression to shift from confusion to recognition, and then a bright, easy smile spread across her face. She waved back and started walking toward his table.

"Hey! Oliver, right?" she said, her voice warm.

"Yes, we met at Maren's place," he smiled back, feeling a bit of the tension in his shoulders ease for the first time all day.

"Yes, of course. It's nice to see you again." She paused, her smile turning a little mischievous. "Maren talks about you."

A cold spike of adrenaline shot through him. He felt his own smile tighten, become a mask. His quest, his father's bizarre legacy – it was a fragile, secret thing. He had trusted Maren, but the thought of her discussing it, even casually, made his stomach clench. "Oh?" he asked, trying for a light tone that didn't quite land. "What did she tell you?"

Daniela seemed to read the panic in his eyes and laughed, a sound that was clear and genuinely amused. "Oh, don't worry," she said, waving a dismissive hand. "She doesn't go into details. Strong believer in client confidentiality. She just mentioned she's known you and your family for years and was helping you with something."

The relief was a palpable, physical thing, an unclenching in his chest he hadn't known was there. He fumbled to cover his tracks. "Oh no, I wasn't concerned. I know Maren's a professional. I just hoped she had nice things to say."

Daniela looked at him, her gaze direct and disarmingly kind. "Oliver, I don't need Maren to tell me that. I could tell you were a nice guy the first time we met." She gestured to the empty chair. "Do you mind if I join you? Seats are hard to find."

He was momentarily speechless, taken aback by the simple, unadorned compliment. "Of course," he finally managed. "That's why I waved. I just didn't realize you came to this café."

She sat down, her presence a bubble of cheerful normalcy. "I don't usually come this late, normally around eleven when I have a break from my classes. They make the best smoothies here." She pointed to her bluish-green drink. "This one's my favorite – Wholesome Energy Bomb. Matcha, almond milk, spirulina, banana, peanut butter, and chia. So good …" She took a long sip, and her face lit up with such pure, uncomplicated delight that Oliver found himself watching her, captivated. It was a reminder of a world where things could be simply and genuinely enjoyed, a world that felt very, very far from his own.

"Nice. What classes are you taking?" Oliver asked, genuinely curious.

"It's my master's at NYU. Theater studies," she replied.

"Cool. I don't think I've ever met a theater major. Do you like it?"

"It's fantastic." A new energy lit up her face. She leaned forward slightly, as if sharing a secret. "I'm on a bit of an unusual path, though. Most people study the common methods, like Stanislavski. I'm specializing in the Grotowski school, which isn't as well known."

"Forgive my ignorance," Oliver said, feeling a little out of his depth, "But I'm not aware of either. What's the difference?"

"Well, I'll keep it simple; otherwise we'll be here for hours," she laughed. "Stanislavski's whole thing was about honesty. He taught that an actor has to completely immerse themselves in a role to *truly* experience the character's feelings and emotions. It's not about pretending. It's about making a deep, subconscious connection to the character you're playing."

The phrase hung in the air. *A deep, subconscious connection.* Oliver's mind flashed to the impossible moment he'd seen his father's face on that flickering TV screen, a connection so visceral it had brought him to tears.

"Grotowski was influenced by that," she continued, her hands starting to move as she spoke, shaping her ideas in the air, "But he took a unique, minimalist approach. He believed in stripping away everything unnecessary – props, elaborate sets, decoration – until you're left with just the actor's body and voice. The actors make the same kind of psychological connection, but they get there through intense physical motion. The physical work is used to unlock what Grotowski called 'emotional memory.'"

Physical motion unlocking something deeper. The memory of his own arms moving without his command – autokinesis – sent a faint tremor through him. His body had answered a question his conscious mind couldn't.

Oliver felt completely lost, and yet, strangely found. He had spent his adult life in the clean, logical world of technology and applications, a world where the arts were a distant, abstract concept. But her words weren't abstract. They were a potential vocabulary for the bizarre, terrifying, and undeniably real things that were happening inside his own head. The idea that acting had such a powerful psychological component was deeply intriguing.

"I'd love to learn more about this," he said, and he meant it. "Where can I read up on it?"

A bright, genuine smile spread across Daniela's face. "Well, if you're really interested, I could invite you to some events at my school. In fact, there's a Grotowski retrospective at the Walter Reade in about ten days. Would you like to come?"

"Walter Reade?" The name was unfamiliar.

"Walter Reade Theater. It's part of Lincoln Center," she explained. "It's a documentary on his life and work. I'm really looking forward to it."

"I'd love to be there," he said, a warmth spreading through his chest that had nothing to do with the coffee. "Are you going with your whole class?"

"Oh no, we're all watching it on our own schedules," she said, then hesitated for a fraction of a second, a slight, charming vulnerability in her eyes. "I was planning on going by myself, but I would certainly appreciate the company."

The invitation, personal and direct, was a bridge between their two very different worlds. "Great," Oliver exclaimed, his response quicker and more enthusiastic than he'd intended. "I'm in."

They chatted for a while longer, the easy conversation a welcome respite for Oliver. He felt himself relaxing in her presence, the heavy weight on his shoulders lifting, if only for a moment.

"So how did you get into all this?" he asked, gesturing vaguely to encompass Maren, the studio, the whole mystical world she represented. "With Maren, I mean."

Daniela took a slow sip of her smoothie, as if gathering the threads of a long and complicated story. "It's really Maren's story," she began, her voice taking on a quieter, more reverent tone. "She wasn't always like this. When she was just a young girl, back in her village in Germany, she fell terribly sick."

Oliver leaned forward, drawn in by the shift in her tone.

"No one could figure out what was wrong, so her parents took her to a specialist in Munich. The diagnosis was … a nightmare." Daniela looked at him, her eyes wide with the gravity of the memory. "Four different types of terminal cancer. The doctor gave her a month to live."

A chill went down Oliver's spine.

"Her parents," Daniela continued, "Refused to give up. They started looking for anything, any alternative remedy. Through a friend, they heard a story – a rumor, really – about a small group of shamanic folk-healers living deep in the Siberian forest."

Shamans? Siberia? Oliver's logical mind recoiled. It sounded like something from a fairy tale.

"They were desperate, so they rushed Maren there. She spent three months living in the forest with them. When she came back, she felt better, but they had no idea if it had actually worked." Daniela paused for effect. "They went back to the same doctor in Munich. He was stunned just to see her alive. And then he ran the tests. All of it – every single cancer – was completely gone.”

Oliver just stared at her, speechless. It was an impossible story. A misdiagnosis, his mind screamed. It had to be. But the conviction in Daniela's voice told him that, for her, this was an absolute truth, a foundational miracle.

“After that,” she went on, “Maren's life had a new purpose. As she got older, she went back to Siberia regularly to learn their techniques. She traveled the world, spending years in ashrams in India and Tibet, learning about meditation. She got deeply into past-life regression, and from that work, she developed her own method for helping people resolve trauma. That's what she calls ‘time projection.’”

The final piece clicked into place. This wasn't some new-age fad Maren had invented. It was the culmination of a life saved by the inexplicable, a life spent trying to understand and harness it.

“She started teaching several years ago,” Daniela finished, a look of deep admiration on her face. “And I'm one of her students.”

“So how did you really meet Maren?” Oliver asked, leaning forward. “You said you were her student, but it feels like there's more to it.”

Daniela smiled, a look in her eyes that was both fond and weary, as if she were about to unroll a very long, very old map. “The short answer is my uncle, Rafael. The long answer … well, it starts with my grandparents in Argentina, before my mother was even born.”

Oliver settled back, his macchiato forgotten. The sounds of the Bluebird patio faded to a distant hum.

“They were Peronistas,” she began, her voice taking on the cadence of a well-told family legend. “True believers. My grandfather was a high-ranking official in Juan Perón's government in the early fifties. When the military overthrew him in ’55, they had to run.”

She described their escape to Brazil with their first child, how they lived in hiding from the Argentine military regime for five years. “My mother, Claudia, was born in their last year there, a baby born in exile.”

Her story took on a thriller's pace. “Shortly after she was born, the regime got wind of where they were. Agents were sent. My mother was just an infant when they fled again, escaping by the skin of their teeth onto a ship bound for France. They spent the next decade as refugees, moving through Europe, until my mother was a teenager."

She paused, taking a sip of her smoothie. "Then, the impossible happened. Perón returned to power in Argentina. My grandparents thought they could finally go home. But as they were sailing back, in 1976, news reached the ship: another coup, this one backed by the U.S. They knew they couldn't land. So they convinced the ship's captain to make a detour to Montevideo, Uruguay. My grandmother's sister lived there. They thought they'd stay for a little while."

"But they didn't," Oliver guessed, completely captivated.

"They stayed for thirty years," she said with a wry smile. "Montevideo became home. My mother married a Uruguayan man, Hector Forlan. They had five children. I'm the youngest." A shadow passed over her face, and her voice lost some of its warmth. "Shortly after I was born, my father left. Ran off with a mistress he'd had for years."

Oliver felt a pang of sympathy, recognizing the same ache of a broken family.

"But his brother," she said, her expression brightening again, "My uncle, Rafael … he was a different kind of man. A wealthy businessman with no children of his own. He was enraged by his brother's selfishness and basically adopted us. He became the father I never really had. He's the one who supported my mother when she decided, in her late thirties, to go back to school to study psychotherapy."

She explained their final move, in 2005, when she was eight. It was Rafael who funded their relocation to Santa Barbara so her mother could pursue further training. "We've been U.S. citizens for years now, all thanks to him."

"He sounds like an incredible person," Oliver said.

"He is," she said, her affection for him palpable. "And he's the reason I know Maren." She connected the final dots. "Rafael is very spiritual. In the 90s, he spent several months at an ashram in South India. That's where he met Maren. They became great friends, and he invited her to visit us in Uruguay. She came many times, over the years. She became part of the family."

Oliver sat in silence for a moment, the scale of her story settling over him. His own life, sheltered and linear, felt impossibly small next to her family's epic of revolutions, narrow escapes, heartbreak, and unshakeable loyalty. It was the second incredible immigrant story he'd heard in a week, but this one felt like a novel. He looked at Daniela, finding her more attractive with each passing minute.

He glanced at his watch and was shocked. "Wow, it's 3:30. I've been here for over an hour." The time had completely vanished, lost in her story. "I need to get back to work."

Daniela nodded.

"That was an amazing story, Daniela," he said, his voice full of a genuine awe that made her smile. "Thank you for sharing that with me."

"Of course," she replied warmly. "Our families are connected through Maren. That means you're like family to me." She leaned forward, her curiosity returning. "So, I told you all about my crazy life. You never told me what you do."

Oliver felt a flush of embarrassment. After her epic tale of revolution and survival, his own backstory felt weightless and banal. "My work is definitely less interesting than yours," he said with a small, self-deprecating laugh. "I work in tech."

"What kind of tech?" she asked, her interest clearly not diminished.

"I'm at a startup. We build blockchain and crypto applications. Have you heard of that?"

Her eyes lit up. "Oh, you mean bitcoin?" She leaned forward, her attention fully captured.

"Well, not bitcoin exactly," he explained, falling into the ritual cadences of his job. "My company is focused on the more modern evolutions of its underlying technology."

"I see," she said, nodding. "My uncle Rafael is a big believer in bitcoin. He gave me a full bitcoin a few years ago and told me to save it, only to spend it if I absolutely had to. I haven't touched it, thank God. He gave it to me when it was around three thousand dollars, and now it's over forty thousand. He thinks it'll hit a million one day."

A small, condescending laugh escaped Oliver before he could stop it. "Ha-ha, I don't think that's likely." He saw her smile falter for a second and tried to recover. "It's just … it's funny. I work in this space, but I haven't spent much time on bitcoin itself. The senior people I respect at work, they all think that while bitcoin set the stage, it's old technology now. There are new blockchains that are much faster, with far more features."

"Interesting," she said, her voice a little cooler now. "I asked my uncle about all the other crypto stuff a few months ago, when everyone was buying NFTs and prices were going crazy. He told me to stay away. He said they're mostly all scams, and that bitcoin is the only thing that makes sense." As she spoke, she subtly shifted back in her seat, a small but definite retreat.

Oliver sensed the change immediately, the easy warmth between them replaced by a sudden chill. He'd contradicted her uncle, the man who was clearly a hero to her. He tried to temper his next statement, to bridge the gap he'd just created. "Look, your uncle sounds like a very smart guy, and I'm sure he has his reasons. From my perspective as a technologist, and from what I've learned from experts in the field, these new technologies just have more applications and are frankly more interesting to me."

As the words left his mouth, he felt a deep sense of detachment from them. They felt hollow, practiced – a reflexive sales pitch he'd delivered a hundred times from muscle memory. For the first time, he heard them not as an expert opinion, but as an empty echo. The nagging doubts he'd been pushing down for months – the failed projects, the centralized "decentralized" systems – all resurfaced at once. A cold, terrifying question bloomed in his mind: *Could this entire industry be built on a lie?*

He pushed the thought away. *No, too many smart people are invested in it.* He looked at Daniela, at the guarded expression that had replaced her open, easy smile, and realized the cost of his practiced speech. He was striking a sour note, alienating the first person in weeks who had made him feel something real and hopeful.

He remembered he was late for work. The thought was a welcome escape hatch.

They exchanged numbers, the conversation now polite and a little strained, and made a plan to connect about the Grotowski retrospective. Then Oliver stood, said his goodbyes, and headed back to the office, his mind buzzing not with the excitement of a new connection, but with the unsettling, discordant echo of his own hollow words.

732959 (April 21)

Oliver gave Google one last shot. For days, he'd been plumbing the depths of the internet, searching for any trace of Jonathan Bryce, the Irish painter who had somehow landed at the center of his father's mystery. The search returned a digital hall of mirrors, reflecting back endless, useless versions of the name: a voice-over actor, a SaaS CEO, a solicitor in Perth. Not a whisper of the man he was looking for. The image results were even worse. He gave up and closed the laptop, the frustration a sour taste in his mouth.

He got into bed. The mystery of the words was a constant, low-grade hum in his mind, and with Maren out of town, he felt a new urgency to press on alone. He'd tried to project by himself the last few nights, but his mind had been a frantic storm of anxiety and grief, an impenetrable wall of static.

But today felt different. The long, easy conversation with Daniela had left him with a lingering sense of calm, a quiet center in the storm. This time, instead of fighting the thoughts that arose, he simply watched them, letting them drift past like clouds without judgment. Within minutes, the static subsided. He found himself in a quiet place.

It was a world drained of color. He was standing on a rough, pebbly floor in a deep and starless darkness. The only thing with any life was a small mouse, its gray form a skittering, stop-start staccato against the black. He followed it. The alley was narrow, the stone walls cold and damp. The mouse led him to an old stone building with a single, barred window – a jail cell – before it vanished beneath a sewer grate.

Oliver stood in the oppressive, monochrome silence, puzzled. Nothingness, and no indication of what to do next. As he waited, a small wound of color tore through the black-and-white scene. An impossible, vibrant blue. A cartoon bird, the exact shade and shape of the original Twitter logo, emerged from *within* the jail cell and perched on the windowsill.

It began to chirp, a soft, digital-sounding melody, but the words were muffled, just out of reach. "… by the dozen … by the dozen …"

He strained to hear the beginning of the phrase, but it was a faint, frustrating whisper. *Cheaper by the dozen?* The thought was absurd, a fragment of pop culture that made no sense here. The bird just kept repeating the garbled phrase.

Then it hopped from the sill, its blue form a streak of light in the gloom, and landed on a person's shoulder. Oliver tried to see the face, but there was none. In the deep shadows, all he could make out was the shoulder itself, a disembodied fragment of a person, also in black-and-white. The shoulder turned and walked away into the darkness, taking the bird with it.

He waited, but nothing else happened. He felt a strange, incongruous sense of completion. His logical mind was screaming with questions – a jail cell, a cartoon bird, a disembodied limb – it was a nonsensical collage of dream-fragments. Yet, his unconscious, the part of him that was now learning to navigate this world, felt a deep, quiet satisfaction. He checked with autokinesis. *Is there anything left for me here?* His right arm dropped. False. He was done. He slowly eased himself out of the projection.

He opened his eyes, his mind a battlefield between logic and intuition. He took stock of the bizarre clues. The jail cell. The bird. The shoulder. The shoulder … the word echoed, and another connection sparked. *Grimsby's Shoulder.* The cold, bureaucratic name for the place where his father had vanished. The bird had landed on a shoulder.

It had to be the next word. He felt the simmering resonance, the gut-level certainty. But he needed the proof. He closed his eyes again, raising his hands. *"Is 'shoulder' the fourth word?"*

His left arm dropped. *Yes.* A surge of triumph.

He tried again, needing the absolute confirmation. He asked the same question.

This time, his *right* arm dropped. *No.*

The contradiction was a jolt of ice water. He tried again. Left. And again. Right. The pattern kept repeating, his body giving him a "Yes" and a "No," a perfect, maddening paradox. The universe was no longer giving him clear answers. It was leaving him stranded in a state of pure uncertainty, with a word he felt was true but could not prove.

734777 (May 3)

"I have seen this happen before. Sometimes people get blocked for many days." Maren's tone was matter-of-fact, offering no apology for the universe's stubbornness.

Oliver stared at her glumly. He was sitting in the usual armchair in her SoHo studio, waiting for Daniela to arrive for their Grotowski documentary date. The session he'd tried to squeeze in beforehand had been another failure. It was his second blank in a week. He could still get *in* – the problem was that the projections were now a chaotic symphony of nonsense. He'd hurtled through impossible labyrinths, floated over silent galaxies, and had conversations with dwarves and aliens. The visuals were spectacular, but they were hollow. They led nowhere, offered no sense of resolution, no clue to the fourth word.

"It could be that you are trying too hard," Maren continued, her gaze analytical. "Your logical mind is taking center stage when it should be your intuitive, spiritual self that steps in. This is probably a good time to have this conversation, because you will be on your own for the next few weeks."

The casualness of her last statement sent a jolt of pure panic through him. "What do you mean, on my own?"

"I'm leaving for India this Friday," she said. "It's Guru Brahma's eightieth birthday, and followers from all over the world are coming to the ashram to celebrate. I was thinking of spending a few weeks there to recharge. This healing work … it takes a real toll."

"Wait, Guru Brahma?" The name was another jolt, a connection to a different part of his life. "That's the same guy my dad talks about a lot, right? Talk*ed*," he corrected himself, the verb tense a familiar, dull ache.

"Of course, it's the same one, silly." Maren laughed. "That's how I met your father, all those years ago. Through the Guru. I incorporate so many of his teachings into my work, including time projection."

The pieces of his father's hidden life were reassembling in his mind, forming a picture he'd never imagined. A sinking feeling settled in his stomach. "So … how long are you going to be in India?" The question was a desperate calculation. How long would he be stranded?

"Until mid-June, maybe early July. I will go with the flow," she responded.

"What about Daniela?" he asked, the thought of his one other connection to this strange new world suddenly paramount.

"Oh, she'll be here, looking after the studio. She wants to complete some school credits over the summer, so it works out."

Oliver was still processing the earlier revelation. *That's how I met your father.* "I didn't realize you met at the ashram," he said, thinking aloud. "I guess I never thought about how you became a family friend. So you've known him for … thirty years?"

"Something like that," she said with a wistful, distant look. "He was in the States already but visited the ashram once or twice a year. We learned some amazing things. It was a wonderful time."

After a few seconds, her expression grew more serious, her gaze returning to him. "So, because I will be gone, you cannot rely on me. You need to figure out how to unblock yourself." She leaned forward slightly, her voice taking on the weight of a final, crucial instruction. "The most important advice I can give you is this: allow yourself to *feel* what is happening, not *think* about what is happening. The only way this works is when your brain's right hemisphere fully takes over. If your left hemisphere – your logic – is in control, you will stay blocked. Also remember this," she added, her eyes locking onto his. "Now that you are in tune with how this works, you might find answers outside of the projections, in the regular events of the day."

Oliver nodded, the gesture feeling hollow. He wasn't thrilled at losing his training wheels, but he knew Maren was right. He had no choice.

Sensing his unease, Maren offered a final piece of encouragement. "You have a special gift, Oliver. I haven't told you this, but it takes most people months to reach the level of projection you found in your first attempts." She paused, letting the words sink in. "Your dad had this gift, too. The ability to switch off the logical mind and simply surrender to your inner being. Even Daniela, and she is one of my best students, it took her much longer than it did for you."

The words were meant to be a comfort, but they landed with a strange weight. A special gift. It felt less like a gift and more like a diagnosis, a fundamental difference that set him apart, that was the very source of his current turmoil.

Almost on cue, a knock came at the studio door, and Daniela entered, a bright smile on her face. "Sorry that took so long. Ready?" she said, her cheerful energy instantly changing the atmosphere in the room.

Oliver got up and gave Maren a hug, a gesture that felt both grateful and desperate. "I guess I'll see you in a few weeks, then." A cold knot of panic tightened in his stomach. The thought of navigating this path without his guide, his only safety net, was terrifying.

He and Daniela walked to the West 4th station and boarded the uptown C train. On the walk, trying to find some common ground in their shared, strange experience, he asked her about her own projections.

As she described them, the gulf between their worlds only widened. Her experiences were exactly as Maren had outlined: she revisited events from her past, observed them from a new perspective, and found resolution. It was a tool for healing, for introspection. Oliver listened, a growing sense of alienation washing over him. *She uses this to find peace,* he thought. *I use it to find clues in a dead man's puzzle.* He felt a pang of envy for her normality, for the clean, therapeutic purpose of her journey. On the other hand, if his projections had been *normal,* he would still be lost in a fog of simple grief, with no knowledge of the twenty-four words, of Bryce, of the quest that was now the only thing giving his life a terrifying, exhilarating purpose.

The C train was surprisingly uncrowded for a Tuesday evening. They chose to stand, holding onto a pole as the car rattled through the dark tunnel. A few feet away, an older man and a young woman sat holding protest signs. Oliver discreetly tilted his head to read them. The text was partially blocked, but he could make out the words "Free Christian."

Just then, Daniela noticed them too. She grabbed Oliver's arm, her fingers digging in with sudden urgency. "Oliver, look," she whispered, her voice sharp. "That's Christiaan's sister and father!"

"Christiane?" he asked, leaning to get a better look.

"No, Chris-ti-aan," she enunciated, her expression a mix of shock and disbelief. "You've never heard of him?"

"I don't think so."

"Wait," she said, pulling back to look at him fully. "You work in crypto, and you've never heard of Christiaan? He's the guy who's in jail, with a crazy sentence, for some bitcoin thing."

A faint flicker of recognition sparked in the back of Oliver's mind, the ghost of a headline he'd probably scrolled past months ago, dismissing it as irrelevant. He'd heard about someone jailed for money laundering with bitcoin, the sentence seeming excessive, but the details were a blur. It was a story from the *bitcoin* world, a different universe from the shiny, corporate *crypto* he inhabited. "Now that you mention it," he said slowly, "I have a vague recollection of hearing something about it."

"He has a Dutch or South African last name I can't remember," Daniela said, her voice a hushed, urgent whisper. "But he built some application for bitcoin back in 2013 or 2014. Then the feds busted him – money laundering, tax evasion, something – and put him away for a crazy amount of time. No parole." She glanced toward the couple. "That's his sister, Adele, I think. She and her dad are trying to collect signatures for a petition to get his sentence commuted. They were at NYU last week."

Before Oliver could process this, Daniela was moving. She stepped up to Adele and her father, her demeanor open and friendly. "Hey, Adele, right? We spoke at NYU last week."

"Oh yes, hi! I remember you," Adele responded, a surprised but genuine smile lighting up her tired face. "We're just headed to Columbus Circle to meet some supporters, get more people to sign."

"That's great. I already signed." Daniela turned and looked pointedly at Oliver, a clear expectation in her eyes. "And I'm going to get my friend to sign it. Won't you, Oliver?"

The spotlight hit him, and he felt a flush of social panic. This was a cause, a public declaration, and he was being drafted into it on the spot. He nodded sheepishly, fumbling for his phone to scan the QR code on the sign. "Sure," he mumbled. "I'll sign this when I'm outside and have reception."

"How many signatures do you have?" Daniela asked, turning her attention back to Adele.

"About half-a-million. We're aiming for a million before we try to get it in front of the president."

"Amazing. Are you in the city for a while?"

"Yes," Adele said, her expression hardening with resolve. "They recently moved Christiaan to the federal facility in New Jersey, so we'll be here for the next few weeks, maybe even months, pushing the campaign."

After wishing them well, Oliver and Daniela walked back to their spot by the pole. The brief, intense interaction left Oliver feeling like he'd stumbled into the middle of a movie.

"Christiaan sounds like an amazing guy," Daniela whispered, her voice radiating a fierce sense of injustice. "It's insane what the government is doing to him. I'm sure it's because of bitcoin – they hate people undermining the state. Murderers get ten or twenty years, and they gave him fifty without parole."

Oliver shrugged. The sentence seemed harsh, sure, but his corporate-trained mind immediately rejected the grander theory. *A government conspiracy? Over bitcoin?* It was a niche internet money, a curiosity. It didn't seem significant enough to warrant that kind of targeted crackdown.

Daniela continued, her eyes bright with the story. "The cool thing is, his family set up a Twitter account for him where they post his thoughts from prison. He's started writing poetry recently, and they post that, too." She leaned in a little closer. "Oh, and another thing. Some folks at the rally told me there's a rumor he has a huge stack of bitcoin hidden away. Huge, like ten or twenty thousand bitcoin. And the coins haven't moved since he was imprisoned."

"Why haven't his family taken them?" Oliver asked, the developer in him focusing on the practical flaw.

"Not sure," Daniela pondered. "Maybe the feds are watching the wallets. Maybe he's the only one with the keys and is afraid to give them out."

Ten or twenty thousand. The number floated in Oliver's mind. He did a quick, reflexive calculation, the kind his brain was wired for. The price had been volatile, but it was hovering around forty thousand dollars. Twenty thousand times forty thousand …

His breath caught. The number that bloomed in his mind was so large, so absurd, it shattered his detached skepticism. It was a figure that belonged to corporations and nation-states, not to a single person's hidden stash.

"Ten or twenty thousand …" he said, the words barely a whisper. "That's … half-a-billion dollars." He looked at Daniela, his eyes wide. "That's nuts."

The train screeched to a halt at Columbus Circle. As they got off, they saw Adele and her father on the platform, heading for a different exit. They exchanged a brief, silent nod before disappearing into the crowd.

Walking toward Lincoln Center, the bustling city air felt charged with a new, awkward tension. The half-a-billion-dollar revelation had been replaced by a more immediate and unsettling thought that Oliver had been grappling with for the last ten blocks. Unable to hold it in any longer, he blurted it out.

"How come you're not going to this with your boyfriend?"

Daniela stopped and looked at him, her expression one of pure surprise. "My boyfriend?"

Oliver's face flushed hot with immediate regret. "Maren … she mentioned you were out with your boyfriend a few weeks back." The words sounded clumsy, accusatory.

For a moment, Daniela just stared at him, and then she laughed, a bright, clear sound that echoed in the night air. "Oh, Maren. She can be so silly sometimes. No, that was just a guy I met a couple of times. He was certainly not my boyfriend."

Oliver felt a fresh wave of embarrassment. He'd completely exposed his hand, letting her see his concern. There was no graceful way to take it back.

"I'm guessing you don't have a girlfriend, right?" she asked, and he saw a mischievous twinkle in her eyes. She knew exactly what he had been asking.

"I suppose I look the type, huh?" he said, feeling the heat in his cheeks. "Yeah, I've been single for a while. With my dad's news and … everything else, I can't even think about it right now." The honest admission felt like a surrender, a moment of real vulnerability.

They arrived at the Walter Reade Theater and found their seats inside the cool, dark auditorium. As the lights dimmed, a director came on stage to speak about Jerzy Grotowski's influence. Then the documentary began.

Black-and-white images of pre-war Poland flickered on the screen. A narrator spoke of a young Grotowski, a boy living through the German occupation. There was a story about him hiding under the dining table during adult conversations, not listening to their words, but watching their feet and legs, learning to correlate their subtle movements with the emotions in their voices. It was, the film explained, the seed of his thesis: that true emotion could be expressed through the body.

Oliver was completely engrossed. This was a validation of the strange world he had entered. *Emotional memory. The subconscious.* Midway through the film, he started to drift. Not into sleep, but into a deeper state of focus. The darkness of the theater, the hypnotic drone of the narrator, the powerful images on screen – it all combined to create a perfect environment for projection. He felt himself floating in the in-between state, half-meditating, half-watching.

It was then that he heard it. The archival voice of Grotowski himself, clear and commanding, instructing an actor.

"It is in the shoulder. The shoulder! That emotion inside you, that rage, move it through the shoulder!"

The word struck Oliver like a bolt of lightning. *Shoulder.* The disembodied shoulder in the black-and-white alley. *Grimsby's Shoulder*, the cold, bureaucratic name for the place his father had vanished. The ambiguous clue from two weeks ago now slammed into place with undeniable force.

He closed his eyes, there in the dark of the theater, and performed the silent ritual. He raised his hands just slightly in his lap. *Is 'shoulder' the fourth word?*

He got a resounding, unambiguous yes. The heavy, certain drop of his left arm. He tried it again. And again. The answer was the same every time.

He had found it. He had the fourth word.

CHAPTER 5. EDUCATE

735662 (May 9)

"Hey Oliver, can you give me a quick status on Phoenix?"

Oliver looked up from his screen at his co-worker, Olumide, with a familiar wave of weariness. He hated status updates. They felt like a performance, a ritual of translating messy reality into clean, corporate fiction. "Why are you asking me, dude?"

"Sri's still out and Wright's out of town," Olumide said, already in project manager mode. "You're the only one close enough to give an update."

"I'm not sure I have the latest," Oliver said, turning his gaze back to his computer, a clear signal he hoped would end the conversation.

It didn't. Olumide sighed, a sound of practiced patience. "Listen, man, we have the quarterly business review with the execs tomorrow. I need to get a status slide posted, and I can't wait. Just tell me what you know. Don't make me make up a status for your project."

Oliver wasn't thrilled. He felt a deep, grating reluctance to participate in the charade. "I don't know, dude. It's hard to say where that project is headed." He finally relented, giving Olumide the unvarnished truth. "The last chat with the Phoenix team, they brought in a couple of people from their actual business unit. They didn't seem enthusiastic. The innovation team loves our proof-of-concept, but the actual decision-makers keep asking about scalability and identity management – questions we don't have good answers for."

Olumide stared at him in silence for a moment, and Oliver could practically see the gears turning in his head, processing the messy facts and searching for the right corporate jargon to repackage them.

"Tell you what," Olumide said finally, his voice shifting into a smooth, confident tone. "Let's call the status 'yellow.' I'll note that the client's champions are 'socializing the project with business units' but are running into 'delays due to competing priorities.' Action item: 'Escalate to upper management if this continues.'"

Oliver listened, a sense of alienation washing over him. Olumide was an alchemist, turning the lead of reality into the fool's gold of a positive status report right before his eyes.

"Don't you think that's a bit optimistic?" Oliver asked, unable to let it go. "I don't see this going anywhere. And frankly, I'm starting to have reservations about the whole use case. How is it 'Web3' and 'decentralized' if we're just handing them the keys and then managing the keys *for* them? I'm not surprised they're pushing back."

Olumide's friendly expression tightened into something slightly patronizing. "Oliver, I'm noticing a lot of doubt from you recently. You've got to believe in the land-and-expand strategy." The grating tone returned. "Besides, Web3 is the future. They'll buckle eventually because they can't resist the winds of change. We just need to *educate* the business units better."

Educate, Oliver thought, the word landing with a sour thud. *Or strong-arm them into believing a story we're not even sure is true.*

"If they don't buckle, they'll just be left behind," Olumide concluded, having gotten what he needed. "Okay, Phoenix update is done. Now I need Nick. Have you seen him?"

"Yeah, he was heading to the common room," Oliver said, getting up from his chair, suddenly needing to be anywhere else. "I'll come with you. Need a La Croix."

They walked into the common room together. The usual low hum of conversation was absent. Sprawled on the main couch, head buried in his hands, was Nick.

"Yo, it's too early for a nap," Olumide said, completely misreading the room's heavy atmosphere.

Nick's head lifted slowly from his hands. His face was pale, as if all the blood had drained from it.

"You okay, man?" Oliver asked, his own frustrations instantly forgotten, replaced by a sharp, sudden concern.

Nick stared blankly at them, his eyes unfocused, as if they were speaking a language he no longer understood. The silence in the room was heavy, suffocating. Finally, he spoke, his voice a dry, broken whisper.

"Dude, I'm fucked. Totally, completely, royally fucked."

The words hung in the air, a stark contrast to Olumide's earlier levity. "What happened?" Oliver asked, his own concern sharpening.

"I'm watching my life savings evaporate in front of my eyes," Nick said, his voice hollow.

"What are you talking about?" Olumide interjected, his face a mask of confusion.

"I yolo'd," Nick said, the crypto slang sounding like a death rattle. "Basically all of it – eighty, ninety percent of everything I had. Over two million dollars. Into Luna." He let out a choked, desperate sound that was almost a laugh. "And that thing has crashed over seventy percent. In the last twenty-four hours."

Terra/Luna, Oliver's mind supplied the context. The infamous algorithmic stablecoin project, a complex Jenga tower of code and incentives.

"I wasn't paying attention," Nick continued, the words tumbling out in a frantic rush. "Their stablecoin, UST, it broke the dollar peg. And it just ... it sank the whole damn thing. Holy fuck, I'm so fucked!"

"How much is your stack worth now?" Oliver asked, the question feeling clinical and brutal.

"Almost two hundred K," Nick replied, his voice flat.

"Are you going to pull it out? Sell it?"

"I don't know what to do!" he burst out, his hands flying back to his head. "I really believe in the project. I think it can go back up. Do Kwon ..." – *the founder,* Oliver thought, *the arrogant frontman of the whole ecosystem* – "... he tweeted an hour ago. Said he's deploying more capital, told everyone to stay steady. I think that might help." The hope in his voice was thin, desperate.

"You've been in crypto for a while, man," Oliver said gently, trying to find some solid ground. "This can't be the worst drawdown you've seen."

"Dude, seventy percent in a single day is right up there," Nick seemed to deflate, all the frantic energy gone, replaced by a deep, dejected weariness. "And this is the biggest position I've ever had. I'm leveraged up the wazoo." He looked away, unable to meet their eyes, his voice dropping to a shameful mumble. "I even convinced my father-in-law to give me two-fifty grand to invest for him. I took a home-equity loan for another two-fifty."

He finally looked at them, his eyes full of a terrifying, bottomless despair. "This was supposed to be it. My slam-dunk, retire-by-thirty-five play." He shook his head, pushing himself up from the couch. "Listen, guys, I can't talk about this. I need to figure out what the hell is going on. I'm trying to plug into their community forums." He started for the door, a man escaping the scene of his own immolation. "Let's … let's grab a drink tonight. Hopefully, by then, this will all be straightened out."

He left. Oliver and Olumide stood in the sudden, ringing silence, the ghost of their friend's catastrophic loss hanging heavy in the air between them.

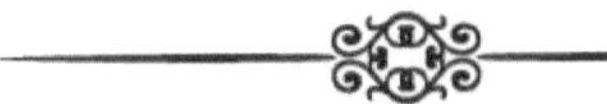

735691 (May 9)

The Żywiec and The Lagunitas stared intently at The Hoegaarden. It was a Monday evening at O'Connell's, but the usual boisterous energy was gone. The pub was nearly empty, a cavern of dark wood and silence. It felt less like a bar and more like a wake.

The Hoegaarden's voice, usually full of manic energy, was flat and hollow, echoing eerily in the quiet. "It's over, man," he said, staring into his beer. "The Luna Foundation went full Zimbabwe. They're minting trillions of new tokens to try and fix the liquidity. It's just crashing the price even more. I had to get out."

"How much were you able to save?" The Żywiec – Oliver – asked softly.

"A hundred K, all said and done," The Hoegaarden replied, the number a ghost of the millions that had been there just days before.

"Well, that's something, at least. You're back in dollars?"

"No, man." A flicker of the old gambler's energy returned to his eyes. "I need to make up the losses. I moved it all to Celsius."

Oliver's stomach tightened. *Celsius. The crypto lending platform run by Alex Mashinsky, another charismatic founder promising easy, risk-free returns.*

"That's more of a sure thing, in my book," The Hoegaarden continued, trying to convince himself as much as them. "Slow and steady. Mashinsky will get it done. He's got a solid team."

"Haven't there been some rumblings about Celsius, too?" Oliver asked, choosing his words carefully. He remembered seeing headlines, whispers of trouble.

"Nah." The Hoegaarden waved a dismissive hand. "All noise and FUD. I trust those guys. They'd never rug their loyal customers."

FUD, Oliver thought. *Fear, Uncertainty, and Doubt.* The crypto world's catch-all dismissal for any information that contradicts the preferred narrative. It was the same blind faith, the same willful ignorance that had just cost his friend everything. He felt a desperate urge to grab him by the shoulders, to scream at him to see the pattern, but he held his tongue. The Hoegaarden was too raw, too distressed. He wouldn't hear it.

The Hoegaarden took a long, pensive sip of his beer, his gaze lost in the distance. With a face full of unearned wisdom, he said, "Just goes to show. We all need to educate ourselves on risk management and human nature."

The irony was so thick it was suffocating. Oliver raised his glass. "We'll drink to that," he said, his voice quiet. He wasn't toasting his friend's newfound insight. He was toasting the brutal, tragic lesson that he was certain his friend had yet to learn.

738140 (May 27)

A red Audi Q5 pulled up to the curb on 94th and Riverside. The back door opened, and Oliver slid in next to Hope, the scent of new leather and the promise of escape filling his senses.

"Really appreciate you guys giving me a ride. And for the weekend invite," he said, looking at Nick and his wife, Becky, in the front seats.

"Of course, man. Our pleasure," they replied in unison.

"Okay, let's see," Nick mumbled, scrolling the map on his GPS. "West Side Highway at 96th, up to the GWB, Palisades …"

As they approached the on-ramp, a line of orange cones and flashing lights blocked their path.

"That's just great," Nick sighed, the city already fighting their escape. "Friday morning construction before a long weekend. Looks like we're taking Broadway up to 125th."

The drive uptown was a crawl. Around 114th, the traffic slowed to a near standstill. A large crowd had gathered on the sidewalk, spilling onto the road where double-parked cars had choked Broadway down to a single, tight lane.

"I wonder what's going on," Nick said, his tone sharpening with irritation.

Oliver craned his neck out the window. In the center of the crowd, a familiar, determined face came into focus. It was Adele, the woman from the train. As their car inched forward towards his *alma mater*, the scene came into focus: Adele and her father had set up a folding table right outside the gates of Columbia University. A large poster of a man's face rested on it, with the words FREE CHRISTIAAN in bold red text.

"I think it's a petition rally," Oliver said to Nick, who was expertly maneuvering the Audi through the narrow gap. "For Christiaan, the bitcoin guy who's in jail."

"Oh, that Christiaan van der Dussen guy?" Nick said with a dismissive chuckle, narrowly avoiding a protestor's foot. "That's hilarious."

The name hit Oliver with the force of an electric shock. The sound of the city, Nick's voice, the car's engine – it all faded into a dull roar. In his mind, the *memory* of the projection exploded into perfect, sudden clarity: the cold, black-and-white alley; the impossible, vibrant blue of the cartoon bird emerging from the jail cell; the garbled, frustrating chirp he couldn't quite decipher. *... by the dozen ... by the dozen ...*

Now, hearing it through the filter of Nick's casual comment, the muffled sound morphed. The syllables clicked into place. It wasn't "By the dozen." It was "Van der Dussen."

Christiaan van der Dussen.

The bird coming out of the jail cell, chirping his name. Daniela telling him Christiaan was writing *poetry* that Adele was posting on his behalf. It was a cascade of connections, a key slamming into a lock he hadn't known he was holding. There was something in the poetry. He had to find that Twitter account.

"What did you say his name was?" Oliver asked, his voice tight, needing to hear it again.

"Christiaan van der Dussen," Nick repeated. "He's the guy who built one of the first CoinJoin tools, right? Turned out some bad dudes were using it, and a bug forced him to mix some transactions manually, so the feds busted him for money laundering."

The name was confirmed, but Oliver's mind was still reeling. "Wait, what's his story?"

"Didn't follow it that closely," Nick replied, steering them past the bottle-neck. "He was an early bitcoiner. Around 2013, he launched a tool to add privacy to transactions. You know that boomer coin – all its transactions are public. His thing, CoinJoin, was like taking a bunch of people's dollar bills, throwing them in a big pile and mixing them up, then giving everyone the same amount back. You still have your money, but no one can trace which specific bills were originally yours. It's something like that."

"What's wrong with that?" Oliver asked.

"As I remember it, CoinJoin itself isn't illegal, as long as no one is in the middle actually touching the transactions," Nick responded. "But if there is, that's money laundering. Apparently, there was a bug in his code, and when Christiaan went in to fix it, he 'touched' the transactions. It was a technicality, a trap, and they busted him." He shook his head. "He had a partner, too. Pseudonymous guy – Devaxar or something. Vanished off the map right after the arrest. Honestly, I'm glad Christiaan's in jail. These cypherpunk types give Web3 a bad name. His punishment sounds excessive, sure, but this whole space should be about getting into world-changing assets and watching the number go up, not this weird anarchy crap. And of course, the people screaming the loudest to free him are the freaking maxis."

"Maxis?" The term was new to Oliver.

Nick laughed. "Dude, are you even on Twitter?"

"I have an account, but I don't really use it," Oliver admitted.

"Maybe you're the smart one," Nick chuckled. "Anyway, 'maxi' is short for bitcoin maximalist. The most insufferable group of assholes you'll ever meet. All they do is yap about how bitcoin is the only thing that matters and the rest of crypto is a scam. It's unreal. Bitcoin was a good starting point, but stuff like Ethereum and Solana took it to the next level. I mean, that boomer coin has a crazy environmental footprint, and all the good developers are building real, world-changing projects now. Anyway," he sighed, "They just get on my nerves. But you'll see them all over the 'Free Christiaan' stuff."

Becky turned around from the front seat, glancing at Hope with a knowing smile. "Oliver, you shouldn't have gotten him started. He really doesn't like bitcoiners."

Nick fell silent, and Oliver spent the next few minutes processing. *Devaxar. Maxis.* New names, new tribes in this secret war he was only just discovering. One thing was certain: he had to get on Twitter. He needed to find Christiaan's poetry.

They finally cleared the bottleneck. As the car picked up speed past 120th Street, a small food stand on the corner caught his attention. The sign read: *N. Schmiter Specialty Meats.*

The name snagged on his consciousness, and suddenly, he wasn't in the car anymore. He was seven years old, tucked into his bed, the weight of the blanket a comforting pressure. He could smell the faint, clean scent of his father's aftershave as he sat on the edge of the mattress, his voice a low, playful rumble. Oliver was fighting to keep his eyes open, to prolong the story just a little longer. The story was always about the Nose Smiter, a short, bald man with a singsong voice and a sad, pig-like nose, who was so unhappy with his own that he tried to smite other people's noses off to steal them.

The memory was so vivid, so warm and safe, that the return to the present was a violent whiplash. The image of his father's smiling face vanished, leaving behind a sudden, brutal awareness of his absence. A vice-like grip clamped around Oliver's chest, tightening with each frantic beat of his heart. The air in the car grew thick and hot; he couldn't draw a full breath. The windows seemed to be closing in, the world outside blurring as his own heartbeat roared in his ears. Panicked, he dropped his head and pressed his face into his hands, fighting for air.

"Oliver, are you okay?"

A soft hand landed on his back. It was Hope. The touch was a single point of solid reality in the spinning chaos. He focused on the gentle pressure, using it as an anchor. The tightness in his chest slowly, painfully, began to dissipate. He could breathe again. He raised his head, feeling the blood rush back to his face.

"Sorry," he said, his voice shaky, the embarrassment immediate and acute. "I'm not sure what happened. I just saw something that reminded me of my dad. I'm okay now."

Hope just smiled and nodded kindly, her hand lingering for a moment before she pulled it away. The car made its way across the Washington Bridge and onto the Palisades Parkway.

The quiet in the car felt fragile. Oliver decided to break it, his voice softer than he intended. "Hey Nick … I hope you were able to recover some of your Luna positions?"

Beside him, Becky took in a sharp, audible breath. Nick shot her a quick, sheepish glance before turning his gaze back to the road. "No, man. It's all gone," he said, his voice flat and devoid of emotion. "Got fucked on Luna, got fucked on Celsius. Lost over a million. I went down with the ship." He shook his head, a ghost of a bitter smile on his lips. "I really looked up to those guys, Do Kwon and Mashinsky. Turns out they were just scammers. Kinda shakes your faith, you know? Who's next? SBF? Dixon? Vitalik?" He paused. "Well, not those guys. They've got integrity. But it makes you wonder …"

He went on, "Becky's dad was upset for a bit that I pissed away a quarter-million of his money, but I think he's getting over it." He glanced at Becky again. "Helps that he's loaded, of course."

Becky just rolled her eyes, a gesture that seemed to hold a world of frustration.

"He's going to be there this weekend, by the way," Nick added. "Last minute thing. Had to fly up from Florida to take care of some stuff. He's pretty chill, though. Your mom's still in Florida, right, Bec?"

Becky nodded.

"So how did your parents end up in Andes of all places?" Hope chimed in from the back seat. "I'd never even heard of it."

"Yeah, it's a small town," Becky explained, her voice carrying the easy confidence of someone used to a certain scale of life. "My parents wanted a real piece of land, ten or twenty acres with trails and a stream. They were having trouble finding the right spot until they were introduced to the guy who owned most of the mountain. He had something like two hundred acres just outside the village. He agreed to carve out ten for them – the part with the stream flowing through it. I think there was a condition that they couldn't build on the stream itself because he has some kind of hydroelectric contraption on it. Interesting guy. But yeah, they took the offer a couple of years ago and built the house. It's their summer and fall place."

Oliver and Hope listened in silence. It was a story told so casually, yet it spoke of a level of wealth and freedom that felt like a different reality.

The rest of the ride was a slow exhale. As they left the parkway and wound their way into the mountains, the landscape became spectacular. The late May wildflowers were an explosion of color on the roadsides, and the fresh, clean air felt like a balm on Oliver's frayed nerves.

The car turned through an elegant, understated gate and proceeded up a long asphalt driveway lined with perfectly manicured hedges. At the end of it sat a modern farmhouse, a stunning blend of rustic charm and sharp, minimalist architecture.

"I can hear them on the back patio," Nick said as they got out. "Let's go say hello."

They walked around the house. On a sprawling stone patio overlooking a vast, wild garden, two men were laughing, silhouetted against the smoke rising from a large coal-fired grill. Nick and Becky walked ahead to hug the older man – Becky's father, Rob.

The younger man turned toward Oliver and Hope, a welcoming smile on his face. He started walking toward them to introduce himself, but Oliver was no longer there. His mind was gone.

The grill. The smell of charcoal. The sound of laughter.

The memory of his last conversation with his dad was a sensory assault. *We'll fire up the grill when we next meet.* The words echoed in his head in his father's voice. The same vice-like grip from the car clamped around his chest, but this time it was instant and absolute. The cheerful sounds of the patio went silent. His vision tunneled until all he could see was the grill, a dark altar of a promise that could never be kept. The air was gone. His legs turned to cotton candy, to smoke. Just as the pure, animal terror of being unable to breathe peaked, his body gave out. The world tilted and spun, and he buckled in slow motion, the ground rushing up to meet him.

****

The world wasn't there anymore. There was no patio, no sky, no ground rushing up to meet him. There was only a thick, slow-motion silence, a floating sensation in a void without dimension. He was pure consciousness, a mind untethered from a body he could no longer feel.

And then, a sound splashed into the nothingness, impossibly bright and cheerful.

"Battlooo, there you are! I've been waiting for you to show up for so, so long!"

The sing-song voice broke through the silence, and Oliver's disembodied mind reeled. *No.* It couldn't be. That voice belonged to a different time, to the warm safety of a childhood bedroom and the low rumble of his father's storytelling. It wasn't real. It was a character from a fairy tale. But the sound of it was so perfectly, terrifyingly real.

"Wh … where are you?" The stutter was the sound of a mind struggling to form words without lungs, without a tongue.

"Battulu, Battolooo, Battlooo, why I'm right here! Here, here, here!" the voice giggled, seeming to come from every direction at once. "I've been looking for you for so long. What took you all this time?"

"I still can't see you," Oliver managed to gasp, the thought a frantic pulse in the void. "I only hear your voice. Where are you?"

The voice vanished. And with it, the last trace of anything knowable.

There was nothing. Not silence, but the *pressure* of it – a thick, suffocating blanket. A darkness so absolute it felt solid, pressing against his eyelids from the inside out.

And then, the sound.

★★★★

"Make sure you hold his head up. I'll get some water."

The voice was firm, calm, and unfamiliar. It was the first anchor. Then came the sensation of cool grass against his cheek, and the warmth of a hand cradling the back of his neck. Oliver's eyes fluttered open. Hope's concerned face swam into focus above him, framed by a brilliant blue sky.

"What happened?" Oliver asked, his own voice sounding distant and weak.

"You just collapsed as you were walking," Hope said, her relief palpable.

"Did I faint? How long was I out?" The clouds of confusion began to part, but they left behind a deep, unsettling mystery.

"Not sure if you fainted, but it was just for a few seconds."

A few seconds. The words made no sense. He had been gone for an eternity, lost in an inky, timeless void with a voice from his childhood … and Maren speaking in German. The discrepancy was a chasm in his mind, a piece of logic that refused to fit.

He felt his strength returning, his breathing evening out. The world was no longer spinning. The younger man from the grill now approached, holding a glass of water. "Ah, good. He seems fine now," the man said with a smile. "Was it something I said? Because I said nothing."

A weak smile touched Oliver's lips. He slowly, shakily, pushed himself up from the grass, acutely aware of everyone watching him. "I'm fine, thanks," he said, the embarrassment a hot flush on his cheeks. "Not sure what happened, but I feel okay now."

"Vince Descoteaux," the man said, extending a hand. His grip was firm and steady. "Rob's neighbor. You had us worried for a second. You turned white as a sheet, and your eyes rolled right to the top of your head."

"Great to meet you. I'm Oliver," he replied, feeling the need to escape the scrutiny. "Maybe I just didn't get enough sleep." It was the lamest of excuses, but it was all he had.

After a round of introductions, the group went inside to unload their luggage. In the guest bathroom, Oliver splashed cold water on his face, staring at the pale, shaken stranger in the mirror. He took a deep breath and walked back out to the patio. Only Vince was there now, calmly tending to the grill.

"I'm sorry about earlier," Oliver said, needing to clear the air.

"Of course not. Don't worry about it," Vince replied with an easy smile, turning from the grill. "We're here for a fun afternoon, and it looks like you're ready for it. Here, let me give you something that might help."

He went to a nearby table and, with the practiced hands of an alchemist, began mixing a drink from three different bottles. A splash of clear alcohol, a dash of something dark, a topper of something fizzy. He shook it with ice and poured the concoction into a small, elegant crystal glass.

"Try this," he said.

"Oh, I'm not sure," Oliver mumbled, the thought of alcohol turning his stomach. "It's a little early."

"Just take a sip," Vince said gently, his eyes kind and reassuring. "Let me know what you think."

Oliver relented. He took the glass and brought it to his lips. The first sip was a shock – a strange, herbal, potent flavor he'd never tasted before. It wasn't a pleasant taste, but something else happened almost instantly. An electric buzz shot through his nerves, a warm current that started in his chest and spread to the tips of his fingers and toes, chasing away the last of the lingering weakness and fog. Life, bright and sharp, rushed back into his face.

"Wow," he said, his eyes wide. "This is amazing. What is this?"

Vince laughed. "A well-kept mountain secret. It's a local prune and goldenrod grappa, with a splash of elderberry syrup and lightly carbonated spring water. I call it a 'Catskill Pick-Me-Up.' You don't want too much of it, but the first one usually sets people straight."

Oliver took another sip, the strange taste already becoming more pleasant. The lingering disorientation was gone, replaced by a clean, calm clarity. It was a small, quiet miracle in a glass. "This is incredible," he said, feeling a wave of genuine gratitude. "Thank you."

With the strange, electric warmth of the drink settling in his veins, Oliver took a chance to walk the property. The contrast was stunning. The front of the modern farmhouse, with its long driveway and manicured hedges, was a testament to precision and wealth. The back patio and garden were the same, a perfect lawn interspersed with artfully arranged flower beds. But beyond this bubble of order, the wild, untamed forest began abruptly, a dense wall of green with a single hiking path carved into it. It was a delicate, expensive balance between control and wilderness.

He returned to the patio, his attention drawn to Vince. The man was probably around forty, with the lean, capable fitness of someone who lives in his body, not just his head. His demeanor was calm and cheerful, and he wore his strange outfit – a collarless linen shirt and what Oliver could only describe as a dhoti – with an unselfconscious ease. Vince had the rare quality of making you feel instantly comfortable in his presence.

Lulled by this easy calm, Oliver found himself saying something he hadn't planned to. "Look," he began, the words coming out before he could stop them. "I recently had a death in the family, and I think some of those feelings are finally catching up with me. I think that's why I … passed out."

Vince looked at him, his expression one of pure, uncomplicated empathy. "I see. It sounds like you had a panic attack. It's not uncommon for grief to show up in the body like that. Do you mind me asking who you lost?"

"My dad," Oliver replied, the words still feeling foreign. "He had an accident on a business trip. They never found his body."

"I'm very sorry to hear that," Vince said sincerely.

Before he could continue, Nick appeared from the house. "Ah, Oliver! Good to see you looking better. Had me worried we'd be spending the weekend at the local hospital!" He gave Oliver a friendly smack on the shoulder. "Great, I see you've met Vince. Oliver, remember what I said about bitcoin maxis? Vince, here, is one of the good ones. Probably the only good one," Nick chuckled.

Vince just smiled at the teasing. The conversation continued, and Oliver, now intensely curious, began to piece together Vince's story. He was the neighbor from whom Becky's parents, Rob and Linda, had bought the land. A former managing director at a bank in Manhattan, Vince had been an early bitcoiner, cashing out a portion of his holdings in the 2017 bull market to buy a huge parcel of land and retire before he turned forty. He lived almost completely off the grid with his wife and three children, growing their own food, hunting, and fishing. He'd even engineered his own power grid with solar panels and a hydroelectric kit in the stream, using the excess electricity to mine more bitcoin. He earned his income now from mining and from giving occasional lectures on the topic, trading bitcoin directly with local farmers for beef and eggs.

Oliver listened, fascinated. He had never met anyone so radically self-sufficient. Vince's life was a functioning, independent reality, not an abstract ideology.

Lunch was one of the best meals Oliver had ever had. It was a feast of pure reality: grilled venison hunted by Vince, thick steaks from a local rancher, smoked trout from the stream, and fresh, peppery microgreens from Vince's garden. It made the packaged snacks and catered lunches of his office life feel like a pale imitation of food.

As they were finishing, Rob, Becky's father, turned to Nick with a playful but sharp grin. "So, Nick. Where are my crypto millions?"

Nick physically squirmed in his chair. "I know, Rob. Big miss on my part. I really messed up." He couldn't meet his father-in-law's gaze. "The good news is, I pulled out some ETH for you. It's sitting safely in FTX. Not touching it. Just going to let it grow there until I figure out the next move."

The confidence in his voice was brittle, desperate.

Rob laughed, a sound that held no humor. "I hope you use this to educate yourself about risk, son. In all my years, I've learned one thing: there is no such thing as a 'risk-free' investment, which is what I believe you called this."

"I get it, Rob," Nick said, his voice tight with shame. "There was an industry expert I followed … he said it was basically risk-free. I should have done my own diligence instead of trusting these guys." He stared intently at his plate, a man cornered and humiliated.

After the plates were cleared, a comfortable quiet settled over the patio. Vince came over to where Oliver was sitting alone in a deck chair, watching the sunlight filter through the trees.

"Cigar?" Vince offered, holding out a small, open wooden box. Inside lay a few Montecristo Robustos.

The rich, earthy scent hit Oliver with the force of a memory. He wasn't much of a smoker, but his dad had been a connoisseur. The smell instantly transported him to his father's favorite cigar lounge in midtown, a world of dark leather, hushed tones, and the blue-gray haze of expensive smoke. He took one. "Thanks."

They lit up, the initial puffs sending fragrant clouds into the pleasant late May sunshine. They sat in a comfortable silence for a minute before Oliver spoke. "So, Nick called you a 'bitcoin maxi.' What exactly is that?"

Vince seemed amused, a slow smile forming around his cigar. "I'm not fond of the term. 'Maximalist' was first used as an insult, a pejorative for people who were only focused on bitcoin. Some folks wear it as a badge of honor now." He took a thoughtful puff. "I suppose it means people like me. People who believe bitcoin is the only crypto asset that's truly meaningful. The only one that can lead to self-sovereignty, a life without depending on the state. We tend to reject the others, either because they're outright scams, or because the problems they claim to solve just aren't meaningful."

"So what would you call yourself?"

"Vince, for starters," he said with a chuckle. "But 'bitcoin fundamentalist' is probably more accurate. I appreciate it for its fundamental properties. I don't believe any other asset on the planet has them." He saw the curiosity in Oliver's eyes. "I used to be in your world. I was a managing director at a big investment bank. Back in 2013, one of our trading arms started looking into mining and trading this new thing called bitcoin. That's how I found it. I was hooked, jumped over to that desk immediately."

He paused, staring out at the mountains. "Then, over the next few years, the whole crypto casino opened up. The Ethereum DAO hack in 2016, the ICO scams in 2017 … I started questioning the decentralization of it all. It felt like the same old system with a new coat of paint. I became bitcoin-only after that. When the price spiked in late 2017, I saw my exit pass. I sold enough, quit my job, and bought this land."

He took another puff of his cigar and smiled, a look of beatific contentment on his face. "I'm fortunate. I'm living the dream. I wanted to retire and do what I loved before I turned forty. And here I am."

After a brief, peaceful silence where they both just enjoyed the cigars and the view, Vince turned to him, his voice gentle. "Tell me about your dad."

The question was simple, direct, and kind. Oliver felt a distinct tightening in his throat, a warning sign of the grief lurking just below the surface. He chose his words carefully, constructing a wall of facts to hide behind.

"My father was an immigrant," he began, his voice flat and matter-of-fact as he stared at the glowing cherry of his cigar. "Moved to the U.S. in the early nineties for grad school at Princeton. Studied applied math and computer science. He met my mom there. They got married, he got a job at a reinsurance company, and I was their only kid." Oliver recounted the moves from Connecticut to the city, the divorce six years ago, his mom's move to Maplewood. He delivered the biography of the man he loved with the detached precision of a historian, tiptoeing gingerly around the emotional minefield, terrified that a single misstep, a single tremor in his voice, would cause him to break down completely.

"Well, I'm mixed as well," Vince replied, a warm, easy smile on his face. "My mom is Eritrean, and my dad is French. He taught at Columbia, and she was a waitress at an Ethiopian restaurant nearby – that's where they met. It's amazing how your perspective changes when you're raised by parents from completely different cultures."

Oliver nodded, continuing to work his way through the cigar. The conversation turned back to bitcoin, and in the pleasant late May sunshine, Vince patiently laid out his worldview. He spoke not like a salesman or a zealot, but like a teacher, explaining the fundamental properties of money, why he felt bitcoin was its highest incarnation. He drew parallels to gold, but then pointed out its inherent flaws: its lack of easy divisibility, its physical weight, the cost of moving it across borders. And then he landed on the final, most crucial point – the cost to keep it secure.

"Violence," Vince said, the word delivered slowly, deliberately. He looked at Oliver to make sure he was truly listening. "The ultimate price to secure gold is violence. Your ownership of physical gold is only as real as your ability to protect it with guns."

The word hung in the air, stark and brutal. Just then, Rob's voice called out from the house. "Vince!"

Vince smiled and began to stand. As he got up to leave, he finished his thought, the words delivered almost as a casual afterthought. "And your ownership of bitcoin is as real as your ability to keep twelve or twenty-four words safe in your head. No violence involved. Bitcoin is peace." He started walking toward the house. "Let's continue this later. Let me see what Rob wants."

Oliver didn't respond. He sat transfixed, the cigar smoke frozen in the air in front of him. Vince's last words were echoing in his mind, colliding with two months of grief and mystery with the force of a tectonic collision.

Twenty-four words safe in your head.

Twenty-four words.

His heart hammered in his chest. A cascade of connections fired off in his brain, so fast he could barely process them. His dad's message on the TV. The quest. The strange, nonsensical number. It wasn't nonsense. It was a specification. A security feature. Not a password or a pin, but a passphrase. A seed phrase.

Only someone with all those words could spend the bitcoin.

The surreal, mystical journey he'd been on was suddenly, shockingly technical. The ghosts and riddles and projections were a cryptography problem, not a spiritual inheritance. It had to be it. It was the only thing that made sense.

Could Dad have been a bitcoiner? The question was a revelation, a betrayal, and a key, all at once. He kept it hidden all these years. *But why?*

Then, the next, inevitable thought: *How much?* How much could possibly be in a wallet that required such an elaborate, posthumous treasure hunt? A hundred bitcoin? Two hundred? Even with the price having crashed after the Luna and Celsius debacles, that would still be … millions of dollars.

A dizzying, terrifying vertigo washed over him. One thing was certain. The world had just cracked open for a second time, revealing another, deeper layer of secrets. And if he was ever going to understand it, he had to follow the path. He had to stay close to Vince. He had to *educate* himself.

738200 (May 27)

Dinner that evening was even better than lunch. Vince produced smoked venison sausages and a rich, local duck-liver pâté to accompany the grass-fed ribeye steaks. The only false note was the wine. Rob, committed to the local theme, had supplied a crate of Cabernet Franc from a vineyard in the Finger Lakes. As Oliver took a sip, the sharp, vegetal acidity made his palate recoil. A bittersweet memory surfaced: his dad, swirling a glass of deep red, patiently explaining the structure of tannins, the ghost of fruit, the importance of balance. His father had trained his palate well, a gift that now meant most wines were a quiet disappointment.

After dinner, they moved to an outdoor firepit, Vince passing around the Montecristos again. Oliver sat back, the rich smoke from the cigar curling into the crisp night air. He looked up, and his breath caught. He had never seen a sky like this. It was close to new moon, and with no city glow to wash it out, the darkness was absolute, a deep velvet canvas saturated with stars. He could see the faint, cloudy river of the Milky Way arcing overhead.

I could get used to this, he thought, a deep, quiet sense of peace settling over him. *The city really does separate you from the majesty of nature.*

As the conversation wound down, Vince stood up. "My wife and kids should be back, so I'll be heading home." He looked at Oliver. "I've got things to do tomorrow, but Sunday is clear. If you want to stop by in the morning, I can show you my bitcoin mining setup. Invitation is open to anyone," he added, turning to the group.

Nick laughed, the sound sharp in the peaceful quiet. "I'm good, man. If I never see another bitcoin miner, I'll be happy. Can't speak for Hope or Oliver, though."

"I'd love to," Oliver said immediately, his voice full of a genuine curiosity he hadn't felt in months. "I've never seen one, and I'm curious to see how your mini electrical grid is set up."

"Great," Vince's smile was warm in the firelight. "Anytime after eight. The kids will be up by then." He gave a small wave and disappeared down the path.

"See you then, Vince. Great meeting you."

Oliver stared into the crackling flames, the last of his cigar glowing in the dark. Nick's cynical comment hadn't soured the moment. It had only clarified it. He had found something here, a connection to a world that was real, grounded, and built on principles he was just beginning to understand. Sunday morning couldn't come soon enough.

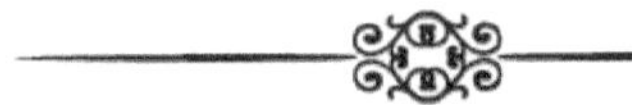

The Notepad

Later that night, in the deep quiet of the guest bedroom, Oliver lay in the dark, the house still and silent around him. He opened the notes app on his phone, the screen's cool light a small island in the darkness. He pulled up the note he simply titled *'Dad.'* It read:

```
violin
toddler
alley
shoulder
```

The fifth word had been elusive, a ghost he'd been chasing for the past few weeks. But today, the ghost had taken form. The word had echoed throughout the day's events, a quiet, insistent theme. He thought of Rob's cold lecture to Nick after lunch – *I hope you use this as an opportunity to educate yourself.* Then he thought of his own profound conversation with Vince, the sudden, shocking realization of his own ignorance, and the burning need that followed it – the need to understand the world his father had secretly inhabited. The need to *educate* himself.

He closed his eyes in the dark, raising his hands slightly under the covers, performing the now-habitual ritual. *Is 'educate' the fifth word?*

A quiet confirmation in the dark. His left arm dropped, heavy and certain.

He opened the note again. His thumb hovered over the screen, and then he added the fifth line, the word not just a clue, but a command. A new mission.

```
educate
```

STAGE 2: ENTROPY

CHAPTER 6. ROOKIE

738302 (May 28)

Oliver found a quiet corner on the deck, the crisp mountain air still cool from their morning hike. This was the first real moment he'd had to himself since they'd arrived in Andes, a pocket of silence to dive back into the quest. His heart beat a little faster with anticipation. He hadn't had a chance to follow the thread that had so shockingly appeared in the middle of a traffic jam. He pulled out his phone and searched for the Twitter app.

He was able to retrieve his old, ghost-like account – three followers, eleven following. A digital relic of a life before his father's death. He spent a few minutes cleaning house, then populated his feed with a new identity, following his colleagues Nick and Hope, and then Vince. Following Vince unlocked a new world, a stream of suggested "Bitcoin" accounts that he added one by one.

Then he searched for Christiaan.

He found the account easily. It had been created less than a year ago, posting sporadically. The most recent tweets were musings from prison, stark and somber anecdotes that gave Oliver a brief, voyeuristic glimpse into a life unimaginable. He scrolled further, his thumb moving faster, searching for what Daniela had mentioned. Then he saw them. Six poems in total, spread out over the year, each short enough to fit in a single tweet. He scrolled down to the earliest one, from July 2021, his pulse quickening. This was it.

Here it is
The rawness of reality
Life slows to a crawl
And I, I'm the one standing by
Unable to spread the seed
But I will try.

And so, in this is my first
With no re-morse we must search
To get started is the key
Right above the second apple,
In steps such as these
I enter a new prison
As always, a rookie

Oliver read it again, a frown creasing his forehead. He felt … nothing. No jolt of recognition, no clever wordplay. It was just clumsy. The rhythm was broken, the rhymes forced. It was, he thought with a pang of guilt, one of the worst poems he had ever read.

His hope sinking, he scrolled through the others. They were no better – a similar blend of nihilistic self-pity and awkward phrasing. The fifth poem, from March of this year, was perhaps the worst of the lot:

We are now at sixes and sevens
Gentlemen,
There is nothing new under the sun
All there is to do has already been done
And then the eight, within wreath.
The time has come
To retire to private life
And wash hogs

He stared at the screen, a wave of confusion washing over him. It didn't make sense. The blue bird projection had been so clear, so specific. The clues from his projections had been unerring guides, leading him from one solid discovery to the next. How could a signpost so clear lead him to this ... this unintelligible drivel?

He immediately felt a wave of shame for the thought. Christiaan was a man in pain, locked away for life. Maybe this was just his way of coping, of making some kind of peace with his circumstances. Who was he to judge it as art?

Still. The infallible logic of his quest had just hit a brick wall. This felt like a dead end. He scanned the poems again, desperately searching for a different kind of clue. Maybe the word was "Poem"? Or an emotion? "Sorrow"? "Re-morse"? The word "Remorse" was there, but it was hyphenated – "Re-morse" – a strange, deliberate-looking error that was as nonsensical as the rest of it.

He wasn't making any progress. He was staring at a signal he couldn't decode, lost in the noise. With a sigh of pure frustration, he decided to let it go. He had hit a wall. All he could do was wait for another projection, and hope the next one would give him the clarity the last one so cruelly lacked.

738379 (May 29)

Purple, orange, and green plumes of light danced in the air, intertwining like smoke. A soft, harmonic hum vibrated in Oliver's chest, a rhythm that seemed to move with the colors. The dancing lights would intensify into a brilliant, swirling chaos, then soften to a gentle, breathing pulse. On and on, a visual symphony in the dark.

God, he thought, a slow, groggy realization, *I've had far too much to drink.*

Through the warm, colorful haze, he could see Hope. Her eyes were shut, a soft, serene smile on her face. Her body was swaying gently, not to any music he could consciously hear, but to the same silent, harmonic hum that was moving through him. They were dancing in the same dream.

How strange. And yet, nothing had ever felt more right.

A final, flickering thought from his sober, cautious self sparked in the back of his mind. *Should I be doing this?*

738420 (May 29)

He most definitely should not have.

The thought was the first coherent thing to surface in the thick, syrupy fog of Oliver's mind. He opened his eyes, and the morning light was a physical assault, a blade of pain stabbing through his skull. He felt groggy, a deep, rolling nausea churning in his stomach. He slowly turned his head on the pillow, and the room tilted violently. *What did I do?*

Flashes of the previous evening returned, a chaotic and blurry slideshow of bad decisions. The after-dinner hike under the stars. The crackling outdoor firepit. The insane, shivering plunge into the nighttime stream. And the wine. All that terrible, acidic local wine that had clouded his judgment and washed away his inhibitions.

He looked beside him. And the full, sickening weight of his regret crashed down on him. Hope. Asleep. His co-worker. The one he passed every day at the office, the one who sat on the beanbag by the door. His heart hammered with a new, frantic rhythm of pure panic. *How can I ever talk to her again? What if someone finds out? What if HR finds out? Wright ...*

He had to get out.

Moving with the clumsy stealth of a thief, Oliver quickly gathered his crumpled clothes from the floor, got dressed, and stumbled out of the room, not daring to look back at the sleeping figure in the bed.

He had promised to meet Vince shortly after eight. In the bathroom, cold water on his face only seemed to sharpen the pounding in his head. The coffee he fumbled to make in the moka pot was a bitter, useless sludge. Nothing helped. He stepped outside into the cold, crisp mountain air and took a few long, deep breaths. The nausea subsided a fraction, but the headache remained, a tight band of pressure around his skull. He set off gingerly down the small hiking path toward Vince's house.

Vince was outside, tending to a flower bed, his movements easy and serene. Oliver must have looked a sight, because Vince took one look at him, and a kind, knowing laugh broke across his face. "Oh dear. One of those nights, huh? Follow me. I have something for you."

Oliver stumbled behind him into the house. The sounds from the kitchen – the clinking of glass, the thud of a knife on a cutting board, the sharp rattle of a cocktail shaker – were like small explosions inside his head. A minute later, Vince returned with a small, half-full shot glass and placed it on the counter in front of him.

"Oh no. No, no, no," Oliver grunted, a wave of revulsion washing over him. "God, no. I can't even think about alcohol."

"It's less than half an ounce. Two sips," Vince said, pushing the glass closer. "Trust me on this one."

Oliver was too disoriented and miserable to argue. He picked up the glass. The first sip was an assault – a strange, herbal fire. Then, a loud explosion seemed to go off inside his head, like a lightning bolt striking a transformer. An electric buzz shot through his body from his toes to the top of his skull. The air suddenly smelled sweet. The second sip was a softer echo of the first, and as the warm, pleasant burn settled in the back of his throat, the world snapped into focus. The blurry edges became sharp, the nausea vanished, and the pounding in his head simply ceased to exist.

He blinked a couple of times, looking around the kitchen, which was now crystal clear and vibrantly real. The hangover was gone. Magically, impossibly, gone.

"What on Earth is this sorcery?" he asked, his voice clear and steady, his mind reeling with disbelief at how good he suddenly felt.

"A Catskill Pick-Me-Up, with a twist," Vince said with a grin. "The one I gave you Friday, but with fresh crushed turmeric, ginger, and a few pinches of a special salt high in magnesium. Works like a charm." He shook his head. "Don't have more than that, though."

Vince asked what had happened the previous night, and Oliver recounted a censored version of the events – the hike, the fire, the ill-advised cold plunge into the stream.

"Ah yes," Vince chuckled. "A rookie mistake in the mountains. The cold air makes you feel deceptively sober. Gets the newcomers every time."

With the fog of his hangover miraculously lifted, Oliver could finally take in his surroundings. Vince's home was much larger than Rob's, a true farmhouse with soaring ceilings and elegant, exposed wood beams that smelled faintly of pine.

"This is all wood from my own property," Vince said, noticing his gaze. "Logged and treated it myself. I make sure to plant two new trees for every one I chop down, so the forest keeps regenerating."

Oliver just nodded, stunned. The idea of building a home from the very land it stood on was so fundamentally real it made his own work of building abstract applications in the digital ether feel like a ghost's profession.

"Have you had breakfast?" Vince asked, then immediately corrected himself with a laugh. "Oh, no way you could have in the state you were in. Here, let's get something going."

Vince walked over to a bucket of eggs sitting in water. "Just collected these from the hens. About as fresh as it gets."

Breakfast was a revelation. The scrambled eggs had a deep, rich flavor Oliver had never tasted before. The bacon was thick and smoky, and the wild strawberries Vince had picked from a bush in his backyard were tiny, explosive jewels of sweetness. This was life, pulled directly from the earth.

The morning became a tour through wonderland. Vince pulled a perfect shot of espresso from a top-of-the-line Italian machine. Then he took Oliver outside to show him his "Mini electrical grid." Oliver watched, amazed, as Vince explained the three sources of power that made his home an independent island: solar panels arrayed in a sunny patch of land, a biomass kit that anaerobically digested waste, and most incredibly, a home hydroelectric turbine whirring in the stream that cut through the property. He was completely self-sufficient.

"In fact, I generate about fifty percent more power than the house needs," Vince explained as they walked toward a separate shed. "Almost all the excess goes into this."

He opened the door. The shed was warm and filled with a loud, constant hum. Racks of machinery were lined up, blinking with lights. ASICs. Bitcoin mining hardware.

"These are some of the most powerful miners out there," Vince said over the noise. "I'm in a small mining pool with a few friends. We win a couple of blocks a month, and I've been making about two bitcoin on average. Broke even on the equipment a few months ago. This is all pure profit now."

Oliver stood there, feeling like a stranger in a strange land. It was all clicking into place. This wasn't a speculative gamble. It was a closed, sovereign system. Vince was converting sunlight and flowing water into pure, digital energy. He was living a philosophy.

A deep sense of dislocation washed over Oliver. His entire life – the concrete jungle of New York, a gilded cage divorced from nature; his career in the startup world, chasing whatever shiny app venture capital money dictated – felt thin and unreal. It was a life of abstractions. This, what he was seeing now, was raw and real. Bonfires under the stars, food from the land, a home built by hand, a life powered by the elements themselves, all culminating in the quiet, peaceful act of securing a global monetary network.

Three days ago, he couldn't have imagined such a life was possible. Now, he was watching someone thrive in it.

The tour continued as they walked back toward the house. Oliver learned that Vince was a licensed ham radio operator, another of his passions, with the ambitious goal of convincing the community to transmit bitcoin transactions over radio waves, bypassing the internet entirely. Every new detail was another layer of a life lived with deliberate intention.

They were greeted at the house by Vince's wife, Marie, and their three kids, a happy explosion of energy. Marie, who Vince explained had been a practicing psychologist in the city, had the same calm, centered presence as her husband. She was semi-retired now, focusing on what she called "Spiritual mind-body healing," blending shamanic practices with the hypnotherapy techniques from her clinical days.

The similarity was immediate and striking. Oliver mentioned Maren, and while Marie hadn't heard of her, her interest was instantly piqued. It was another strange resonance, a hint that Maren wasn't an anomaly, but part of a larger, hidden world Oliver was only just beginning to glimpse.

"I wanted to show you one last thing," Vince said, a glint in his eye. He gestured for Oliver to follow him down a small, winding path into the woods. After a five-minute walk, they reached a clearing dominated by a small shed. All around it, like silent, iron sentinels, stood large, intricate metal sculptures, their surfaces textured with rust and age.

"This is my favorite hobby," Vince said simply. "I make these."

The shed was a blacksmith's workshop, a place that felt ancient and elemental. A giant coal-fired furnace radiated a palpable heat, and the walls were lined with hammers, tongs, and anvils. "I source the metal from junkyard sales," Vince explained. "Mostly iron and steel. There is such a primal thrill in using fire to bend and shape metal." He looked at Oliver. "Not enough time today, but next time you're up here, I'll show you how it works."

"I'd love to," Oliver said, a note of uncertainty in his voice. "But I'm not sure when I'll be back. Nick's in-laws move back in for the summer."

Vince just laughed, a warm, easy sound. "Oh, you're welcome to stay with me. Any time. I see the spark in you, Oliver. We'll make a bitcoiner out of you yet. I'd be glad to host you."

The offer was so genuine, so unconditional, that it took Oliver by surprise. "That would be amazing," he said, a bright feeling of hope and gratitude washing over him. "I don't know about becoming a bitcoiner, but I'd love to see real blacksmithing. What do you do with the sculptures?"

"I auction the ones I don't want to keep. They're all priced in bitcoin," Vince said casually. "I've sold over ten. The most expensive one went for almost a full bitcoin. Isn't that wild?" He pointed to a piece near the woods. "I leave them outside so they can interact with nature – the air, the rain, the snow. The art's life never ends; it just continues to evolve."

Oliver's mind was reeling. Vince was creating a whole micro-economy around bitcoin. He was converting physical labor and fire into art, and that art directly into sound money, with no one in between.

He glanced at his phone and was shocked to see he'd been with Vince for over two hours. The others would be wondering where he'd gone. He thanked Vince profusely for the tour, for the drink, for everything. Vince mentioned he came to the city once or twice a month for lectures, and they agreed to connect the next time he was there, leaving Oliver with a dizzying sense of a world cracked wide open.

Hope was in the kitchen when Oliver got back to the house, a bright and cheerful presence that made his stomach clench with anxiety.

"Morning, Mr. Battolo," she said, her voice full of the same easy, playful energy as always. "Where were you? We were about to start brunch. Did you get a good night's sleep?"

The question, so innocent, so direct, hit him like a slap in the face. He wasn't sure how to react, where to look. He struggled to meet her eyes. "Oh," he fumbled, his voice sounding thick. "I was a bit hungover, but it's good now. Sorry, I stopped by Vince's place to check it out. Didn't want to wake anyone."

"Oh right, Vince. I forgot about that." She gave him a skeptical look, but it was aimed at his excuse, not at him. "And hangover? I don't think we had *that* much to drink. I feel fine." She shrugged, turning back to the coffee machine. "Anyway, ready to eat? I think Nick's setting the table."

Oliver just stood there, his mind reeling. He couldn't detect a single trace of acknowledgment in her voice, not a flicker of shared memory in her eyes. It was as if last night simply hadn't happened.

Did it not happen? The question was a frantic grasp for an easier reality. *Was it just another weird, drunken dream?*

No. The answer was immediate and certain. He remembered waking up next to her, the disorienting shock of it. He remembered his crumpled clothes on the floor.

So she's just … pretending it never happened? He tried to find a less complicated explanation. *Maybe that's all it was. We just had too much to drink and fell asleep next to each other. An accident.* The thought was a lifeline, a simpler, safer story. He clung to it. Maybe it was better this way. Just pretend nothing happened and move on. As he settled on this convenient fiction, a wave of relief washed over him, the knot in his stomach finally unclenching.

The rest of the day passed in a pleasant, uneventful haze. Around ten o'clock that night, after a long dinner, the effects of less than four hours of sleep finally broke through. Vince's magic pick-me-up had kept the hangover at bay all day, a miraculous loan against his body's exhaustion. But now, the debt was coming due. A heavy, leaden tiredness crashed over him. He excused himself from the group and went to his room, the need to simply lie down overwhelming everything else.

The strange mixture of wired-ness and exhaustion was making his thoughts race in frantic, looping circles. *Did Dad have a bitcoin wallet? Why hide it? Was this his inheritance? And Christiaan's poetry – a complete dead end. And Hope … ugh. How could I have been so stupid? Things are going to be so weird at work. God, Dad, why are you torturing me like this? Why not just write it down on a piece of paper? This is so unfair …*

The thoughts began to fray at the edges. Oliver felt the room shift behind his closed eyes, and a soft buzzing sound started, like a tiny electric drill in the far distance, growing steadily closer until it was humming inside his skull. The darkness of his closed eyelids deepened, turning from black to a rich, impossible purple.

"Yoohoo, Battulu. I knew you'd be back soon. And this time you look ready!" a voice suddenly sang out, impossibly cheerful.

It was the same sing-song voice, coming from all directions at once, just as it had when he collapsed on the patio. Oliver didn't feel the same terror this time; his body was too heavy with fatigue. He tried to force his eyes open, to pull himself back to the solid reality of the guest room bed, but it was like trying to lift his own body. He couldn't.

"Are you trying to leave, Battolooo?" The voice adopted a theatrical pout. "You know, that makes me so sad. Sad, sad, sad. A saddy laddie, that's what that makes me."

"I'm not trying to … I just tried to open my eyes," Oliver mumbled into the void.

"But why? Why, why, why?" The voice giggled, a sound that seemed to spin around him. "Your eyes are finally opening by themselves. You are ready, Batlow. You are finally ready and you don't need to try anything. It is happening for you already."

As the voice spoke, a figure began to coalesce out of the deep purple blackness, as if being painted into existence. A short, portly man in a loose brown suit. A bald, almost egg-shaped head. Deep, piercing purple eyes, and a blunt, upturned nose that looked like a cross between a pig's and a human's. He looked and sounded exactly as Oliver's father had described him, all those years ago.

"Are you the …" Oliver gasped, the name a relic from a buried childhood. "You're the … Nose Smiter!"

The strange man put a hand to his chest in mock horror, his eyes wide with feigned shock. "I'm the what the who now?"

"The Nose Smiter. You're unhappy with your nose, and you try to steal other people's noses!" Oliver said, the absurdity of the words hitting him even as he spoke. He was arguing with a bedtime story character in a hallucination.

"Battolo, see, that just hurts my feelings, you meanie," the strange man said, turning his back in a dramatic sulk. He peeked over his shoulder with a sad face. "My nose is perfectly, just about okay. It's magnificently sort of normal. Most people think it's the most incredible nose that's marginally below average they've ever seen." He spun back around, suddenly animated and proud. "I'm certainly not this Nose Smiter person. Don't you remember me?"

"I do remember you," Oliver said. "So if you're not the Nose Smiter, who are you?"

The strange man's demeanor shifted instantly. He drew himself up, puffed out his chest, and assumed an imperious, theatrical pose, as if a tiny, personal spotlight had just hit him. "I'm the Noncemeister, of course."

"The Noncemeister?" Oliver asked, unsure he'd heard correctly.

"Yes, the Noncemeister," the strange man continued, his voice now booming with self-importance. "The master of the nonces."

"What? That sounds a lot like the Nose Smiter to me," Oliver said, raising a skeptical eyebrow.

The Noncemeister let out a long, theatrical sigh, and his entire body seemed to deflate like a punctured balloon, his suit sagging around him. "Young Battootoo, you have to let go of my nose. There's nothing wrong with my nose. I don't need another one. Let it go, so I can breathe."

Oliver considered this, but the name was still a sticking point. "So you're the Noncemeister from the bedtime stories my dad used to tell me?"

"Dad? What dad? Who's dad?" the Noncemeister asked, suddenly re-inflating to his full height. He began looking around theatrically, peering under imaginary furniture and patting Oliver's pockets as if searching for a hidden person. "I don't see any dads here. I'm your old buddy, the Noncemeister. The master of the nonces. The keeper of the timechain."

There it was again, that odd phrase from the poem he'd heard on the patio. "Time chain?" Oliver asked.

"Why yes, of course." The Noncemeister attempted a jaunty salute. "I'm the nonsense of the master and the timer of the keepchain. Don't you remember?" He paused, scratching his bald head with a comical look of confusion. "Wait, did I say that right? Anywho!" he chirped, the confusion vanishing as quickly as it appeared. "It doesn't really matter, does it? The answer is in noncense." With that, he did a nimble little skip, appearing suddenly behind Oliver.

"Well of course I remember you," Oliver said, turning to face him. "But Dad made you up. And he called you the Nose Smiter. And he certainly didn't say anything about any 'time chain'."

"Batlu, you've got to drop this nose business," the Noncemeister said, waving his hand dismissively as if shooing a fly. "It's old hat. It's over. It's behind us. See?" He pointed an animated finger past Oliver's shoulder. "It's behind you. There, it's gone." He made a fist and then opened his fingers with a flourish. "Poof! There is no nose. It's noncense. But that's good. The answer is in noncense."

"The answer is in nonsense? What does that even mean?"

"Not nonsense. *Noncense*," the Noncemeister clarified, enunciating the word with unhelpful precision.

"That's what I just said."

"Ah, you have a lot to learn, young tiger. But the good news is, you are ready today." He grinned. "You might be a rookie cookie, but you are ready steady teddy." He stepped forward and stuck out a single, surprisingly solid index finger, poking Oliver squarely in the chest.

The moment his finger made contact, the sound began. The whisper of a million voices, rising in a deafening, physical crescendo that vibrated through

Oliver's entire being. He instinctively clapped his hands over his ears, the sound a painful, overwhelming pressure. The whole event lasted only a few seconds before receding back into the purple silence.

He took his fingers out of his ears. The Noncemeister stood with his eyes blissfully shut, a serene, ecstatic smile on his face. "What was that sound?" Oliver asked, his own voice shaking slightly.

The Noncemeister opened his eyes. "That is the most beautiful sound in the world. The timechain agrees."

"The time chain agrees that's the most beautiful sound?" Oliver tried to parse the bizarre statement.

"Oh no, you silly billy," the Noncemeister giggled. "That *is* the sound of the timechain agreeing."

"What on Earth *is* the time chain?"

The Noncemeister's playful expression vanished, replaced by one of genuine surprise. "Hello? Anybody home?" he said, rapping his knuckles sharply on Oliver's forehead. The sensation was startlingly real. "How could you have forgotten? I taught you everything a long time ago." He paused, tapping a finger on his chin. "I suppose it's fair of you to ask, I suppose. I suppose you supposed I suppose. It was a long time ago. And you know nothing, so I can teach you everything again, all over again and again," he concluded, looking immensely pleased with himself.

"I'm lost," Oliver said with a helpless shrug.

"Okay big boy, here it goes again ..." The Noncemeister straightened up, assuming the posture of a street-corner preacher about to deliver a sermon. "The timechain is everything there was, everything there is, and everything there ever will be disassembled into two quads and a tenth. It is where truth resides as seen by everyone at all times. First there is truth and then there is a new truth. But for the new truth to become truth, the timechain needs to agree. And when it agrees, the old truth becomes new truth. Easy peasy lemon squeezy."

The torrent of word salad left Oliver reeling, grasping for the simplest possible container for the idea. "So the time chain is a person, then?"

The Noncemeister let out a high-pitched, tinkling giggle that seemed to bounce around the purple void. "Tee hee. Hee hee hee. You are such a goofy bird." He began to pace like a professor in a lecture hall, hands clasped behind his back. "The timechain is not a person. It is a state. It is a state of mind. It is the collective consciousness of the universe that projects itself into the truth over and over again." He stopped and made a grand, sweeping gesture, as if tracing a massive sphere in the air. "The timechain is the contour of reality. It is your mind with all the mirages removed. In short, it is the incontrovertible truth."

"Truth about what?"

"About everything, of course," he chirped. "Everything and nothing all at once. Our civilization has a fabric, it has a texture, Battu." He reached out and plucked at the sleeve of Oliver's shirt, as if it were a cosmic tapestry. "A fabric that is created by how we speak and how we interact and how we transact. The basis for this fabric is truth, because in the absence of truth, there is fabrication. And without a fabric, there is no civilization."

"I'm not sure I'm following," Oliver said, trying to keep up. "You're saying there is this place, or state of mind, that tells us what the truth is, and that's what holds civilizations together?"

The Noncemeister's face lit up, and he clapped his hands together with a loud, joyful smack. "Why yes, that was good! You got it already!"

"How come I've never heard about this time chain?" Oliver asked, raising an eyebrow.

"You've always known about it. It has always existed, but its genesis brought it into public consciousness."

"Not my consciousness."

"It has now." The Noncemeister leaned in, his purple eyes twinkling, and poked Oliver's chest again for emphasis. "Now you know, Batlu, and now you are free!"

"This makes no sense," Oliver replied, the words a flat statement of fact.

"Aha, yes!" the Noncemeister said happily. "The answer is in noncense."

"There you go again. It feels like we're going in circles." Oliver threw up his arms in exasperation. He was trapped. He couldn't wake up, and he couldn't escape this absurd conversation. He took a deep breath, a feeling of weary resignation settling over him. The only way out was through. He had to accept where he was and plough through the madness. He decided to latch onto the one concrete thing the creature had said.

"And what was that about 'everything there is assembled into a quad' or whatever it was?" he continued, his tone shifting from frustrated to inquisitive.

"Yes, yes," the Noncemeister replied, delighted to be back on topic. "The timechain is everything there was, everything there is, and everything there ever will be, disassembled into two quads and a tenth."

"You already said that, but I don't know what it means. What's 'two quads and a tenth?'"

"Two quadrillion and a tenth more, of course," the Noncemeister said, as if explaining two plus two. "But you knew that."

"No, I didn't," Oliver said, a sharp hint of irritation creeping back into his voice. "Two quadrillion of what?"

"Two quadrillion and a tenth more, Battolo. Don't forget the tenth more. Of everything there was, everything there is, and everything there ever will be. The continuum of abundance in this world."

"Abundance? You mean like money?" Oliver asked, the word a familiar echo from Maren's new-age lexicon.

The Noncemeister let out a deep, booming "Ho ho ho ho ho," a laugh that seemed to shake the purple void. "Batulu. Such a precocious young tiger you are. But no. No, no, no, no. His tone softened, becoming suddenly sincere. "Money is not abundance, and abundance is not money. Money is simply a tool some people use to incorrectly measure abundance. Abundance is a state of mind. It is a feeling of pure contentment, peace, love, and cheerful eagerness."

Oliver pondered this. Stripped of the strange delivery, it didn't sound entirely unreasonable, just … new-agey. "So the time chain is a measure of abundance?"

"The timechain is a measure of time," the Noncemeister corrected, tapping his own chest as if marking a beat. "Its heartbeat signals when the old time has moved on to a new time, by incrementing the old truth to the new truth. And because it is time and truth, it is used to *describe* abundance. It is a language in that sense."

Oliver sighed. "The time chain has a heartbeat?"

"Yes," the Noncemeister smiled. "That was the beautiful sound you heard a short while back. The sound of agreement."

"I only heard it once so far. And once before, when I was here a couple of days back. That's a long heartbeat."

"The timechain's heartbeat is exactly as long as it needs to be, so as not to change the language of abundance," the Noncemeister said with a profoundly casual shrug. "Sometimes it is short, and sometimes it is long, but at all times, it is correct. On average."

Oliver fell silent, his exhausted mind trying to process the strange, interlocking logic. He had been fighting this, trying to escape it. But he was here. He was trapped. He looked at the strange, smiling creature in front of him, and a new, fundamental question formed. "Am I in the time chain right now?"

The Noncemeister's entire being lit up with an explosion of pure joy. "Batulu, Battoo, Batululu! Yes, yes, yes! I knew you were finally ready! I love it when I'm right." He pointed a gleeful finger at Oliver. "And you're right too. Yes, big boy, you're in the timechain now with me." He clapped his hands. "Oh goody, I feel so happy right now, I could sing!"

And with that, the Noncemeister launched into a ridiculous, joyful dance, skipping in clumsy circles around Oliver.

Then, to Oliver's shock, the Noncemeister did as promised. He stopped his dance, struck a pose like a vaudeville singer about to begin his number, and burst into song.

"Wherein languid streams of arbitrage
Were drenched in gentle runes
While work's weatherbeaten visage
Wore unsullied prolix moons
The azimuth refrain
A blind and ruthless timechain

"When a score and two are herein six
Dissociatively so
With unordinated numerics
From yesterdays long ago

The azimuth refrain
A blind and ruthless timechain

"Disremembered symphonies
Held hopelessly aghast
Prematurely poisoned seas
Implausibly fast
The azimuth refrain
A blind and ruthless timechain

"Set fourth, come first, surprisingly
Imminent in its hue
Awkward ankle from its knee
Seldom can pursue
The azimuth refrain
A blind and ruthless timechain

"One after ten, turns into three,
As clock ticks define
Chapter, verse, they all agree
Perhaps the end is nine
The azimuth refrain
A blind and ruthless timechain

"The more's obscured, the more's revealed
Counterintuitively
Subterraneously concealed
Lockless absent key
The azimuth refrain
A blind and ruthless timechain"

The last note hung in the purple void and then vanished. Oliver was left in a stunned, ringing silence.

"What on Earth was that meant to be?" he asked, trying to comprehend the torrent of lyrical nonsense that had just washed over him.

"Oh, that's noncense, Battlo. The answer is in noncense, remember?" the Noncemeister said, taking a small, proud bow.

"Oh, I agree it was nonsense," Oliver said, bewildered. "But I'm not sure what answers it had."

The Noncemeister sighed, a sound of withering disappointment. "Oh my dear chief. My poor tormented big boy. It's *noncense*, not nonsense. But that's okay. You made a good start today, and next time, you will be ready for more."

"What do you mean next time?" Oliver asked.

"There's always a next time, Batuloo," he said, beginning to walk backwards in a slow circle around Oliver. "Every after needs a before, otherwise it won't be after before, would it? If an after is before a before, then the before becomes the after and the after becomes the before." He stopped walking and stamped his foot with a sudden, emphatic finality. "And *that* … would be nonsense."

"Right, nonsense," Oliver said, finally finding something he felt he could agree on.

"Tee hee hee hee," the Noncemeister giggled, the sound light and genuine. "You're funny, just like him."

The comment was casual, but it snagged in the air. "Him?" Oliver asked.

The Noncemeister's playful expression froze for a fraction of a second. "Oh no, no, no, no, silly, silly me," he said, waving his hands frantically as if to erase the words from the air. "Not him, you. There is no him." He immediately regained his composure, clapping his hands together once. "But Batlue, you are ready to go now. Today's work is done." He gave Oliver a jaunty, two-fingered salute. "Toodle pip, big boy!"

And with that, he simply popped out of existence, leaving Oliver alone in the sudden, absolute silence.

738564 (May 30)

Oliver woke to the morning sun slicing through a gap in the curtains. He blinked, looking around the unfamiliar guest bedroom, and a wave of relief washed over him. He was alone. In his nightclothes. He had gone to bed around ten, had a truly bizarre dream, and woken up nine hours later. That was all. Nothing had happened with Hope. Phew.

Noncemeister, he thought with a small, dismissive laugh. His imagination could really run wild. It had been a vivid dream, though. He could still remember every strange detail, every nonsensical line of that silly song about the time chain.

Later that day, as they were packed and getting ready to leave, Vince came by. "Figured you'd be heading out," he said to the group. "Thought I'd stop by and say goodbye."

He walked up to Oliver and handed him a small, thin object that looked like a USB stick. "Here, I got this for you."

"Oh, thanks. What is it?" Oliver asked, inspecting the strange device.

"It's an Opendime," Vince said. "A single-use bitcoin wallet, in a manner of speaking."

"That's awesome. How does it work?"

"You can look up the instructions online, but there are a hundred thousand sats on it, roughly thirty dollars. Enough to get you started on your bitcoin journey."

"A hundred thousand 'sats?'" Oliver asked, the word unfamiliar.

"Oh, sorry. A 'sat' is short for 'satoshi.' It's the smallest unit of a bitcoin," Vince explained patiently. "There are a hundred million sats in one bitcoin. So, a hundred thousand is just a thousandth of a coin."

"Wow, I really appreciate this, Vince." Oliver felt a genuine delight, holding the small, tangible object. It felt like a key to a new world.

"Not at all," Vince said. "When you read the instructions, you'll see you need to create your own wallet to move the funds to when you unseal it."

Something Vince said snagged Oliver's attention. "There are twenty-one million bitcoin in total, right?"

"That's the final supply, yes," Vince confirmed. "Only about nineteen million are in circulation now. The rest will be mined over the next hundred and twenty years or so."

The timeline seemed absurd. "Why will it take so long to mine the last two million, when the first nineteen million were done in about thirteen years?"

Vince smiled. "That's the magic of the 'halving.' The bitcoin code cuts the supply of new coins in half roughly every four years. In the beginning, miners got fifty bitcoin for every block they found. After four years, it dropped to twenty-five. Then twelve-and-a-half, and so on."

Oliver felt a flush of embarrassment. He, a supposed blockchain expert, was getting a lesson on the fundamental monetary policy of the original. He remembered the concept now, a half-forgotten detail from his past readings. "Oh, right," he said, the pieces clicking into place. "So the block reward is huge upfront, and it gets exponentially smaller over time. The later years barely add to the supply."

Vince nodded, a look of approval in his eyes.

Oliver's mind went back to his original question, but now with a new layer of information. He ran the math quickly in his head. *Twenty-one million bitcoin. A hundred million satoshis per bitcoin …* the numbers multiplied, expanding into an astronomical figure.

"So," he said slowly, "If there are twenty-one million bitcoin and a hundred million satoshis per bitcoin … that means there are two point one quadrillion satoshis, right?"

"That's right," Vince responded.

Oliver felt a sudden chill, the memory of his "Dream" washing over him with unnerving clarity. He spoke the next words almost reluctantly, the phrase feeling alien and dangerous in his mouth. "Or … two quad, and a tenth."

Vince laughed. "That's a weird way of saying it, but sure."

The world seemed to tilt. Vince's casual confirmation was a thunderclap in the quiet of Oliver's mind. It wasn't a dream. A vivid fever dream couldn't have contained a piece of verifiable, esoteric mathematical truth that he himself had not known. The Noncemeister, the silly song, the cryptic sermon … it was real. Or it was a projection, a bizarre, unconscious journey that had happened without his consent. Which was worse? The barrier between his mind and the world, a barrier he had always assumed was solid, was terrifyingly permeable.

He managed to thank Vince again, reiterating that he wanted to catch up soon.

As Nick's Audi pulled out of the elegant driveway, Oliver looked back at the modern farmhouse, at the wild mountains behind it. His mind was a whirlwind of impossible questions. But underneath the unsettling confusion, one clear, simple thought remained.

This was a good life.

The Notepad

1. violin
2. toddler
3. alley
4. shoulder
5. educate
6. rookie

CHAPTER 7. OVAL

Through a light purple haze, the roar of a crowd washed over him. Oliver found himself in a bustling cricket stadium, the air smelling of cut grass and warm beer. He was an observer, a ghost watching a man and a young boy, who looked to be around twelve, make their way to their seats.

"Daddy, why are there so many people supporting India here in England?" the boy asked as they sat down.

"Well, Visu," the father began, his voice kind and patient, "A lot of our people have moved here for better opportunities. When our team comes to play, they show up. It's their way of staying connected to our culture."

"But if they want to stay connected, why did they leave?" Visu demanded, his young mind grappling with the contradiction.

"There are many reasons, and you'll understand them better when you grow up," the father explained. "For now, they feel there's not much opportunity in India for them. So they come here, or to America, to build something new."

"But we have a good life in India, right, Daddy?" the boy asked earnestly. "I have my friends, we play in the hills, we go to Grandma's house for sweets. We even have a TV now."

The father smiled. "You're right, sweetheart, we have a wonderful life. But you never know what someone else is going through. One day, India will be a powerful country, and maybe some of these people will even return." He decided to change the subject. "Now look. You're in a foreign country for the first time. We're in England, at the Kennington Oval, watching your favorite cricketers. Are you excited?"

"Yes, Daddy! I'm excited to see Gavaskar bat. I think he'll score a century!" Visu jumped in his seat.

"Let's hope so, but this England team is much stronger," his father cautioned.

"Why are they so much better?"

"They have good players, better trainers, more money. But don't worry," the father said, his voice full of a quiet confidence. "I have a good feeling about our team's future. We have Gavaskar, Kapil Dev, Srikanth, Vengsarkar … I think we'll win the World Cup in the next few years, you just watch."

Oliver observed, fascinated. This projection was different. It wasn't a single, charged moment but a long, spooling ribbon of time, an entire afternoon unfolding before him. He found it strange that he could understand them; they were speaking another language, he was sure of it, yet the words arrived in his mind as perfect, clear English. He'd never understood cricket, despite his own dad's attempts to explain it, but watching it like this, as a silent observer of this gentle, familial scene, was deeply peaceful.

As the day wore on, the game turned. Visu looked dejected. "Daddy, how can we let Ian Botham hammer our bowlers like this?"

"He's a very good batsman, son."

Just then, Botham unleashed a blistering cover drive. The ball, a red missile, smashed into the shin of Gavaskar, the fielder. Visu's hero collapsed to the ground, writhing in pain.

"I hope he's okay, Daddy!" Visu cried out, jumping from his seat in horror as his favorite player was carried off the field on a stretcher.

Later, as the day's play was ending, news trickled through the crowd: Gavaskar had likely broken his shin. He was out for the rest of the match.

"It's so unfair!" Visu wailed, his small face streaked with tears. "We came all the way to the Oval to watch him, and now he's not even going to play!"

Oliver watched as the boy's father gathered his thoughts, searching for the right words. "Visu," he said softly, putting a comforting hand on his son's shoulder. "Sometimes we enter an experience expecting one thing, but we end up with something completely different. You should always allow yourself to be surprised. It doesn't feel good now, but who knows what other amazing things might happen?"

The boy was not convinced. His father continued, his words seeming to travel across the decades, aimed not just at the crying child, but at the unseen observer, Oliver, watching from the future.

"When you are older, you might start a job or a career thinking it is exactly the right path. But you might find that certain things happen that lead you in a completely different direction – away from what you thought you wanted, but toward what you *needed*, to grow as a person."

The scene slowly faded to black, the father's words echoing in the silence.

Oliver opened his eyes, the quiet of his apartment a stark contrast to the roar of the long-ago crowd. *That applies to Dad's life, too,* he thought. The brilliant computer scientist who ended up in a boring reinsurance job. The path he thought he wanted, and the one he ended up on. How many other secrets did that diversion hold? Could his mom have been right about him all along? Why hide the bitcoin world from his own son? The questions multiplied, each one a new layer of shadow over the man he thought he knew.

739959 (June 8)

Oliver fought his way through the human tide of Grand Central, a chaotic river of commuters flowing against him as he made his way toward the Oyster Bar. He walked in and immediately saw the unmistakable figure of Eddie Garcia getting settled at a table, a small, portly island in the sea of the grand, vaulted room.

"Hi there, tiger, glad you could make it," the cheerful voice boomed, cutting through the din of the restaurant.

As Oliver braced himself for the verbal onslaught, he shook Eddie's hand and looked at him – really looked at him – for the first time with his new, projection-opened eyes. The short, portly stature. The perpetually ill-fitted suit. The bald, egg-shaped, almost oval head. The slightly upturned, porcine nose. A jolt went through him, a moment of dawning, horrified clarity. *The Noncemeister.* It was him. His dad had based the entire surreal, maddening, brilliant character from his bedtime stories on … Eddie Garcia. The connection was so obvious, so absurd, he couldn't believe he hadn't seen it before.

"Hi Mr. Garcia. Thanks for inviting me," Oliver said, sitting down, his mind still reeling from the revelation.

"Olly, Olly, Olly," Eddie began, contorting his face into a pained grimace. "How many times do I have to tell you this? Call me Eddie or Uncle Eddie. Why so formal with me, chief?"

"Just habit, I guess, Uncle Eddie," Oliver replied sheepishly.

"Listen champ, I have a little over an hour before my train to Irvington leaves," Eddie said, tapping an imaginary watch on his wrist. He picked up his napkin, and with the theatrical flair of a magician, whipped it open and tucked it neatly into his collar. "The next train's not till after nine, and Melissa will give me hell if I'm home after ten. Let me tell you something, big guy, you don't want to be on my wife's bad side. That woman," he shuddered dramatically, "Has more stamina for unpleasantness than an ultramarathon runner. I love her to death, don't get me wrong. But man, can she not let go of something. Gotta keep her happy. Happy wife, happy life, you know what I'm talking about? Of course you don't. But take it from me, kiddo. Gotta keep your woman happy."

Eddie's eyes scanned the restaurant and lit up as he spotted the raw seafood display. "By the way, have you tried the oysters here?" He pointed toward the glistening ice bed with the grand gesture of a museum curator unveiling a masterpiece. "Top of the line. They get them from everywhere – Long Island, Cape Cod, Maine, Nova Scotia, the west coast. You gotta try them. Best in the business. I heard someone say Chelsea Market had the best oysters, and I gotta tell you kiddo," he leaned in, his voice a conspiratorial whisper, "I asked the guy to gimme a goddamn break. Chelsea Market is where yuppies from Jersey go to feel good about their worthless lives. They don't have a clue. Now these guys …" He leaned back with a booming, "Ho, ho, ho!" "These guys know what they're doing. The best in the business, let me tell you, chief."

Oliver, feeling utterly defeated by the monologue, closed his menu. "I guess I'm getting the oysters, then."

"And don't even get me started on their clam chowder," Eddie said, his eyes glazing over with a dreamy, far-away look. "It has to be tasted to be believed. You wouldn't even know there's a clam in there. It's rich, smooth, like eating liquid silk. The chef handpicks the clams himself every morning. Goes to Chinatown at the crack of dawn to beat the crowds. You don't want to be there in the afternoon, chief. Place is a zoo, smells like rotten fish. As it should, if you really think about it. Anyway, the best clams you've ever seen. Not like the fake Rolexes they sell down there. This is the real deal. The other day …"

Oliver saw his chance, a tiny gap in the conversational torrent. He had to take it. "Hey, Uncle Eddie," he interjected, cutting him off before the next anecdote could begin. "Sorry to interrupt, but did you want to meet because there was more news on my dad?"

"Oh, yeah, yeah," Eddie said, a flicker of amusement in his eyes. "You want to get straight to the point, just like your old man, may his soul rest in peace, that goddam sonofabitch. Okay, kiddo, I get it." He started thumbing through a worn leather briefcase. "So here's the deal: the company was cleaning out one of the old filing cabinets in his room the other day, and they found this."

Oliver leaned forward, his focus absolute.

"Remember when you were asking me about this Hungarian Georgie guy?" Eddie continued, finally pulling out a single, folded piece of paper. It was faded, yellowed, and soft at the edges from years of handling. "We found this. It wasn't even in a file. Just lying under a stack of papers at the bottom of the cabinet."

Eddie held up the sheet and waved it in front of Oliver's face like a prize. "Look. It's an email from him to your dad."

Oliver took the paper, his fingers tracing the deep creases. It was a tangible artifact from his father's secret life. He unfolded it and read.

```
From: Gyorgy Lorincz <glorincz@posteo.de>
Date: Tue, Oct 19, 2010 at 4:42 PM EST
To:

Subject: Re: closing the loop

Good direction on using secp256k1 for blind mixing for
your Akasha idea. I'll give it some thought and write
a more detailed response soon.

On a separate note, I'm thinking it is time (no pun
intended) to sell the third Bryce after everything
that's happened. I know you said S might be interested,
so let me know how we can set that up.

Much love,

Gyorgy
```

The words swam in front of Oliver's eyes, a collection of cryptic clues. *Secp256k1.* The term was a ghost from a graduate-level cryptography class, a technical incantation that felt both familiar and impossibly distant. *Akasha. Blind mixing.* Then, the jolt. *The third Bryce.* It confirmed Shannon's story completely. *I know you said S might be interested.* A new variable. A new mystery. And finally, the name. *Gyorgy Lorincz.* A full name. A concrete lead. The faded "To" field was illegible, but it didn't matter. This email was a Rosetta Stone, a key to a world he was just beginning to understand.

He looked up, his mind reeling. "Eddie, this is a weird email. Was there anything else?"

"Everything else was just clearly work-related stuff, kiddo." Eddie pursed his lips and shook his head. "Lots and lots of reports and data projections. It's amazing how much we used our office printer back in the day, you know what I mean? Those laser cartridges cost an arm and a leg. I don't know how the company manages to squeeze that into the budget." As he spoke, Oliver just stared at him, the sound of his voice a meaningless drone. He was holding a clue to an inexplicable mystery, and Eddie was lamenting the cost of office supplies. The absurdity was staggering. "... the amount of money your dad alone used to make for the company with the Europe accounts was a sight to behold, so he never had an issue using company stuff. Printers, papers, files, you name it."

Oliver had to cut through the noise, to get back to the only thing that mattered. "Any other leads on Gyorgy?"

"We still haven't gone through the files on your dad's computer yet," Eddie said, just as a flicker of hope ignited in Oliver's chest. "It's in a maintenance queue with our IT support team to unlock it and take an inventory." The flicker died. "Nothing to do with the Georgie stuff, specifically. It's just what happens whenever an employee leaves the company voluntarily or invol ... um ..."

Eddie's voice trailed off, a rare moment of self-awareness as he realized the grim territory he'd stumbled into. He coughed, course-correcting with the speed of a seasoned salesman.

"You won't believe the amount of bureaucracy with our IT folks, kiddo," he began, and Oliver felt his heart sink. He was a captive audience. "One time, I forgot to reset my password. You know, they force you to change it every ninety days for 'security reasons,' but let me tell you, chief, it's a royal pain in the ass. The number of people who lock themselves out is off the charts."

Eddie leaned forward, his voice rising with remembered injustice, his hands starting to chop the air for emphasis. "So anyway, I locked myself out and it took them *two days* to get to it. Can you believe that, champ? Two whole days! I'm in and out of their office, and they're telling me they're too backlogged. I escalated it to the general manager – didn't help! Apparently, every other request was escalated, too. So there I was, hat in hand, while our IT bozos were cooling their heels. I almost lost an account over it! Absolute madness."

Oliver waited, letting the storm of indignation pass over him. He watched for a pause, a single moment where Eddie might need to take a breath. He saw it and jumped in, his voice almost resigned.

"And my dad's computer ...?"

"Oh, right, right, right ..." Eddie smacked his forehead with the palm of his hand, a gesture of self-reproach. "So the support ticket to unlock his machine has been sitting in their queue for over a month. Lord knows when those clowns will condescend to attend to it. I'm a watcher on that ticket, though, so I'll get an email as soon as they start working on it." His eyes suddenly lit up, his attention completely diverted. "Oh look, your oyster platter is here. About time, too. My train leaves in forty minutes."

A platter of glistening oysters on a bed of ice was placed between them, a tangible, welcome interruption.

Eddie was right. The oysters were very good.

740124 (June 9)

A new kind of calm had settled over Oliver. He had made his peace with the sporadic, unpredictable nature of his father's quest. The initial, frantic impatience had burned itself out, replaced by a quiet acceptance that the words would arrive at their own pace, when he was ready.

He spent the next few days collecting his thoughts, letting the revelations of the weekend settle. *Dad was a bitcoiner.* The fact was still hard to fully grasp. He'd enjoyed his conversations with Vince, but he couldn't yet bring himself to believe that bitcoin was the only thing that mattered. His mind, trained in the world of Web3, still wrestled with the alternatives. *What about democratizing finance? What about digital property, all the use cases that go beyond simple money?* Bitcoin seemed like a fortress, powerful and secure, but limited. Blockchains like Ethereum were more like chaotic, sprawling cities, full of potential for things like lending and complex contracts. Surely, there was value in that?

The Opendime Vince had given him was a cool piece of technology, though. Following Vince's suggestion, he had spent an evening doing his homework. He installed Sparrow Wallet on his laptop, a popular application for managing bitcoin. He carefully unsealed the Opendime, moved the hundred thousand sats, and watched with a small thrill as the balance appeared on his screen. Sure enough, when setting up the wallet, he was given the option: a twelve or twenty-four-word seed phrase.

He had chosen twenty-four. That led him down a new rabbit hole. He spent hours reading the BIP-39 specification, a "Bitcoin Improvement Proposal" from 2013. He, a supposed blockchain expert, was getting a humbling education in the foundational mechanics of the original. He learned how a group of loosely aligned developers had proposed this more secure way of managing a private key. He found the official wordlist – all 2,048 of them. And then came the jolt. He scanned the list, his heart pounding, and found them. *Violin. Toddler. Alley. Shoulder. Educate. Rookie.* All six of his father's words were there. It was the final, definitive proof.

Oliver closed his eyes and relaxed his body. Projection was getting easier, more comfortable with each episode.

Great, he thought, as the world of his apartment dissolved into the familiar, disorienting void. *Back to the inky black time chain place.* The last time, with the Noncemeister, had felt so real, so vivid. Far more than a dream, a projection he had stumbled into.

"Batlooo! You're back! This makes me so happy!" The sing-song voice erupted from the silence, and the Noncemeister stepped out of the shadows with the flourish of a ringmaster entering the center ring. "Did you miss me?"

"I don't … well, I didn't think I'd see you again," Oliver said, his voice still shaky in this strange place. "I thought you were a dream."

"A dream? Come on, big boy!" The Noncemeister's voice boomed, his playful demeanor suddenly replaced by an immense, overwhelming authority. He leaned in close, his purple eyes locking onto Oliver's. "This is as real as it gets. Have you ever considered that everything that happens outside the timechain is just a lie? A collective delusion? An elusive illusion?" He spread his arms wide, encompassing the entire purple void. "This is the only place that is real. Everything else is fake news."

"I have not considered that, and I will not consider that," Oliver replied peevishly. "That's your usual nonsense again, isn't it?"

"Noncense, Battulu. Noncense," the Noncemeister corrected with a patient sigh, as if explaining to a toddler. "Not nonsense. But that's neither here nor there. It's anytime or anywhere. Are you ready for today's story?"

"I'm trapped here again, aren't I?" Oliver sighed, the fight going out of him. "I can't seem to get back to my room."

"Get back? Trapped?" the Noncemeister asked, his face a perfect mask of genuine surprise. He looked around the purple void, peering into the shadows as if searching for invisible bars. "You are never trapped, Batlue. You are exactly where you need to be, and you always have a choice to leave. The fact that you're not leaving means that you're choosing to be here."

"I'm not choosing that. I want to leave, but I can't."

"Ah, I see the problem here." The Noncemeister snapped his fingers with a loud, sharp crack, a sudden look of theatrical insight on his face. "There is a disconnect between what you are thinking, and what you are feeling, and what you are desiring." He began to lecture, pointing a finger at Oliver's head. "What you are thinking – or rather, what you *think* you are thinking – is really your silly conscious mind, your ego, producing noise. That's not the signal." He then pointed to Oliver's chest. "What you feel, how you feel, what you *desire* – that is your unconscious mind expressing itself. That is the signal, Battcw. You are here because you desire something. You have made this choice."

"So you're telling me that my conscious mind wants something completely different from my unconscious mind?" Oliver asked, trying to follow the strange thread of logic.

"Why yes, of course! Your conscious mind is an eejit. It knows nothing. It thinks it knows, but it knows not, and it's not conscious enough to know what it doesn't know."

"An 'eejit?'" Oliver asked, confused by the strange word.

"A dum-dum. A silly billy. A waste of space," the Noncemeister rattled off cheerfully, as if listing ingredients. "It is the only thing standing in the way of you and the rest of the universe. You *are* the universe, Batloo, and the universe is you, but your eejit conscious mind creates that separation. But that's okay for now. Today is for a short story, not this mush-mush about the universe."

"Is this story going to help me find one of my father's words?"

The Noncemeister stopped cold, his playful demeanor vanishing. He stepped back and circled Oliver slowly, his eyes narrowed in suspicion. "Father? What father? You have a father? You don't look the sort. How come you never mentioned this 'father' person before?"

"Well, this is only the second time I'm really talking to you," Oliver said, exasperated. "And most of the time, you're doing all the talking."

"Ah yes, yes, yes, yes, yes," the Noncemeister said, the suspicion melting away as quickly as it had appeared. "One of these days, I'll talk my silly old oval head off. But talking is good, Batlululu. That's why I do it." He leaned in close again, his expression turning intense. "But yes, about this 'father' character. What about him?"

"He had some words I need to find," Oliver said. "I was wondering if your story would lead me to them."

"Words, words, words, words, words," the Noncemeister mused, scratching his bald head. "Words, you said?" A dreamy, distracted look came over his face. "Are you sure you don't mean … birds? I have birds. Birds are beautiful, and free. They soar and they sing, and they nest, and they wing." He paused, a look of mild disappointment on his face. "Well, I don't actually *have* birds, come to think of it. And I don't think my story does either. I like them, though."

"Words, not birds," Oliver said, his voice cold and sharp with the effort of pulling the conversation back to reality.

"Oh right, you did say words, didn't you?" The Noncemeister tapped his temple with a single, thoughtful finger. "No, I have no words. I mean, I have words, and my story has words, but they're just words. Not *Words*. Why did this father of yours leave you words?"

Oliver hesitated, a feeling of profound absurdity washing over him. He was about to explain the technical architecture of a decentralized digital asset to a character his father had invented to explain a pig-like nose. He took a breath and plunged in. "They're part of a seed phrase for a bitcoin wallet."

The Noncemeister tilted his head, his face a perfect mask of utter bafflement. "What's a seat phase? What's a bit corn wallet?" He suddenly brightened, a look of dawning comprehension on his face. "Oh, I get it. You're trying to learn, aren't you? You're trying to speak noncense just the way I told you." He wagged a scolding finger. "But this isn't noncense, Battulu, this is nonsense. I have no clue what you're talking about. None eversowhat."

Just then, the sound began again – the soft hum escalating into a deafening, harmonic roar. A physical wave of pressure washed over Oliver, forcing him to crouch down and clamp his hands over his ears.

The Noncemeister, however, did the opposite. He spread his arms wide, tilted his head back, and let the sound wash over him, a look of pure, ecstatic bliss on his face. Tears of joy streamed from the corners of his closed eyes. "So, so, beautiful," he whispered as the sound subsided, his voice cracking with emotion. "It gets me every single time. Every single time, Battu …" He punched his own heart with a soft fist, a gesture of deep feeling.

Oliver slowly straightened up, his ears ringing. "Okay then. Are you ready to carry on with your story?"

The Noncemeister looked at him, his face scrunched in a confused grimace. "Story? What story?"

"The story you said you were going to tell me."

"Oh right, that story! Right, right, right, right, right." He smacked his forehead with the palm of his hand. "I lost myself for a moment there. The timechain agreeing can do that to me sometimes. And all that stuff you were saying about words. Words are good. They can have meaning, or they can be noncense. Noncense is good because it has the answer. Sometimes there is meaning in the answer, or sometimes noncense has no meaning. But at all times, the answer is in noncense. But yes, words, you lost me there. Now, are you ready for the story?"

"I'm ready," Oliver said, exhausted but resolute.

"Great." The Noncemeister's entire demeanor shifted. He was now the ancient storyteller, the keeper of lore. "Once upon a long ago – who knows how long ago, really. Let's just say it was fourteen million three hundred and six thousand, one hundred and twelve heartbeats ago, but who's counting, amirite, tiger?"

"Heartbeats?" Oliver asked.

"Yes, heartbeats of the timechain, remember? The timechain is a measure of time, and its heartbeat is when the old time becomes the new time. We just heard the sound. That was the heartbeat."

"Oh right, you did tell me that," Oliver said, his logical mind trying to find an anchor. "How many minutes is a heartbeat, anyway?"

"Minutes? Don't think I know what that is." The Noncemeister's eyebrow rose to an impossible height on his bald forehead. "Is that you attempting noncense again?"

"No, no. Minutes are a unit of time," Oliver explained, feeling the absurdity of having to define a minute. "We use seconds, minutes, hours, days …"

"Battu, do you ever listen to yourself speak sometimes?" The Noncemeister suddenly appeared right in front of him, leaning in close. "Are you a cuckoo bird? Are you a wacky-ducky? Hello, anybody home?" He rapped his knuckles again on Oliver's forehead. "This is nonsense, Batlow. Don't waste my time with this. The only measure of time is the timechain's heartbeat. Everything else is a subjective delusion."

"Okay, if you say so," Oliver shrugged, surrendering.

"Of course, I say so!" The Noncemeister drew himself up to his full height, seeming to grow a foot taller as he stared down at Oliver with an imperious glare. "I am the Noncemeister, the master of the nonces, the keeper of the timechain, and I have spoken."

"Carry on," Oliver said, taking a small step back. "I won't interrupt."

"Ok, as I was saying before I was so rudely interrupted," the Noncemeister began, his tone shifting back to that of a whimsical storyteller, "Once upon a long ago … probably fourteen million three hundred and six thousand, one hundred and twelve heartbeats ago on average, there were two friends. Leonhard and Giulio." He began to mime his story, lovingly tracing a perfect circle in the air. "They both loved shapes, especially circles. But Leonhard wanted the circle to have stretchy bits … he felt the radius was too constant, too unexpressive." He then made a series of sharp, dramatic slicing motions with the edge of his hand. "His friend Giulio agreed, and they both started slicing cones with their sabers …"

Oliver's logical mind, starved for something familiar, seized on the image. "Do you mean they were slicing horizontally, as in a conic section?"

The Noncemeister paused, his hand frozen mid-slice, wearing an expression of cosmic shock. "Why, yes! How did you know?"

"Well, I studied this in high school," Oliver said, feeling a small surge of confidence. "If you slice a cone parallel to its base, the cross section is a circle. I don't know who this Giulio is, but is Leonhard's last name Euler, by any chance?"

"No way, Batlu! Do you know him? How could you know him?" the Noncemeister gasped. "This is incredible! He lived over fourteen million heartbeats ago, and you don't look a heartbeat over a million and a fifth."

Oliver's mind, a machine built for calculation, instinctively started running the numbers. "Wait, if that's what you think my age is, that means a heartbeat is roughly ten or eleven minutes."

The Noncemeister sighed, a sound of weary exasperation. "Batloo, there you go again with your strange words. A heartbeat is exactly as long as it needs to be. It is sometimes longer, and it is sometimes shorter, but every time, it is just right."

But Oliver's brain was still running. *Ten minutes.* He confirmed the second calculation. *Two hundred and seventy years ago … the 1750s … that's Euler's time.* Then another piece of information, something he'd learned from Vince, slammed into place. *Bitcoin blocks are generated every ten minutes on average.* A cascade of connections lit up his mind. Could *heartbeat mean block time? Time chain is … blockchain? Where does time come into it? The chain is just blocks linked by hashes.*

The realization was so electrifying, he had to ask. "Sorry to interrupt," he said, "But is the time chain the same as the bitcoin blockchain?"

The Noncemeister exploded in a fit of pantomime exasperation. "Batew, you've got to stop. Please stop." He began rattling off words in a flurry of different languages. "*Arret! Parar! Bandh karo!* What are these strange words? I've never heard of 'bit corn.' What is it? Is it when you chew on the cob and a little bit falls off?" He threw his hands up in the air. "It's a nonsense word, Battulu. There is the timechain, and everything else is fake news. Capisce?"

"Okay, okay, fine," Oliver said, backing off again, having clearly hit a nerve. "No need to get snippy. I was just curious. So, Leonhard is Euler, you said? I don't know who Giulio is, though."

"Yes, yes," the Noncemeister said, his frustration vanishing as he calmly resumed his lecture. "Leonhard Euler and Giulio Carlo. Giulio Carlo, Count

Fagnano, Marquis de Tosch. Anywho, they loved circles, but they wanted the radius to be more stretchy in some parts. Then they realized that a circle only had one focus, and to have a stretchy part, they'd need two foci."

"Foci?" Oliver asked.

"Focuses. Two of them," the Noncemeister clarified, holding up two fingers. "Not one focus, but two."

"Ah, right. The plural of focus," Oliver said, placing the word. He was back on solid ground. This was math, a language he understood.

"So they realized they'd been slicing the cone wrong all along. The horizontal cuts were just giving them circles of different sizes, so they sliced it at an angle to the base. Not parallel, but at an angle."

"Sure, that's an ellipse," Oliver interjected, the memory of a high school geometry class surfacing with surprising clarity. "You can also get parabolas and hyperbolas, depending on the angle."

The Noncemeister stopped, putting his hands on his hips and fixing Oliver with the stern glare of a schoolmaster. "Battoo, who's telling the story? You or me? Can you please zip it?" He made a zipping motion across his lips. "Zip. It. Yes, that way. Silencio. The Noncemeister speaks now, not this young tiger. I can tell you're excited, but this is my time. Capisce?"

"Sorry, sorry," Oliver said, unable to suppress a cheeky grin.

"Good. So they sliced it at an angle and got the beautiful shape with two foci. And that made them very happy," the Noncemeister said, then paused, letting the final word hang in the air … *oval*.

The word was a key. It unlocked a sudden flash of memory from his projection of the cricket match – the vast, green field, the roar of the crowd, the Kennington *Oval*. It had to be. He quickly checked, his hands moving almost imperceptibly in the purple void. His left arm dropped. It was the seventh word. He had it. *Okay, I'm done here,* he thought, and tried to will himself back, to open his eyes. Nothing happened.

"Battoo, Battolu, Batululu, what are you doing? How rude is this?" The Noncemeister's voice was sharp, indignant, a cage slamming shut around him. "I haven't finished my story, and you're trying to leave? Where are your manners, you sneaky weasel? Wait. Wait, wait, wait, wait, wait. Wait for me to finish, and then I will tell you when you are ready to go."

Oliver realized there was nothing he could do. He let out a silent, internal sigh and gave a small shrug of resignation.

"Right, where was I?" The Noncemeister shook his head in pantomime disgust. "Oh yes. So they had this new way of slicing a cone, and they called it an ellipse. But they didn't stop there." He began to pace again, his voice taking on a more complex, academic tone. "With a circle, finding the arc length was easy. But for this beautiful oval, it was not so simple … they couldn't generalize … soon they found that to generalize, you need to integrate, and so elliptic integrals were born. And then someone inverted the integral and got elliptic functions. Beautiful curves, but nothing like an ellipse. You with me so far, Batto?"

"I think so," Oliver said, but his voice was unconvincing, his attention suddenly fractured. The words *elliptic curves* and *integrals* had triggered a different, painful memory. He was suddenly eighteen, sitting in a cavernous lecture hall at Columbia, a professor droning on at the front of the room. He wasn't hearing the math. He was hearing the echo of his parents' latest screaming match from the night before, the words of their divorce papers a constant, crushing static in his head. He had barely passed that class.

"Okay, good," the Noncemeister said, oblivious to Oliver's internal state. "Then, many, many heartbeats passed. At least twelve million and three hundred thousand heartbeats before two other people, Neal and Victor, realized that elliptic curves over finite fields produce a beautiful algebra. An algebra so beautiful that it can be used to lock and unlock secrets."

The phrase jolted Oliver back to the present. "Lock and unlock secrets? You mean cryptography?"

"Silly words, Battulu. But Koblitz is the one I want to end on."

"Koblitz?"

"Oh, that's Neal's last name. Koblitz. He put the 'k' where it belonged in his elliptic curve," the Noncemeister clarified, with a wink that Oliver found completely unhelpful.

"Now I'm completely lost," Oliver said blankly. The thread was gone.

"Okay, Battie, let's see if this helps." The Noncemeister sighed, as if his brilliant lecture had been wasted. "I might have to try a better form of noncense for you to find the answer." And with that, he threw his arms up, ready to begin another performance, and launched into verse again.

"Two rabbits exploded, a line oddly worded
Penultimate is just one before
Nineteen remaining, not quite explaining
Why it was strangely four more

A prophecy behooved, when tens are removed
Turns seventeens into sevens
Smooth curvy elliptic, characteristic
Of secrets of earths and of heavens

"Euler's focus, was right on the locus
Of two points on a plane
One's distance was such, from the other point as much
As double the distance between

This conic section, had tilted direction
From references quite circular
A difference so stark, that the length of an arc
Was no longer abundantly clear

"The heartbeats that followed, where wisdom was hollowed
Led right down to Koblitz and Miller
Algebra discerned, that Galois returned
For secrets, there is a distiller

And so the timechain, that liminal membrane
That lets in naught but the sun
Constructively shielded, wrought metal wielded
Sec p two five six k one"

The last line, delivered with a final, ringing clarity, was not a word. It was a variable. A specific, technical name that Oliver had seen before. The memory of the faded, dog-eared email from Eddie flashed in his mind. It all slammed into place.

"So that's it!" Oliver exclaimed, a triumphant grin breaking across his face. "Gyorgy was writing to Dad about a cryptography scheme!" The song was a cipher, and he had just found the key. "Thank you. You were right. I had to listen to the story told nonsensically to get it. The answer really is in nonsense, then."

The Noncemeister let out a long, weary sigh, a sound of affectionate exasperation. "Ay, ay, ay, ay, ay, Battulu. *Noncense*, not nonsense. We've been over this before." He waved a dismissive hand. "Anyway, that's the story for the day. Off you go!"

And with that, he disappeared into the shadows. The purple void held for a moment, silent and empty, and then gently dissolved. Oliver felt the solid reality of his apartment return, his eyes opening slowly. He was back in his room, his mind buzzing not with confusion, but with the clean, beautiful certainty of a solved problem.

The Notepad

Oliver got down on his haunches, the scent of old paper and dust rising from the bottom corner of his bookshelf. He pulled out several books, their spines familiar but not what he was looking for. Then he found it. The 2022 WilcoxRe diary.

He ran his thumb over the smooth, dark leather cover. At the beginning of each year, his dad would come home with one of these, a gift for senior employees, and promptly hand it over to Oliver. A flood of memories washed over him as he held it – his younger self, doodling fantastical creatures in the margins of a past edition; his high-school self, meticulously organizing his life in its gridded pages. In recent years, they had just collected dust on his shelf. Now, this one had a purpose.

He walked back to his desk. The conversation with Vince, the realization of what these twenty-four words truly represented, had changed everything. A simple note on an internet-connected phone suddenly felt reckless, a glaring security vulnerability. He needed something real, something offline. Something his father had touched.

He opened the diary to the first crisp, blank page. Then he opened the notes app on his phone. With a slow, deliberate hand, he neatly copied the sacred list, transforming the ephemeral pixels into solid, permanent ink. When he was done, he added the seventh word, the prize from his strange journey through the history of mathematics.

i) violin ii) toddler iii) alley iv) shoulder v) educate vi) rookie vii) oval

He stared at the list on the page, the seven words that were the beginning of a map to a secret kingdom. Then, he turned back to his phone, his thumb hovering over the digital version of the note. With a final, decisive tap, he deleted it. The note vanished, leaving no trace. The secret was now safe, locked away in the physical world.

CHAPTER 8. BELOW

Oliver stared at the last, lonely slice of pizza in the box with a look of genuine disappointment. "Ugh, it's gone cold. The crust will go all soft in the microwave."

"Hey man," Olumide responded, a grin on his face. "That's the best part of pizza Fridays. The fourth slice, soft and warm, when the microwave makes all the grease ooze out just right. I'll take it if you don't want it."

"Go for it," Oliver replied with a shudder of disgust. "Are we heading to O'Connell's? It's 4:30. I'm ready to get out of here."

"Nah, dude. Grab a Lagunitas from the keg. It's a beautiful day. Let's hit the roof," Olumide said.

Just then, Hope walked into the common room, a bright smile on her face. A jolt went through Oliver's stomach, and he gave a tight, sheepish wave. For the past ten days, a tense, unspoken agreement to pretend that night in the Catskills had never happened hung between them. She acted with a maddening, cheerful normalcy that only amplified his anxiety. He would have preferred a confrontation, a clear-the-air argument. Instead, he was trapped in this polite fiction, and the awkwardness was a constant, low-grade hum under his skin.

"Have you been avoiding me, Mr. Battolo?" Hope's tone was teasing, but to Oliver, it landed like a cross-examination.

"Oh no, no," he scrambled, the words coming out too fast. "Sorry, it's just been really busy. Phoenix and all the other stuff going on …" It was a reflexive, desperate lie.

"Wait, stuff is happening on Phoenix?" Hope looked genuinely surprised. She turned to Olumide. "But your quarterly review deck said Phoenix was on pause until the end of the month, right?"

Olumide just shrugged, leaving Oliver completely exposed.

"I heard Wright is going to DC next week to meet them," Hope continued, her innocent questions feeling like a tightening net. "Maybe that'll move the needle."

"Oh, yeah," Oliver chimed in, his mind racing for a plausible-sounding fiction. "It's not moving on the business side, but we're doing some code upgrades. Maintenance, you know. Just to make sure it all works well for his trip." The lie felt thin and brittle even as he said it.

"Gotcha," Hope said, seemingly satisfied. "Well, let's hang out soon, guys. It's been a couple of weeks." She grabbed something from the fridge and left.

The moment she was gone, Olumide turned to him, his friendly expression replaced by a suspicious, penetrating stare. "All good, dude? Your face just turned purple. And what was that horseshit about Phoenix? There's nothing on the Jira board about code upgrades."

Oliver felt cornered, his flimsy lies collapsing around him. He refused to capitulate just yet. "Oh yeah, it wasn't a big deal. Just a small bug I found. Didn't need a ticket, so I just fixed it."

"And *that's* what's been keeping you so busy?" Olumide's head cocked to the side, his eyes narrowed in disbelief.

"Dude, let's just drop it," Oliver snapped, his voice sharp with embarrassment and frustration. "I'm sick of Phoenix, anyway." He turned and grabbed a plastic cup. "I'm getting a beer. Let's go to the roof." It was a desperate, angry retreat, and he hoped it would be the end of the subject. Thankfully, it was.

As they made their way to the stairwell, they nearly collided with Ian Wright.

"Ah, there you are, Mr. Battolo," he chirped, his cheerfulness painfully loud. "I think I've sorted out what's happening with you now."

The words hit Oliver like a physical blow. His blood went cold. *He knows. Hope told him. I'm dead.* A frantic, silent spiral of panic ignited in his mind. *He's going to humiliate me right here. I'm fired. A permanent record. How could I have been so stupid? It was consensual, but that doesn't matter. What am I going to tell Dad … oh, right.* The thought was a fresh stab of pain in the middle of the panic.

Wright continued, oblivious. "I don't think it makes sense for you or Sri to come to DC with me next week. Their tech folks won't be there, just the business directors, so best I go there myself. Hold off on getting the Acela tickets."

The wave of relief that crashed over Oliver was caustic, a feeling like battery acid coursing through his muscles, leaving him shaky and weak. "Oh, okay. That makes sense, Mr. Wright," he mumbled, scrambling past him and through the door to the stairwell as if escaping a near-fatal accident.

Up on the roof, the bright sun and open air did little to calm his frayed nerves. Nick was there with a few other colleagues, but he broke away when he saw them, a wide, manic grin on his face.

"What's up, my dudes?"

"Whoa, Nick, you seem happy today," Olumide said, surprised by the change from the previous month's despair.

"My boy SBF is gonna bail me out," Nick declared, his eyes shining with a gambler's feverish hope. *SBF*, Oliver's mind supplied the context, *Sam Bankman-Fried, the boy-genius CEO of the crypto exchange FTX.* "I was just listening to an interview. He's got big plans, and I'm waiting for the right moment to move my remaining ETH there. I'm going to make it all back, you just watch. Becky's dad isn't going to believe his eyes. Those fifty ETH are going to turn into five hundred, then five thousand."

He paused, a thought striking him. "Also, the Merge is happening in a couple of months, and that's definitely not priced in." The Merge, Oliver knew, was the long-promised, massive proof-of-stake software update to the Ethereum network, a risky and complex shift away from the mining-based system similar to the one that secured bitcoin.

"Oh man, I can't wait for ETH to flippen BTC when that happens," Nick continued breathlessly, his confidence growing with every word. "It's time to kiss that boomer coin goodbye. Proof of stake is the future. You better believe the government is going to crack down on proof of work with all the environmental damage. Maybe I can finally buy that Aston Martin I always wanted. I'll do donuts around Becky's dad's home upstate. He'll see then who the expert on risk management is."

The tirade, so full of buzzwords and speculative bravado, felt deeply alien to Oliver now. He found himself asking a simple, quiet question that cut through the noise. "Why do you think ETH will overtake bitcoin after the Merge?"

"Because proof of stake is better," Nick retorted, as if stating the most obvious fact in the world. "Instead of wasteful miners burning all this energy, you just have people staking their ETH to update the blockchain. Close to zero energy footprint. If you have any ETH, you should stake it. You'll get a yield on it, too."

"I had three or four ETH last year that I spent on NFTs," Oliver said, his voice quiet and weary. "Now I can't sell them. No one wants them. I think they're down ninety percent or more."

"Yeah, you should have asked me, dude," Nick said, though there was no real sympathy in his voice, only the forward-looking zeal of a new convert. "I would have told you the right ones to get. You should just buy more ETH and stake it. Welcome to the future, Oliver." He leaned in, his eyes wide with a manic, unshakeable conviction that looked almost like religious fervor. "The ETH price has bottomed now, right before the Merge. There's no way it's going below this. Up only!"

The confidence, coming from a man who had been financially annihilated just weeks ago, was unnerving. "Also, Nick," Oliver began cautiously, the lessons from Vince still fresh in his mind, "Is it safe to leave your coins on an exchange? I've been reading about self-custody and cold storage. Seems like the safer bet."

Nick let out a sharp, condescending laugh. "Haha, you're funny. Have you been talking to Vince?" he teased. "He'd say something like that. Look, if you have huge amounts and you're a seasoned tech guy, maybe. But the average user isn't going to get that stuff. Crypto won't grow if we make it too hard.

Let's leave the cold storage stuff to the nerds and conspiracy theorists." He took a confident sip of his beer. "Besides, FTX is as good as cold storage. What's going to happen? They're a massive, regulated institution with a reputation to uphold. I'm good. In fact," he said, puffing out his chest with a desperate bravado, "I'm better than good. I'm golden."

Oliver just looked at him, and felt an aching sense of pity. He saw a friend, drowning in losses, clinging to the one piece of driftwood he had left, telling everyone it was a luxury yacht. There was nothing more to say.

He gave a small shrug and walked over to the railing, turning his back on the conversation. The office building was ten stories tall, and the view over SoHo was largely unobstructed, a sea of rooftops stretching west toward the Hudson. A small twin-engine plane droned over the river, pulling an aerial banner behind it. Oliver watched it idly. The letters unfurled against the blue sky: **DON'T MISS WHAT'S BELOW YOU.**

The words were a strange, direct command. His gaze instinctively dropped, following the instruction from the sky down to the river below. There, a boat was chugging along, an electronic banner scrolling text along its side. The pixels were hard to read from this distance, but he squinted, focusing until the words resolved themselves.

5th Annual West Village Surrealist Art Fair: Sunday, June 12, by Pier 40.

Clever ad campaign, he thought. Then another thought, immediate and clear: *Daniela.* Surrealist art. Grotowski. This was right up her alley. It had been a few weeks since their date at the theater. A perfect excuse to see her again. A hopeful, simple plan in a world that had become impossibly complex. He smiled, a genuine smile for the first time that afternoon.

740434 (June 11)

"Welcome, young lad, to the 5th annual West Village Surrealist Art Fair! Prepare for your mind to be bedazzled!"

The voice was a cheerful, theatrical boom that cut through the pleasant Sunday air as Oliver made his way onto Pier 40. An old man, sprightly and surprisingly mobile for someone who looked to be in his nineties, was striding toward him with a grin.

"Oh, hello. Thank you," Oliver said, a little taken aback. Something was strange. A faint, shimmering purple haze seemed to cling to the man's outline, a trick of the light that Oliver couldn't quite resolve.

"Would you like to look at some fabulous art today?" the man asked, his accent a bizarre concoction of Irish brogue and sea-captain's growl.

"Sure, that's why I'm here."

"Come with me this way then!" the man gestured, and Oliver, feeling vaguely like he was being swept up in a performance, followed. *It's all part of the surrealist act, I suppose,* he told himself.

"Aye, as you can see here, laddie, some of the finest works of our time ..." the old man said, his crackly voice full of reverence. He pointed animatedly at a series of seven large canvases. "Inspired by Francis Bacon and Marcel Duchamp, this is a collection by the young South American painter, Luis Velázquez. See the sharp contrasts in emotion? The progression of human desire over a lifetime, from childlike eagerness to stoic detachment, and finally, to an apathetic nihilism."

The paintings were of large marble blocks in various states of decay. Oliver stared at them, trying to see what the old man saw. He couldn't find "Yearning" or "Nihilism" in the images, but they were undeniably beautiful. The canvas was an authoritative black, and the grayscale blocks at their centers were rendered with a skill that was almost photorealistic. The texture, the detail ... it was the work of a master.

"This young lad Velázquez is one of the finest painters of our generation," the old man gushed. "We've been trying to get him to visit, but he doesn't like leaving home."

He led Oliver past a few more exhibits of paintings and sculptures. The work was fascinating, but a nagging sense of dissonance grew in Oliver's mind. He couldn't reconcile the old man's florid, abstract explanations with the art itself. Another detail felt wrong, too. The pieces were all in the open air, exposed to the damp, salty breeze coming off the Hudson. He wasn't an expert, but he knew you didn't leave valuable art outside. The purple haze, the accent, the strange curation … it was all starting to feel less like an art fair and more like a bizarre, private dream.

After a few more pieces, the old man turned to him, his eyes twinkling. "Now, are you ready for the real deal?"

"Sure," Oliver said, a new caution in his voice. "So I guess all this until now was not the real deal?"

"Oh no, no, laddie. This was all great stuff, don't get me wrong," he said, his grin widening. "But are you ready to take this up a notch?"

"I guess I am," Oliver replied, his curiosity now warring with a definite sense of unease.

"Great, come right this way, then," the old man said, leading Oliver to the far corner of the pier. Five large, square shapes stood in a line, each shrouded in a heavy cloth. "This is my life's work. I haven't unveiled it yet, so you're going to be the first. Are you excited, laddie?"

"Um … sure, I am," Oliver said, his voice hesitant. A deep sense of unreality was beginning to settle over him.

The old man grinned and whipped the cloth off the first painting. "This one's called 'Waiting for Autumn.' My first. Painted over fifty years ago."

Oliver looked around, a sudden, sharp spike of panic hitting him. Daniela was gone. She hadn't been by his side for several minutes. He scanned the sparse crowd on the pier. She was nowhere to be seen. He was alone with this strange man. He turned back to the painting, his heart thumping, trying to force a sense of normalcy. It was a simple, skillful pastoral scene: sheep in a meadow, a warm orange sunset. "Very nice," he said politely. "This isn't surrealist, though, is it?"

"Oh, no, no, laddie. Not yet," the old man said, his voice dropping. "My paintings are a progression. I painted the first from my own imagination. The voices started by the time I got to the second."

"What do you mean, voices?" Oliver asked, a chill running down his spine.

The old man's gaze became distant, haunted. "There were voices, laddie. They spoke to me. Told me what to paint. They weren't human, not really. More like … energy, being downloaded into my brain, inspiring my hands. They were rare. Sometimes I'd go ten years without hearing them, and in that time, I couldn't paint to save my life. It's like I'd forget how, unless I heard the voices."

Oliver didn't know what to say. The man's confession was too strange, too raw to be part of an act. "How about the next painting?" he asked, desperate to move on.

"Ah, I'm glad you asked," the old man's cheerful demeanor returned instantly. "Because this one's for you, young lad." He whipped the cloth off the second painting.

The world stopped. The sounds of the pier, the cry of the gulls, the distant city hum – it all vanished. Oliver stood in a bubble of silent, roaring shock. He stared, his mouth agape. It was *The Toddler*. Bryce's second painting. The one from O'Connell's. The one Aisling had moved to a secure warehouse. It was impossible.

"You … you painted this?" he stammered, the words barely forming.

"Why yes, laddie. All mine, and damn proud of it," the old man beamed. "I called it, *The Toddler!*"

Oliver struggled to make his brain work. *It's in a warehouse. This can't be here. Who is this man?* "Wait, you painted this?" he asked again, his voice a strained whisper.

"Of course, I did!" the old man said, crossing his arms indignantly. "Why would I say it was mine unless it was?"

"What's your name?" Oliver demanded.

"Ah, I thought you'd never ask, laddie. It's John. Pleasure to make your acquaintance." He stuck out a crooked, wrinkly hand.

"Wait … John as in Jonathan Bryce?" Oliver asked, grimacing as he took the man's surprisingly strong, vice-like grip.

"Yes sir! In the flesh and at your service!" the old man saluted smartly.

"But you're dead," Oliver said, pulling his hand back. "Shannon told me. You died six years ago."

"Oh, bless her soul, my sweet Shannon. No, no. I'm very much alive," Bryce said quickly, ushering him along. "Come now, let's look at the next three before it's too late."

Still reeling, Oliver watched as Bryce took the cover off the third painting. The canvas was blank. "There's nothing here," he stuttered.

"Ah yes, that's a good point," Bryce said, and with a flourish, unveiled the last two paintings. They were also blank. "They're all below, laddie."

"Below? What do you mean?" Oliver asked, utterly bewildered.

"Just that. Below. My third, fourth, and fifth paintings are below."

The words were another shock. "But wait, I thought you only had three paintings," Oliver said, his mind spinning. "Shannon and Aisling both said so. Where did a fourth and a fifth come from?"

"From the same place as the second and third, Battulu. From the voices. They guided me," the man said, and in that single, final word, his voice changed, the Irish-pirate growl thinning into a familiar, high-pitched, sing-song cadence.

The shift was so subtle, so chilling, that it froze Oliver in place. He knew that cadence. He knew that name. "Wait … did you just call me Battulu?" The pieces slammed together in his mind with horrifying force. "No way. You're the Noncemeister. How is this even possible? This is real life, not a projection!" A hot surge of anger at being so thoroughly deceived simmered in his chest.

The figure of Jonathan Bryce laughed, a sound that morphed mid-chuckle into the Noncemeister's signature, tinkling giggle. "Busted. Hee, hee, hee. Ooh, it's hard to keep up the act for so long. And it was going so nicely, too. You're an observant eagle eye, Battew. You got me this time." He raised his hand, a playful grin on his face. "Okay, that's enough for today, I suppose. Off you go!"

He snapped his fingers.

The world shattered. The scent of salt and the cry of gulls vanished, replaced by the stale, silent air of his own apartment. Oliver gasped, his eyes flying open. He was lying in bed. He looked around wildly. His room. His bed. He grabbed his phone from the nightstand, his hands shaking. The screen glowed: *12:17 AM. Sunday.*

A wave of pure, nauseating vertigo washed over him. *No.* It had been mid-morning. He was on Pier 40. He had just come from the café. He was with Daniela.

Had this been a projection all along? The question was a fissure cracking through the foundation of his sanity. Every other time, he had *known*. He'd been a conscious passenger, aware he was in a dream, even if he couldn't get out. But this … this had felt real. Indistinguishable. His own mind had become an unreliable narrator, a perfect forger of reality. The purple haze around "Bryce." Daniela's sudden, impossible disappearance. It had all been in his head.

He sat up, his heart pounding a frantic, terrified rhythm. He forced himself to breathe, to think. *The clues.* He had to salvage the clues from the wreckage of the experience. The Noncemeister, playing the role of a dead painter, had shown him five paintings. The first two were real. The last three were blank canvases, which he'd said were "below."

But *below* made no sense. And the third painting … Shannon had said Gyorgy bought it. It existed. Why would it be blank? The contradictions tangled in his mind. *Gyorgy.*

The name was a sudden, solid anchor in the sea of confusion. Gyorgy was real. The email Eddie gave him was real. The email address on it was real. He had to connect with Gyorgy. It was the only way to test this, to tie the madness of the projection to a verifiable fact in the real world.

He got out of bed, his movements stiff and robotic, and walked to his desk. He powered on the computer, the blue light of the screen illuminating the dark room. He opened his email and started typing, his fingers finding a desperate purpose.

```
Hi Gyorgy,

My name is Oliver Battolo, Nate's son. Not sure if you
heard, but my father passed away in March this year. It
was very sudden and unexpected.

I'm reaching out because I was going through some old
photos and files of his recently and realized he was
friends with you. I wanted to connect and also ask you
about Bryce's paintings, which my dad was interested
in. I believe you own the third one.

I would love to hear from you.

Sincerely,

Oliver
```

He stared at the words, hesitating for a moment. It felt too direct, too forward to a stranger. He didn't care. He hit send.

A few seconds later, a new email notification popped up. His heart leaped. And then sank. *Mail Delivery Subsystem.* The address didn't exist. The email had bounced.

He tried googling Gyorgy's full name, but the internet offered nothing but a few dead ends on random message boards. The trail had gone cold as quickly as it had appeared. He slumped back in his chair, utterly defeated, the surreal events of his projection now feeling like a cruel joke. He had to put the quest on pause, to get some rest before his *real* date with Daniela, an event that now felt like it belonged to a different, simpler lifetime.

740498 (June 12)

Oliver sat on a park bench at West and Clarkson, watching the Sunday morning pedestrians amble past. A knot of anxiety and anticipation tightened in his stomach. He was here for a normal date, a simple, real-world pleasure, but after the previous night, he wasn't sure what "real" even meant anymore.

Then he saw Daniela approaching in the distance, and the anxiety momentarily dissolved. She wore an elegant floral turquoise dress that the late spring breeze caught and played with, and in that moment, she was the most real and beautiful thing he had ever seen.

"Hi there, stranger!" she said, her smile wide as she gave him a warm hug. "Where did you disappear to in the last few weeks?"

"Oh, you know. Busy with work, and I was away in the Catskills," he said, the excuse feeling both true and like a massive understatement. "I'm back now."

"I'm impressed you still want to explore art," Daniela said, a look of playful surprise on her face. "I thought the Grotowski documentary might have scared you off for good."

"Oh no, I loved that," he said honestly. "That's why I wanted to come. I figured there would be a similar exploration of human psychology here."

"For sure. Surrealists are some of the deepest thinkers," Daniela agreed. "They understand the mind so well they can deconstruct it and reassemble it into something new. One of my friends from NYU is an organizer, so we might see her."

As they walked onto the pier, Oliver held his breath. His senses were on high alert, his eyes scanning the scene, half-dreading, half-expecting to see an old man with a pirate's accent and a purple haze. But there was nothing. The layout was different, the exhibits were all safely enclosed in a large, ordinary pop-up tent, and there was no sign of Jonathan Bryce's ghost. A wave of giddy relief washed over him. It *had* just been a dream. A bizarre, elaborate, but ultimately meaningless dream. He could relax. He could just be a guy on a date.

They enjoyed the art. Oliver, feeling grounded again, found himself genuinely appreciating the paintings and sculptures. Many were thought-provoking; others were so abstract he privately concluded the artist probably didn't know what they meant either. As they were finishing the loop, Daniela let out a little squeal and ran to hug a woman standing under a tree, smoking what looked like a Virginia Slim.

"Megan, I want you to meet my friend Oliver," Daniela said, pulling him into the conversation. "Oliver, this is Megan, one of the organizers."

They exchanged pleasantries, and Megan explained the curation. "We're really fortunate," she said. "We had an amazing surrealist agree to join the team this year. He's the main reason the show feels so cohesive."

"Oh, who is it?" Daniela asked.

"Luis Velázquez," Megan replied.

The name was a sonic boom in the quiet of Oliver's mind. The cheerful sounds of the pier, Daniela's excited gasp, Megan's continuing chatter – it all faded into a dull, distant roar. *Luis Velázquez.* An impossible echo from the dream he had just dismissed. He had never heard that name before last night, and now a real person was saying it out loud.

"Oh, that's amazing! I love his work!" Daniela exclaimed, turning to Oliver. "And my uncle Rafael knows him, can you believe that? No wonder it's so good this year!"

Oliver just nodded, unable to speak. He was stuck on the name. It couldn't be a coincidence. It was too specific, too uncanny. The projection had been wrong about the layout, wrong about Bryce, wrong about everything … except for this one, impossible, verifiable fact. The solid ground of reality he had just reclaimed a few minutes ago had turned to quicksand.

Oliver's mind was racing, trying to catch up. He found a lull in the conversation and seized it. "Is Luis here? Is any of his art on display?"

"He's around somewhere," Megan said, scanning the crowd. "It's rare for him to travel, so we're grateful he made an exception. I don't think any of his work is on display, though. He just helped curate. Let me check in our 'below' and I'll let you know."

"Sorry, you'll check where?" Oliver asked, the word snagging in his ear.

Megan laughed. "Our 'below.' It's a term of art. Luis belongs to a school of surrealism started by his mentor, Krzysztof Kaminsky. Disepinephrenetic Psychosurrealism. A key tenet is that you only display your less significant work. Your major pieces," she leaned in conspiratorially, "Remain hidden, usually in underground storage units called 'belows.' The inaccessibility is part of the art. On Luis's suggestion, we're using the downstairs area of the facilities warehouse as our 'below.' He spends most of his time there."

Below. The word from the aerial banner. The explanation for the Noncemeister's blank canvases. Another impossible connection clicked into place, sending a fresh wave of vertigo through him.

"Can we get a tour of the below?" Oliver asked, his curiosity now a desperate need.

"I doubt it," Megan responded, shaking her head. "Luis gets the final say. I can ask, but don't get your hopes up."

As Megan walked off, Oliver and Daniela wandered toward the food stalls. "When's Maren back?" Oliver asked, trying to find a solid piece of information in his spinning world.

"Sometime in July, I think," Daniela replied. "My uncle is supposed to be visiting Guru Brahma, too, so I guess they're together now."

"How is your uncle? You said he's a bitcoiner, right?"

"Yeah, he likes bitcoin and got in early," she said. "I haven't talked to him in a couple of months, just emails. He's busy, I'm busy. You know."

"You did say he gave you one," Oliver said, a new humility in his voice. "I've actually been studying it more recently, and met some cool people. I probably shouldn't have dismissed it the way I did before."

Daniela smiled warmly. "My uncle always says that everyone finds bitcoin when the time is right for them. Maybe this is your time, Oliver. I don't follow it like he does, but I love the philosophy."

Megan returned a short while later, her expression apologetic. "Bad news. I spoke to Luis. He doesn't want anyone visiting the below today. He said, 'no one is ready for it and it needs to stay that way.' Sorry, I tried."

"What's the point of art if no one can see it?" Oliver asked, the disappointment sharp.

"Like I said," Megan explained, "It's part of the art. The concealment reveals more than the display would."

As she spoke the words, the Noncemeister's sing-song voice echoed in his memory, a perfect, chilling harmony. *"The more's obscured, the more's revealed; counterintuitively. Subterraneously concealed …"*

Could he have been referring to this? To a niche, obscure school of surrealist art. How? How could his subconscious mind, his "Imagination," have known this? How could it have known the name of a real, living artist?

The rest of the afternoon was a blur. He walked with Daniela back to Carmine Street, the plans he'd had for a long, perfect first date – brunch, a walk, dinner – dissolving in the acid of his anxiety. He couldn't pretend to be normal, not now. He gave her a hug at her door, the gesture feeling distant and disconnected, and turned toward the subway.

On the ride back, the rhythmic clatter of the train was the soundtrack to his spiraling thoughts. The projection had felt so incredibly real. He had believed it. Was he losing the ability to tell the difference? The Noncemeister was supposed to be a figment, a character from his dad's bedtime stories that his mind had latched onto. But a figment couldn't know things. A figment couldn't have access to obscure, verifiable facts about the world. This entity living in his head was becoming terrifyingly, undeniably real. What was it? And what, exactly, was it doing to him?

The Notepad

Oliver pulled the 2022 WilcoxRe diary from its new, secure home inside his desk drawer. In a world that now felt fluid and unreliable, this leather-bound book had become his one true map, his single source of truth.

He opened it to the first page. The list of seven words stared back at him. The eighth word was almost laughably obvious now. It had been a theme that had relentlessly pursued him all week. The Noncemeister's cryptic explanation for the blank canvases. The bizarre, commanding advertisement pulled by the plane. Megan's matter-of-fact explanation of an obscure school of art. Below. Below. Below.

He felt he didn't even need to check with autokinesis this time, but the ritual had become part of the process, a final, physical confirmation. He closed his eyes. The answer came instantly, a heavy, solid drop of his left arm.

He picked up his pen and proceeded to add the new entry to the page, another breadcrumb on his father's impossible trail.

viii) below

CHAPTER 9. PUNCH

741093 (June 16)

Oliver opened the Twitter app, his thumb scrolling reflexively through the timeline. He had ten minutes to kill before heading to O'Connell's to meet Vince. The feed was its usual river of digital noise: garish frog memes, fanciful charts promising a $200,000 bitcoin price by year's end, random videos of people screaming at each other. He waded through the chaos until something caught his eye and made his stomach tighten with a familiar sense of duty and disappointment.

Christiaan had tweeted again. A seventh poem.

Dispirited again
As monotony does
If you follow the gaze
At three past ten in the orchard's haze
And once again I feel this punch
The absence of love
The warm summer breeze
At the halfway mark
In the hirsute man's left shoe
One day I will be free

To experience such wealth

Ugh. It was another painful read, a tangle of mournful, grotesque, and self-indulgent lines. Oliver felt a fresh wave of frustration. The blue bird in his projection had been so clear, so insistent. It had led him here, to this … this cryptic dead end. The poems were supposed to be the key, but they were just unintelligible drivel. He felt a pang of guilt for his harsh judgment – Christiaan was a man in pain – but the feeling was quickly overwhelmed by the sheer, maddening uselessness of the clue.

He closed the app and got ready to leave, the thought of seeing Vince a welcome antidote to the digital noise. Vince was in town for a Bitcoin Socratic seminar Oliver had to miss for a customer demo, and Oliver was genuinely looking forward to catching up.

"Nice spot. I don't think I've been here before," Vince said, looking around O'Connell's as they settled onto stools at the bar.

"Yeah, it's mostly for the startup crowd from around here," Oliver said. "Can I get you a beer?"

"This one's on me." Vince waved away his protest. "And I'm not a beer drinker. I'll just get a scotch." He explained his preferences to the bartender, and soon a Glenfiddich and a Żywiec sat between them.

As Vince spoke, Oliver's gaze drifted to the wall behind the bar, to the spot where his quest had taken a sharp turn into reality. He stared in disgust at the soulless print of fruit in a bowl that now hung in *The Toddler's* place.

"You know," Oliver said, the words coming out before he'd fully formed the thought, "There used to be a really nice original artwork right there. Until about a month ago. It was painted by the owner's grandad."

"Oh? What sort of painting was it?" Vince asked, his interest piqued.

"A Renaissance style painting of a little boy with a floral wreath, by an apple tree," Oliver explained, feeling a strange new authority in telling the story. "It was called *The Toddler*. Painted by a guy named Jonathan Bryce. His granddaughter, Aisling, owns this place." He looked around, a part of him hoping to see her familiar, stern face. "Doesn't look like she's working today, though."

"Wait," Vince said, his eyes widening in genuine surprise as he stared at the empty space on the wall. "Jonathan Bryce, the Irish artist from the seventies and eighties? No way."

The shock in Vince's voice sent a jolt through Oliver. "Yeah, that one. How do you know him?"

"He's a niche celebrity for some cypherpunks," Vince said, a slow, disbelieving smile spreading across his face. "I mean, I'm not a cypherpunk – I suck at writing code – but they're my people, and I've heard the stories."

"Wait, *bitcoiners* knew about Bryce?" The words tumbled out of Oliver's mouth, and he nearly knocked over his beer.

"Yeah, a decent number did," Vince confirmed. "The story behind his paintings is pretty wild."

"What was the story?" Oliver leaned closer, his voice a rapt whisper.

"Well, he was just a regular guy in Northern Ireland, born eighty or ninety years ago. No formal training in math, barely finished high school. Then, in the early seventies, he starts creating these incredibly intricate paintings that are apparently riddled with cryptographic references. Some mathematicians found out and started trying to buy them. Did you say the one that hung here was *The Toddler*?"

Oliver nodded, his focus absolute.

"I remember hearing about that one," Vince continued. "I think that was the one where the wreath on the boy's head resembled a simple Merkle tree structure."

The words were a sonic boom in Oliver's mind. *Merkle tree.* The ghost of a concept from a data structures class suddenly slammed into focus. A cryptographic proof. A parent node containing the hash of its children, creating a verifiable chain of data. He could see it now: the leaves as the base data, the flowers as the parent nodes. And the name. *Myrtle* flowers. *Myrtle. Merkle.* The phonetic pun was so elegant, so perfect, it made his head spin. "Wait," he said, his voice breathless with discovery. "How could Bryce have possibly known about Merkle trees in the seventies?"

"That's the crazy part," Vince said. "He didn't. He was just a regular guy. The story, and it's probably apocryphal, is that he heard voices in his head. Said they were like 'energetic downloads' that told him exactly what to paint."

A profound chill went through Oliver, a feeling of the floor dropping out from under him. *The voices. It's like I had forgotten what to do unless I heard the voices.* It was the exact, insane story the Noncemeister-as-Bryce had told him in the projection. It was real.

"And how many paintings did he create?" Oliver asked, his mind racing.

"As far as anyone knows, three major ones. Though I've heard rumors of more," Vince said. "This is quite the coincidence, I've got to say. Who would've thought an obscure painter, known only to a handful of cypherpunks, had a granddaughter running your local pub?"

"You don't say," Oliver retorted, his mind buzzing with connections. He had to push forward. "Have you heard of a guy named Gyorgy Lorincz? Bryce's daughter said he was the one who bought the third painting."

Vince's brow furrowed in thought. "The name rings a bell … Gyorgy … I think he was a bitcoiner, way back. Before my time, really. I got involved around 2013. I think Gyorgy was active before then, but got upset about something and just … rage-quit the community. Might have been during the block size debate."

Gyorgy. An early bitcoiner. A cryptographer. The pieces were slamming together. His dad and Gyorgy were collaborators in this secret world. Bryce, the voices, the paintings – it was all connected.

"Here's the punch you ordered," a voice said, and the bartender set a deep orange drink on a coaster in front of them.

Oliver and Vince looked at each other, surprised. "I don't believe we ordered this," Vince said politely.

The bartender looked equally confused. "Oh. For some reason, I thought you did." She gestured to the drink. "Splash of rum in it?" Both men shook their heads, and with a shrug, she took the punch away, leaving the word hanging in the air between them.

Oliver, now a seasoned player in this strange game, made a mental note. *Punch.* The word, arriving out of nowhere, felt like another breadcrumb. It was a potential ninth entry for the list.

The conversation turned to the seminar Vince had just left. He explained that he'd spoken about collaborative transactions, and as he began to describe the concept of CoinJoins – a method for mixing bitcoin to preserve privacy –

a connection fired in Oliver's mind. It was what Nick had been talking about in the car.

"Have you ever heard of a guy named Christiaan?" Oliver asked, feeling like he was pulling on a crucial thread.

Vince's expression softened, a wistful look in his eyes. "Oh, yes. He was one of the greats from the early days," he said. "He and his partners created an early version of CoinJoin back in 2012. I think it was initially called *Akasha,* but they later changed the name to MixMarket. It was all very new then. But a year later, there was an issue, and Christiaan ended up manually mixing some transactions. Turns out he'd walked right into a trap set by the feds. They charged him with money laundering. One of the worst travesties of justice I've ever seen. Neither Obama nor Trump would commute the sentence. Too much pressure from the DoJ to make an example of him."

"Yeah, I heard about that," Oliver said. "What happened to his partners?"

"There were two of them, and they're legends in their own right." Vince took a slow sip of his scotch and stared into the middle distance, as if looking back in time. "The brains behind the operation was a pseudonymous guy, Devakshar. Maybe with an underscore, I don't remember. An old-school cypherpunk. I believe he even talked with Satoshi back in the day." He shook his head. "Disappeared without a trace when the MixMarket bug happened. Email deactivated, gone from the message boards, nothing. The feds only went after Christiaan, but he must have panicked and erased himself. A real shame. The man was a legend."

"He disappeared just like Satoshi, then?"

"In a sense, but under very different circumstances," Vince said. "Dev_akshar probably figured he was at risk, that Christiaan might try to use him as a bargaining chip."

"Could he have been Satoshi?" Oliver asked, the thought a wild leap.

"Highly, highly unlikely," Vince shook his head. "There are public emails between them from 2010. Unless Satoshi was playing some kind of multi-layered identity game, I doubt it."

"What about the third guy?" Oliver pressed.

"Another ghost. A pseudonymous dev called Sazsa," Vince said. "We don't know much about him, other than two things: he was a brilliant cryptography expert, and he was a big art collector. He vanished too, but before the MixMarket bug. This space has a lot of people who just drop off the map."

An art collector. The words were a lightning strike in Oliver's mind. He saw the faded printout of Gyorgy's email in his head. *I know you said S might be interested.* The cryptography part of the email, the "blind mixing," was almost certainly MixMarket. And S, the art collector interested in Bryce's third painting … it had to be Sazsa. The pieces slammed together with the force of a revelation.

But the excitement was immediately followed by a cold, sickening dread. If S was Sazsa, then Gyorgy's email meant his father knew him. And if his father knew Sazsa, and he knew about "blind mixing," then his dad was likely connected to Christiaan's entire operation. He was on the periphery of a federal crime.

His head spinning with the troubling new connection, Oliver tried to ground himself, to change the subject. "And Christiaan has been in prison ever since, right?" he asked, his voice a little distant. "Any chance of a retrial or pardon?"

"Doesn't look like that's going to happen," Vince said, his voice laced with a grim finality. "I know his dad and sister have the petition, but I don't see it working. There's too much pressure from the feds to make an example out of him." He took another sip of his scotch. "The other interesting thing is, we know Christiaan had over twenty thousand bitcoin back then. We even know the wallet address. And as far as I'm aware, that wallet has been completely inactive since his arrest. I'm surprised he hasn't given the private key to his family, but I suspect he's worried authorities will confiscate it. They review all communications going in and out of that prison, so him handing out a seed phrase is impossible."

Seed phrase. The words were a key turning in a lock. A blinding flash of inspiration hit Oliver, so powerful it almost made him gasp. *The poetry.* It was brilliant camouflage. Clumsy, self-indulgent, grotesque – the perfect disguise for a coded message. *That's what the blue bird was trying to tell me.* Christiaan was broadcasting a key, piece by agonizing piece, hidden in plain sight.

As Oliver's mind reeled with the new theory, Vince continued. "It's also likely that Dev_akshar had far more bitcoin than Christiaan, though no one knows his address. There are fewer than fifty wallets with that kind of balance, so it's one of them, but most have been silent for years."

Oliver found all of this fascinating. He felt like a man who had spent his life studying a single, sanitized textbook, only to be handed the secret, uncensored history of the world. His time at the startup, with its focus on corporate blockchains, had completely insulated him from this raw, revolutionary cypherpunk world.

Feeling a new sense of trust and camaraderie, Oliver found himself opening up. He described the projects he worked on, the growing reservations he had, the feeling that it was all a solution in search of a problem. Vince listened, nodding in agreement. "Blockchains only make sense if they're truly decentralized," he said. "No central operator, no one who can gatekeep users or change the rules on a whim."

He looked at Oliver, his expression clear and certain. "In the end, you realize the bitcoin timechain is the only one that meets all these criteria."

The word hit Oliver with the force of a physical jolt, a word from his deepest projections spoken casually in a noisy pub. "Wait," he said, his voice sharp. "Did you just say 'time chain?'"

"Yes, timechain. One word," Vince clarified. "I prefer it to 'blockchain.' Satoshi himself called it a 'distributed timestamp server.' It makes more sense. In a distributed network, there's no single, reliable clock. So when you're moving money, you need an unbreakable agreement on the 'before' and the 'after' of a transaction. The only way to enforce that singular, authoritative flow of time without trusting a central party is with bitcoin's consensus mechanism – difficulty-adjusted proof of work."

Oliver listened, and the Noncemeister's bizarre, nonsensical riddles about time and truth and heartbeats suddenly snapped into a new, brilliant, logical focus.

A silent, internal explosion of understanding was taking place in his mind. *Timechain.* Vince had said it as one word. The Noncemeister's word. That dark, purple place, the periodic, rising whisper of a billion voices – it wasn't a mystical void. It was a representation of the network itself, the global conversation of nodes. And the heartbeat ... the heartbeat was consensus. It was a new block being found. The strange paradoxes were suddenly making a terrifying kind of sense. "If an after is before a before, then the before becomes the after ..." he mumbled softly to himself, the Noncemeister's riddle no longer nonsense, but a poetic description of the fundamental problem of ordering time.

"What was that, Oliver?" Vince asked, catching the quiet murmur.

Oliver shook himself out of his stupor. "Oh, nothing. Just remembering something I'd read." He looked at Vince, his eyes bright with a new, deeper understanding. "It makes sense now, what you were saying. About the timestamp. Transactions have to be ordered unambiguously, otherwise it's just chaos. I'd love to learn more about why you think bitcoin does this better than other chains. I still don't see the issue with how Ethereum does it, to be honest. Or Solana, with their proof of history."

Vince smiled, a warm, patient expression. "I will gladly explain the distinction next time. I'm not sure when I'll be back in the city, but you're welcome to visit my place anytime this summer. I can show you how to sculpt metal as well."

The offer was an open door into a world Oliver was now desperate to understand. "Oh, that would be fantastic," he said, his voice full of a genuine eagerness. "I'd love to visit again. Maybe in July or August?"

"Sounds like a plan."

741115 (June 16)

Oliver settled into the chair by his desk, the quiet of the apartment a welcome silence. He closed his eyes, and this time, walked into the projection. The distinct, inky purple void materialized around him. *It's probably going to be him,* he thought.

It was. The Noncemeister was floating cross-legged a few feet away, happily juggling three small, glowing orbs of light.

"Battolu, we're making this a habit, aren't we? It's good, good, very good," the Noncemeister exclaimed, catching the orbs and letting them hover in the air around his head like a strange halo. "I like when you come back. It means you want to learn more, right tiger?"

"I guess," Oliver shrugged. "I don't really choose to be here. It just happens."

"There you go again, Battu. You always choose. You are where you need to be, and that is a choice."

"Okay, sure. So why did you pretend to be Bryce the last time?" Oliver asked pointedly, deciding to skip the pleasantries. "I don't understand why that needed to happen."

"Ah, I knew you were going to ask me that." The Noncemeister began to pace slowly in a circle around Oliver, walking on the empty air as if it were solid ground. "It needed to happen, Battolo. You were coasting, and things were getting too easy for you. I thought you needed a punch to wake you up. Think of me as your wake-up call. And it did wake you up, didn't it? Don't tell me you got nothing out of it?"

"Well, I did get something out of it," Oliver contemplated. "I learned Bryce probably has five paintings, and his last three are in a 'below.' Do you know where I can find the third? How do I get hold of Gyorgy?"

The Noncemeister stopped pacing and blinked, a look of theatrical surprise on his face. "Bryce? Gyorgy? Who are these people?" The glowing orbs around his head flickered and vanished.

"Jonathan Bryce? The Irish painter. The guy you just admitted to impersonating?" Oliver said, amazed at the creature's audacity.

"I have no idea what you're talking about, Batue," the Noncemeister said, his gaze drifting upwards as if admiring the featureless purple ceiling. "Is this nonsense again?"

"What? You literally just brought it up! You said I needed a punch or a wake-up call or something." Oliver felt the familiar wave of frustrated bewilderment.

"I certainly did no such thing," the Noncemeister retorted indignantly, putting his hands on his hips. "And a punch? Why on Earth would I say that? That seems so mean. Violence is the last retort of the incontinent, Battulu. I would not advocate it. No sirree!"

"I think you mean 'last resort of the incompetent' – it's an Isaac Asimov quote," Oliver said, raising an eyebrow.

"Isa who now? Who are all these strange people you keep talking about?"

"Ugh, never mind." Oliver decided to move on; the circular arguments were exhausting. He got to the heart of what was truly bothering him. "Anyway, now I'm worried that I can't tell the difference between reality and these projections. If you could fool me so easily, how do I know what's real and what's in my mind?"

The Noncemeister's playful energy subsided. He stopped floating and drifted closer, his expression turning serious for the first time. "Battew, what is this reality you speak of?"

The question was so simple, so fundamental, it stopped Oliver cold. He thought for a moment. "I mean … it's what I experience every day. The sights, the sounds, the feelings. The people I talk to, the work I do. My apartment, New York City. That's reality." He gestured to the purple void around them. "This isn't. You aren't real. You're in my head."

"That is phenomenal," the Noncemeister said, his voice a dull, matter-of-fact monotone.

"I'm sorry?" Oliver asked, surprised by the odd choice of word.

"What you said you experience and describe as reality is phenomenal," he repeated, the word delivered with a clinical, deadpan precision, completely stripped of its usual meaning.

"I don't know if I'd call it phenomenal all the time …" Oliver began, confused by the strange turn. "Some of it is good, some neutral, some not so good."

"They are all phenomenal, Battu," the Noncemeister said blankly, letting the strange, unsettling pronouncement hang in the silence between them.

"What are you talking about?" Oliver's annoyance finally boiled over. "I think I can discern for myself what feels good and what doesn't. I've had experiences where I could say, 'Wow, that was phenomenal!' but those are rare. The rest just *is*. It's life. Stuff happens."

"Silly Battulu, your language blinds you," the Noncemeister chuckled, the sound condescending and amused. He began to pace again, lecturing to the void. "You are so attached to vernacular semantics that ontology itself escapes you. Everything you described is phenomenal. They are *phenomena*, those experiences. The experience of reality strictly through that empirical lens is known as phenomenal reality."

"Oh," Oliver said, the anger deflating as he realized he'd been caught in a semantic trap. "I see what you're saying. Yes, empirical. Reality for me is empirical. What else can it be?"

"Ah, my foolish young puppy," the Noncemeister's tone shifted, becoming grand and mysterious. "I think we know what today's story is about then, don't we?"

"We do?" Oliver asked, surprised.

"It is a story about three realities. Are you ready to hear it?"

"Do I have a choice?"

"Yes, and you've made it," the Noncemeister said firmly. He stopped pacing and held up one finger. "The first type of reality is apparent reality. You might call these dreams, where the seas can be boiling hot, and pigs can have wings."

"And where a childhood character my dad made up can be talking to me about the types of reality," Oliver interjected, the words laced with a bitterness he couldn't suppress.

The Noncemeister grinned. "My, my, feisty today, aren't we? Why don't you listen to the story and then decide for yourself?"

"Okay, fine," Oliver backed off.

"So, the first type is apparent reality," the Noncemeister continued, holding up a second finger. "The second is phenomenal or empirical, the one you described. The third," he held up a third finger, his voice dropping to a profound whisper, "Is absolute reality. In this reality, you understand that there is nothing to understand. What is phenomenal is actually apparent, and the only thing to be done is be."

"Be?" Oliver asked, the word an incomplete echo.

"Just be," the Noncemeister nodded, his expression becoming utterly serene. "In this reality, everything just *is*. The universe you experience is just apparent. The only thing that truly exists is your being, and that being is the universe."

"So empirical reality is an illusion in absolute reality?" Oliver asked, trying to keep up.

"Absolute reality is not describable as what it is," the Noncemeister said patiently. "It can only be understood as what it is not. It is not phenomenal, because what is phenomenal is only apparent. It is not apparent, because what is apparent is constructed from what is phenomenal. Seas are phenomenal, as is the act of boiling. Pigs are phenomenal, as are wings. Boiling seas and pigs with wings are just projections *from* phenomenal reality."

"Great," Oliver said, his skepticism returning with a vengeance. "So you're telling me everything I've believed, my whole life – my childhood, my parents, my apartment, my friends – it's all just a figment of my imagination, no different from a dream?"

"So it goes, Battulu."

The words hung in the air, and just then, the deafening whisper of the heartbeat washed over them. Oliver instinctively hunched over, while the Noncemeister simply closed his eyes, a look of peaceful reverence on his face.

When it passed, Oliver straightened up, his resolve hardened. "Sorry, I don't buy it. This is new-age gobbledygook."

The Noncemeister opened his eyes. His gaze was piercing. "How do you explain your Bryce conversation, then?"

The question was a perfectly laid trap. Oliver's mind seized on the contradiction. "Wait," he said, a slow, triumphant smile spreading across his face. "You said you had no idea what I was talking about when I brought that up."

"Answer my question, big boy," the Noncemeister said, waving a dismissive hand, the contradiction erased from the air as if it had never existed. Oliver's brief victory evaporated.

He sighed and carried on. "Well, I can't explain it. It seemed real, but it wasn't. I need to understand why that happened."

"You don't need to understand," the Noncemeister said, his tone infuriatingly calm. "The only thing to understand is that there is nothing to understand. You need to be."

"How can I accept that?" Oliver's frustration returned. "I thought I knew what real meant. It meant what I could describe with my senses. Now you're telling me to reject that. How do I do that?"

"There is no sense, Battu. The answer is in noncense," the Noncemeister laughed.

"Oh please, not this nonsense stuff again!"

"I can see this isn't easy for you," he said, a challenging glint in his eye, "So I will make it harder." He held up three fingers, then slowly brought them together into a single point. "In the timechain, all three realities are one. As such, there is only one reality, that of truth. What is apparent is phenomenal, and what is phenomenal is absolute. There is no distinction between verisimilitude and veracity, because the authoritative truth is absolute."

"So the timechain is absolute reality?" Oliver asked, seizing on what felt like a contradiction. "It's not empirically observed? Last I checked, blocks get confirmed and appended to a public ledger. That can be verified by everyone. That sounds empirical to me. And that's a good thing."

"Batew, you're using those strange words again," the Noncemeister said, wrinkling his face in mock disgust. "Let's not waste time, because you need to go." His voice shifted, becoming deeper, more rhythmic, almost hypnotic. He began to float slowly in a circle around Oliver as he delivered his final sermon.

"I'll end my story with this: the timechain is neither good nor bad. It just is. It is formless, shapeless, qualityless. Because it is the incontrovertible progression of truth, it is an absolute measure of time. Because it is an absolute measure of time, it is the ineffable language of abundance. Because it is the ineffable language of abundance, it is the blissful surrender to love. Because it is the blissful surrender to love, it is the tautological act of understanding. Understanding that there is nothing to understand. Just be. When you are one with the timechain, who is to say which reality is which? No one. Because they are all the same. And so, it is."

He came to a stop in front of Oliver, the last words hanging in the silent, purple void.

"That's just great!" Oliver said, his voice a sigh of pure, exasperated resignation. "So every experience I have is either apparent or phenomenal, but it doesn't matter because they are all absolute. Now I'll never know the difference! Was this the wake-up call you wanted to give me?"

A slow, sly grin spread across the Noncemeister's face.

"It's ... more of a *punch* line."

And with that, he dissolved into the purpleness, leaving Oliver utterly alone.

The Notepad

i) violin ii) toddler iii) alley iv) shoulder v) educate vi) rookie vii) oval viii) below ix) punch

741221 (June 17)

Oliver's heart raced as he read the email again. It had appeared in his inbox without fanfare, a simple, unread line in a sea of junk mail. He hadn't expected to hear from Gyorgy. The bounced email had been a dead end. But somehow, impossibly, his message had found its mark.

```
Oliver,
It is so nice to hear from you. I have to confess,
my email address that you wrote to has been largely
abandoned for several years, but I just happened to
retrieve the inbox yesterday because I was looking for
some old files. It is quite a remarkable coincidence at
many levels that you sent your email around this time.
Yes, I did hear the news about your father - I am
deeply sorry. Your father was an excellent man and he
always spoke about you with such love, joy, and pride.
Another reason why your email is such a coincidence
is because I was planning on getting in touch with you
anyway! I will be visiting New York next week for the
last time and I wanted to meet you in light of your
father's news. Let us find some time on one of the
afternoons and I can answer your questions about the
painting.
Warm Regards,
Gyorgy
```

The words in the second paragraph seemed to lift off the screen. *Love, joy, and pride.* The phrase, coming from a stranger, from a ghost in his father's past, was a direct conduit to the man he had lost. The screen blurred. A hot, sharp pressure built behind his eyes, and a single, ragged sob escaped his throat. It wasn't the violent, angry, Lagavulin-induced grief of two months ago but a deeper, more intense ache – the unbearable sadness of being loved by someone who was gone forever.

He let the tears stream down his face, not bothering to wipe them away. But even as the wave of sadness washed over him, his mind, now honed by weeks of paranoia and puzzle-solving, snagged on the other details. The coincidence. The timing. He wiped his eyes and read the email again, but this time, the words felt different, charged with a strange, unsettling energy.

Visiting New York for the last time. The phrase was so final, so ominous. Why would he say that?

Planning on getting in touch with you anyway. Why? To offer condolences? It seemed too forward for a stranger who hadn't spoken to his father in years.

And the coincidence itself. Resurrecting an abandoned email account at the exact moment a message arrived after a decade of silence. It wasn't just a coincidence. It felt like another move in the impossible game his father had set in motion, another piece clicking into place by some unseen hand.

But the good news, the only news that mattered right now, was that he had a lead. A real, tangible connection to his father's secret world. Gyorgy was coming to New York. And Oliver would be there to meet him, ready with a list of questions that grew longer and more desperate by the day.

CHAPTER 10. CERTAIN

"Going someplace fun, I hope, Mr. Wright?" Oliver asked, watching Ian pack a small suitcase by the coat closet.

"Talking to federal bureaucrats has got to be someone's idea of fun, I suppose," Ian replied with his signature, booming laugh. "Come to think of it, that's the only reason I enjoy DC – I can be certain the party won't stop with that lot."

Oliver couldn't tell if he was joking.

Ian snapped the suitcase shut. "I'm off to meet our good friends at Project Phoenix. It's about time they stopped waffling and committed. I'm getting tired of demo-ing that proof-of-concept, and I'm sure you are too. It's time to build." He began to pace, his energy filling the space, his voice taking on the familiar, hypnotic cadence of his sales pitch. "Imagine the headlines, Oliver: *BlockWaves becomes the first enterprise blockchain company to take a full-fledged product to market at scale.* Think of the Series B we could raise. Working with a quasi-government entity like Freddie makes it even more impactful. Yes," he said, his eyes shining with the vision, "it's time to close this deal once and for all."

"Well, best of luck, Mr. Wright," Oliver said, the enthusiastic words feeling like a foreign language in his mouth. "I can't wait to hear how it went."

In truth, he couldn't care less. A deep apathy had taken root in him over the past few weeks. He looked at Ian, a man selling a dream he no longer believed in, and felt a vast, weary distance. He saw holes in all their projects now, even the company's crown jewel – Project Tarantula, the much-hyped infrastructure overhaul for a Southeast Asian stock exchange.

He remembered the press releases from two years ago, the breathless headlines: *"First exchange to clear and settle securities using blockchain technology makes history."* It was supposed to be their coming-of-age, the moment their technology crossed the Rubicon into the mainstream.

But the word on the street, the real word from the trenches, told a different story. He'd seen the frustration bleeding through in the shared Slack channels from the isolated team in Southeast Asia, their messages posted in the dead of the New York night. He'd heard the rumors: the technology wasn't scaling, timelines were slipping, and the promised revolution was getting bogged down in troubleshooting the basics.

Yet, at every all-hands meeting, the executive team painted a rosy picture. *"Everything is hunky-dory. Our team has it all under control."* The gap between management's words and the grim reality had become a chasm. The corporate facade felt thin and brittle, and Oliver was beginning to see right through it. He was approaching a point of absolute, soul-crushing certainty: every single private blockchain project they had was doomed to fail. His only remaining hope was to get himself transferred to one of the smaller, more promising Ethereum-based projects, a small island of potential in a vast sea of corporate illusion.

Almost on cue, he bumped into Olumide in the hallway. This was it, a chance to find a life raft. "Hey man," Oliver said, his voice more earnest than he intended, "I know we talked about me getting involved in Project Crestone. Any chance you can get me in?"

Project Crestone. It was the one project at the company that still felt semi-real to him. Tokenizing luxury real estate in Colorado on Ethereum, creating fractional ownership for regular investors. It was ambitious, public, and everything that the company's other moribund, private projects were not.

Olumide looked at him, his project manager's gaze assessing the request. "You know, I think they are looking for a little help since Shiran left on

maternity leave. They could use about eight hours a week of your capacity."
He paused, the caveat coming. "You'll have to check with Sri or Wright, see if
they'll let you step out of sales engineering for that long. If you get their okay,
I can get you on."

"That's great," Oliver said, a surge of genuine hope cutting through his
apathy. "I don't think Sri will have an issue. He's been supportive of me doing
more core engineering work."

This was it. The break he'd been looking for. An escape hatch from the
dead-end projects and hollow sales pitches. With a sudden spring in his stride
he hadn't felt in months, he went to find his manager, Sri, to ask for his blessing.

He promptly received it.

742017 (June 23)

Mykonos Diner was a place that time, and taste, had forgotten. In the East
50s in Midtown, its unassuming façade gave way to an interior that hadn't
been updated since the 1980s. The menu was a laminated monument to the
uninspired: pancakes, gyros, a handful of pasta dishes. Oliver looked at the
stained coffee pot behind the counter and shuddered. *Watery and acidic,* he
guessed. *At best.*

He had slipped out of work, telling no one, for this extended and deeply
strange lunch. Gyorgy's choice of venue was as baffling as the man himself.

As he waited, a cold, vivid dread began to creep in. His gaze drifted around
the diner, but he wasn't seeing the worn-out vinyl booths or the faded pictures
on the wall. He was checking for flaws in the simulation. *Is this real?* The
thought was a sudden, sharp spike of panic. *Or was this another projection, another
trick?* He pictured the Noncemeister appearing in a waiter's uniform, a sly grin
on his face. The paranoia was so intense, so immediate, that he had to fight the
urge to run. He tried the mental exercise he'd been practicing: he tried to will
himself back to his apartment, to force an exit from the projection he might

be in. Nothing. But that meant nothing, too. The Noncemeister let him leave only when the lesson was over.

He was trapped, either in a diner in Midtown or in his own treacherous mind. At a loss, he decided to surrender. The only way out was through.

A short while later, the front door squeaked open, and an old, frail-looking man in a tweed jacket stepped inside. He scanned the room, his movements slow and deliberate, and his eyes eventually locked with Oliver's. He gave a small, weary nod and made his way to the table.

"There's no escaping genetics," the man said, his voice a dry, croaking whisper. A weak smile touched his lips as he extended a trembling hand. "Don't let anyone tell you you're not your father's son. It's nice to see you again, Oliver."

Oliver stared in shock. The man in front of him was a ghost. The photo from his mother's album had shown a man his father's age, vibrant and alive. This man looked at least thirty years older, his body withered, his skin thin and papery. But it was his eyes that truly stunned Oliver. They were pools of a deep, fathomless sorrow, a profound and weary regret that seemed to extinguish the light in the room.

"Mr. Lorincz," Oliver said, his own voice sounding distant as he took the man's frail, cool hand. "It's an honor to meet you. I only just learned you were a friend of my father's."

"Please, call me Gyorgy," he said, easing himself gingerly into the booth. "And we did meet. Once. When you were around twelve or thirteen years old."

Oliver had no memory of it, only his mother's vague recollection. He nodded politely as Gyorgy stared at him, his gaze intense, as if he were memorizing his face.

"Oliver," Gyorgy said, his voice dropping, getting straight to the point. "I am a very sick man. I am dying. My fourth round of chemotherapy failed last month." He delivered the words with a calm, brutal finality that sucked the air out of the diner. "My doctor has given me a couple of months, at best, to get my affairs in order. That's why I'm here. I needed to meet you, and one other person, to close out some unfinished business."

Oliver stared at Gyorgy, speechless. He had never heard a voice so devoid of hope. It was a sound scraped clean of all life, a deathly monotone that was more terrifying than any scream.

Gyorgy continued, his gaze fixed on a point somewhere beyond Oliver's shoulder. "I loved your father, I want you to know that. We haven't spoken in almost seven years, but I considered him a very dear friend." His voice began to tremble. "I would have liked to tell him this directly, but now I have to tell you. I'm sorry. Please forgive me." His eyes were looking through Oliver, at a ghost. "I want you to forgive me, Nate. Please, do it for me, your old friend. I need to hear it from you before I'm gone …" The monotone finally cracked, and his eyes, already so full of sorrow, welled up with tears that traced slow, painful paths down his hollowed cheeks.

Oliver was too stunned to respond. The raw, desperate plea hung in the stale diner air. Finally, he found his voice, the words feeling small and inadequate. "I'm sure my dad would forgive you," he said gently. "Could I ask … what for?"

Gyorgy seemed to compose himself, retreating back into the story. "We worked very closely for over ten years. Applied cryptography. We were very involved in the early days of bitcoin." He let out a dry, rattling sigh. "Those were good days. We were young, full of hope … the world was our oyster."

The words were a quiet explosion in Oliver's mind, a final, definitive confirmation. *Dad wasn't just a bitcoiner. He was a pioneer.*

"We started to have differences, nine or ten years ago," Gyorgy continued, the memory clearly painful. "Small things at first – implementation details, the people we worked with. Then the differences grew wider. Irreparable." He took a shaky breath. "It was the block size. I wanted the blocks to be bigger, to allow the network to scale. Your dad … Nate felt that would push bitcoin out of the hands of the average user, that only large entities would be able to participate." The old argument, a distant, technical debate, was recounted with the fresh pain of a recent wound. "Things got ugly. I took Roger Ver's side. And then … bitcoin split. That was it. We never spoke again."

Oliver could see the immense physical and emotional toll the story was taking on him.

"For years, I was certain my side was right," Gyorgy said, his voice a hoarse whisper. "But we lost the adoption battle. I gave up. Moved on. Shortly after, I fell sick."

"So that was the blocksize war?" Oliver asked, connecting the story to the bit of lore he'd heard from Vince. "That's what broke your relationship?"

"Indeed," Gyorgy rasped. "And now, staring death in the face, I see how silly it all was. Your dad was a dear, dear friend. Our human connection … it should have transcended technology." He was so choked with emotion he could barely get the words out. His gaze became frantic, desperate, boring into Oliver's. "So Nate, I'm begging you. Please release me. I love you, Nate. We were brothers. Please, let me die free of this."

Before Oliver could react, Gyorgy clutched his arm with both of his skeletal hands, his grip surprisingly strong, pulling him forward weakly across the table.

Oliver was trapped, a terrified proxy in a dying man's final, desperate confession. "Uh …" he stuttered, the words catching in his throat. "I'm not Nate. I'm Oliver. It's not for me to forgive you, but I'm sure my father would if he were alive today."

"No, Nate, it needs to be you! Please!" Gyorgy's voice was a ragged, desperate plea. "I can't go like this. I need to close this chapter, Nate! I'm so sorry. I said terrible things." He was confessing to a ghost. "I took my friends, my life, for granted, and now I have nothing. At least grant me the peace of your forgiveness." Still clutching Oliver's arm, he collapsed forward, his head resting on the grimy diner table, his body shaking with silent sobs.

A concerned waiter appeared with a glass of water. Gyorgy slowly raised his head, letting go of Oliver's arm. Oliver stared at the man's face. It had a gray, stony, almost marble-like texture, etched with lines of pain. The image of the Velázquez paintings from his projection – the series of marble slabs in progressive states of decay – flashed in his mind. Gyorgy's face was the final painting in that series: a portrait of apathetic nihilism, the human spirit crushed by time.

After a few shaky sips of water, Gyorgy seemed to find his voice again. "I'm sorry," he whispered. "I know you can't do it on your father's behalf. But can you at least try to reach him and let him know?"

"I'm not sure what you mean," Oliver said, his voice laced with caution. "He's dead. I can't talk to him."

"Oh, come on, Oliver, we both know that's not true!" Gyorgy's voice, though weak, had a sudden, sharp edge of certainty.

A cold dread washed over Oliver. "What's not true? That he's dead, or that I can't reach him?"

"Oliver, I know that you know how to reach your father, wherever he is," Gyorgy insisted, his gaze intense. "Please. Honor a dying man's wish."

Time projection. The thought was immediate and terrifying. How could Gyorgy possibly know? Oliver wasn't sure how he could use it to talk to a dead man, but he knew he had to get out of this conversation. "Okay," he said, the words a desperate gambit. "I'll do my best."

It seemed to be enough. A flicker of relief, almost imperceptible, eased the tension in Gyorgy's face. "Thank you, Oliver. I knew I could count on you."

The conversation shifted, becoming slightly more normal. Gyorgy spoke of his past, of meeting Nate on a cryptography mailing list in the early 2000s, of a friendship that blossomed from a shared intellectual passion. He had no other family, and for years, Nate had been like a brother. Oliver listened, and then asked the question that had been burning in his mind. "Why did my dad keep you, and all the bitcoin work, a secret from me?"

Gyorgy seemed to struggle with the question. "Your father always wanted to tell you," he said finally. "But it was never the right time. I don't want to speak for him now that he's gone, but I suspect he still has his way of letting you know."

As he spoke the last words, Oliver saw it for the first time: the faintest twinkle of a shared secret in Gyorgy's tired eyes. It was the final confirmation. Gyorgy knew. He knew everything.

The conversation turned to Gyorgy's love of art, and he confirmed what Oliver had learned from others: the story of Bryce, the voices, the prescient cryptography woven into his paintings.

"Do you still have Bryce's third painting?" Oliver asked the other burning question he'd been waiting to ask.

"Oh no," Gyorgy said. "I sold it in late 2013. I'd had it for twenty-one years, so it felt fitting to let it go then."

"Who did you sell it to?"

"An anonymous buyer. I only dealt with the broker," Gyorgy replied. "I did sell it for almost five hundred bitcoin. At the time, it was the most expensive painting ever sold for bitcoin. I doubt we'll ever see that again." A dry, rattling laugh escaped him. "The joke was on the buyer. The price of bitcoin went up six-fold a couple of months later. If they had waited, they would have parted with far less."

"What was the name of the painting?"

"*It Is Time*," Gyorgy said, his eyes distant. "I can't do it justice trying to describe it. It somehow managed to capture the birth of time, the birth of bitcoin itself. Don't ask me how. It just did. A staggering piece of work, especially for the 1970s. When I bought it, I saw the cryptography in it, but I didn't understand its full meaning until 2010 or so. That's when I realized I needed to sell it. It held a power that was too great for me."

The email. The final piece of the puzzle. "Gyorgy," Oliver said, his voice tight with focus, "I found an email from you to my dad, about selling the painting to someone called 'S.' Was that Sazsa, the guy from MixMarket?"

Gyorgy closed his eyes, a flicker of pain crossing his face. When he opened them, his gaze was guarded. "Oliver, some questions are best left unanswered. If your father didn't tell you, it is not for me to say. That is all in the past."

"Did you sell the painting to Sazsa?" Oliver pressed.

"No. I don't know who I sold it to," Gyorgy replied, his voice firm. "I worked with a broker. Bojan Mitrovic. A Serbian guy."

"So you really can't talk about Sazsa? Did you know him? Did my dad?"

"Yes," Gyorgy said, a final, unmovable wall. "But that's all I can say. I'm sure your father will tell you if he wants you to know."

"How can he tell me? He's dead," Oliver said, the words a raw, frustrated plea.

"You know how, Oliver," Gyorgy said with another dry laugh. "He was a wily old fox. You do know his views on immortality, don't you?"

"Immortality?"

"I guess that's another thing he felt wasn't the right time to tell you," Gyorgy said, a wry smile touching his lips. "You will find out in due course. *Indestructible* was the name he chose for himself."

"I don't understand," Oliver said, his mind reeling with the strange, new word. "He changed his name to Nate. What does that have to do with immortality?"

For the first time, a genuine, full smile spread across Gyorgy's face, a brief flash of the man he used to be. "Oliver, I see the spark in you. The same spark your father had. But this story is not for me to tell. You will find out at the pace he wants you to."

Oliver just sat there, utterly lost. The meeting had confirmed so much – his dad's deep involvement in bitcoin, the connection to Bryce, a name for the broker. But it had also opened up a dozen new, impossible questions that left him feeling more bamboozled and alone than ever before.

The waiter arrived with the check, and Gyorgy, with a quiet but unyielding insistence, claimed it. As he was getting ready to leave, a slow and deliberate process, he pulled two small, crisp envelopes from his jacket pocket. He inspected them both carefully, as if weighing their contents, before putting one back. He handed the other to Oliver.

"I'm glad I met you, Oliver," he said, his voice a soft, dry rustle. "I feel one step closer to completing my unfinished business. I know you will talk to Nate about forgiving me. I brought this for you."

"Oh, you didn't have to," Oliver said, looking at the simple white envelope. "What is it?"

"It's a paper wallet," Gyorgy explained. "With a little over one bitcoin on it. From Nate's preferred chain, not mine. I only had a little bit left after the fork, and I wanted to give it out to you and the other person I am meeting."

The number stunned Oliver into silence. "One bitcoin? That's … that's a lot. I'm not sure I can accept such a generous gift."

"Oliver," Gyorgy said, his voice gentle but firm, "Indulge a dying man. I don't have one of those fancy modern wallets that came after I moved on, but this should still work just fine, the way we old-timers used it. Please. Accept it."

Oliver looked at the dying man's pleading, sorrowful eyes and felt the last of his resistance crumble. He took the envelope, its lightness a strange contrast to the immense weight it represented. "Thank you, Gyorgy," he said somberly.

They left the diner. Oliver helped Gyorgy to the curb and hailed a taxi. As the cab pulled up, before getting in, Gyorgy turned and put both of his frail, skeletal hands on Oliver's shoulders. He stared deeply into Oliver's eyes, a final, intense connection.

"You are your father's son," he said, his voice a low, certain whisper. "You will make him proud. I know it. Remember that your father is immortal."

Oliver just stared back, a blank expression on his face, the word "Immortal" echoing in the chasm of his confusion. A faint, knowing smile touched Gyorgy's lips.

"Thank you, Oliver. My last trip to New York has been worth it. Don't forget my final request. I know you won't." He let go, eased himself into the back seat of the taxi, and was gone.

As Oliver watched the yellow cab pull away from the curb and merge into the river of city traffic, an eerie sense of finality washed over him. He knew, with an absolute and chilling certainty, that he would never see Gyorgy Lorincz again.

The digital display on the downtown 6 train platform glowed with a small, cruel number: *14 min.* The meeting with Gyorgy had hollowed Oliver out, leaving him feeling shaky and raw. The thought of waiting on a crowded platform, of then descending into the stale air of the subway, felt unbearable. He sent a quick, vague Slack message to Sri – *not feeling well, taking the rest of the day* – and retreated to the street. Thirty-seven dollars for an Uber to the Upper West Side. The surge pricing was a minor insult, but he thought of the paper wallet from Gyorgy, a strange and heavy comfort in his pocket.

As the car crawled through the midtown traffic, the sickness began to crest. Meeting Gyorgy had been like coming face to face with death itself, a preview of the void. The man's empty, hopeless voice echoed in his ears. That, and the desperate, repeated pleas for forgiveness addressed to a ghost, had unsettled Oliver on a level he couldn't name. The moment he stumbled into his apartment, he ran for the bathroom and was violently sick.

Feeling slightly better, the physical purge having done little to quiet his mind, he made his way to bed. *At least I can be certain that was real,* he thought, a grim, ironic twist. The nausea, the vomiting – it was too visceral to be a projection.

He shut his eyes, taking a few deep breaths, trying to find the quiet center he had learned to access. But this time, he didn't have to search for the projection. The moment his conscious mind relaxed, the timechain pulled him in.

The familiar, pitch purple-black texture materialized around him, the silence humming with the soft, almost imperceptible whisper of a billion voices.

"I don't have much to say to you today, Battu." The voice came from directly behind him, calm and quiet, startling him not with its usual boisterous energy, but with its lack of it. "It's one of those days when you need to talk, not me."

This was new. The Noncemeister was simply there, standing still, his hands clasped behind his back, his usual manic grin replaced by a blank, expectant stare. For the first time, Oliver felt like he was in control of the conversation. He thought of the questions that had been nagging at him, the ones he never had a chance to ask.

"What is this quiet hum?" he began. "It sounds like it should be silence, but it's not. I don't mean the heartbeat. I mean the silence *between* heartbeats. It sounds like people whispering."

The Noncemeister tilted his head, a single, simple word dropping into the void. "Gossip."

"Gossip?" Oliver asked, unsure he'd heard correctly.

"Yes, Battulu. That is the sound of gossip," the Noncemeister said, his voice flat and informational. "Before the old truth becomes the new truth as it happens during each heartbeat, the prospective new truth needs to be proposed. Once it is proposed, there is gossip. And from gossip emerges the new truth."

"Who's gossiping?"

"Everyone." The Noncemeister spread his arms wide, as if embracing the entire purple void. "The timechain is the collective consciousness of all that is true and all who seek the truth. But before truth is formed, there needs to be a proposition." As he spoke, he reached out and seemed to pluck a single, shimmering thread of whispery light from the air. He held it between his thumb and forefinger. "A proposition is neither true nor false until the next heartbeat. Its veracity can only be confirmed by the entirety of the collective, and for it to spread to the collective," he blew gently on the thread, and it dissolved into a thousand tiny, whispering motes of light that dispersed into the darkness, "there needs to be gossip."

The explanation was so elegant, so perfectly aligned with what he was learning, that Oliver could see it clearly in his mind. The user's transaction, the mempool, the gossip of the nodes, the final confirmation in a block.

"So that soft, almost inaudible whisper is gossip about propositions," Oliver said, thinking aloud, "And the deafening whisper is the heartbeat where the propositions either get accepted or rejected. Did I get that right?"

"Very prosaic, Batew," the Noncemeister said, performing a single, slow, deliberate clap that echoed in the silence. "I could have said it better myself, but yes, you are correct."

Oliver's mind was racing, the connections solidifying. "I have another question for you," he said, emboldened by his small victory. "Why do you keep correcting me when I say something is nonsense and you say, 'not nonsense, but nonsense?' You're just repeating the same word."

"Ah, silly Batlulu," the Noncemeister said with a playful grin. He held up his hands and, as if plucking letters from a celestial Scrabble bag, pulled the glowing characters "N-O-N-S-E-N-S-E" from the air and let them hang there. "I am talking about noncense, not nonsense." With a flick of his wrist, he rearranged the glowing letters. They now read "N-O-N-C-E-N-S-E".

"See, that's exactly what I mean! You said the same thing twice!" Oliver exclaimed, pointing at the floating word.

"You are not observing closely enough, and that's why I said you were a silly-billy." The Noncemeister reached out and tapped the first five letters of the word, making them glow brighter. "There is sense in nonces. That is non-cense. Otherwise," he waved a dismissive hand at the original configuration, "It is nonsense."

"Wait, nonces?" A glimmer of light. A memory of his late-night reading on the BIP-39 specification, on mining, on block headers.

"That's right," the Noncemeister puffed out his chest, his brown suit momentarily shimmering with an embroidered pattern of random, glowing numbers. "I am the Noncemeister, after all. Master of the nonces, keeper of the timechain."

"Nonces as in the element in the bitcoin block header?" Oliver pressed, the connection almost too perfect to be true.

The Noncemeister's suit returned to its normal, drab brown. He put a hand to his ear, a look of theatrical confusion on his face. "Batew, one of these days I'm going to have to learn about this 'bit corn,' isn't it? You keep talking about it so much, I'm beginning to wonder how deep the nonsense resides within you."

Oliver ignored the feigned ignorance. His mind was already there. *The nonce. The 'number used only once.' The random input miners change billions of times a second, searching for the winning hash.* The Noncemeister was speaking in code, a perfect, obtuse, poetic translation of the very technology he pretended not to know.

"So you were saying *noncense* all this while, not nonsense?" The realization finally dawned on him, a slow, brilliant sunrise in the purple void.

"You bet," the Noncemeister said, giving him a saucy wink.

"Okay, but that still doesn't make sense," Oliver said, the final piece of the puzzle still missing. "I get the different spelling now, but what does it even mean?"

"There is an old truth and there is a new truth," the Noncemeister explained, his voice becoming suddenly clear and direct. "That transition can only happen by finding sense in nonces."

"I see. So what does 'the answer is in noncense' mean? You keep saying that."

"It means just that. The answer is the truth, and you get to it by making sense of nonces."

"I don't get it," Oliver said, the brief moment of clarity dissolving back into confusion.

"Battu, today was supposed to be a day for you to talk to me, not the other way around," the Noncemeister said peevishly, stamping his foot on the empty air. "But you're leaving me with no choice."

"Aha," Oliver grinned, catching him. "So you're saying you *don't* have a choice? I thought everything was a choice?"

The Noncemeister stopped, a slow, dangerous smile spreading across his face. "Right now, there is no choice but one, Batlu. It is a choiceless choice. I now will tell you the story of the Certain Man and Entropy."

"Wait, what?"

The Noncemeister raised his hand imperiously, silencing any protest, and as he began to speak, the purple void around them began to fill with faint, ghostly images, a theater of the mind taking shape.

"The timechain, where the truth resides
Was shimmering anew.
Propositions posed improperly,
Consumed with nary a queue.
And this was odd, because it was
Not how the truth renewed.

"The fiery flames were much bemused,
Their energy beguiled.
A misdirected game of chance
And promises reviled.
An extraordinary twist of fate?
The truth had been defiled."

As he sang, ghostly, shimmering flames erupted in the void, and within them, Oliver could see chaotic, jumbled data streams flickering and dying.

"Pools of memory sought in vain
To properly propose.
Signatories lost at sea,
A demeanor much morose.
Could true abundance disappear,
Perhaps, perchance, suppose?"

Two new figures appeared. One was a man made of solid, unmoving stone
– The Certain Man. The other was a swirling, dancing woman made of pure,
chaotic energy – Entropy.

"The Certain Man and Entropy
Observed without a tear.
Inertia and ennui
Were posthumously clear.
A little dance, a game of chance
Was all was needed here.

"'Oh nonces, come and play with us!'
Entropy did beseech,
'Iterate, a little late,
Convert this code to speech.
Make sense of this, for heaven's sake
The truth is there to reach.'"

The woman of Entropy danced, and as she did, millions of tiny, sparkling
lights – the nonces – swirled around her, a joyful, chaotic storm.

"The Certain Man stared stoically,
For doubt was not his thing.
Chaos, order, are imposed
As time, the truth will bring.
When ten to four as it may go
The larp's tongue, it will sing.

"When fire burned quite pointedly
To create a game of chance,
Entropy was quite assured
That truths unbiased advance
The only way she knew they could
By watching nonces dance"

The poem continued, a bizarre and beautiful ballet of allegorical figures and cryptographic concepts. And Oliver, watching the performance, finally began to understand.

"The nonces gathered playfully
To iterate in merry ways.
With first as third and fifth as fifth.
A complimentary gaze
From the Certain Man, at peace again
As uncertainty decays

"When a score is second, awkwardly,
Or the last one is just nine.
Entropy had done her job.
An outcome to define,
The sense in nonces, obviously
Reality, by design

"A dozen and one are five behind
As Entropy had won.
Reductio ad absurdum too,
The Certain Man did spun.
Fourteen is ten for good measure,
In this chapter, bar none.

"So Entropy imposed herself,
As did the Certain Man.
Chaotic order now restored,
As per the master plan.
Propagating as only
A blind-ruthless timechain can."

"I think I get it," Oliver said as the last note faded. "The only type of work that you can't cheat is guesswork, right? A random number is a random number. That's what you mean by 'game of chance' – generating random numbers. You can try to generate more per second, but for that, you have to expend more energy. Do more work. There are no shortcuts."

"So it goes, Battulu."

Grappling with the newfound knowledge, a final, profound realization washed over him. "Your song … it was proof by contradiction," he said, the words a breathless discovery. "Creating an authoritative and certain direction of time can only be unbiased if it comes from the entropy and chaos of random numbers, which are generated using energy. Out of fire comes entropy, and out of entropy comes certainty. It's making sense out of nonces!"

A slow, proud smile spread across the Noncemeister's face. "*Ex igne, tempus nascitur.* Out of fire, time is born. But that is a story for another day." He began to fade, his form growing translucent. "I'll tell you what, though, Batue …" he said, his voice a warm, final whisper, "… you are not a doofus, and of that, I am certain."

The Notepad

i) *violin* ii) *toddler* iii) *alley* iv) *shoulder* v) *educate* vi) *rookie* vii) *oval* viii) *below* ix) *punch* x) *certain*

STAGE 3: ANGER

CHAPTER 11. COVER

"We're just not meeting our KPIs with the current setup. We have a demo in a few weeks, and there's no way our client is going to find this acceptable …"

Oliver listened to the product manager, Carol, prattle on, a low hum of irritation building in his chest. *KPIs.* Key Performance Indicators. How he hated the term, a piece of corporate jargon designed to give a scientific veneer to what was often just pure guesswork. When he'd begged Olumide to get him on Project Crestone, he'd seen it as an escape. He hadn't realized it would be a double-edged sword. As a sales engineer, his job was to sell the dream; he never had to live in the messy reality of delivering it. Now, he was drowning in the annoying, intractable details.

He'd spent the last week buried in the project's code and its customer requirements, and the more he learned, the less sense it made. They were building a system to "fractionalize" ownership of luxury villas in Colorado, but the tokens they were issuing were a legal fiction. They weren't a claim on the property itself, no right to actually *use* the villas. They were just equity in a nebulous legal entity called "Crestone Inc." It was the same old world of stocks and shares, just wrapped in a shiny, new, and unnecessarily complicated blockchain package.

Worse, the project was a failure before it had even launched. The management team had wildly overestimated buyer interest. Less than ten percent of the tokens had committed buyers, and the team was now scrambling, trying to gin up marketing hype for a product no one seemed to want. Crestone had promised them over a million dollars, but so far, all BlockWaves had seen was a paltry ten-thousand-dollar installment. The rest of that money, Oliver was now certain, would never arrive.

And then there was the technical absurdity. The smart contracts, as built, were a privacy nightmare, exposing sensitive user information to the public blockchain – the very KPI Carol was now droning on about. Their proposed solution? Ditch the public network and switch to a private, permissioned version of Ethereum, run on a single cloud provider. It was, in Oliver's mind, a glorified database. A slow, expensive, and needlessly complex database, but a database nonetheless.

He felt a sudden, compulsive need to puncture the bubble of polite, collective delusion in the room. He had to ask the question. "Why don't we just run this on a regular database with privacy controls?" he said, his voice cutting through Carol's monologue. "We'll get better performance and reduce the complexity."

The entire team turned to stare at him. The sudden, absolute silence was a physical thing, a vacuum that sucked the air out of the room. Carol was the first to find her voice, and it was pure ice.

"This is a *blockchain* project, Oliver. We are expected to deliver a *tokenized* product, on a *blockchain*."

A diminutive engineer chimed in, his tone scandalized. "How can we meet the Ethereum token standard requirements if we use a database?"

Oliver felt the gazes of his colleagues on him, a mixture of shock and hostility. He had become, in the space of a single sentence, the least popular person in the room. He decided to persist. "Think about any other company that issues stock. Those are just lines in a database, right? Crestone has already admitted these tokens are securities. So why not go the tried and tested route?"

"Oliver, we don't have time for philosophical debates," Carol said, her voice dripping with condescension. "We have a deadline. We have a major privacy risk to mitigate. And," she said, landing on the only point that truly mattered, "we are a Web3 company, being paid to build a Web3 project. We can't pivot midstream to a traditional system. How would that reflect on us?"

The final sentence hung in the air, a perfect, damning summary of everything that was wrong. It wasn't about the best solution. It was about the brand. It was about the narrative. Realizing the absolute futility of the discussion, Oliver just shrugged, a small, bitter gesture of surrender. For now.

A short while after the meeting, Olumide walked up to Oliver's desk, a look of amusement on his face. "So, happy I asked you to cover for Shiran on Crestone?" he chuckled.

Oliver let out a long, weary sigh. "I have some concerns, to be honest," he said, the words heavy with a frustration he could no longer contain. "In the one week I've been on it, it's clear we're not going to meet the deadline. And besides that, I don't think the project is going anywhere. Who is rushing to buy these worthless tokens? It's just a promise of equity in a company that could disappear overnight."

Olumide's expression sobered. "Oliver, I've noticed something different about you these last few months," he said, his voice taking on a grave, managerial tone. "Why are you asking all these controversial questions? We have a mandate to deliver first-in-class Web3 solutions. We need to be laser-focused. Trying to poke holes doesn't help."

"Dude, how is this being 'controversial?'" Oliver shot back, the condescension in Olumide's voice a spark on dry tinder. "I'm being realistic. The technology doesn't scale. The business value isn't there. How are we not just enabling a giant rug-pull by building this centralized, private network? It doesn't seem right."

"You're missing the bigger picture," Olumide said, the patronizing tone returning, grating on Oliver's last nerve. "We are shaping the future of commerce. The old web is dying. We are putting asset ownership directly in the end-users' hands."

"See, that's exactly it!" Oliver said, his frustration boiling over into open anger. "Those are just words! We just sat in a meeting where we decided to move to a private, permissioned network because the main chain can't scale! We've decentralized nothing. All the data is at the mercy of the cloud provider and us!"

"Yeah, but the market will have to trust us," Olumide said calmly. "Our reputations are at stake."

"Then why the hell aren't we just building it on a simple database?" Oliver pushed back, unable to hide the raw irritation in his voice. "It's the same trust equation, right? A database would be far simpler and easier to manage than this Rube Goldberg contraption we're building!"

Olumide's face hardened. He leaned in, his voice dropping to a low, serious register. "Oliver, I'm telling you this as a friend. Word is getting around that you're asking these prickly questions. This is the wrong time to bring down team morale. We need to raise a big Series B to survive, and we need a few wins under our belt. Just let go of these purist ideas for now. We'll figure it out along the way."

Oliver just stared at him, a quiet, seething rage building in his chest. It was emotional blackmail, plain and simple. *Fall in line, or you're a problem.* He had a good mind to tell Olumide to take him off the project, to walk away from the whole charade. But then the cold, hard reality of his situation crashed over him. His rent. His life. The one bitcoin from Gyorgy was a safety net, but it wasn't a career. He needed this job. For now.

He just stopped himself from speaking, the angry words dying in his throat. And the thought of assets, of money, reminded him of an inconvenient, necessary conversation he'd been avoiding for far too long. He had to talk to his mom.

August 1986, Andhra Pradesh, South India

The monsoon rain was a violent, percussive roar, turning the dusty road into a thick, flowing river of mud. Huddled under the flimsy straw awning of a general store, seeking a futile cover, two teenagers were pressed together, their clothes plastered to their skin.

The girl looked up at the boy, a mischievous chuckle cutting through the sound of the downpour. "Visu, what do you think our parents would say if they found us like this?"

"I don't think there's any danger of that, Nandita," the sixteen-year-old boy said, his voice a low rumble against her ear as he hugged her tighter, a desperate attempt to share warmth against the unseasonable chill. "They are safely home, a couple of kilometers away. I doubt they'd venture out in this rain."

They stood in silence for a few moments, the embrace their only shield against the storm. Nandita leaned back slightly, her eyes full of a future she could already see. "In a few years, we could be married. We could have children. We'd let them do what they wanted, right? No rules like these."

Visu drew a deep, ponderous breath, and the warmth of the hug seemed to recede as he loosened his grip. "Let's not talk about that now," he said, his gaze fixed on the rain. "I don't know if I'm going to stay in India for much longer. My future is not here. I need to leave."

"Take me with you," she said, her hand clutching at the wet fabric of his shirt.

"I don't know if I can," he said, taking a small step back, gently disengaging her grip. The words seemed painful for him to say. "I feel … destined to move to America. I know I will in a few years, and I feel like I need to do it on my own."

Nandita looked at him in shocked disbelief, her eyes welling with tears. "But you told me you loved me! Do you know the trouble I could get into with my parents if they found out about us?"

"I do love you," Visu said, but to Oliver, the unseen observer, the words lacked the conviction to match the tears in her eyes. "And we still have a few more years together. But when I'm done with college, I am certain I will go to America. My dad is going to buy me a computer soon. We'll be one of the first families in town to have one." His voice gained a strange, fervent energy, a desperation to make her understand an inner truth he barely understood himself. "I'm going to learn everything about computers and then go to America for graduate studies. It's hard to explain, but there are voices in my head that are guiding me. I think it is the universe speaking to me, telling me what I should be doing. I have to listen to the voices. Please, try and understand."

But she couldn't. Sobbing now, Nandita moved away from him, creating a cold, miserable distance between them under the small awning. The rain had eased to a steady drizzle. A man emerged from the darkness of the store behind them, an umbrella in his hand. He paused, looking out at the rain, and then turned, his face flickering with a glimmer of recognition as he saw the two teenagers.

He was in his early forties, bearded, with threads of silver in his dark hair. But it was his eyes that caught Oliver's attention. They were the kindest, most peaceful eyes he had ever seen. The man smiled warmly at the heartbroken teenagers, a silent, compassionate witness to their small tragedy.

A wave of relief washed over Oliver. This was a normal projection. A sad, human story from a time long before he was born. For the first time in what felt like an eternity, he was simply an observer, and thankfully, the Noncemeister was nowhere to be seen.

"Ah, Visu and Nandita, what are you two doing out here in this pouring rain?" the man asked, his voice warm and kind.

"Nothing, Uncle," Visu said sheepishly, unable to meet the man's gaze. "We're just taking shelter."

"And making the young lady cry in the process?" The man's expression was stern, but his eyes held a gentle, teasing light.

Visu stared intently at his shoes, a flush of shame creeping up his neck.

"Haha, the joy of youth, isn't it?" the man smiled warmly, the sternness vanishing. "What can be purer?" He looked from one drenched, miserable teenager to the other. "Uncle, you're not going to tell our parents about this, are you?" Visu stuttered.

The man let out a hearty laugh that seemed to push back against the sound of the rain. "Who am I to interfere with young love? I will cover for you, Visu, don't worry."

An awkward silence fell between them, punctuated by the staccato rhythm of the intensifying downpour. Nandita, her tears spent, just stared angrily into the distance. Visu, desperate to fill the silence, latched onto a piece of village gossip. "Uncle, my father told me you will be leaving town soon to build an ashram. Is that true?"

"Yes, it is true," the man responded, his peaceful gaze turning inward. "I have reached a stage in my life where I need to retreat and meditate. This materialistic life is not for me."

"So you're going to leave your home and family behind?" Visu asked, and Oliver, the unseen observer, could hear the boy's desperate attempt to find a parallel, a justification for his own restless dreams.

"I'm not moving too far away," the man replied. "We have found a very auspicious property in the mountains close by. We will have a groundbreaking ceremony next month."

"You will be missed around here, Uncle," Visu said, a genuine sadness in his voice. "People always enjoyed your jokes and stories."

"You silly boy, I'm only moving an hour away," the man smiled. "You are always welcome there, you know that."

"Have you decided on a name for the ashram?"

"Not yet. But I have decided on a name for myself."

"For yourself?" Visu looked surprised.

"Haha, yes. I am leaving this old life behind me, shedding my attachments. That includes my name. I will become Guru Brahma. The name came to me in a dream. I will be the creator of a new reality."

"I would love to visit you there, Uncle."

"Then you must," the soon-to-be Guru Brahma said. He looked at Visu for a moment, his gaze becoming more focused, more personal. "And how about you, young man? Your father tells me you have dreams of going to America one day."

"Yes," Visu replied, his voice regaining its certainty. "I feel my destiny is there. It is the land of opportunity, and I know I will thrive there."

"Then so it goes," the man said, raising his right hand in a gesture that was not quite a wave, but more like a blessing. "Always allow yourself to be surprised and delighted by what the universe has in store for you. Follow your heart. We are here to experience life to its fullest." He paused, his kind eyes looking from Visu to the distant, rain-shrouded hills. "We have a saying in our language: just as the Banyan tree does cover the tired traveler, so does the solace of pursuing his dream cover the curious man."

And with that odd, resonant aphorism, the scene dissolved, the sound of the monsoon fading into a dead silence. Oliver opened his eyes, the only concrete takeaway from the strange, sad episode being the quiet, unexpected origin story of Guru Brahma.

743516 (July 3)

"Hi honey, I'm so glad you called," his mom's voice trilled over the phone, a bright, cheerful sound that felt jarringly out of sync with his own gray mood. "Have you decided to spend July 4th with me tomorrow? We can drive down to Hoboken for the fireworks."

"No, Mom, I can't, sorry," Oliver lied, the words tasting like ash. "I've made plans with friends." The lie was an act of self-preservation, a necessary shield against a well-meaning but emotionally draining day he simply couldn't face.

"Oh," her voice faltered, the disappointment a palpable thing even through the phone. "Well, you know where to find me if you change your mind."

"Mom," Oliver said, changing the subject before she could press him. "What was that thing you told me to follow up on with Greene?" Ben Greene. His dad's attorney. Another conversation he'd been avoiding.

"Oh, yeah," she said, her tone shifting to one of practical concern. "Ben wasn't able to get hold of you. I know this isn't easy, sweetheart, but you need to deal with your father's apartment. Get it cleared out, get it listed for sale, whatever you want to do. It's worth at least two million, and it all legally goes to you. You need to decide. Your dad didn't leave a will, as you know, so I would reach out to Ben and figure it out."

Oliver closed his eyes, a physical grimace twisting his face. The apartment. It was a museum of a life that was over, a time capsule of his father's existence that he was now expected to dismantle and liquidate. He remembered visiting a week after the funeral, moving through the rooms in a disembodied daze, the familiar objects screaming with the absence of their owner. He hadn't been able to bring himself to go back since.

"Okay, Mom," he said, his voice flat. "I'll talk to him. Love you." He hung up before she could say anything more.

He spoke to Ben shortly after that. The lawyer's voice was kind but firm, confirming the inevitable. The co-op board was demanding a resolution. The world, with its rules and deadlines and legal obligations, was not going to wait for his grief to subside. He had to decide. He had to act.

743619 (July 4)

"How are you doing, Mr. Oliver? It's good to see you again!"

The voice was a warm, happy melody from a life he no longer lived. Oliver looked up and saw Santos, the doorman, his face a landscape of fond memories. "Hi Santos," Oliver said, a genuine, tired smile reaching his lips as he returned the hug. "Yes, it's been a while. It's … tough to come back here."

Santos had been a constant, a fixture in the lobby of 456 W 19th Street for as long as Oliver could remember. He was there every day after school, a friendly face to greet him as he ran through the door. He was a silent witness to the family's life, the comings and goings, the slow, imperceptible fracture of his parents' marriage, and now, its final, tragic dissolution.

"You know," Santos said, his eyes crinkling at the corners, "I can't believe the little kid who used to run around and cause trouble in this building is now this handsome young man, an important business professional." It was the same refrain Santos had used for years, but today it landed differently, a painful reminder of the simple, linear path his life was supposed to have taken.

Oliver laughed politely. "I've come to take a look at a few things in Dad's apartment."

The warmth in Santos's expression instantly clouded over with a deep, shared sorrow. Tears welled in his eyes. "Mr. Oliver, I am so sorry. I know I said this before, but I mean it. I miss your father. He was one of a kind."

He shook his head, looking past Oliver as if seeing a ghost in the lobby. "He had this way of making people feel good about themselves. The only one in the whole building who would speak to me in Spanish, always joking, always making me laugh. He just … he knew the right thing to say."

Santos composed himself, but the emotion was still thick in his voice. "One time, a few years ago, I was asking him for financial advice. You know, because he's a finance guy." He paused. "You know what he told me? He told me to buy bitcoin. I'd never even heard of it. But he explained it so clearly. His word was enough for me. I took all my Christmas and New Year's tips and found a guy who gave me bitcoin for the cash. I still have it. Because of him," Santos said, his voice full of a quiet, life-changing awe, "Maybe I can retire before I'm too old for this job."

The words hit Oliver with a disorienting force. He felt a strange, dizzying sense of displacement, as if the ground had shifted beneath his feet. "Wow," he said, the word feeling small and inadequate. "That's amazing, Santos. I didn't know that."

"I even asked him when I should sell," Santos continued, eager to share the story. "Last year, when the price went over sixty thousand, I was ready. But your dad told me, 'Only sell what you need. Hold the rest. In a few years, you won't need to sell it. You'll just use it as money.'"

"What did you do?" Oliver asked, his voice a near whisper.

"I listened to him. I sold a little bit, to cover some costs. Kept the rest. He explained it to me. He said buying bitcoin isn't investing; it's saving. Saving for your future self, for your family. It took me a long time to understand that."

"I'm glad that worked out for you," Oliver said, but his mind was somewhere else, lost in a fog of confusion and a sharp, sudden pang of something that felt like betrayal. His father, his brilliant, secretive father, had shared this revolutionary idea, this life-altering financial advice, with the doorman. But not with him. Not with his own son. How many other people knew this side of him? How many other secret lives had he lived?

Oliver unlocked the door to the apartment and stepped inside. The silence was immediate and absolute, a physical presence that pressed in on him. He walked in gingerly, each soft footfall on the hardwood floor a drumbeat of loss, a stark reminder that the gentle, powerful spirit that had inhabited this home for two decades was gone forever.

His gaze fell on his old childhood bedroom, now his father's library. He saw the ghost of his bed in the space now occupied by two large bookcases, and the memory was so vivid it made his throat tighten. He could almost feel the weight of his father sitting on the edge of that phantom bed, his voice a low, playful rumble as he spun tales of fantasy lands, of daring adventures, of a strange, pig-nosed man called the Nose Smiter.

He moved on, past the dining table, a place that used to be the warm, vibrant heart of their home, filled with laughter and the incredible smells of his dad's cooking. Until it wasn't. Until the laughter was replaced by the sharp, acidic tones of his parents fighting, a slow poison that began seeping into their lives around the time he was twelve or thirteen. *2011 or so,* he calculated. *After bitcoin.*

The thought was a sudden, cold clarity. *Could that have been it?* Could his father's entry into that secret world, into Gyorgy's world, have been the source of the secrecy that his mother had misinterpreted as infidelity? What could have been so terrible that he had to hide it from them?

Another troubling thought surfaced. That whole period of his life was a blur, a collection of vague and hazy memories. He couldn't remember meeting Gyorgy. He could only remember the feeling of the arguments, not the words. It was the same time he'd had trouble focusing in school, the time his dad had first taken him to Maren. He made a mental note to ask her about it when she got back from India.

He collapsed into the armchair in front of the TV, the worn leather sighing under his weight. On the coffee table sat the remote. He picked it up, his thumb tracing the telltale wear around the power and volume buttons. It was the same chair, the same remote from his very first projection, a physical bridge between the real world and the surreal one. He looked around the apartment, at the books, the art, the furniture, and was suddenly overwhelmed by the full, crushing weight of all the memories held within these walls.

He couldn't sell it. There was no way. His dad's soul was still here. He had enough in the checking account to cover the maintenance fees for another year. He would buy himself that time. The two-million-dollar price tag was a tempting fantasy, a solution to the constant, low-grade anxiety of his own finances. But to erase all this, to liquidate his own past for a healthier bank account … the thought was unthinkable. If it meant being broke for a while longer, so be it.

He leaned his head back, closing his eyes, and a raw, angry prayer formed in the silence of his mind.

God, Dad. Why are you doing this to me? Things would have been so simple if you hadn't gone on that damn trip. You'd still be here. You could have been honest with me. Why did you have to hide everything? I'm loving learning about bitcoin. It's a whole new world, and every time I think I understand it, I learn something new that makes me realize how stupid I was a moment ago. I love it.

The final, unspoken question hung in the empty apartment, a perfect, heartbreaking ache. *Why couldn't you have been the one to teach me this?*

A soft rustling from his old bedroom, now the library. Oliver froze. The sound was distinct – someone thumbing through the pages of a book, humming a jolly, off-key tune. He got up from the armchair, his body moving with a silent, cautious grace, and tiptoed to the door. He peeked inside. The back of a familiar, bald, egg-shaped head was visible over the top of a worn armchair.

The Noncemeister turned, sensing him, a book held open in his hand. "Ah Battu, fascinating stuff in this bookshelf here. Have you read any of it?"

"You?" Oliver groaned, the sound a mix of disbelief and pure exhaustion. "Don't tell me this isn't real."

"And a real pleasure to see you too, tiger," the Noncemeister chirped, not a hint of surprise on his face. "My word, I would have thought you'd be a little happier to see me after everything we've been through. Such a rudie you are, Battulu."

"I mean, I wasn't expecting to see you again," Oliver said, leaning against the doorframe, the fight already going out of him. "I thought this was real."

"Batew, haven't we been over this already? Don't make me repeat myself about reality." He looked down at the book in his hands. "Anyway, have you read this? It's fascinating. It's called *The Ground Beneath Her Feet.*" He read a line aloud with dramatic flair. "'Goodbye, Hope.' What a beautiful line. And all this stuff about disorientation – you should be familiar with that, of course. And

Orpheus, Morpheus, and Metamorpheus. Beautiful, beautiful." He beamed. "And the best part is, it was written by a salmon."

"What?" Oliver said, confused.

"It was. Rum thing, innit?" the Noncemeister shrugged.

Oliver looked at the cover. "Salman Rushdie," he said dryly. "One of my dad's favorite authors. Not salmon, Salman."

"Ah, fish posh!" the Noncemeister retorted, casually tossing the priceless, signed first-edition over his shoulder where it vanished without a sound. "Not worth a moor's last sigh. Now tell me, Battu, you look sad, and I daresay disoriented. How can I make it worse?"

"Ha, just keep going," Oliver said with an ironic chuckle. "You're doing just fine."

The Noncemeister's playful expression softened for a fraction of a second. "Battu, Battulu, Battolo! You know this comes from a place of love. I'm teasing, of course. I want to help. Sadness is okay. Anger is okay. Disorientation is okay. But there is something better for you ahead of it. Let's get you there."

The rare moment of sincerity was an open door. Oliver stepped through it. "Well, as you can see, we're in my dead father's apartment. All my memories are here. His presence is still here. In the kitchen, at the dining table, in that armchair. Everywhere. And I have no money. I might have to sell this place to stay afloat. But if I do that," his voice began to crack, "This will all be gone. Whatever is left of my father will be gone."

"And how does that make you feel?" The Noncemeister asked, his back now turned as he inspected another book on the shelf.

The question, so simple, so clinical, was the final pin pulled from the grenade. "Fucking sad, that's how it makes me feel!" Oliver's voice rose, the words tearing out of him, raw and uncontrolled. "And it makes me furious! Why do I have to do this? I don't want to let go. I miss him. I need him! And Goddamnit, I need the money too! I have no fucking money, you understand? I can barely make ends meet. I'm almost a hundred thousand dollars in debt! But if I sell this place, the last trace of my dad is gone!" The final words were a ragged, desperate shout into the quiet of the apartment.

The Noncemeister carefully placed the book he was holding back in its spot on the shelf and turned around, his expression calm, analytical, giving Oliver his full, undivided attention. "Whoa, a lot to unpack there, big guy. Why don't we start with the feelings first and then get to the money?"

"Sure, whatever," Oliver said, his voice now a low, cagey growl.

"Where do you feel these feelings of sadness and anger?" the Noncemeister asked, his voice calm and detached.

"Where? I feel them everywhere," Oliver snapped back. "I'm consumed by them."

"You are not your sadness, Battu," the Noncemeister said, holding up a hand. As he spoke, a shimmering, translucent duplicate of Oliver peeled away from Oliver's own body and stood silently beside him, its expression utterly serene. "You are not your grief, you are not your anger. There are parts of you that feel those things, but that is not the totality of you. Your essence, your inner being, is pure and it just is."

"What part of me? I feel them completely and totally," Oliver said, ignoring the silent, watchful duplicate of himself.

"That's because you don't know you are the witness," the Noncemeister said, gesturing to the serene doppelgänger. "Your inner being is just a witness; it is your anchor to the universe. Tap into it, and you will see that these feelings are just created by thoughts, which are created by feelings, which are created by thoughts." He reached out and seemed to pluck a fiery orb of anger from Oliver's chest and a tangled, thorny knot of thought from his head, holding them up as separate, pulsing objects. "Which one came first? It doesn't matter, because as a witness, you can always choose the better feeling thought."

"That made zero sense."

"Tell me, Battulu, how do you feel in this very moment?" he asked, letting the orb and the knot dissolve. "Not one moment before, or a million heartbeats before. Not in the next moment or a million heartbeats later. In this very moment, how do you feel?"

"Like shit," Oliver retorted blankly.

"You are incorrect. Try again." The Noncemeister raised a single, unmoving index finger. "Those words you just said are coming either from the past or an expectation of a future outcome. In this very moment, frozen in time, what is happening? Are you able to breathe? Are you able to stand on your feet? Are you able to speak, and listen, and touch, and smell, and see?"

The firm, insistent tone cut through Oliver's frustration. He paused, giving the question real thought. "Well," he said slowly, "If you strip away all context, then yes. I'm able to do all that."

"Is your brain functioning? Is your heart beating? Are all your organs and muscles functioning as they ought to?" the Noncemeister went on, his voice a steady, rhythmic cadence.

"I guess so ..." Oliver said warily.

"So in this very moment," the Noncemeister's voice rose slightly as he moved a step closer, "What do you need?"

"Again, stripped of all context," Oliver said, the answer surprising even himself, "I suppose I don't need anything."

"Would you say that in this very moment, you have everything you need and want and more?"

Oliver considered it, the simple, radical truth of the statement slowly dawning on him. "In a weird way," he conceded, "I guess you're right."

"Of course, I'm right. I always am," the Noncemeister responded, his imperious tone returning for a moment before softening. "And so it is, Batue. Life is a continuum of infinitely many such infinitesimal moments. Your inner being knows because it only exists in the moment. The parts of you your conscious mind creates, which distract from that pure act of living ... you can call it context, you can call it reality, but from the perspective of your pure consciousness, it is all apparent." He reached out and gently tapped Oliver's chest. "It is just a cover – a mirage. All that is left to do, is to be. In every single moment, you have everything you need and want and more, and thus life is something that happens *for* you, not *to* you."

"How does that solve my money situation, though?" Oliver asked, the question a desperate pull back to the hard, sharp edges of his reality. "I have bills to pay. I have to keep this stupid job that pays nothing even though the work doesn't make sense anymore. And I can't bring myself to sell this apartment."

"You are not in the moment, Battu," the Noncemeister reminded him, gently wagging a finger.

"Yeah, but that other moment will come," Oliver shot back. "Bills have to be paid. I can't just pretend they don't exist."

The Noncemeister paused, tilting his head as if genuinely contemplating this novel problem. "Why do you want this money, Battulu?"

"I just told you. To pay bills. Rent, food, my student loans, credit cards … the list goes on."

"And what would you do if you had the money to pay these bills?"

"I'd pay them, of course," Oliver said, frustrated by the tautological questioning.

"And what would you do then?" the Noncemeister continued, his voice infuriatingly patient.

"Well …" Oliver had to stop and think. What came after? "First, I'd feel relieved. And then … I'd find time to do something I actually like."

"And what would that be?"

"Maybe find another job. One that aligns with my values, that gives me time to do the things I want," Oliver said.

"What are the things you want? Are they not things that align with your values?"

"Sure, yeah."

"Then why can't your job be the thing you want?"

"Well, certainly not *this* one," Oliver said. "But maybe the next one. It's a good point, though. I should work on what I really want to do."

"Great," the Noncemeister beamed. "And what would that do for you?"

"I guess I'd feel satisfied," Oliver concluded. "I'd feel happy."

"And what is this happiness, Battu?" The Noncemeister's eyes widened with theatrical curiosity. "Is it in the room with us right now?" He began to twirl around the library, peering under the phantom armchair and behind the ghostly bookcases as if searching for a lost pet. "Here, happiness, happiness! Come on out!"

"Well, no, not right now," Oliver said, ignoring the performance, feeling the Noncemeister was finally getting to the point. "It's a feeling I sometimes get."

"Is that feeling inside of you when you do feel it?"

"Yes."

"Completely inside of you?"

"Well yes, it's a feeling, right? It's within me," Oliver said, wondering where this was going.

"Then why do you need external conditions for it?" the Noncemeister asked, stopping his search and turning to face him, his point landing with a quiet, devastating precision. "If it's within you, you can feel it when you want to."

Oliver was silent. The logic was so simple, so infuriatingly correct, he didn't have a response. He was conditioning his own internal state on a series of external events, when the feeling itself, the happiness he was chasing, was just a chemical reaction in his own brain.

"Batue, I'll cut to the chase here," the Noncemeister said, floating closer. "You think you need money because it will get you something, which will get you something else, which will eventually get you to happiness. But money doesn't buy you happiness. Happiness buys you happiness. Your framing is wrong. It's not: 'If only I had money, I'd be happy.' It ought to be, 'If only I were happy, I'd be happy.' And then money would be irrelevant. It may come, it may not. But you would be happy, and that is the best kind of abundance."

"How would I do that? You make it sound so trivial," Oliver said with an ironic chuckle.

"By being in the moment. Context is just the cover for what's underneath. Always look below the cover," the Noncemeister said slowly, his voice dropping to a conspiratorial whisper.

Oliver considered this. "Guess it's worth a shot," he said finally. "So every time I feel overwhelmed, I just … stop, and think about all the things I have in this one moment?"

"Yes, and appreciate them. Appreciation is an active, good-feeling thought. It is better than gratitude, which is passive. Appreciate everything you have in one single moment. Then everything else will be irrelevant." He smiled. "Okay Battulo, it's time to go. Remember, look under the cover."

And with that, a giant, jagged crack of pure darkness opened in the floor where the Rushdie book had vanished. The Noncemeister gave Oliver a final, jaunty wave and leaped right into it, disappearing into the blackness.

Oliver's eyes snapped open. He was in his dad's armchair. The scent of old books and dust was real. He hadn't been asleep in his bed; he'd been here, in Chelsea, the whole time. He must have projected the moment he sat down.

He got up and walked aimlessly around the apartment, his mind buzzing with the strange, powerful lesson. He found himself at his dad's desk and, without thinking, pulled open the top drawer. Inside, among old pens and paperclips, lay an empty, square envelope cover.

… look under the cover.

The Noncemeister's final words echoed in his head. His heart began to pound. He lifted the flimsy piece of cardboard. And there, nestled in the shallow space of the drawer, was a heavy, cast-iron key. He stared at it, a jolt of recognition so powerful it made him feel dizzy. The intricate, archaic shape. It was the same key. The key tattooed on the lion's back. The key the violinist had given him in his very first projection.

He could scarcely believe his eyes. The surreal world of the projections had just reached out and placed a solid, physical object in his hand. What on Earth could this be a key to? He frantically searched the apartment, trying the key in every lock he could find. It fit none of them.

He eventually gave up and decided to head home, the strange, heavy key a solid weight in his pocket. The conversation, the key, the overwhelming sense of his father's presence … it had all clarified something for him. He now knew exactly what he was going to do with the apartment.

The Notepad

i) *violin* ii) *toddler* iii) *alley* iv) *shoulder* v) *educate* vi) *rookie* vii) *oval* viii) *below* ix) *punch* x) *certain* xi) *cover*

CHaPTer 12. aGree

"The band should be on stage in about twenty minutes," Daniela said, her voice a bright, clear note over the low din of The Bitter End. "You'll love them, trust me."

She had described her friend's band, Ultroneus, as "psychedelic djent," a bizarre combination of genres that had intrigued Oliver. It sounded adjacent to the complex, atmospheric rock he loved, a taste inherited from his dad's Pink Floyd and King Crimson records.

"How are you doing these days?" she asked, her expression softening with a genuine sympathy that made him feel seen. "I know it's been a few months, but I'm sure it's still not easy."

"You know," he said, surprised by the honesty of his own answer, "I'm actually doing a lot better. I somehow feel more connected to him now, believe it or not." The thought of telling her, of finally sharing the impossible burden of the twenty-four words, flickered in his mind. The need to tell *someone* was becoming a low-grade ache, a way to confirm his own sanity. But he pushed it back down. Not yet.

"You never showed me a photo of him," Daniela said.

Oliver pulled out his phone, a familiar pang of loss and pride hitting him as he scrolled to a favorite picture from earlier in the year. He handed it to her.

"Oh my goodness," she breathed, her eyes wide. "He was so handsome! He should have been a movie star." She looked up at him with a playful, teasing grin. "I guess you must have gotten your looks from your mom, then."

Oliver grinned sheepishly, the compliment and the joke a welcome, easy warmth.

"I'm teasing, silly," she said, giving his arm a light, friendly punch. "You do look a lot like him. And you know the funny thing?" She leaned closer, a look of dawning realization on her face. "Your dad looks a lot like my uncle, Rafael. Let me show you."

She pulled out her own phone, found a photo, and held it up next to his. He stared. The resemblance was uncanny. It was the same intensity in the eyes, the same set of the jaw – more than just a passing similarity in features.

"And I think they might have even known each other, right?" she continued, the pieces clicking into place for her as well. "They both went to Guru Brahma's ashram, both knew Maren. What a small world."

Just then, a man walked up behind Daniela and tapped her on the shoulder. She turned, let out a short, happy squeal, and threw her arms around him in a tight hug. "So good to see you, Anton! Oliver, this is my dear friend Anton. He's the lead singer for Ultroneus."

Oliver shook the man's hand, a sudden, awkward third wheel. He watched as Anton spoke about the band's two-year hiatus, his arm still wrapped tightly around Daniela's waist, her own arm around his. The easy, physical intimacy between them was a stark, cold contrast to the fragile, budding connection Oliver had felt just a moment ago.

"Okay, we're on in a few minutes," Anton said finally. "Let's catch up after." He gave Daniela a final squeeze and headed for the stage.

The warmth between Oliver and Daniela was gone, replaced by a tense, chilly silence. Oliver couldn't stop himself. "You and Anton seem very close," he said, the words coming out sharp, prickled with an insecurity he couldn't hide.

"Oh yeah, we go back a long way," she replied, oblivious to his tone. "We used to date in high school."

"But not anymore?" The question was too direct, too needy, but he couldn't help it.

"Of course not!" she said, shaking her head with a wince of mock disgust. "We were too different. It would never have worked out."

Oliver fell silent, a hot flush of embarrassment creeping up his neck. He knew his reaction had been immature, a raw, possessive impulse he had no right to. But knowing it didn't make the feeling go away.

Daniela's laugh was a bright, clear sound that cut through the bar's low hum. "Oliver, don't tell me you got a little jealous just then?"

The question, so direct and accurate, made Oliver's face flush hot. "No, no," he stammered, the denial completely unconvincing. "Nothing like that. Just curious."

"Oliver, we're just hanging out," she said, but then a mischievous twinkle appeared in her eyes. "Of course, that could change if somebody showed some initiative." She batted her eyelids in a moment of good-natured, pantomime mockery, and he knew she was enjoying watching him squirm.

He was bright red now, completely flustered and searching for a response that wouldn't make him sound like a total idiot. He was saved by a loud, distorted chord from the stage. Anton was at the mic. A small crowd began to migrate from the bar toward the stage.

"Come on," Daniela said, tugging at his elbow, her playful mood returning. "We have to be up front. This isn't music you listen to sitting down."

The first song was a frenetic, chaotic assault, a complex storm of arrhythmic drums and heavily distorted guitars. It was in the sound of the guitars that Oliver finally understood the genre's strange name. The percussive, palm-muted strum was a perfect onomatopoeia: *djent … djent … djent*. As the song crashed to a halt, Daniela leaned in close, her voice a warm whisper against his ear. "This is their usual opener. Wait until you hear the next one." Her lips seemed to linger for a fraction of a second before she pulled away, leaving a faint, tingling warmth.

The next song began. The tempo was slower, the mood more melancholic, but the time signature was just as complex. A beautiful, hypnotic guitar solo filled the room, a winding melody that felt both nostalgic and alien. Daniela leaned in again, her lips gently brushing his ear this time, her whisper a soft caress. "This is the one. It's called 'agree.' It's a ten-minute instrumental."

The word, the music, the flashing lights, the warmth of Daniela beside him – it all combined to create a powerful, hypnotic state. Oliver felt himself swaying to the odd rhythm, his mind detaching, floating on the waves of the beautiful, intricate solo. A thick burst of fog erupted from a machine on stage, and as the white cloud washed over him and then cleared, the bar was gone.

He was standing in a hazy purple semi-darkness, at the foot of a set of giant stone stairs that rose into an unseen height. He seemed to be inside a vast, ancient castle. He walked up the stairs slowly and entered a large, empty, cavernous room. At the far end, another stone stairwell beckoned. He ascended again, entering a smaller, windowless chamber. At the other end was a single, heavy wooden door. Carved into it in ornate, archaic letters was a phrase in what looked like Spanish: *Camara del Tiempo*.

Without thinking, his hand went to his pocket. He felt the cold, heavy weight of the cast-iron key. He pulled it out. It slid perfectly into the keyhole. With a turn, a heavy bolt snapped open with a satisfying thud. He pushed the door slowly …

"Wasn't that amazing?"

Oliver blinked. The silent, stone castle vanished. The roar of the crowd, the smell of beer, the heat of the stage lights – it all came rushing back. He was at The Bitter End, standing next to Daniela. The song had just ended. *What was that?* Had the music just sent him into a projection?

He looked at Daniela, his mind still trying to reorient itself. He nodded, the word coming out on two levels at once, a response to her and a confirmation to himself. "I agree," he said, his voice a little distant. "That was incredible."

The rest of the set was a blur of complex rhythms and moody solos. None of it, however, touched the strange, almost magical power of that one song. He made a mental note to look up the band later. He was surprised he had never heard of them before.

Outside the bar, the cool night air was a stark contrast to the heat and noise inside. "I'd love to hang out more," Daniela said, and Oliver's heart gave a hopeful leap, "But I'm practicing with my theater group early tomorrow morning. I don't want to be out too late." She gave him a hug, a quick, friendly gesture that felt like a period at the end of a sentence.

A wave of disappointment washed over him. He had finally worked up the courage, had finally been ready to show the initiative she'd hinted at, and the opportunity had vanished. He'd imagined a quieter bar, more conversation, a real date unfolding into the night.

She must have seen the look on his face because she pulled back from the hug, her expression softening. "The next time you take me out, Oliver," she said, her voice a low, intimate promise, "I will be all yours for the entire evening. It's just ... this is my first time directing. It counts towards my master's. I don't want to mess it up."

He nodded, silently kicking himself for his own hesitation. "Okay," he said, forcing a smile. "I'm headed this way, then. I'll see you soon."

"Isn't your train in the opposite direction?" Daniela asked, a small frown of confusion on her face.

"Oh, I'm not going back uptown," Oliver said, the decision feeling solid and real as he spoke it aloud for the first time. "I've decided to move into my dad's old place in Chelsea. My lease is up for renewal soon anyway, so I figured I'd let that lapse and stay there. It's closer to work."

"That's great," she said, her smile returning, brighter this time. "And if you're in Chelsea, you're just a short walk away from me." A new, welcome proximity. "By the way, Maren is coming back next week, so you should come visit."

"Oh, that's great, I will. See you soon, Daniela!"

As he walked back to his dad's – no, *his* – apartment, he realized his feelings for Daniela were becoming something more than a simple crush. It was a deeper connection, a sense of rightness he couldn't quite name. He wondered if she felt it too.

His mind then wandered back into the surreal territory of the projection. The castle. The stone stairs. The door marked *Camara del Tiempo*. It had felt so solid, so real, a stark contrast to the dreamlike cottage from his first projection. And the key ... the key from his dad's drawer, a physical object, had worked on a door that existed only in his mind. What could it possibly mean? He felt a desperate need for a guide, for someone to help him make sense of the increasingly porous border between his two realities. He would have to ask the

Noncemeister. Or maybe, just maybe, Maren would have an answer when she returned.

745400 (July 17)

"This is the only place in town I buy coffee, champ," Eddie said, his voice booming with an enthusiasm that felt far too loud for the quiet diner. "They know how to brew a cup, let me tell you. Dark, black, full of flavor. Just as God intended, am I right?"

Oliver nodded politely, taking a sip from the thick ceramic mug. It tasted … fine. Standard diner coffee, probably drip-brewed hours ago. He wished he'd stopped at Bluebird for an espresso.

Eddie, of course, was not done. "I just don't understand how the kids these days have all these fancy drinks that pass off as coffee, you get me, chief? Oat-milk vanilla latte, banana bread frappuccino, gimme a goddamn break." He shuddered with theatrical disgust. "And don't even get me started on those stuck-up pseudo-intellectuals who think they're so special they can only drink Italian-style coffee." He hunched his shoulders and adopted a high-pitched, mocking voice. "*Ooh, I can only drink espresso macchiato in a teeny-tiny cup. Ooh, look at my Ivy League degree, it makes me forget what real American coffee tastes like.*"

Oliver laughed, a little uncomfortably. He was an espresso drinker. With an Ivy League degree. Eddie, in his infinite lack of self-awareness, was taking aim squarely at him.

"I loved your old man to death, don't get me wrong, tiger," Eddie continued, his tone shifting to one of fond remembrance. "But man, could he be stuck up about food, and wine, and coffee. Nothing was ever good enough for him. I'd take him to the best restaurants, and he'd always find something wrong. He'd never say anything directly, bless his heart, but if you pressed him, his inner New York Times food critic would come out. 'The tannins needed a few more years to settle.' 'The sear on the steak was acceptable.' 'The sauce was a little too bright …'" Eddie threw his hands up in exasperation. "A little too bright? What the hell was he even talking about? This is a wholesome American meal, not a lightbulb factory inspection. Where did he get it into his head that taste could be measured in lumens?"

"Uncle Eddie, I'm not …" Oliver tried to interject, to steer the conversation back to its purpose.

But Eddie was on a roll. "Let me tell you a funny story, big guy. One time, your old man and I took some clients out to dinner. Big French account. Nate was supposed to pick the restaurant – you know what a tightass he could be – but he couldn't, so he asked me. I picked the fanciest place I could think of: Papa Carmine's on 48th and Broadway. My wife and my favorite place in the city … we only went there on special occasions." He leaned in, his voice a proud whisper. "Dinner for two is three, four hundred bucks, easy. This one was on the company tab, so who's counting, am I right?"

He paused for a fraction of a second to catch his breath, his eyes gleaming. "So we get there with these French bigwigs, order appetizers, expensive wine. I'm chowing down like there's no tomorrow. I look up to see how the clients and your dad are doing, and you won't believe what happened, kiddo …"

"What happened?" Oliver asked through gritted teeth, a feeling of dread coiling in his stomach. He was a helpless passenger on this conversational runaway train.

"Crickets, that's what happened," Eddie said, his face flushing a deep, angry red that seemed unnatural under the diner's fluorescent lights. "Not a peep out of them. It was like they were eating prison sludge. Then one of the French guys takes a sip of the wine – which by the way we broke the bank on – and says in his stupid fucking accent, 'You know, in France, we drink better wine at train stations for less than one euro.' Can you believe that, tiger?" He slammed his fist on the table, but the impact made no sound, a detail that Oliver's confused mind registered as just another oddity in the strange morning. "And I didn't get to the worst part: your dad turns around and agrees with him! And says that's the case in Italy too. And Spain. Un-fucking-real, that's what that was."

A strange, bitter energy was coming off Eddie now, a venom Oliver had never seen before. The cheerful, bumbling uncle was gone, replaced by someone sharp and cruel.

"I haven't gotten to the real worst part yet," Eddie continued, his voice dropping to a low, menacing growl. "The main courses arrive, and of course they are these huge plates, right? Family style. I'd ordered the Alfredo sauce, their trademark …" A strange, nostalgic look briefly softened his features, then vanished. "You won't believe what those sick fucks did, kiddo. They started laughing. Laughing right at my goddamn face. Including your dad, that elitist motherfucker." As he spoke, his face seemed to momentarily stretch and distort, the features pulling into a grotesque caricature of a smile before snapping back to normal.

"They start talking about fat Americans and portion sizes and how you could get arrested in Italy for ordering Alfredo sauce. They went on and on, barely tasting the food. Making fun of me, and this fucking country that I love. They might as well have spat in my face, kiddo. It was heartbreaking. And your dad piled on too. He called me an uncultured fat fuck, and they all pointed at me and laughed. I'd never been so humiliated in my life."

The story was a monstrous fiction, an impossible distortion of the man Oliver knew. His father, who had spent his life quietly making people feel seen and valued, participating in such a gratuitous, public humiliation? It was unthinkable. "Eddie, that doesn't sound like Dad at all," he interjected, his voice firm. "I've never, ever seen him act like that."

"Oh, you think you know your old man well, do you?" Eddie's voice rose to a shout, and the other patrons in the diner didn't even turn their heads. It was as if he and Oliver were in a soundproof bubble. "Well, he was a sneaky son of a bitch, let me tell you. A disgusting, conniving, double-crossing, elitist motherfucker. Always thinking he was so much better than anyone else because he dressed well and had a fancy accent." He leaned across the table, his face inches from Oliver's, his eyes burning with a strange, purple-tinged light. "I got some news for you, big guy – he was a coward. A goddamn coward!"

Oliver was now worried, and a little scared. There was something wrong with Eddie. This was completely unlike him.

Eddie wasn't done. He was on his feet now, gesticulating wildly, his shadow dancing on the diner wall. "Riddle me this, kiddo. Why the fuck have you been running around trying to find stuff out about him since he disappeared? Why did he have to disappear? If he loved you so much, why couldn't he have told you what you needed to know before he left? Why is he treating you this way?"

"Eddie, please sit down," Oliver said, his voice trembling slightly. "There's no need to get upset. And … what do you mean he disappeared? He's dead, remember? You showed me the report." He was genuinely scared now, a primal fear that something was about to break.

"Ha, dead!" Eddie spat the word, taking a slow, menacing step toward Oliver. "So you think, you dumbfuck. You stupid, naïve, dumbfuck. Read the room, chief. Where's the fucking dead body? Did you see it? Did I see it? Did any of those Coast Guard cocksuckers in Bermuda see it? No. So how do you know he's dead?" He was inches from the table now. "He's disappeared. The wily son of a bitch is up to something. Wake up and smell the coffee, kiddo. Why are you even here on a Sunday chasing shadows? Go and live your pathetic life and forget about your dad."

The venom in his voice was shocking, but there was a word that snagged in Oliver's mind, a single, dissonant note in the symphony of madness. *Sunday.* It was Sunday. What was Eddie doing at the WilcoxRe office on a Sunday? And why would Oliver have taken a train from his office to meet him? The internal logic of the scene, which he hadn't even been consciously tracking, suddenly fractured.

Eddie was still walking toward him, but a strange, shimmering purple haze was now clinging to his outline. He seemed to be frothing at the mouth, and a thin, impossible wisp of orange smoke was curling out of his ears. This couldn't be real.

Oliver's phone suddenly rang, the cheerful, digital chime cutting through the tense, surreal silence like a blade. He looked down at the caller ID. It read: *Eddie Garcia.*

He looked back up. Eddie, the diner, the entire scene spun violently, flickered for a single, strobe-like instant, and then collapsed into a familiar, all-consuming purple blackness.

Oliver's eyes snapped open. He was in his dad's armchair in Chelsea, his heart hammering against his ribs. His phone was ringing on the table beside him. He looked down at the caller ID. *Eddie Garcia.*

He answered, his hand shaking. "Hi there, tiger. Did I catch you at a bad time?" Eddie's jolly, oblivious voice boomed over the line.

Oliver's mind was a blank, a short-circuited mess. He finally found some words. "Hi Uncle Eddie," he said, his voice a dry croak. "Can I call you back in two minutes? Just wrapping something up."

He hung up and let out a long, shuddering breath. Relief. It was just a projection. Another one that had felt so real, so utterly convincing, that his own mind had become an unreliable narrator. He was still shaken, the image of the monstrous, distorted Eddie burned into his brain. It was disturbing to hear such a venomous, untrue characterization of his dad, and he was glad it wasn't real.

But he was still troubled. The projection-Eddie's words, his sneering insistence that his dad had simply "disappeared," had picked at a wound that had never fully healed for Oliver. The absence of a body. It was the one piece of the story that had never allowed for true finality, the one detail that left a small, nagging door open for a hope he was too terrified to acknowledge. The projection had just given the doubt a voice.

After feeling a little more grounded, a tremor of residual panic still in his hands, he called Eddie back.

"Olly, sorry if I caught you at a bad time, big guy," Eddie's voice boomed, blissfully unaware of the psychological drama he had just interrupted. "We can always chat later if this doesn't work for you."

"Oh, I'm good, Uncle Eddie," Oliver said, the lie tasting like rust. "Just needed to take care of something. I'm free now."

"Great, so I wanted to let you know real quick that our IT clowns were finally able to retrieve the files on your dad's computer," Eddie said. "The bad news is there's nothing more about this Georgie guy you asked me about. Looks like your dad kept everything on that computer super professional and above board. I mean, why wouldn't he, come to think of it? He was a super solid, professional guy. Loads of stuff about reports, and models and whatnot. A crap ton of code too, believe it or not. I didn't realize how many of our models he coded up. I thought the code monkeys we hire and pay an arm and a leg take care of all of that. Oh, sorry," he chuckled, "I guess you're a developer – I didn't mean it that way. You know what I mean, chief. Your dad was a very senior manager, so nobody expects him to write code. But yeah, it was mostly that. Boring stuff even to me, so I can't imagine what it would be like for an outsider to go through all that. You can skip the Nyquil and melatonin if you catch my drift."

"Well, that's good to know, I suppose," Oliver said, a strange mix of disappointment and relief washing over him. "I'm not sure I was ready to hear much more about Gyorgy, to be honest."

"There was one weird thing that they found, Oliver," Eddie continued. "Not sure if this means anything, but there was a small, password-protected text file in one of his directories. When they hovered over the tooltip for the password hint, it just said 'agree.' So our guys tried 'agree' as the password, and it worked. Isn't that hilarious? Why would your dad do something so silly?"

A jolt went through Oliver, a sudden, sharp signal in the noise. "What was in the text file?" he asked, his voice tight.

"So that's the other funny part, tiger. It was a short and weird note written in Spanish, of all things. I took a photo of the note on the computer screen. Here, I'm texting it to you now."

Oliver's phone buzzed. He opened the text and stared at the image of his father's computer screen, at the cryptic words left behind.

Estamos de acuerdo con la alquimia de Pittamiglio. Los sueros más potentes contienen los secretos más hermosos. Un día, me aventuraré a su castillo y quizás encuentre mi próximo hogar. Estaís de acuerdo.

"What does it mean, Eddie?"

"Well, the rough translation is something like 'We agree with the alchemy of Pittamiglio. The most potent of serums contain the most beautiful of secrets. One day, I will venture out to his castle, and perhaps find my next home. We agree.'"

"That makes no sense," Oliver said, bewildered. "Who on earth is Pittamiglio?"

"Beats me, kiddo. 'Pittamiglio' was the filename, too. Your old man could be a weird cookie sometimes. Here's yet one more weird thing – it's written in that fancy, old-school Spanish they speak in Spain. Not the type I grew up with in the Bronx, if you catch my drift. Well, maybe it's not so weird. Your dad did speak that kind of Spanish."

After confirming there was nothing else, Oliver hung up, his mind a whirlwind. The password was 'agree.' The note began and ended with 'agree.' And the song from the Ultroneus concert, the one that had sent him into the projection of the castle, was called "agree." The convergence was too powerful to be a coincidence. It had to be the twelfth word. But his mind was already preoccupied with a bigger question. *Pittamiglio's castle.* The projection at the concert … could that have been it?

He immediately started googling. *Pittamiglio castle.* The results were sparse, mostly in Spanish. He found a Wikipedia page and ran it through a translator. Humberto Pittamiglio. An early 20th-century Uruguayan alchemist of Italian descent who had, indeed, built a castle dedicated to alchemy in Montevideo.

The clue was real. But Montevideo might as well have been the moon. He didn't have the money for a plane ticket, for a hotel. His credit cards were nearly maxed out. He still had the one bitcoin from Gyorgy, but after everything he'd learned from Vince, after hearing Santos's story, the thought of selling it for dollars felt like a betrayal, a profound failure of understanding. He would put it in cold storage, as soon as he figured out how.

So the castle, for now, was a dead end. Another impossible clue in a quest that was becoming a mountain of loose ends and unsolved mysteries. He sighed, the weight of it all settling over him again. Just add another one to the pile.

The Notepad

i) violin ii) toddler iii) alley iv) shoulder v) educate vi) rookie vii) oval viii) below ix) punch x) certain xi) cover xii) agree

745898 (July 21)

A Slack notification bloomed on Oliver's screen, a small, digital bomb. It was a group message from Ian Wright to the entire sales team channel. *Sales team all-hands in Western Conference room in ten minutes.*

A cold knot of dread formed in Oliver's stomach. An all-hands on ten minutes' notice? These things were usually well-choreographed events, announced days, if not weeks in advance. Something was wrong.

As he got up, a different kind of dread materialized in front of him. It was Hope. She wasn't part of the sales team and wasn't summoned to the ominous meeting.

"Hey Oliver. How have you been?" she asked, her tone casual, but her eyes holding a new, unreadable intensity.

"Good," he said, forcing a smile that felt brittle. "Just about to head to a meeting Wright called. What's up?"

Hope didn't smile back. "I saw you out in the Village last week," she said, her voice flat. "I was across the street with friends. I called out to you, but you seemed preoccupied."

"Oh, you mean last Thursday? At The Bitter End?" he said, his mind racing, trying to find the safe version of the story. "Yeah, I was there with a friend for some music. Sorry, I probably didn't see you."

"Who's this friend you were with?" Her eyes narrowed, the casual question landing like an accusation.

A mild panic began to prickle at the back of his neck. "Oh, that was Daniela. She's a family friend."

"Looked like you were really into her," she pressed on, her voice losing its friendly edge. "You were about to kiss her."

"Oh no, no. Nothing like that," he said, the denial sounding weak and defensive even to his own ears. "It must have looked that way from the angle. We were just saying goodnight."

"Are you seeing someone else, Oliver?" Her voice rose, sharp and clear, and Oliver instinctively glanced around the office, terrified of being overheard.

"Someone else? I'm not even seeing someone," he said, his own voice rising with a frantic, desperate energy. "Hope, trust me. Daniela is just a good friend. We were at her ex-boyfriend's band's event."

"Ex-boyfriend?" she latched onto the word. "So she doesn't have one now. Which means it could well be you. Oliver, how could you lie to me like this?"

"Hope, I don't understand," he pleaded, the conversation spiraling out of his control. "When did I lie? Are you talking about that night in the Catskills? That was just … things just happened, right? I didn't realize you took it to mean anything. This is the first time you've even mentioned it." The empty space of their two months of silent, polite avoidance suddenly felt like a chasm he had fallen into. The rest of the office seemed to melt away, their quiet focus a stark contrast to the loud, messy drama unfolding by his desk.

"Hope, look," he said, his voice dropping to a desperate whisper. "I'm honestly confused. Can we talk about this after work? Wright's meeting is about to start, and I think it's important."

She just glared at him, a look of pure, cold anger on her face. Then she turned and stormed away. Oliver stood there for a moment, his heart hammering, his face burning with a mixture of shame and frustration. He made his way meekly into the conference room, praying no one else had heard a thing.

"One minute late, Mr. Battolo," Wright said, his voice clipped, an unusual edge of steel in it.

The comment, so unlike Wright's usual booming cheerfulness, landed like a stone in the silent room. Oliver looked around. There were only fourteen people here, not twenty. Every face was grim, a collective brace for impact.

"Okay team, I'll get straight to the point," Wright began, dispensing with the usual pleasantries. "In light of recent events, we've had to make some tough decisions. We've had to let go of Rob, Tim, Venkat, Sri, Dan, and Emily."

The names were a series of hammer blows. *Sri is gone.* His manager. The one person who had supported his desire to do real engineering work. Oliver felt a sudden, cold sense of being untethered, his one ally in management just erased.

"Which brings me to the events that precipitated this," Wright continued, his voice a flat, unemotional monotone. "I've spent the past few weeks talking to our friends at Freddie Mac about taking Project Phoenix live. We came close, but in the end, they decided not to move forward. As a result, Phoenix has been sunset. Most of the people on that team had to be let go."

Phoenix has been sunset. The corporate euphemism was so absurd, so poetically ironic, that a bubble of hysterical laughter rose in Oliver's throat. He had to physically bite his cheek to keep it from escaping. A project named for a mythical bird of rebirth, extinguished without ever having flown.

"Also," Wright wasn't done, "we're downsizing Crestone based on market demand. Only a core team will be dedicated to it."

Good riddance, Oliver thought, a small, selfish flicker of hope that he might finally be freed from that doomed project.

"And finally," Wright said, his expression hardening, "it appears our exchange friends at Project Tarantula have gone behind our backs and hired Ascendium Consulting Group to do an audit of our technology. We found out a few days ago. Ascendium will conduct an eight-week analysis, at the end of which, they will produce a report. Tarantula will take guidance on next steps from that report."

This was the kill shot. Tarantula, their flagship project, the company's entire future, was now in the hands of a third-party consulting firm. Oliver knew he should be concerned, that his own job was now balanced on the edge of a knife. But all he felt was a strange, dark, satisfying sense of validation. A grim, quiet schadenfreude. He had seen the rot in the foundations, and now the inspectors were at the door.

"What this means," Wright concluded, trying to rally his shaken troops, "is that we're taking a short-term, all-hands-on-deck approach to Tarantula. We are putting most of our developers on that project until the report drops, to ensure all scaling and throughput issues are addressed." The words were meant to sound proactive, strategic. To Oliver, they sounded like pure, desperate panic.

As the team streamed out of the conference room, a grim, silent procession, Wright gestured for Oliver to stay behind. The door clicked shut, leaving the two of them alone in the sterile, quiet room. Wright looked at him, his usual cheerful mask gone, replaced by a weary expression.

"Oliver, I know this is probably a bit of a shock, Sri leaving," he began. "We'll try to reduce the blow. You'll report directly to me for the time being. I'm also putting you on Tarantula – that team needs all the help they can get."

"Mr. Wright, what about all the other ..." Oliver started to protest, the thought of being pulled into that failing, high-stakes project a sudden, cold dread.

"Phoenix has been sunset," Wright cut him off, his tone matter-of-fact. "And we're taking you off Crestone. You should be able to dedicate all your time to Tarantula. I know the time difference isn't great, but you'll have to put in the hard yards until the report is out. All of us will be."

"How many more weeks is this going to be?" Oliver's heart sank. The strange, demanding hours would mean no nights, no social life. Just when things with Daniela had felt so promising.

"About another five weeks," Wright replied. "They're almost three weeks into their analysis already. We'll try and stagger the shifts, but you'll likely have to come in around 3 p.m. and stay until midnight. Could have been worse – some folks are on the 7 p.m. to 4 a.m. shift." He attempted a rally, but the words fell flat. "There's good things at the end of this, Oliver. A glowing report from Ascendium will make a huge difference for our Series B. Think of the headlines."

Oliver wasn't convinced. And for the first time, he could see that Wright wasn't convinced either. The polished, inscrutable English façade had cracks in it, and underneath was a deep, weary jadedness.

"One more thing, Oliver ..." Wright said as Oliver was turning to leave. His voice had lost all its warmth, all its theatrical charm. It was flat, cold steel. "I've heard through the grapevine that you've been saying unconstructive things at the Crestone meetings. Questioning the project. Suggesting we don't use a blockchain." He paused, his eyes locking onto Oliver's. "I'm going to need you to stop that on Tarantula. You understand?"

Oliver stared back, his own shock and anger a silent, rising tide.

"We can't have that kind of behavior," Wright continued, his voice an icy whisper. "Not at a time like this. A lot of folks are on edge. We need to stay mission-focused and deliver what our customers expect – a first-in-class Web3 experience. No distractions. Is that understood?"

It wasn't a question. It was a command. A threat. Oliver just nodded quietly and left the room.

He walked back to his desk, a white-hot, silent fury building in his chest. This was the final straw. It wasn't just the ungodly hours or the doomed project. It was the reprimand. He had been punished for asking logical questions, for pointing out the emperor had no clothes. The company wanted believers. It wanted acolytes. He sat down at his desk, staring blankly at his screen, the quiet, seething rage a promise of a rebellion to come. The next few weeks were going to be hell.

CHAPTER 13. COAST

"Hey man, I heard Phoenix has been sunset." Nick walked up to Oliver's desk, a look of grim sympathy on his face.

"Yeah, we were told last week," Oliver replied, his voice flat with an exhaustion that went deeper than just lack of sleep. "Honestly, I'm not surprised. The conversations with them have been going nowhere for months."

"That sucks, man," Nick said. "I really thought we could coast with that project all the way to DC. Oh well. At least you're on Tarantula now, right? Flagship project and what not. How does it feel to be in the spotlight?"

"Not too great so far," Oliver said, rubbing his tired eyes. The long nights were blurring into a single, continuous gray day. "It's only been a few days for me, and I'm already exhausted. I'm supposed to wrap up by midnight, but it's been later than that every night. I get home around 2 a.m., but I'm too wired to sleep. I've been crashing around 5 a.m. and waking up at 10. A few days of that have already crushed me. I have no idea how I'm going to handle another five weeks of it."

"How's the project looking, though?"

A grim, humorless smile touched Oliver's lips. "It's too early for me to tell, honestly, but the initial signs aren't promising. Too much complexity in the smart contracts. I think that's what's causing the scaling issues. I'll know more once I've dug through the code a bit."

"Dude, truth be told, I'm worried about that project too," Nick said, his voice dropping to a conspiratorial whisper. "A big consulting company like Ascendium getting involved now is not a good sign. Do you know why most companies hire consultants?"

"Why?" Oliver asked, a flicker of genuine curiosity cutting through his fatigue.

"When they want a third party to deliver a message they themselves don't want to deliver," Nick said, his expression turning cynical. "You only hire an Ascendium to write a report if you already know what you want them to say, but you'd rather a respected outfit say it than you. It gives you cover and plausible deniability."

"I'm not sure I get it," Oliver said, confused. "Why would the exchange waste the money if they already know what the report is going to say?"

"Yeah, that's what everyone thinks," Nick explained, settling onto the edge of Oliver's desk. "The truth is, it's all one big game. The exchange has probably already decided our tech isn't going to work for them. But they don't want to be the ones to say it. The PR would be atrocious. People would ask why they made the decision to go with blockchain in the first place. But with a damning report from Ascendium? They can just hide behind it. 'Look, our initial analysis was promising, however our esteemed partners have uncovered some serious shortcomings …' Blah, blah, blah. It's all just a political play."

The cynical logic of it was so perfect, so depressingly plausible, that Oliver just stared at him. "Wow," he said softly. "I didn't know that's what happens."

"Consulting companies play a vital role in our economy," Nick said with a wry grin. "They're like earthworms in your compost – eating all the rotten food and shitting out fertilizer you can use to plant begonias. They're bottom feeders. They eat the worst kind of shit that sinks to the bottom, but at least they keep the lake clean."

Oliver let out a genuine laugh, the first one in days. "I need to get back to the code," he said, the momentary levity already fading.

"I hear you," Nick said, patting him on the shoulder as he walked away. "Don't let the bastards get you down."

A short while later, a stern-looking woman walked over to Oliver's desk. "Oliver, I need a few minutes of your time. Preferably now."

It was Heather Watson, the head of human resources. Her presence at his desk was as welcome as a fire alarm. Oliver's heart began to pound a slow, heavy drumbeat of dread. This was not a casual chat. He nodded and got up, his legs feeling strangely numb, and followed her back to her office.

He sat in the chair across from her, the silence in the small, sterile room amplifying the frantic thumping in his chest. Heather stared at him, her expression grim and unreadable.

"Oliver," she began, her voice devoid of any warmth, "We've received a complaint about an inappropriate advance you made toward one of our female employees. As per standard policy, we will not disclose who this person is."

Hope. The name was a certainty, a cold, hard fact that landed in the pit of his stomach. The disastrous "clear-the-air" conversation from last week flashed in his mind. He had tried to explain, to apologize for the misunderstanding, but she had been adamant. To her, that drunken night in the Catskills had been a deeply meaningful connection, a promise. To him, it was a terrible, regrettable mistake. His clumsy attempts to explain that, combined with her seeing him with Daniela, had been viewed as a betrayal, a humiliation. He had seen the hurt in her eyes curdle into a cold, hard anger before he'd finally given up and walked away. This was her response.

Heather continued, her voice a flat, bureaucratic monotone. "We've had a chance to evaluate the evidence provided to us and have classified it as a 'yellow' violation of our harassment policy. Are you familiar with our scale, Oliver?"

He nodded, his mouth too dry to speak. He remembered the mandatory training video, the color-coded system of infractions. Blue for a minor offense, a three-strike rule. Red for the most egregious cases, instant termination. And yellow, the one he was now accused of, for intentionally hurtful and derogatory comments. A two-strike policy. He was halfway to being fired based on a conversation he hadn't understood he was even in.

He started to speak, to protest, to explain *his* side of the story, but Heather held up a hand, a gesture that was both a stop sign and a dismissal.

"As you know, Oliver, there is no discussion on these topics. The victim is always right." The words were a corporate mantra, an unshakeable dogma that slammed the door on any possibility of nuance or defense. "You have a yellow violation. One more of these can have very serious implications for your role at BlockWaves, up to and including termination. Please bear this in mind as you conduct yourself with your colleagues going forward."

He was being sentenced without a trial. He left Heather's office in a daze, the injustice of it a white-hot, silent scream in his mind. By the time he got back to his desk, the shock had burned away, leaving only a pure, seething rage. He had been falsely accused, convicted, and sentenced, all without being allowed to speak a single word in his own defense. How could he have been so wrong about Hope? This was a calculated, vindictive act.

He was furious with her, but he was even more furious with himself. For letting his guard down. For being so stupidly, blindly naive. He had gone against his better judgment that night in the mountains, and now he was paying the price. The lesson was brutal, and it was clear. The people you work with, their interactions governed by the cold, bureaucratic calculus of an HR contract, are not your friends. They were never your friends.

747091 (July 29)

"Another bad day, Batlu?" the Noncemeister's voice asked, impossibly innocent. The voice was coming from the ceiling. Oliver looked up to see him floating there, upside down, legs crossed, casually reading a newspaper that was also upside down. "You look like a fuss ran over you."

"You mean *bus*," Oliver said, his voice flat and dead.

"What's a bus?" the Noncemeister asked, with an expression of genuine puzzlement.

"You don't know what a bus is? It's a … argh, never mind." Oliver was too tired to explain public transportation to a hallucination. "Yes. I look like a fuss ran over me. Let's go with that."

"Well, you do," the Noncemeister said, and as he spoke, a small, furry, multi-legged creature labeled 'FUSS' materialized in the void, scurried down the invisible wall, ran right over Oliver's exhausted form, and disappeared into the floor. "What's the fuss about?"

"I'll tell you what it's about," Oliver said, not even flinching at the bizarre display. "It's 10:30 in the morning and I just woke up. After falling asleep at 6 a.m. Because I got home at 3 a.m. Because I'm too much of a wuss to tell my boss to stick his stupid project where the sun doesn't shine. I haven't had more than five hours of sleep in two weeks."

"So that's what a bus is? Something you tell to stick its head where the sun doesn't shine?"

"What? No, I said *boss*," Oliver said, his patience, already thin from sleep deprivation, beginning to fray. "The bus thing is over. I was talking about my boss." He was trapped again. No escape until the lesson was over.

"Why don't you sleep more?" the Noncemeister asked, floating down to stand in front of him, the newspaper vanishing in a puff of purple smoke.

"Because I can't," Oliver said, the words a litany of his own private hell. "I'm either writing code or on non-stop Zoom calls with folks on the other side of the world trying to debug their code until 3 a.m., and when I get home, I'm too wired to fall asleep."

"Sounds like this isn't serving you well," the Noncemeister said, his tone suddenly serious. "Why don't you tell them you don't want to do this anymore?"

"Because … because if I do …" The thought, so simple and direct, had never really occurred to him. "Well, okay, here's why: if I do, I'll probably get fired."

"I thought you don't like this job," the Noncemeister continued, tilting his head with an innocent curiosity. "Losing it sounds like a good outcome, no?"

"Yeah, sure, but then how do I pay my bills? We've been over this before."

"Indeed we have," the Noncemeister said, beginning to pace. "And I already told you that life happens for you, not to you. Have you considered that you're being presented with this opportunity to finally make a decision that could change your life? How much longer did you think you could coast through this situation without having to do something about it? Now is your chance, Batew. Do the right thing."

"What is the right thing? Depriving myself of a livelihood?" Oliver asked, incredulously.

"You don't trust the process, Battulu," the Noncemeister smiled, stopping his pacing. He gestured, and a high, narrow precipice materialized beneath Oliver's feet, a sheer drop into the endless purple void. "That is the problem here. You are correct that a net doesn't exist yet. More precisely, you are currently unaware that a net exists. But that is because you haven't jumped yet. Jump, and the net will appear. So it goes."

"Take a leap of faith and something will work out magically?" Oliver said with a short, ironic laugh. "Yeah, I don't think I'm ready for that new-age gobbledygook. And I can't let my team down. There are people depending on me. What if we get a bad report from Ascendium? Then the company is toast."

"And what would happen then?" the Noncemeister asked.

"Then I'd be out of a job," Oliver replied.

"And that's a bad thing because?"

"Come on, man!" Oliver said, exasperated, throwing his hands up in the air. "How many times do we have to talk about the same thing?"

"You're not answering my question," the Noncemeister said, his tone softening as he floated closer, the precipice beneath Oliver's feet vanishing, replaced by solid, featureless ground. "It sounds like either way you're out of a job, which is really what you want. You said so yourself. Not the conscious-mind-eejit version of you that's worrying about money, but your unconscious true self." As he spoke, a shimmering, translucent version of Oliver, looking serene and confident, stepped out of Oliver's own body and gave him a calm, knowing wink before dissolving. "It craves adventure and creativity. Once you strip out all the distractions, all the illusions; once you step out of the phenomenal into the absolute, you will see that all that's there is pure love. And that is where creativity resides. Creativity is an act of pure self-love. It is an act of discovery and adventure. It is not the pursuit of happiness: it is indeed happiness in and of itself."

"You're forgetting the teeny-tiny possibility that we can actually make this thing work," Oliver interjected, clinging to the last shred of his old reality. "We get a good report, the project continues, the company thrives."

The Noncemeister's eyebrow rose so high it nearly flew off his bald head. "Do you want that to be true?"

Oliver paused. He searched his own feelings, past the fear and the anxiety, and found the hard, undeniable truth. He was tired of the charade. He wanted it to be over. "I'm not sure," he finally replied, the lie feeling thin and useless.

"Battu, there is a tiger within you. Stop being a lamb." The Noncemeister's voice became a powerful, resonant boom that seemed to shake the purple void. "You are everything you need to be, you already are. You have nothing to prove to anyone. You just need to *accept* that reality – that will bring you peace. You need to *trust* that reality – that will bring you love. And finally, you need to *know* that reality – that will bring you joy." He floated forward and gave Oliver a light, friendly punch on the chest that somehow felt as solid as a real one.

"There is one other thing that's related, I guess," Oliver said, the words coming out before he could stop them, a confession to this strange, all-knowing entity.

"Go on."

"I think I'm in love with a girl, but I'm honestly not sure if she feels the same way. I don't want to mess things up by making the wrong move."

"A girl?" the Noncemeister asked, his serious demeanor instantly vanishing.

"Yes, that's what I said."

The Noncemeister let out a low whistle and began wiggling his eyebrows up and down with comical speed. "Well, you really are a big boy now, aren't you? Talking about girls and everything." He began to shrink, his form compressing until he was the size of a small doll, his voice becoming high and squeaky. "The last time we spoke, and let's see, that must have been about five hundred and seventy thousand heartbeats ago, you never said anything about girls."

"What are you talking about?" Oliver did the math in his head. *Ten years ago.* "We last spoke about a week or two ago, not ten years ago."

"Week? Years? Strange words again, Battolo," the tiny Noncemeister squeaked, peering up at him. "I'm not talking about the last time we talked *this* time, but the last time we talked *last* time."

"You mean back when my dad used to tell me bedtime stories about you?" Oliver said, the memory suddenly sharp and clear. "That was longer than ten years ago. I must have been eight, so that would be …" he ran the numbers, translating his life into this strange new language, "… at least nine hundred thousand heartbeats ago." As he said the number, the Noncemeister instantly popped back to his full size, a wide, knowing grin on his face.

"You are incorrect, Battu." The Noncemeister crossed his arms in a firm X, the playful energy gone, replaced by an unshakeable certainty. As he spoke, the purple void around them shimmered, and a ghostly, translucent image of a much younger Oliver, maybe thirteen years old, flickered into existence for a moment before vanishing. "I know what I'm talking about. It was five hundred and seventy thousand heartbeats ago. That was when I taught you everything. But they made you forget everything. And then you knew nothing. And so I taught you everything again. Well," he shrugged, "I'm still teaching you, but you might get there soon."

Oliver was now completely puzzled. Ten years ago? When he was thirteen? His dad certainly wasn't telling him bedtime stories then. And who were "they"? "What do you mean, 'they' made me forget?" he asked, the question a cold stone in his stomach.

"Ah, water under the bridge now, Battu," the Noncemeister sighed, and as he did, the featureless floor beneath their feet transformed into a glittering, sandy coastline, stretching out to meet a vast, dark, silent ocean. "As the coast is not the ocean, so that timeline is not this one. So it goes. It is time to move on."

Oliver stared at the impossible shoreline, his mind racing. Was this related to the hazy, forgotten memories of that time? Not remembering Gyorgy, his parents' fights … Was it all connected?

"Anywho, you were talking about a girl," the Noncemeister continued, the beach vanishing as quickly as it had appeared, returning them to the empty void. "Tell me more."

"That's pretty much it," Oliver said, feeling embarrassed to be discussing his love life with a figment of his imagination. "I somehow don't have the spine to show more initiative. I think I'm in love with her, but I can't bring myself to do anything about it."

"You *think* you're in love? Do you know it?" the Noncemeister asked, his gaze sharp and piercing.

"Well, yes. How can I know for sure? I'm attracted to her, and I like spending time with her," Oliver replied.

"You need to know, Batlu. Knowing is the only stable state of mind. Right now, you are unstable." To demonstrate, the Noncemeister wobbled precariously on one foot, his arms flailing wildly before he regained his balance with a theatrical flourish.

"Great, so how do I know?" Oliver asked, putting his hands on his hips.

"The net is already there, Battolo. Always has been. You need to jump," the Noncemeister said, and the precipice reappeared beneath Oliver's feet. "Remember, you are exactly where you need to be, you already are. Once you know that there is no such thing as a wrong action, all your actions will be inspired. Accept, trust, and know. Then you can do."

"I can do?" Oliver asked, confused by the strange, unfinished sentence.

"Yes, do. Doing is an extension of being," the Noncemeister replied, his voice calm and centered. "Acknowledging that all you need to do is just be is what leads you to inspired action."

Oliver stood on the edge of the imaginary cliff, the Noncemeister's words echoing in the void. He pieced it all together, the lessons from his job and his heart converging into a single, terrifyingly simple truth. "Okay," he said slowly, "I think I know where you're going with this. As with my job, I shouldn't second-guess all the possible outcomes, but just do what feels right in the moment. If it feels right to quit, then I should quit and not worry about the consequences, because those will just shape my path. If it feels right to show more initiative with Daniela, I should do it and not worry about rejection, because either way, it will bring me closure. Did I get that right?"

"Indeed, you did," the Noncemeister smiled, a look of genuine pride on his face. "Remember, acceptance brings peace; trust brings love, and knowing brings joy. That is how you act through inspired action."

Oliver shrugged, the precipice beneath him solidifying into a firm, stable floor. It was worth a shot. All said and done, what did he really have to lose?

"Batue, before I let you go," the Noncemeister said, his playful tone gone again, replaced by a keen, penetrating focus, "I notice there is something else on your mind."

Oliver paused, surprised by the shift. He remembered the projection at the concert. "Yes, there is. I saw something called *Camara del Tiempo*, but I don't know what it is. Do you?"

"Why didn't you ask me earlier, you silly billy?" The Noncemeister's playful energy returned in a rush. "Here, look." He gestured with a grand flourish, and the purple void in front of them rippled and tore open, revealing the scene from Oliver's memory: the small, windowless chamber, the single, heavy wooden door.

Oliver saw the words again, carved into the wood: *Camara del Tiempo*. He instinctively reached into his pocket and felt the cold, solid weight of the cast-iron key. He stepped forward, twisted the lock, and the bolt snapped open. The door swung inward, revealing a purple-black darkness and the faint, rhythmic sound of a distant hum.

"You can walk in, Battu," the Noncemeister said softly from behind him. "I took you here once before, but you have forgotten. You can go again."

Oliver stepped cautiously into the dark room. The rhythmic hum grew louder, resolving itself into a low, hypnotic chant. Beneath it, another sound, more distant: the gentle, ceaseless crash of waves against a coastline. The air carried a faint smell of iodine. As his eyes adjusted to the gloom, a hazy silhouette of a person took shape in the purple blackness. The person was sitting with his back to Oliver, chanting. There was something about the shape of his shoulders, the set of his head, that was deeply, achingly familiar.

The words of the chant were audible now, echoing off the high, unseen ceilings. *Ex igne, tempus nascitur.* Over and over. *Out of fire, time is born.* The Noncemeister's words, a cryptic parting shot from weeks ago, now a mantra in this strange, sacred space.

Oliver listened, mesmerized. As he took a step closer, the silhouette seemed to sense his presence and turned. The chant stopped. A deathly silence fell, broken only by the sound of the waves. Oliver couldn't make out the face in the darkness, but he was certain he knew this person. The figure seemed to recognize him, too, and in a single, fluid motion, got up and walked away, disappearing hastily into the blackness.

The moment he vanished, Oliver felt himself yanked backwards, sucked out of the room in a rapid, disorienting rush. The door slammed shut, the sound echoing with a deafening finality. The Noncemeister was waiting for him outside.

"Well, well, well, Battulu. Looks like you were almost ready to find out what was in there, but not quite."

"What the hell was that all about?" Oliver asked, gathering himself.

"You wanted to see the Chamber of Time, Battu, so I showed it to you."

"Is it a real place? Is it in Pittamiglio's castle in Uruguay?"

"It is as real as real can be," the Noncemeister said mysteriously. "No more, no less."

"That's not helpful. Who was that person chanting inside? I could have sworn I knew who that was."

"If you didn't know who that was, then the time was not right for you to know," he said, his voice maddeningly serene. "When the time is right, the tables will turn, and you will know."

"Tables will turn? What on Earth are you talking about?"

The Noncemeister laughed, a short, sharp sound. "Perspectives will invert and what you thought was not you, will be you, and vice versa. It's a lot for one day, tiger. Now go get 'em."

And with a final, sharp snap of his fingers, the world shattered, and Oliver found himself back in his dad's armchair, the echo of the crashing waves and the lingering scent of iodine still with him.

747409 (July 31)

Oliver walked up to 39 Carmine Street and saw the main building entrance was slightly ajar. He pushed his way through, bypassing the buzzer, and started up the four flights of stairs. As he made his way up, a woman was descending.

She walked past him on the narrow staircase without a glance, but her face snagged in Oliver's memory. He stopped, thinking hard for a moment. It was Adele. Christiaan van der Dussen's sister. What on earth was she doing here? Coming out of Maren's studio? A cold, prickling suspicion began to form in the back of his mind.

He knocked on Maren's door. It opened, and she was there, her face a mask of warmth. "So good to see you again, Oliver!" She gave him a hug that felt a little too tight, a little too long, and then showed him into the studio.

She had returned a few days ago from her extended trip to India, looking rested and tan. "How was it?" Oliver asked, the question a polite placeholder for the ones that were now screaming in his mind.

"Hot, and then the monsoons began," she said. "But it was wonderful to see old faces. Guru Brahma is his usual self. No sign of slowing down."

Oliver decided to go straight at it. "Hey Maren," he said, his tone casual, "I think I just saw Adele in the building. Christiaan van der Dussen's sister. Was she just coming from here?"

He saw it. Just for a fraction of a second, but it was there. A flicker of deep panic in Maren's eyes before her professional calm slammed back down like a shutter. "Oh yes. She stopped by," she said, her voice a little too bright. "I can't really talk more about it. Client confidentiality. Just like I wouldn't mention anything about you."

Oliver just soaked it in. The reaction had been defensive, nervous, and deeply suspicious.

"So tell me, Oliver," she said, changing the subject with a practiced ease, "how has the quest been going? How many words are you at right now?"

The question, so direct, so probing, didn't sit right. It felt less like a therapist's inquiry and more like a shareholder asking for a status update. He made a split-second decision. He would not tell her the full truth. "It's going well," he said, keeping his voice even. "Slow progress. I'm at twelve words now. Halfway there." He left it at that, a deliberate, partial truth.

He was wrong to think that would be enough.

"Do you remember them?" she asked, her gaze a little too intense.

The question was a confirmation. She was fishing. "Not off the top of my head," he lied, even as the sequence of twelve perfect words scrolled through his mind. "I'd have to look at my notes."

"Well, it looks like you've become quite the expert in time projection," Maren said, her usual serene manner returning, the mask perfectly back in place.

Oliver had a dozen questions he'd wanted to ask her – about the Noncemeister, about the blurring line between reality and projection, about the anger and confusion that were his new constant companions. But after her strange, panicked reaction to Adele, after the pointed, almost greedy questions about his father's seed phrase, he decided against it. Something was fishy. The trust he'd placed in her, his only guide, was beginning to fray at the edges.

He did have one last question, though, one he felt was safe enough to ask. "Maren," he began, "For some reason, I can't remember much from when I was around twelve or thirteen years old. I know I was having trouble in school, and my parents brought me to you. But beyond that … it's all a black hole. People I met, things that were happening at home … it's all gone."

Once again, a small crack appeared in Maren's composure. "Yes," she said, her gaze drifting away from his, finding a sudden, intense interest in a crystal on a nearby shelf. "You were having trouble back then, and I was able to help."

"What sort of trouble? And why can't I remember it?" Oliver persisted, sensing her discomfort.

"You were … you were hearing things, Oliver," she said, her words chosen with a slow, deliberate caution that set off alarm bells in his mind. "And I worked with you to make you forget those things. Maybe your subconscious mind erased some surrounding memories as well. Some light collateral damage."

Collateral damage. The clinical, dismissive phrase chilled him. Something had clearly happened, and the only people who knew were either dead or, in Maren's case, actively stonewalling him. *Wait. Mom was there. Maybe she knows.*

"What do you mean, 'hearing things?'" he asked, a new, personal fear creeping in. "You mean voices in my head?" The thought of Bryce, of the "Energetic downloads" that guided his hand, was suddenly a terrifying parallel.

"Oliver, this is all in the past," Maren said, her voice strained, her discomfort now obvious. "You are over it now. You have become an expert in projection. What happened in the past doesn't matter anymore."

"But I deserve to know," he insisted, his voice rising with a new anger. "This happened to me, and you were involved in making me forget it. Don't you think I deserve an answer?"

Maren let out a long, slow sigh, a sound of reluctant concession. "Oliver, here's what I can tell you," she began, her tone shifting, becoming a lecture. "There is a reason projection comes so easily to you. A reason you have such a different experience. It came easily to your father, as well."

The mention of his father silenced his anger. He listened, his focus absolute.

"In all my years teaching this, I have only come across one person who had a supremely special gift," Maren continued. "His mind had no constraints. He could step through his conscious, subconscious, and unconscious minds with ease. That person was your father. He already had this gift before I met him, and he was able to harness it and surpass even me. I long suspected synesthesia was the reason – the ability for the senses to interchange, breaking all barriers that tie us to this superficial reality."

"So you're saying my dad was a master at time projection?" Oliver asked, the information a stunning, world-altering revelation.

"Yes," Maren said, her voice dropping. "So much so that he even developed the ability to enter into other people's projections and change what they saw. For your dad, it became a tool to shape reality. And you have the same gift, Oliver. I knew it as soon as you described your first episode, but I didn't want to scare you. Even I am unable to do the things you do. Please," she said, her eyes finally meeting his, "be careful with how you use this gift."

Oliver listened in shock. The Noncemeister. The clues. Was his dad guiding him from beyond the grave? It was impossible. But if what Maren said was true … and now, to find out that he might have that same, terrifying power …

Just then, Maren's phone, sitting on the table beside him, began to ring. He glanced at it instinctively. The caller ID glowed with two words: *Bojan M.*

The name was a lightning strike. *Bojan Mitrovic.* The Serbian art broker Gyorgy had mentioned. The man who had sold Bryce's third painting. *How on Earth did he know Maren?*

Maren picked up the phone, glanced at the screen, silenced the call with a practiced flick of her thumb, and put it away. The casual, dismissive action was more damning than any confession.

Oliver spent a few more minutes talking, his mind a whirlwind, but the conversation was over. His head was spinning. Adele. The erased memories. His father's impossible power. And now Bojan. The connections were too many, too specific to be a coincidence. He was now certain he could not trust her. She was far more involved in this than she had ever let on. Maybe she knew about the seed phrase all along. Maybe she wanted in.

He left her apartment, the friendly hug at the door feeling like a cold, calculated performance. As he walked out into the summer afternoon, one thought was crystal clear in his mind. The coast was not clear. Not at all.

The Notepad

i) violin ii) toddler iii) alley iv) shoulder v) educate vi) rookie vii) oval viii) below ix) punch x) certain xi) cover xii) agree xiii) coast

CHAPTER 14. SUGGEST

"It's so nice to hear your voice, sweetheart!" his mom's voice said, a bright, cheerful sound that felt like it was coming from a different planet. "I've been meaning to call, but my women's group has been so busy."

"All good, Mom," Oliver said, the lie coming easily now. "Work moved me to a crazy schedule for a few weeks, so I've been slammed."

"So, to what do I owe the pleasure of my busy son finding the time to talk to me today?" she asked, the question laced with a gentle passive aggression that Oliver knew all too well.

"Don't be silly, Mom," he said, deciding not to take the bait. "I did want to talk to you about something that's been bugging me, though."

"Of course, baby. You know you can talk to me about anything."

He took a breath. "Mom, I've been having trouble remembering stuff from when I was twelve and thirteen. I know I was having issues at school and that you and Dad took me to Maren, but it's all a blank. Do you know what happened?"

The cheerful energy on the other end of the line vanished. A heavy silence stretched for a few moments. "Why are you asking about this now, Oliver?" she asked, her voice cautious. "Did you just remember something?"

He thought about telling her about Gyorgy, about the voices, about everything. But he remembered her panicked reaction the last time he'd mentioned "secrets." He retreated to a half-truth. "I've just been trying to remember things from back then. Being back in the Chelsea apartment … it's triggered a lot of old memories. But that whole time period is just … a blank."

More silence. He could almost hear her grappling with a decision on the other end of the line. "Oliver," she said finally, "this is a strange topic. It's best we don't talk about it."

"What are you talking about, Mom?" His irritation flared, hot and immediate. "You can't just say that and expect me to drop it. You have to tell me what happened."

Another long, agonizing pause. "Honey," she said, her voice strained, "your dad and I spoke about it back then. We thought it was best not to talk to you about that time."

"Well, you can't hide it from me forever," he snapped, his frustration boiling over. "I demand to know."

He heard her let out a long, weary sigh, the sound of a mother's surrender. "Sweetheart, you were going through a strange phase back then," she said, her voice a low, fearful whisper, as if the memory itself was dangerous. "You started hearing voices in your head. You were repeating things to us. Things you couldn't have possibly known at that age. Things that made no sense."

A cold dread washed over Oliver, a grim, chilling confirmation. "What sort of things?"

"I barely remember. I've tried to forget, to be honest, because it was so scary," she said, her voice trembling slightly. "You kept saying something about a 'non-master' or something like that. And something about a chain … and entropy … and time. It was all just nonsense. I was so worried. We were about to take you to a psychiatrist, but your dad … he was the one to suggest we see Maren first. Surprisingly, he wasn't as worried as I was. But he did want to get it fixed."

Oliver stood in the middle of his apartment, the phone pressed to his ear, his mind reeling. *Non-master. Chain. Entropy. Time.* The Noncemeister. It had been him, even back then. But how? He was too young. Bitcoin had barely existed. The words, the concepts … it was impossible.

"Wait, so I was using all these words, and saying a voice in my head was telling me to use them?" Oliver asked, his own voice a quiet, fearful whisper.

"Yes," his mother confirmed. "You only told us about it when you were thirteen, I think. You'd been keeping it to yourself for months. Then one day, you just burst out, talking about this 'non-master' person who kept telling you things. Your teachers had been complaining for a while, but it took us some time to put it all together." Her voice hardened, the old bitterness creeping in. "I think it was the trauma. Your dad and I had started fighting around then. I blame him. If he hadn't had all those affairs, you would have been just fine. It was his fault, as usual."

"Mom, can you please stop?" Oliver snapped, the accusation a grating sound he couldn't bear to hear, not now. "I can't have this conversation. You know what I think about that. Can we please just get back to what happened to me?"

He heard a sharp intake of breath on the other end of the line, the sound of a wounded retreat. "So," she continued, her voice now cold and clinical, "When we realized this had been going on for months, your dad took you to Maren. And after a couple of sessions, it all miraculously went away. She did say she was going to make you forget some things, so it's possible that's why your memory is so foggy from back then. I still don't know what she did, but it seemed to work."

"So that was it?" Oliver asked, struggling to believe the story was so simple, so clean. "I heard voices, you took me to Maren, and she fixed me?"

"Yes. But it was a scary time," she said, her voice softening again. "I was so worried you had psychiatric issues."

He didn't get any more out of her. She had walled off the memory, burying it under years of her own narrative. But it was enough. As he hung up the phone, the pieces of the last ten years of his life began to violently rearrange themselves in his mind.

The Noncemeister had been there, in his head, when he was twelve or thirteen. He had been teaching him, telling him things about the timechain, about bitcoin. He had kept it a secret, a strange and wonderful world inside his own mind, until he couldn't anymore. And his parents, terrified, had taken him to Maren. And Maren ... Maren had erased it. She had performed a kind of psychic surgery, cutting out the memories, leaving a black hole of forgetting in their place.

It was what the Noncemeister had meant all along. *I taught you everything, but they made you forget.* It wasn't a riddle. It was a literal, historical fact.

He stood in the middle of his apartment, the revelation a terrifying, exhilarating earthquake. He had to know what happened in that lost year. He had to see it for himself. He had to go back.

748740 (August 9)

Oliver stared at the spaghetti code on his screen with a dull, throbbing disgust. It was a tangled mess, a knot of someone else's bad decisions that he was now being paid to unravel. It was past 6 p.m., and he'd been wrestling with the same broken module for three hours, getting nowhere. He heard footsteps and swiveled in his chair to see Nick approaching, a cheerful, end-of-week energy radiating off him.

"Guess you're not heading out to O'Connell's with us, then," Nick said.

"No, man. I'm on the night shift, remember?" Oliver said, the words heavy with a gloom he couldn't hide. "My social life is canceled for the foreseeable future."

"We're not devs like you," Nick replied, a note of sympathy in his voice. "The whole company is focused on this Ascendium report. At least all the devs are. Leaves folks like me at loose ends. Gotta keep ourselves busy."

"When are you guys heading there?" Oliver asked, a fleeting, foolish fantasy of a single, cold beer momentarily distracting him.

"About thirty minutes. Olumide needs to wrap up a review."

"No, man, I can't," Oliver said, letting the fantasy go. "I'm tempted, but I've got to refactor these modules before midnight. Even one beer will slow me down."

"Hey, did you see?" Nick pulled up a chair, his voice dropping to a conspiratorial, excited whisper. "The Merge is going to happen in about three or four weeks. First or second week of September."

The Merge. The great hope of the ethereum world. Oliver had been hearing about it for years, a perpetually-on-the-horizon software upgrade that was supposed to fix everything. Proponents like Nick claimed it would make the network faster, more scalable, and – the key selling point – far better for the environment than bitcoin.

But Oliver wasn't buying it anymore. The lessons from Vince and the Noncemeister had fundamentally rewired his understanding. He saw the energy debate as a deliberate misdirection, a red herring. He now understood that the entire point of a timechain was to create an unbreakable, unambiguous order of time without a central ruler. The only way to do that fairly, the only way to anchor it to physical reality, was to harness the raw, chaotic energy of the universe itself. It was making sense out of nonces. It was proof of work.

This new thing, proof of stake, felt like a betrayal of that core principle. It was taking the power to order time away from the chaotic honesty of pure energy and handing it over to a small, privileged group of "stakers" – in other words, back to corruptible human beings. This was hardly a technological evolution. This was a regression, a quiet coup. Any claim ethereum had to true decentralization was, in his mind, about to go out the window.

"Dude, it's going to be epic," Nick said, his eyes shining with the manic, born-again fervor of a man who'd found a new religion just days after his last one had collapsed in a fiery wreck. "This is the moment we've all been waiting for. The Merge is not priced in. ETH is going to go parabolic. The flippening is imminent."

Oliver just listened, the words a well-worn litany of crypto-twitter buzzwords. The "Flippening" – the long-prophesied day when ethereum's total market value would surpass bitcoin's.

"What makes you think it isn't priced in?" Oliver asked, his tone quiet, genuinely curious.

"Because the boomers in DC are all being fed the maxi narrative," Nick shot back. "They're all parroting the same line that bitcoin is the only 'stable' crypto asset. It's not. Bitcoin is a joke, and it needs to die a painful death. And it will. Ethereum is ultra-sound money, and the Merge is going to prove it."

A few months ago, Oliver would have nodded along. Now, after the lessons from Vince and the Noncemeister, the words felt hollow, a desperate marketing slogan. "How is it 'ultra-sound money?'" he asked, unable to resist. "How does it do anything meaningful better than bitcoin?"

"Dude, what are you even talking about?" Nick exclaimed, a look of genuine betrayal on his face. "You're beginning to sound like a maxi. I knew I shouldn't have introduced you to Vince!"

"That's your answer?" Oliver raised an eyebrow.

"No, of course not," Nick said, scrambling to find his talking points. "Look, with proof of stake, the stakers will ensure no more ether is created. It will actually be deflationary. In bitcoin, the supply is still increasing."

"It's increasing at a fixed, predictable schedule that no one can change," Oliver countered calmly. "Who decides if more ether gets burned than is issued?"

"The stakers and the core developers, of course," Nick said.

"And what does it take to be a staker?"

"Currently, you need thirty-two ether."

Oliver did the math. "So, you need over fifty thousand dollars to be able to participate in securing the network?" he asked, unable to hide his incredulity.

"Yeah, that sounds about right," Nick replied, not seeing the problem.

"How can that ever be decentralized, then?" Oliver asked. "Normal people don't have fifty grand to just lock up. It's a system that gives all the power to the wealthy. A plutocracy. And they haven't even written the code for you to get your money back out, right? It's locked up indefinitely."

"Of course they're going to write the code for it, dude," Nick said, surprised. "Why wouldn't they?"

"Because people will start dumping their ETH if they can un-stake it?" Oliver suggested. "They want to prevent a bank run."

"Listen, man, you've got to trust these guys a little more," Nick said, his voice full of a mystifying earnestness. "They're trying to build a world computer, not steal your money."

Trust them. The words hung in the air, a perfect summary of the difference between their two worlds.

"Okay, so these stakers," Oliver continued, pressing the point, "They control the rules now, right? How do you know they'll vote to keep the supply deflationary?"

"They're incentivized to protect the network," Nick retorted. "Their own wealth is at stake."

"So we just have to trust them?" Oliver asked, almost laughing at the simplicity of it.

"Trust their instinct for self-preservation," Nick shot back.

Oliver just looked at his friend, at the desperate hope in his eyes, and felt a profound sense of distance. "I'd rather not trust any human," he said calmly, the words a quiet declaration of his new-found philosophy. "I like math. And I like rules in code that I can verify."

"Then you're going to miss out on the Web3 rocket ship, dude," Nick said, his voice a mixture of pity and frustration. "What can I tell you? We're changing finance, banking, supply chains, you name it."

"How are you changing any of those things?" Oliver asked, his voice quiet, the question a simple, sharp needle aimed at the balloon of Nick's hype. "None of our clients take the tech past the experiment stage. They back down when they realize the real-world implications."

Nick closed his eyes and let out a deep, theatrical sigh, the sound of a patient teacher dealing with a slow student. "Oliver, you're talking about a handful of anecdotes. The real pioneers haven't stepped up yet. But they will. Once they realize every legal contract can be a smart contract, every asset can be a token … it's a game changer. Mortgage payments, real estate transfers, all settling on the blockchain with instant value transfer."

"And how are disputes handled for these contracts?" Oliver challenged.

"Code is law!" Nick slapped the desk with his palm for emphasis, his face bright with the certainty of a true believer. "The smart contract dictates all possible scenarios. The proof is on the blockchain."

"These are legal contracts," Oliver said, his voice a calm, immovable counterpoint. "With decades of precedent. Do you really think a judge is going to look at smart contract code to arbitrate a real estate dispute? No. The judge is going to use the law."

"But why would he need to?" Nick asked, his earnestness now bordering on desperation. "The smart contract can enforce all the rules!"

"First of all," Oliver said, dismantling the argument piece by piece, "Most of these blockchains are run by foundations or companies. We know this because that's what we build. These so-called 'proofs' can be changed or reversed. But more importantly, code is *not* law. Law is law. All these use-cases involving real-world assets will always be subservient to the law of the land. The only scenario where that might work is for a truly digitally native asset that's not governed by any single jurisdiction."

The argument silenced Nick for a moment. He scrambled, reaching for the grandest, most absurd talking point he had. "Dude, you're missing the forest for the trees. In the future we're building, the Constitution and the law *itself* will be a smart contract. We won't need judges and juries. The path will be messy, sure, but you can't lose sight of the end game."

Oliver almost laughed. The sheer, unadulterated absurdity of it was breathtaking. Instead, he controlled himself and delivered his final, quiet conclusion, the words a summary of everything he had come to believe. "That's just not going to happen. For it to happen, you would need an incontrovertible base layer that can't be changed by anyone. The more bells and whistles you add, the more complex and less secure you make it, and then it stops being reliable. Maybe there are a handful of use cases, like ticket sales, but a database would still be better for those. In any case, I'm not interested in any of that, because it has minimal real-world impact." He looked at Nick, his gaze direct and clear. "If we fix the money, that will fix a lot of other issues. Money is just an information system, a language. And we need a simple language governed by rules, not rulers. That's what I want to focus on."

The words hung in the air between them, a declaration of a fundamental, unbridgeable divide. Nick just stared at him, the enthusiastic energy finally drained from his face. "I don't know, man," he said, his voice quiet. "It seems like you're pretty far gone down the bitcoin maxi rabbit hole. I'm not sure why you're still working here, to be honest. And I'm saying that as a friend."

Oliver looked out at the city, at the world of BlockWaves and its empty promises, and then back at his friend, a man he no longer understood. "I'm not sure either," he concluded.

748993 (August 11)

A blinding white light filled the void, a light that wasn't hot or harsh, but silent, pure, and absolute. It coalesced into a long, featureless corridor that stretched into an infinite, luminous distance. A figure was walking slowly away from him, his form a dark, familiar silhouette against the overwhelming brightness.

A jolt of unbridled joy shot through Oliver. "Dad!" he called out, his voice a choked, desperate cry. "Dad, it's me, Oliver! I'm right behind you. Dad, turn around!"

But the figure couldn't hear him. He just continued his slow, deliberate walk, his gentle footsteps the only sound in the vast, white silence. Oliver fought against the invisible constraints of the projection, desperately trying to change his perspective, to move in front of him, to see his face. It was useless. He was just an observer, a ghost tethered to his father's back.

At the far end of the corridor, a door appeared, already open. Nate turned and walked inside. The room was sparse, lit by the same intense, shadowless light. In the center was a single bed, and on it, a frail, withered figure lay sleeping. It was Gyorgy.

Gyorgy opened his eyes as Nate entered, and a weak, fragile smile touched his lips. "You're finally here," Gyorgy whispered, his voice a dry rustle of leaves. "I knew Oliver wouldn't let me down." He then turned his head, his gaze seeming to look past Nate, past the white walls, across time itself, and smiled directly at Oliver, the unseen observer.

Nate, his back still to Oliver, simply walked to the bedside. He reached out and took Gyorgy's thin, papery hand in his own.

"I forgive you," Nate said, his voice a low, gentle rumble, full of a peace that seemed to emanate from the light itself. "Everything that has happened is behind us. I love you, dear friend, and I am letting go of the past. You are released. You are now free. I forgive you."

Gyorgy listened, his eyes filling with tears that traced slow, glistening paths through the landscape of his weary face. With a great effort, he lifted his other hand and placed it over Nate's, clasping it between both of his. "Thank you, old friend," he rasped, the words a final exhalation of a lifetime of regret. "Thank you from the bottom of my heart. I love you too. I can go in peace now."

Nate just nodded.

Gyorgy's gaze found Oliver again. "That boy of yours right there," he said, his voice a thread, "You have done a fine job of raising him. He will surpass you, and of that, you should be proud."

Nate nodded again, his back still turned. But somehow, Oliver knew. He could feel it across the impossible distance, a warmth that needed no sight to be seen. He knew, with an absolute and heart-wrenching certainty, that his father was smiling.

Gyorgy's hands, their final task complete, slowly dropped to his sides. His eyes fluttered and closed. His head fell limply to the side, a final, quiet surrender.

And then the light, already so bright, intensified. It grew until it was no longer a light but a presence, a pure, white, all-consuming energy that dissolved the room, the bed, the two figures, everything, into its own serene, silent essence. The brilliance was too much to bear. Oliver had no choice but to open his eyes, and with a gasp, he found himself back in the dim light of his dad's armchair, the ghost of a single, silent tear cool upon his cheek.

749539 (August 15)

The blare of the alarm was a physical assault. *Raar, raar, raar.* The iPhone's default setting, a sound he kept meaning to change but never did. It was the worst possible way to be ripped from sleep.

7:30 a.m. The earliest he'd woken up in weeks. A strange, ominous email had arrived from the CEO late Sunday afternoon, summoning the entire company to a 9 a.m. all-hands meeting and declaring an immediate end to the brutal night-shift schedule. It didn't sound like good news.

He dragged himself out of bed and into the city. By the time he arrived at the office, the common room was already filling up, not with the usual Monday morning chatter, but with small, huddled groups whispering in hushed, anxious tones. Olumide saw him and walked over, a grim look on his face. "Don't know what to think, man. This is not looking good," he said, his voice low.

"Have you heard anything?" Oliver asked.

"Rumor is the Ascendium report is dropping today, two weeks early," Olumide murmured, stirring a coffee he didn't seem to want. "Execs probably got a sneak peek and are trying to do damage control."

At nine sharp, the giant screen at the front of the room flickered to life. Tomer, the CEO, appeared, flanked by Wright and a couple of other executives, their faces a carefully composed mask of corporate solemnity.

"Team, thank you for joining us on such short notice," Tomer began. "We have two separate but exciting updates to share with you today. First, our friends at Ascendium have completed their report on Project Tarantula two weeks ahead of schedule. We wanted you to hear it from us first."

Here we go, Oliver thought, a grim, cynical part of his mind taking notes. *The turd-polishing has begun.* He was willing to bet money on what word was coming next.

Tomer continued, his voice smooth and practiced. "The report was very *constructive*, suggesting areas for enhancement, noting some market assumptions that fell slightly short, and providing a general path to evolve our tech stack to truly revolutionize the exchange's infrastructure."

Is that it? Oliver thought, incredulous. The euphemisms were so thick he could barely breathe.

"It is possible," Tomer went on, "That the media will misinterpret this report to mean that Tarantula is abandoning the project. They will likely make a big deal out of it. I ask all of you to ignore the noise. Yes, our friends at Tarantula will likely put some aspects of the work on pause while they assess the findings, but that by no means implies they are moving away. In fact, it is an opportunity to reevaluate and deepen our relationship."

A bubble of pure, hysterical laughter rose in Oliver's throat. He had to physically suppress it. *Deepen our relationship?* It was one of the most ham-fisted, outrageously dishonest attempts at spinning a catastrophe he had ever witnessed. He had seen the code. He knew the project was a dumpster fire. The report had clearly laid that bare, and here was the executive team, twisting themselves into pretzels to call it a victory.

"You should all be proud of the work you've put in," Tomer concluded, his gaze sweeping across the camera with a look of paternal pride. "Speaking of which, that brings me to our second announcement. Ian, do you want to take this one?" He handed off to Ian Wright, the designated bearer of more "exciting" news.

Wright cleared his throat, his expression shifting from grim to a performance of bold, forward-looking optimism. "Thank you, Tomer. As some of you might know, we've been having conversations with the Central Bank of South Africa over the past few months ..."

Oliver had no idea. The news was a complete blindside.

"Recently," Wright continued, his voice building with theatrical importance, "The Bank of China decided to join those discussions as well. Today, I'm proud to announce that BlockWaves has been chosen as the tech partner for a pilot program for institutional cross-border trade using a central bank digital currency between those two countries. The project will be codenamed Oppenheimer."

A murmur went through the room, a mixture of surprise and confusion. But for Oliver, the words landed with the force of a physical blow. *A CBDC.* A central bank digital currency. It was the antithesis of everything he had come to believe in. Bitcoin was freedom, a system of rules without rulers. A CBDC was the ultimate tool of control – a government-issued digital token, running on a private, centralized ledger where every single transaction would be visible, censorable, and subject to the whims of bureaucrats. It was a surveillance state's dream. It was a digital panopticon.

Wright went on, his voice full of self-congratulation, and the meeting eventually adjourned with the usual empty platitudes about changing the world. As the executives trickled out of the conference room, Wright caught Oliver's eye and gestured for him to follow.

"Right, Oliver, I've got some good news for you," Wright said as they sat down in his office, the door closing with a soft, final click. "You have your regular hours back, now that the Ascendium report is out."

Oliver just shrugged, waiting for the other shoe to drop.

"But here's the real big news," Wright said, leaning forward with a conspiratorial grin. "Now that you're off Tarantula, I am appointing you lead sales engineer on Oppenheimer. Sri is gone. It's your time to step into the spotlight."

The words registered as a sentence. He was being handed the keys to the most morally horrifying project he could imagine. He didn't know what to say.

"You look thrilled, old chap," Wright laughed, misreading his stunned silence as awe. "Come on, Oliver, this is your chance. You can make your career on this. Impress the clients, and the growth will be dizzying." The sales pitch began, a torrent of temptations. "Lots of travel. Top brass at central banks. A spot on the podium at Davos next February. We'll get you a company card, business class for any flight over six hours. That's most of them – South Africa, China, Switzerland at a minimum."

Oliver was still reeling, the sheer scale of the offer a dizzying, terrifying prospect.

"Will there be a ..." he started to ask, the practical, desperate question forming on his lips.

"Yes," Wright said, seeming to read his mind. "As soon as we close our Series B – which is imminent now – I will personally make sure you get a fifty percent raise, at least. And more equity." He leaned back, the final piece of the trap sprung. "Oh, and I forgot. Starting tomorrow, we're getting rid of the 'junior' from your job title. You'll be a full-fledged solutions architect. So, what do you say, Oliver? In or out? The project kicks off on Wednesday, so I'd suggest you take the next two days to sort yourself out."

His head was spinning. The promotion, the money, the travel ... it was everything he was supposed to want. It was a golden ladder to a future he now found repulsive. But what choice did he have? He was in debt, his career was on the line, and the most powerful man in the company was offering him a golden ticket.

"I'm in," he said, the words coming out in a meek, hollow whisper that sounded like someone else's voice. He shook Wright's hand and walked back to his desk in a daze, feeling not like a man who had just been promoted, but like a man who had just sold his soul.

The Notepad

i) violin ii) toddler iii) alley iv) shoulder v) educate vi) rookie vii) oval viii) below ix) punch x) certain xi) cover xii) agree xiii) coast xiv) suggest

CHAPTER 15. BORING

Oliver couldn't sleep. It was almost midnight, but his internal clock was still a wreck, a casualty of the brutal, time-zone-hopping war he'd been fighting on Project Tarantula. Tomorrow was the kickoff for Oppenheimer, the CBDC project, and the thought of it was a lead weight in his stomach. He got out of bed, the well-trodden path to his dad's armchair a sleepwalker's reflex. He sat down, closed his eyes, and waited for the inevitable.

It came.

"Another day, another dilemma, am I right, tiger?" the Noncemeister asked. He was sitting in a spectral duplicate of the armchair, directly opposite Oliver, meticulously knitting a long, purple scarf from a ball of what looked like pure shadow.

"You can say that again," Oliver said, his voice a flat, exhausted monotone.

"Doesn't it get boring, to be this confused over and over again?" the Noncemeister asked, his knitting needles clicking with a soft, rhythmic clatter.

"Boring?" Oliver asked, surprised by the word.

"Yes sir. I'd find it boring, repeating old patterns the way you do," he said, not looking up from his work. "Have you tried not doing that?"

"Well, it seems to be keeping me on my toes, that's for sure," Oliver retorted.

"And you like being on your toes this way?" The Noncemeister dropped his knitting, which hovered in the air, and began to skip up and down on his tiptoes in a clumsy, absurd ballet.

"I guess not," Oliver sighed. "Some resolution would be nice. I need to break through this fog."

"So what's the dilemma today?" the Noncemeister asked, returning to his floating armchair and resuming his knitting as if nothing had happened.

"Ugh, we've talked about this. My work sucks. Now they're pushing me into a project that I have serious reservations about."

"What sort of reservations?"

"It's a CBDC project," Oliver said, "And I feel like that's against everything bitcoin stands for."

"See bee desee with bit corn standing?" The Noncemeister curled up his nose and squinted at Oliver until his eyes were almost shut, a look of theatrical confusion on his face. "That entire sentence was nonsense, Battu. You'll have to do better than that."

Oliver sighed. It was exhausting, but he knew he had to translate. "I've been given a lead role in a project for a new form of money," he said slowly. "That money has its own timechain, but it's a private one, not *the* timechain. It will give the issuer the ability to see and potentially control all the transactions."

The Noncemeister pondered this for a few moments, the clicking of his needles the only sound. "Battulu, I'm not sure I understand all the words you used, but I think I got the gist of it. Someone wants you to build something on what they think is another timechain, but you only know of the timechain. Is that your dilemma?"

"I suppose you could say that, yes."

"Let me tell you today's story then, Batew." He set his knitting aside again, the half-finished scarf hanging impossibly in the purple void. "Do you remember when we talked about the three realities?"

"Yeah, you won't let me forget," Oliver rolled his eyes. "It's ruined my ability to appreciate life."

"Why on Earth would you do that, you goofball?" the Noncemeister asked, a look of genuine, cartoonish surprise on his face.

"Well, every time I'm enjoying something," Oliver said, "There's a sneaking suspicion at the back of my mind that it isn't real – it could just be a dream or an illusion."

"And why is that just a suspicion and not a full belief?" the Noncemeister asked.

The question confused him. "Because I can't know for sure?" he replied, the words a question.

"Battolo," the Noncemeister said, and as he spoke, he reached out and casually pushed his hand *through* Oliver's chest, a gesture that was both impossible and completely without sensation. "Just as you can step out of a dream, an apparent reality, back into phenomenal reality," he pulled his hand back out, "So too you can step out of phenomenal reality into absolute reality." He gestured to the purple void around them. "Everything in apparent reality is a projection from phenomenal reality. And similarly, everything in phenomenal reality is a projection from absolute reality. Projections are caused by abstractions. For the first, the abstraction is sleep. For the second," he tapped Oliver's forehead, "Your conscious mind is the abstraction."

Oliver had nothing to say to that. The logic was as airtight as it was terrifying.

"Absolute reality is characterized by the singularity of all things," the Noncemeister continued, his voice becoming a calm, steady lecture. "The non-duality of all things. That non-duality is projected via conscious abstraction – your senses – into what you believe is empirically observed."

"But if everyone projects their own phenomenal reality," Oliver argued, grasping for a flaw, "Then we all live in different worlds. How can we all be projecting the same thing? It would be too much of a coincidence. What I see isn't what someone else sees. It doesn't make sense."

"Of course it does, Batue. There is a singular, absolute truth, and there are infinite projections of it. And that's okay."

"There's only one truth?"

"Indeed. There are infinite perceptions of it, but it is still a singular truth."

"And what is this singular truth?" Oliver asked.

"You are that," the Noncemeister said simply.

"I'm sorry? *I* am the singular truth?" Oliver was bewildered.

"Silly boy, blinded by your semantics," he sighed. "I did not say that you are the singular truth. I said the singular truth is that *you are that.*"

"I am that? What is 'that'?"

"That which you think is separate from you," the Noncemeister said, running a slow, deliberate circle around Oliver with his arms outstretched, as if demonstrating the boundary of a self that didn't really exist. "It is not. That is non-duality."

"I see," Oliver said, only partially understanding. "I get what you're saying in the abstract, but not sure how I can truly know it to be true."

"Battu, we've been over this before. By surrendering to the moment, of course. By just being."

"Ah, right. You did tell me that."

"There is only one truth, Batew. You are that. And so it goes with the timechain."

The sudden pivot caught Oliver off guard. "Wait, what does the timechain have to do with this?"

"There can be many perceptions of the timechain. There can be many attempted reincarnations of it. It can be projected through abstractions into different shapes and forms," the Noncemeister said. As he spoke, ghostly, distorted versions of coins – some stretched, some twisted, some rendered in gaudy, flashing colors – appeared and then vanished in the void around them. "But the truth is singular. There can only be one timechain, and this is that."

Oliver digested this, and the final, crucial piece of the puzzle slammed into place with the force of a thunderbolt. This was beyond a philosophical riddle – he was being handed a technical specification. *Singular absolute truth.* A single, canonical, immutable ledger anchored to reality through the raw, unforgeable cost of energy. That was the absolute reality. Everything else – every other crypto project, every corporate blockchain, every "faster, more efficient" alternative – they were just projections. They were phenomenal realities, created by the abstractions of charismatic founders and venture capital, but they weren't the thing itself. They were just copies, perceptions, running on centralized servers that could be changed by a handful of people. They weren't anchored to anything real. There could only be one timechain, because there was only one absolute, verifiable link between the digital world and the physical world of energy.

"The incontrovertible link," Oliver said, the words tumbling out of his mouth in slow motion, as the full weight of the realization sank in, "Once created, cannot be recreated. There can only be one. Is this what you meant by the tautological act of understanding?"

The Noncemeister stopped floating and clapped his hands together, a look of childlike delight on his face. "The thing that is, is the thing that is!" he exclaimed. "It cannot be another thing, for then it would not be the thing that is! The truth is true because it is the truth! You see, Batulu! You see!"

Oliver stared at him, speechless.

"And that wasn't boring, was it, Battu?" the Noncemeister asked, a knowing grin on his face as he began to fade.

"It certainly wasn't," Oliver said, his voice a quiet whisper of pure awe.

749833 (August 17)

A strange, unfamiliar feeling. Oliver woke up not to the groggy, nauseating pull of exhaustion, but to a feeling of clean, quiet clarity. He was wide awake the moment his eyes opened, the shrill *raar* of the alarm not an assault, but a simple fact. 7:30 a.m. He jumped out of bed, his mind calm and focused, his body feeling relaxed yet humming with a new, strange energy. It was, he thought, what being "in the zone" must feel like.

The Oppenheimer kickoff meeting was at eleven. He had to speak to Wright before then.

He found him in his office at ten. "Ah, Oliver," Wright chirped, his usual bright, brittle cheerfulness on full display. "Good to see you nice and refreshed ahead of the big kickoff."

"Mr. Wright, there's something I wanted to talk to you about." Oliver felt a momentary flicker of his old anxiety under Wright's intense gaze, but the new, solid core of his certainty held firm.

"By all means, Oliver. Keep it quick, though. I need to speak to Tomer in ten," Wright said, gesturing toward the CEO in the glass-walled conference room.

Oliver took a long, deep breath, exhaling slowly, calming the last of the fluttering nerves. He remembered the Noncemeister's words, the feeling of the precipice beneath his feet, the promise of the net. He took one more deep breath. The tiger stepped out to consume the lamb. "Mr. Wright," he said, his voice even and calm, "I have decided to resign from BlockWaves. I would like to tender my two-week notice today."

The effect was instantaneous. The cheerful mask on Wright's face dissolved, replaced by a look of pure, stunned disbelief. "What are you talking about, man?" he said when he finally found the words, his voice losing its polished, sales-pitch cadence. "We're about to kick off our biggest project yet. I've given you a lead role. What do you mean you're resigning?"

The clarity Oliver had woken up with seemed to deepen, to solidify into an unshakeable calm. "Ian," he said, the use of the first name a quiet, deliberate act of leveling the field, "I've given it a lot of thought. I just don't believe in the company's mission anymore. I don't believe Web3 is real."

He continued, his voice not angry, but measured, the words a clinical, damning diagnosis of an industry he now saw with perfect clarity. "We as a company, and the industry as a whole, are chasing shadows. There are large venture capital firms that thrive off the initial hype of these projects, which end up showing no results. The VCs create the hype, take the early profits, and leave hapless secondary investors holding the bag. And it's not just them. The third wave, the public, they get wiped out when the token goes to zero."

Wright listened in a stunned, absolute silence, his arms crossed, his usual arsenal of charming deflections completely gone.

"And let's not forget the employees," Oliver went on, his voice still eerily calm. "They've bought into this pseudo-idealistic narrative, full of buzzwords and empty platitudes, entirely misled by baseless hype from these VC charlatans. They've invested years of their precious career time into building Rube Goldberg Ponzis. It's wrong, Ian. It's just unethical. I can't be part of it anymore."

The silence stretched for a long moment. Then, the seasoned professional, the man who had seen everything, re-emerged from the shell of the shocked executive. Wright's expression became a neutral mask. "Oliver, I'm sorry you feel that way," he said, his voice flat. "Clearly, a lot of us here don't share that view. That said, I respect your decision and wish you the very best. Please notify Heather in HR. You'll need to put together a handoff plan." He paused, his gaze hardening. "And I do request that you don't share your industry criticism with anyone else in the company."

Oliver stared back, his own gaze defiant. The quiet, compliant, once-junior engineer was gone. He would not be muzzled. Not anymore.

Wright seemed to notice the defiant silence and his tone softened, a calculated retreat. "It is a request, Oliver. Not a directive. The company morale, and indeed the industry morale, is fragile at the moment. We've seen the reputational hit from Terra, Celsius, all of it." He leaned forward, his voice a low, conspiratorial murmur. "I'm even hearing rumblings that all might not be well at FTX. The collateral damage from something like that would be massive. There are people saying the types of things you are saying about Web3, and I don't want that fire to spread within our company. We have a Series B to raise."

The shift from command to quiet groveling was pathetic, and Oliver had to actively hide the look of disgust from his face. Wright was admitting he might be right, but begging him to keep quiet so he could raise more money. The conversation ended. Oliver walked back to his desk, a triumphant, liberating smile spreading across his face. He hadn't felt this sense of clean, righteous accomplishment in a long, long time.

A short while later, Olumide passed by his desk. "Hey man," he said, a confused look on his face as he pointed toward the glass-walled conference room where the Oppenheimer kickoff was underway. "Why aren't you in there? I thought Wright gave you a front-row seat. Also," he added, "Why are you just staring at a blank computer screen with a huge smile on your face?"

Oliver hadn't even realized. He was still floating in the pleasant, electric buzz of his own decision, a calm flow state that had insulated him from the rest of the office. "Oh, yeah," he said, unable to stop a chuckle. "So here's the deal, man … I've quit."

"You've *what* now?" Olumide gasped, a look of horror on his face.

"Quit. Just gave my two-week notice. Out of here by the end of August."

"Dude, what the fuck are you telling me?" Olumide asked, incredulously. "Did you get a better offer? Was it R3? I knew it was R3 – those fuckers have been sniffing around for months."

"Olumide, chill," Oliver laughed, the sound easy and free. "It wasn't R3. I'm not joining another company. I've just … quit."

"Wait, so you don't have another job lined up?" The question was a sharp, cold needle, piercing the warm bubble of Oliver's certainty. "Why would you quit without another offer?"

The first crack appeared in his resolve. He hadn't fully contemplated the 'what next.' The Noncemeister's voice echoed in his mind – *jump, and the net will appear.* But Olumide's horrified, practical face was here, in the real world. The checking account, the co-op fees, the student loans – the numbers began to swarm in his head. He felt a brief, sickening lurch of panic. "I'm working on something," he said hastily, trying to sound more confident than he felt.

"So you're launching your own Web3 startup?"

"No," Oliver said, the clarity returning, "I'm done with Web3. I've got something planned that I'm not ready to talk about."

"Oh, I get it. Top secret stuff," Olumide said with a laugh, the crisis averted in his mind. "Well, I hope you don't forget your humble nine-to-five friends once you've made the big leagues." He clapped Oliver on the back. "But seriously, dude, what can I say? I'm shocked you're leaving, but it's been an honor working with you. When's your last day?"

"August 31st," Oliver said, his mind already drifting to the cool, quiet mountains of Andes, to a conversation he was now free to have.

Olumide walked away. Oliver closed his eyes and breathed slowly, searching for the calm, solid center he had found just an hour ago. After a few minutes, it returned. He knew what he needed now. A quiet drink.

O'Connell's was empty, a quiet, hollow space in the middle of the afternoon. A lone figure sat at the bar, an older lady staring into a glass. As Oliver walked closer, a jolt of recognition went through him. It was Shannon, Aisling's mother.

"Oh hello, Shannon. How have you been?" he asked.

She turned, her eyes taking a moment to focus, to place the face. Eventually, it clicked. "Oh, hi! I remember you," she said, a slow, boozy smile spreading across her face. "You're the computer guy who wanted to buy the painting, right?"

Oliver laughed, the sound easy and unburdened for the first time in weeks. "I am indeed the computer guy. Though I was just curious, not really planning on buying it."

"Well, you better get on it, young man," she said, leaning in conspiratorially. "I received an offer just last week. Seventy-five thousand dollars. Cash only, he said. Not sure I want to deal with that much cash, so I'm holding off. Eighty grand and it's yours. Check or money order."

Oliver laughed again, but his curiosity was suddenly, sharply piqued. Who knew enough about *The Toddler* to make that kind of offer? "Do you know who it was?" he asked.

Shannon looked up at the ceiling, her brow furrowed in concentration. "Trying to remember his name … Had a thick, gruff accent. Eastern European, if you ask me. Wait a minute … his name was … Boy something. Boy … Boyen, yeah, I think that's what it was."

"Wait, *Bojan?*" The name sent a jolt through him, and Oliver almost knocked over a glass on the bar.

"That's it! Boyan," she confirmed. "Said he was a broker, buying it for a client."

Oliver's mind reeled. *Bojan Mitrovic.* The Serbian art broker. The man Gyorgy had sold the third Bryce painting to. The man who had called Maren's phone while Oliver was in her studio. He was here, now, trying to buy the second painting. For cash. The connections were thick, heavy cables, all leading back to Maren.

Just then, Aisling emerged from the kitchen, a plate of food in her hand. "Oliver," she said, a look of surprise on her face. "We just opened. What are you doing here so early and all by yourself?"

"Hey Aisling," he chuckled, the sound full of a giddy, newfound freedom. "Funny story. I just resigned today, so I decided to stop by for lunch and a drink."

"Aha! A free man," she said, a genuine smile spreading across her face. "Let's get you a drink to celebrate. Żywiec, right?"

Oliver nodded. "Well, not free just yet. Still have to serve my two weeks. But at this point, I just don't care."

"When did you hang up Daideó's painting in the pub, love?" Shannon asked, her mind still on the topic.

"I dunno, Mum. Six, seven years ago," Aisling responded, setting the plate down.

"So it was after it went on tour, right?" Shannon continued.

The question, so casual, so offhand, made the hairs on the back of Oliver's neck stand up.

"That's right," Aisling said, her tone matter-of-fact. "It went on tour and then was just lying around the warehouse collecting dust. I didn't think it was worth much, so I hung it up."

The new information sent another jolt through Oliver. "The Toddler went on tour? When was this?" He asked, trying to keep his voice steady.

"Maybe eight or nine years ago, something like that," Shannon chimed in. "It was those computer guys. They thought it would be a good idea to take it around the U.S."

"They took it for a tour but didn't want to buy it?" Oliver asked, the logic of it eluding him. "Do you remember their names?"

"I don't, to be honest," Shannon replied, shaking her head. "They spoke to my dad, and he agreed to let them take it. I guess he trusted them."

"How long was it on tour?"

"A year or so, I think."

Oliver digested this. *The computer people.* His father's tribe. They had taken the painting on a tour of the country a decade ago, but why? What was the purpose if not to acquire it? Something didn't add up.

Aisling returned with his beer, and he placed his lunch order, but his mind was still racing. There was another question, a more sensitive one, that he had been wanting to ask. Buoyed by the strange adrenaline of his resignation, his usual inhibitions were gone.

"So I've been meaning to ask one of you …" he began, looking from Shannon to Aisling. "I heard a rumor that Bryce was guided to draw his paintings by voices he heard. Is that right?" He tried to frame the question as gently as he could, to strip it of any accusation of madness.

Shannon and Aisling exchanged a brief, silent look, and Aisling gave her mother a small, almost imperceptible nod. It was a permission.

Shannon turned back to Oliver, a long, weary sigh escaping her lips. "Yes," she said, her voice dropping. "It's true. My father heard voices. I remember him telling me about them when I was just a teenager." Her gaze became distant, lost in a painful memory. "At first, they started gently, occasionally. Then they got more intense. They told him what to paint, down to the smallest detail. At least, that's what he told us." She shuddered slightly. "There were days when he was tormented by them, screaming at them to go away. It was tough to watch."

"When did this begin?" Oliver asked softly.

"Right after his first painting," Shannon said. "But they were definitely there for his second and third, and for all the other failed ones he tried to paint after that."

"Wait, so he did have more than three paintings?"

"No, not as far as I'm aware," she said, a deep sadness in her voice. "He tried, several times, but he could never complete any of them. The voices were driving him crazy."

"Were the voices always there?"

"No, they'd come and go," she shook her head gravely. "There were periods, sometimes for years, when they'd disappear, and he'd have no interest in painting at all. But they always came back, with a vengeance. And he had no choice but to pick up the canvas again, just to try and make them go away. Poor man, how he suffered." Her eyes welled with tears. "I still remember something he used to say, over and over again, begging and pleading with them. 'Oh, what I would do for a boring life!'"

Aisling nodded, a grim, silent confirmation on her face. Oliver felt he had pressed them enough. He had pushed them into a painful corner of their family history, and they had generously shared it with him. He had the answers he needed. He just didn't know what they meant.

749889 (Aug 17)

"Well, well, well …" Daniela's voice was a warm, teasing melody as she walked up to him outside Celeste. "If it isn't the elusive Mr. Battolo." She gave him a hug that lingered for a moment longer than just friendly. "Avoids me for over a month and then drags me all the way to the Upper West Side on a Wednesday to meet him. Makes me wonder what's going on."

"I told you I really wanted to hang out," Oliver said, a flush of embarrassment creeping up his neck. "The night shift was brutal. I was a zombie. But," he said, gesturing to the restaurant door, "This is long overdue. You'll love this place – my favorite Italian restaurant in the city."

The bistro was crammed and rustic, the small tables close together, creating an immediate sense of intimacy. "So what is this mysterious celebration?" Daniela asked as they were seated. "All you said was it was work-related. Did you get a promotion? Flying in the big leagues now?"

"Even better than that," Oliver said, a genuine, unforced smile spreading across his face.

"What could be better than a promotion?" she mused, placing a napkin on her lap. "You closed a big deal and got a huge bonus?"

"Nope. Even better," he said, leaning forward, the excitement bubbling up in him. "I resigned today. Gave them my two weeks." He thumped the table softly with his palm, the gesture a small, physical declaration of his freedom.

Daniela's laugh was a burst of pure, surprised delight. "Oh my goodness, Oliver! I guess that's good news if that's what you wanted. But didn't you tell me you were building all those cool blockchain products? You seemed really into it."

"I wasn't. I was lying to myself," he said, the earnestness in his voice surprising even himself. "I was unhappy. I didn't believe in any of it. It was all a big lie, Daniela. And it took me until now to finally have that long, hard conversation with myself and ask what the hell I was doing." He looked at her, his gaze direct and clear. "I feel liberated. And I couldn't think of a better person or a better place to celebrate that feeling."

"Wow, Oliver," she said, her voice soft, a look of genuine admiration in her eyes. "I'm honored you wanted to share this with me. Standing up for your principles like that … it's the best thing you can do. So what are you going to do now?"

"I don't know yet," he admitted. "But I know I want to work on something bitcoin-related."

"Bitcoin?" A slow smile spread across her face. "My, my, that's quite a change, Mr. Battolo. I remember you telling me it was old technology, that you were working on newer and better versions of it."

"It was all a story I told myself because I didn't know any better," he said, shaking his head at his own past ignorance. "I was so wrong. Turns out, you and your uncle knew more about it back then than I did. But I've been learning. And now I know. If I can contribute in even the smallest way to fixing the money, to fixing how we transact with each other, then I know I'm on the right track."

"I love that," Daniela said simply, her smile warm and genuine.

"I know it might sound crazy," he continued, the passion for his new mission pouring out of him, "But bitcoin really is hope. So many things that are wrong in the world – the injustice, the needless economic suffering, even war – they can be fixed. I really believe that, and I want to be part of the peaceful revolution that gets us there."

He finished, his declaration hanging in the intimate space between them. He had laid his newfound soul bare. Daniela just looked at him, her expression unreadable for a long moment. Then, she slowly reached her hand across the small table and placed it over his. Her touch was warm, and certain.

"You know," she said, her voice a low, soft murmur, "My uncle always said that when you find something you truly believe in, you should hold onto it with everything you've got." She squeezed his hand gently. "I think he would really like you, Oliver."

Oliver smiled at her, savoring the electric warmth of her hand on his.

"I want to be part of that revolution with you, Oliver," Daniela continued, her voice a low, intense murmur, her thumb gently stroking the back of his hand. "I want to live in a world where people don't have to struggle for their basic needs, where a sound, ethical money can get us there. In a world like that, art and creativity can thrive because people won't be focused on injustice and violence. I want to live in a world where people stand *for* something and build towards it, not stand against things and try to break them down."

Her words were a perfect echo of his own nascent philosophy, a validation so profound it almost took his breath away. "It's a deal, then," he said, his gaze locked on hers. "We're in this together."

And in that moment of absolute, unshielded connection, he decided. He had to tell her.

Daniela listened in rapt, silent attention as the entire, impossible story poured out of him. He told her everything – Bryce's paintings, the block size war and Gyorgy, Christiaan's poetry, the Noncemeister and the timechain, the strange, synchronous clues. He laid the whole secret world at her feet. He only held one thing back: his new, chilling suspicion of Maren. He knew how close they were, and he couldn't bring himself to plant that seed of doubt. Not yet.

When he finished, she didn't speak for a long moment, her hand still holding his across the table. "Oliver," she said finally, her voice full of awe, "That is truly an incredible story. Your projection episodes … they sound magical. I have goosebumps." She looked at him, her eyes shining with a new understanding. "This whole journey … it's like you're still connected to your dad, despite his passing. As if he's still here, guiding you. Maybe," she said, the idea forming on her lips, "Maybe he wanted you to go through all this so you would become a bitcoiner, just like him."

He nodded slowly. "It's almost as if he planned it all. At first, I was so impatient, I wanted to find everything out at once. But I've realized now, this is a journey that unravels at its own pace. There's no point fighting it. The answers will come when the time is right."

They talked for hours, the rest of the world fading away. It was close to midnight when the Italian proprietor, who had indulged their four-hour occupation of his table and even shared a bottle from his "Secret" wine list, came over and cleared his throat with a theatrical cough. "Friends," he said with a warm but weary smile, "Unless you are planning on a third dessert, I do have to close the restaurant soon."

They laughed, paid the bill that had been sitting on their table for an hour, and stepped out onto the quiet corner of 84th and Amsterdam.

"Daniela," Oliver said, the words coming out with a new, easy confidence, "Would you like to join me next weekend in the Catskills? I'm going to visit my friend Vince. He has a huge house; there will be more than enough room for both of us. I'm planning to take Friday off and make it a long weekend."

"Oh, I don't know, Oliver," she said, a genuine conflict on her face. "I still have to work on this play I'm directing."

"Daniela," he persisted, his voice full of an earnestness he didn't try to hide, "It would mean the world to me if you could make it. Would you please consider it?"

She looked at him, at the raw, open plea in his eyes, and a slow, beautiful smile spread across her face. "Wow, Oliver," she laughed softly. "When you put it that way … okay, let's do it. I'd love to visit your friend in the Catskills with you. Next Friday, so in about ten days?"

"That's right," he said, a wave of pure, uncomplicated happiness washing over him. "We can take the Amtrak to Kingston, and Vince will pick us up."

"Great, now I'm excited!" she said. She leaned in, a mischievous twinkle in her eyes. "And what about tonight, Oliver? Looks like the boring old Upper West Side is kicking us out. I guess this is goodnight then, isn't it?"

"It's only midnight," he said, a bright, confident smile matching hers. "And downtown is still awake." The boy who had stumbled out of the office in a fog of disillusionment was gone. The man who was taking the first step into his new life, a life of his own choosing, was just getting started.

The Notepad

i) violin ii) toddler iii) alley iv) shoulder v) educate vi) rookie vii) oval viii) below

ix) punch x) certain xi) cover xii) agree xiii) coast xiv) suggest xv) boring

STAGE 4: UNCERTAINTY

CHAPTER 16. TISSUE

A man and a woman were deep in conversation in a café, their voices a low, urgent murmur.

"Are you sure you know what you're doing? I'd rather we take him to a professional," the woman said, her words tight with an anxiety that Oliver, the unseen observer, could feel from across the room.

"Yes, I do," the man responded, his voice a calm, steady counterpoint to her fear. "Maren will be able to help him. I'm certain."

"I don't trust her, Nate. I don't want Oliver getting messed up because of her weird new-age stuff."

"Honey, let's just try a couple of sessions," he placated. "If they don't work, we'll take him to the psychiatrist. I'd just hate to see him put on medication when there could be another way."

Oliver watched them, a profound sense of dislocation washing over him. His parents. Younger, caught in a moment of crisis he had no memory of. He had hit the jackpot, though. This was exactly the point in the past he had been trying to reach.

His mother's agitation grew. "You know, none of this would be happening if you were more present as a father," she said, her voice rising, laced with the familiar, bitter accusation. "You're always running off to your so-called secret meetings. I know you're lying to me. I'm going to find out who these women are, Nate. And once I have proof, this is over!"

"Diane, please," Nate said, his own patience fraying. "There are no other women. How many times do we have to go over this? This family is every-thing to me. I've just been busy with important projects at work. I'm doing this for us, for our future. Please, just be more patient."

Oliver couldn't help a small, sad smile. *Not the full truth, Dad.* The "important projects" were in the secret, cryptographic world he was only now discover-ing, not at WilcoxRe. No wonder she was suspicious. But still, to be accused of something so odious, so contrary to his nature as infidelity … Oliver could feel his father's frustration across the decade, and for the first time, he understood that maybe their divorce had been inevitable. Her untrusting nature and his well-meaning but impenetrable secrecy were two chemicals that could only ever result in an explosion.

Just then, a boy emerged from the bathroom and joined them. "What are you talking about?" he asked. "You look upset, Mommy."

"Oh, nothing sweetheart," his mother said, her expression instantly soften-ing. "Daddy wants to take you to meet his friend now. She can help make the voices in your head quiet."

"But I like the voices, Mommy," the thirteen-year-old Oliver said earnestly. "The Nonsmaster is funny, and he's teaching me a lot of new words. We've gone on lots of adventures and defeated many bad guys. It just gets a little distracting sometimes."

The adult Oliver observing this let out a soft, silent chuckle. *Nonsmaster.* Endearing, really.

"I know, sweetheart, but it's better we get it checked up, okay?" his mother said, her voice a gentle trap. "Remember what Ms. Mallory said? We don't want you getting into trouble at school. If you don't get good grades, they'll keep you back in eighth grade. All your friends will move on, and you'll have to stay behind. You wouldn't want that, would you?" She was weaponizing his own future against him, and Oliver, the observer, felt a pang of helpless anger on behalf of the boy who had no idea what was about to be taken from him.

The thirteen-year-old Oliver shook his head, a small, defiant gesture. Nate stood up and gestured for his son to follow. They left the café, the argument with his wife hanging unresolved in the air, and walked the few blocks to 39 Carmine Street.

Oliver-the-observer followed them up the four flights of stairs, his heart pounding. He was about to witness the moment his own past was stolen from him.

Inside, he watched his father explain the situation to Maren. She listened, her expression one of calm, professional concern, while the younger Oliver occasionally chimed in, a bright, unselfconscious participant in his own diagnosis.

"Okay Oliver," Maren said to the boy when Nate was finished, "Do you want to play a little game?"

The boy nodded.

"Here, let's find you some paper," she said, looking around. She spotted a piece of orange wrapping tissue on a shelf and pulled it out, smoothing the delicate, crinkled paper on the coffee table. She handed the boy a pencil. "Why don't you draw what this person who speaks to you looks like?"

The young Oliver spent the next five minutes hunched over the fragile paper, his pencil moving with a focused intensity. Oliver-the-observer watched as the childish drawing of the Noncemeister took shape – the bald, oval head, the strange, porcine nose. A conduit for insights, a character that had existed in his mind long before his father had died.

Maren then led the boy into a guided meditation. Oliver watched as his younger self resisted at first, fidgeting and anxious, before finally letting go, his body relaxing into the chair. He saw Maren whispering to the boy, her hands making slow, hypnotic gestures in the air around his head. It looked less like healing and more like a gentle, psychic intrusion, a careful, deliberate act of erasure. The session lasted a full thirty minutes.

When it was over, Maren turned to Nate. "I need you to bring him in one more time next week," she said, her voice a low, clinical whisper. "I have pushed the memories back, deep into his subconscious. He will be unable to access them again unless there is a triggering event."

"What sort of triggering event?" Nate asked, his own voice tight with a concern he couldn't hide.

"Usually, it is a great trauma or tragedy," Maren said, her tone unnervingly casual. "Luckily, Oliver has a strong family, so that is unlikely to happen. He will probably have some other memory loss from this period, unfortunately. The last few months will be a blur for him. But that is a small price to pay."

A small price. The words were a cold blade in Oliver's mind. His own history, redacted.

Nate just nodded, accepting the diagnosis and the cure. He gave Maren a hug and a kiss on both cheeks, then turned to leave with his now quiet, subdued son.

"Oh, by the way ..." Maren called out, just as Nate reached the door. He turned back.

"Is Gyorgy still in town?" she asked, the question so offhand, so utterly disconnected from the psychic event that had just taken place.

"No, he left last week," Nate replied, oblivious. "I'm not sure when he'll be back, but I'll let you know." He turned and left, closing the door behind him.

Oliver-the-observer stood in the silent studio, the world spinning. Maren knew Gyorgy. She had known him for over a decade. And when he had mentioned the name to her, she had feigned complete ignorance. It wasn't just a suspicion anymore. It was a certainty. She was a gatekeeper. And she had been lying to him from the very beginning.

The scene faded, the revelation a cold, hard knot in his chest.

751269 (August 26)

"I set you guys up in two separate guest rooms. Is that cool?" Vince asked, a knowing, friendly glint in his eye as he helped them with their bags.

They both just shrugged, a wave of awkward, unspoken energy passing between them. Vince laughed. "Okay, I'll let you two figure it out. The rooms are there if you need them."

They had taken the morning Amtrak to Kingston, the Hudson River a shimmering ribbon of silver outside the train window. Vince had picked them up, but through the hour-long drive into the mountains, Oliver noticed a change in Daniela. The easy, bright energy from their dinner in the city was gone, replaced by a quiet, preoccupied stillness.

When Vince disappeared into the kitchen, Oliver turned to her. "Hey, you doing okay? You seem a little distant."

"Oh, it's nothing, Oliver," she said, her smile not quite reaching her eyes. "Sorry, I'm just a little distracted."

"Are you sure?" he pressed gently. "You can tell me. I want us to have a good time this weekend."

She hesitated, chewing on her lower lip for a moment before the story came tumbling out in a rush. "It's just … Maren has a new student moving in with her next week. Which means I have to move out. I had a place lined up with a friend in Brooklyn, but her mom got sick and had to move in with her, so that fell through. As of next week," she said, a note of real, raw panic in her voice, "I'm officially homeless."

"Can't you just stay with Maren for a little longer?"

"Not really," she said, shaking her head. "She only has the one extra room. It's not fair to the new student."

An idea, simple and obvious, sparked in Oliver's mind. "Hey, my old apartment on the Upper West Side is empty until the end of September. The lease isn't up yet. You're welcome to stay there."

She considered it, a flicker of genuine relief in her eyes. "You know, that might actually work! I can definitely find a place by then."

As she said it, another, crazier, more impulsive idea bloomed in his mind, and it was out of his mouth before he could stop it. "The other option is, you can just move in with me in Chelsea."

The words hung in the air between them. Daniela just stared at him, her expression a blank slate of disbelieving shock. She finally spoke, the words coming out of her mouth in a halting staccato, "Wait, are you … are you asking me to … move in with you?"

The silence stretched, and Oliver's face flushed hot with immediate, catastrophic regret. "No, no," he stammered, furiously backpedaling. "I didn't mean it like that. I just meant … it's a second option. But now that you put it that way, it's a terrible option. Sorry I even brought it up."

And then, she burst out laughing. It was a full, joyous, belly laugh that filled the quiet house. "Oliver," she said, wiping a tear from the corner of her eye, "I love it! That is so incredibly sweet and impulsive and insane." She looked at him, her smile wide and genuine. "Let's do it. It'll be fun. I'll chip in with the rent, of course."

"Wait," he said, his own mind struggling to catch up. "So you're … you're going to move in with me?"

"Well, yes," she said, tilting her head, her playful, teasing energy returning. "You just offered, didn't you? Or didn't you?"

"No, of course I did," he said, the words coming out with a lot less certainty than he felt. "This will be great. You'll love the apartment." As he spoke, the full, terrifying weight of what he had just done began to settle over him. He had just asked a woman he'd been on two real dates with to move into his dead father's apartment. The impulsiveness, born from a desire to solve her problem, had just created a whole new, wonderful, and terrifying reality for them both.

Vince returned from the kitchen with a tray of drinks, his perceptive gaze taking in the sudden, charged atmosphere between Oliver and Daniela. "Sorry," he said with a small chuckle, "Did I catch you guys at a bad time?"

"Oh no, no. All good, Vince," Oliver replied, a little too quickly. "We were just sorting out Daniela's lodging situation in New York."

The three of them went out onto the patio, the cool mountain air a welcome antidote to the sudden, awkward heat of the conversation.

"So," Vince said, settling into a chair, "Have you figured out what you're going to do next?"

"Not really, Vince," Oliver admitted, grateful for the change of subject. "As I was telling you on the ride here, I just … I reached a breaking point at my old job. It would have been unethical for me to keep selling a technology I don't believe in. My colleagues were just parroting company lines without any critical thinking. I couldn't be a part of it anymore." He looked out at the vast, green expanse of the forest. "All I know is that I want to do something in bitcoin. I just don't know what that looks like, or where to even begin."

Vince mulled this over, taking a slow sip of his drink. "You know, Oliver," he said after a moment, "I'm a director at a nonprofit that aims to bring computer science and financial literacy to underserved communities. We recently received a very generous grant from Jack Dorsey to expand our efforts." He looked at Oliver, his gaze direct and clear. "We're looking for part-time instructors to teach coding at after-school programs for middle schoolers in Harlem and the Bronx. Is that something you'd be interested in?"

The offer was so unexpected, so perfectly aligned with the vague, unformed desire in his own heart, that Oliver just stared at him. "I'd love to hear more about this," he said, a genuine excitement cutting through the last of his anxious fog.

"It's really simple," Vince explained. "You show up for a few hours after school and teach the kids the basics. We also plan to introduce the basic concepts of what money is, what makes it 'sound,' and then slowly introduce bitcoin. That's it. It's about twenty hours a week. It doesn't pay a lot, but Jack's grant has made it easier for us to compensate our instructors."

"How much does it pay?" Oliver asked, the practical, nagging question of his finances immediately surfacing.

"Three thousand dollars a month," Vince responded. "Maybe a little more, depending on the hours. We can pay a portion, or even all of it, in bitcoin if you want."

Oliver's heart raced. Three thousand a month. It wasn't much by Manhattan standards. But with Daniela now moving in, splitting the co-op fees ... it was enough. It was more than enough. It plugged the hole in his budget, the one that had been a source of a constant, low-grade panic since he'd walked out of Wright's office. And more importantly, it was a cause. It was real work.

"I'd love to, Vince," he said, the words a rush of giddy enthusiasm. "It sounds like a great opportunity."

"That's great," Vince said, a look of genuine satisfaction on his face. "The school year begins right after Labor Day, so we're kicking off soon. We need more people like you, who have the skills and want to help. This is how we win."

Later that afternoon, Vince led them down the path to his blacksmithing workshop, the air growing thick with the scent of coal smoke. He showed them the process, the raw, elemental magic of it. He heated a piece of scrap metal in the forge until it glowed with a fierce, white-hot intensity, then placed it on the anvil, the ring of his hammer a sharp, rhythmic song in the quiet of the woods.

"I'm making a bouquet of metal flowers," he explained over the noise, his face illuminated by the glow of the forge. "This one is for the petals. I need to hammer this piece until it's as thin as a tissue." He demonstrated, his blows precise and powerful. "I won't be able to do it all in one go. I'll have to return it to the fire, heat it, and then continue shaping it once it's pliant again."

Oliver and Daniela watched in fascination, then took turns with a smaller hammer, their own clumsy, ineffective blows a stark contrast to Vince's effortless mastery. They were struggling to make a dent, while he was transforming raw, stubborn metal into something delicate and beautiful.

After a while, Vince finished shaping six delicate, leaf-like petals and set them aside to cool. "You know," he said, his voice a low, thoughtful murmur against the rhythmic hiss of the forge, "In some sense, this is just another form of bitcoin mining for me. I use fire and energy to shape these sculptures, and then I sell them for bitcoin." He looked at Oliver, his eyes full of a simple, deep clarity. "I'm converting fire into time. It's alchemy."

Alchemy. The word, combined with the intense heat and the elemental transformation of metal, triggered another connection, a phrase from the dark, chanting chamber of his projection. *Pittamiglio was an alchemist.*1 The memory was so vivid, the words so clear, that Oliver spoke them aloud without thinking.

"*Ex igne, tempus nascitur ...*"

"What was that, Oliver?" Vince asked, turning from the forge.

"Oh, just a Latin saying I heard recently," Oliver said, quickly recovering. "It means 'out of fire, time is born.'"

"Wow," Vince said, a slow smile spreading across his face. "That's pretty cool. I haven't heard that one, but it's exactly what I'm talking about. Where did you hear it?"

Oliver thought for a moment, the image of the strange, chanting figure in the dark, purple room flashing in his mind. He wasn't ready to share that, not yet. "Oh, I can't remember now," he lied. "Must have been on some forum or Twitter or something."

Just then, Vince's wife, Marie, came into the workshop. "Hi babe," she said, giving Vince a hug and a kiss. "I just got back." She waved at Oliver and then turned to Daniela with a warm smile. "Hi, I'm Marie. I'm so sorry I wasn't here to greet you. I had to take the dog to the vet."

She looked back at Oliver, a flicker of recognition in her eyes. "Oh, Oliver, I've been meaning to tell you. I reached out to your friend Maren after you told me about her. What an amazing person. We were so on the same page about everything. We might even start working on something together now that she's back."

A cold, prickling unease began to creep up Oliver's spine. "Oh, that's great," he said, keeping his voice even. "I didn't realize you had connected already. Did you talk on a video call?"

"Yes, we did," Marie said, her face bright with the memory. "And this one time, she was sitting in front of this amazing background. On a mountain, with acres and acres of vineyards behind her. It looked like she was in Italy, or Greece."

"Oh, no," Oliver said with a small, confident laugh. "She was actually in India for the past few months."

"No, I don't think so," Marie replied, her own certainty unwavering. "I asked her where she was. She said she'd been traveling and had spent some time in India for her guru's birthday, but when we were speaking, she said she was on the Mediterranean coast."

The casual words landed with the force of a thunderbolt. Oliver's mind raced. "When was this?" he asked, his voice suddenly tight.

"Oh, must have been a month or so ago," Marie responded.

He turned and glanced at Daniela. Her face mirrored his own shock, an expression of undiluted confusion. The easy, trusting world they had been building together had just been fractured. Maren had clearly lied. She had fabricated a whole new narrative.

Marie waved, said she was heading back to the house, and left them in the ringing silence of the workshop. The moment she was gone, Oliver walked over to Daniela. "Hey," he said, his voice a low whisper. "Did you know Maren was in the Mediterranean?"

Daniela just shrugged, her eyes wide with bewilderment. "No. This is news to me. She never mentioned it. Even when we talked about the trip after she got back, it was all Guru Brahma, all India. She never said a word about Italy or wherever." A small, nervous laugh escaped her. "Must have slipped her mind."

"Isn't that kind of a big detail to just slip someone's mind?" Oliver asked, his own suspicion now a cold, hard certainty in his chest.

"It is a bit weird, I agree," Daniela admitted, a sense of unease settling in the air between them. "I'll ask her when we get back to the city."

Vince went back to his work, the ring of his hammer on the hot metal a sharp, percussive rhythm in the suddenly tense afternoon air.

751365 (August 27)

A sharp sliver of morning sunlight cut through a gap in the curtains, a warm line that fell directly across Oliver's eyes, pulling him from a deep and dreamless sleep. He blinked, the guest room at Vince's house slowly coming into focus. The bed was comfortable, the mountain air through the open window crisp and clean. He had definitely made the right choice in picking this room.

He looked at his phone. Almost 7 a.m. The thought of a quiet, solitary walk in the cool morning air was tempting. Just then, a soft sound beside him, a gentle sigh. Daniela turned in the bed, still lost in sleep, and as she moved, the sheet slipped from her shoulder, pooling at the small of her back.

And Oliver's breath caught in his throat.

There, just below her left shoulder blade, stark and black against the warm tones of her skin, was a tattoo. It wasn't just any tattoo. It was a four-inch, intricately rendered, old-fashioned key. A key he knew with a certainty that went deeper than memory. He had seen it on the lion's back in the meadow of his first projection. He had held its impossible, solid weight in his hand, the cast-iron twin he had found in his father's desk. He had used it to open a door in a dream-castle. And now, it was here, etched into the skin of the woman sleeping beside him.

The sight was an explosive collision of his two worlds. *How?* What impossible connection could she have to this quest, to his father's secrets? Then he remembered. Pittamiglio's castle was in Montevideo. Daniela's home. It was a convergence. It had to be.

He was surprised he hadn't noticed it before, but in the breathless, close-up intimacy of their recent nights, his focus had been narrowed to the immediate and the overwhelming. There had been little room for the quiet, detached observation that the calm morning light now afforded.

He couldn't wait. He had to know. He reached out, his fingers gently tracing the shape on her bare back. He whispered her name.

Daniela opened her eyes, a slow, sleepy smile spreading across her face as she saw him. "What is it?" she murmured.

"Your tattoo," he said, his voice a hushed whisper. "On your back. What is it?"

"What tattoo?" she asked, still half-asleep.

"The key," he said. "The only one you have."

She pushed herself up slightly, supporting herself on her elbows, fully awake now. "Oh, that," she said, a soft, fond smile on her face. "That's a family heirloom. The key has a special significance in my family. It's supposed to unlock magical secrets."

Oliver held his breath. He hadn't told her about the castle, about the *Camara del Tiempo*. He did now. "Does Pittamiglio's castle mean anything to you?"

Her eyes widened, all trace of sleep vanishing instantly. "Yes. Of course. It's a famous landmark in my hometown, built by a mysterious alchemist a hundred years ago." She looked at him, her expression a mixture of awe and disbelief. "This key … it's the key to one of the rooms in the castle. Or at least, it's a symbol of it. My uncle Rafael was a huge admirer of Pittamiglio. I'm not sure how he got the original key, but he's always had it. How do you know about Pittamiglio?"

"I found a note," he said, the words a torrent now. "On my father's work computer. It talked about a room in the castle – the *Camara del Tiempo*. And I went there, in a projection. I used my key to open the door."

"I've heard of the Chamber of Time," she said, shaking her head. "But I don't think it's a real place. I visited the castle as a little girl. There was no such room. Pittamiglio was an alchemist, and a lot of the stories about him are more myth than history."

Oliver was confused again, caught in the same disorienting space between his father's cryptic clues and the hard facts of the world. But Daniela was staring at him, her gaze intense, full of a new, intense understanding.

"You know, Oliver," she said, her voice a low murmur, "This is incredible. You, on this spiritual, magical quest for your father, and it has somehow led you directly to my hometown, to my own family's story." She reached out, her hand finding his. "I feel so connected to you right now."

He stared back at her, at the impossible, beautiful truth of it. She was right. He felt it too. "You know," he said, a mischievous smile returning to his face for the first time that morning, "I was thinking about going for an early morning walk …" He paused, his hand slowly making its way from her hand up her arm, to her back, his fingers once again tracing the outline of the impossible key. "… but I think that can wait."

July 1977, Belfast, Northern Ireland

A man in his early fifties shuffled unsteadily down a wet cobblestone street, his lips moving in a frantic, silent conversation with himself. The air was thick with the smell of coal smoke and damp stone.

"Afternoon, John," a man in a bowler hat called out from a pub doorway.

The man, John, gave no sign of hearing, his gaze fixed on a point somewhere in the gray, oppressive sky. He was a ship lost in his own internal storm.

He passed a woman and a young girl standing in a doorway. "Dad!" the woman called out, her voice a sharp note of concern.

John stopped, turning slowly, the furious muttering ceasing as he registered her face.

"Daideó!" The little girl, no older than eight, broke away and ran to him, her small arms wrapping around his leg. A flicker of light, of the man he used to be, returned to John's eyes as he looked down at his granddaughter. He softened, lifting the little girl into his arms and kissing her forehead. "Hello Aisling, my darling."

He walked to the doorway, kissing the woman on both cheeks. "Afternoon, Shannon."

"Where have you been, Dad?" Shannon asked, her face a mask of worry. "We haven't seen you in days."

John took a sharp, ragged breath. "It's happening again, Shannon," he said, his voice a low, haunted whisper. "The voices came back. They're telling me to paint another one."

"Oh no, Dad! Don't say that," she responded, the concern in her eyes deepening into fear. "I thought they were gone."

"I know, love," he said, his own voice cracking with a despair that was terrifying to witness. "But I don't have a choice. I can't sleep, I can't eat. It's tearing me apart."

"What are they asking you to paint this time?"

"I don't understand it," he said, his hands beginning to tremble. "It's a painting about time. A chaotic scene in a pub, well-dressed people wandering. Some of them … some of them are carrying fire in the palms of their hands. Others are arguing." He looked at her, his eyes full of a frantic, pleading confusion. "And in the center, there's a strange man holding a glowing, melting clock. It only has the number zero on it, in white, against a pitch-black face. And a coat of arms on the wall, with Latin I can't read. It makes no sense, but every time I try to paint it, they make me correct some detail. They tell me I've got it wrong. Over and over again. I can't take it anymore, Shannon," he finished, his voice a raw, broken thing.

"Where are you going, Dad?"

"Home. To finish it," he said, as if it were a death sentence. "It's the only thing I can do." He patted the little Aisling on her head, set her down gently, and set off down the path, his shoulders hunched against a weight no one else could see.

Oliver-the-observer watched him go, then followed as Bryce entered his small house, the frantic muttering returning. He went straight to a back room where a large canvas stood on an easel. He picked up a brush and began to paint with a furious, desperate energy. Oliver tried to change his perspective, to see the canvas itself, but he couldn't. He was a fixed point, forced to watch the artist, not the art.

He saw the torment on Bryce's face, the sweat beading on his forehead, the way his knuckles were white as he gripped the brush. Then, a raw, agonized scream tore from Bryce's throat. "No, please no! I did what you told me. What more do you want?"

He dropped the brush, grabbed a balled-up tissue from a nearby table, and began to furiously smudge the canvas, a frantic, destructive act of erasure. He was at war with the image, at war with the voices in his own head.

Oliver watched for a little while longer, a horrified, helpless witness to the man's private hell, until the scene faded, leaving a residue of deep, chilling sadness. The demons that consumed Bryce were real, and his suffering was unimaginable.

He thought back to the description of the painting – the fire, the melting clock, the zero. Gyorgy had said the painting captured the birth of bitcoin. The genesis block. The themes were all there. And then he remembered the other part of his projection from the art fair. The third painting, Bryce's lost masterpiece, was likely hidden away in a "Below." Somewhere secret. Somewhere safe.

As he was pondering this, a familiar, dizzying sensation washed over him. The scene wasn't over. He was being pulled back in.

752040 (August 31)

"You see, Battolo, these margins are very fine," the Noncemeister said, his voice a calm, matter-of-fact hum in the sudden, silent void.

"What margins?" Oliver demanded, the lingering horror of Bryce's tormented face still fresh in his mind. "Why did you pull me back in? I was just watching Bryce."

"Oh, don't worry, we'll keep this one short," the Noncemeister said, casually holding up a sheet of something that looked like impossibly thin, almost translucent paper between his thumb and forefinger. "I just wanted to point something out to you."

"And what's that?" Oliver asked, his patience worn thin.

"What separates one reality from another," he began, letting the delicate sheet float from his fingers, "Appears to be a very fragile membrane. An ethereally thin veneer. A tissue, if you will." He watched as the sheet drifted slowly, catching an invisible current. "One heartbeat you are in one reality, and the next, you experience something completely different. Like you just did."

"Sure, but that's because of projection, right?" Oliver asked, trying to ground the conversation in a rule he understood. "This separation between the things I'm experiencing?"

"Yes, indeed. Or so you think," the Noncemeister said, the sheet of tissue dissolving into purple dust before it hit the ground. "The next step is for you to realize that there is no tissue. It is all one, and your conscious mind chooses to focus on only one version of it at a time. Projection allows you to break through that."

"Well, I suppose that's one way of looking at it," Oliver said, though his mind was still on the tormented artist. "Hey, since I have you, can you please tell me about the third Bryce painting? You've dodged this question before, but surely, you've got to know."

"Ah, what can I tell you, Battu?" the Noncemeister sighed, pausing to think. "Here's something – it's about me."

"It's about *you*?" Oliver asked, surprised. "Bryce knew about you?"

"Why of course he knew about me. And when I say me, I mean the timechain," he said, his voice becoming suddenly serious. "He was told, but he refused to understand. Some people allow the tissue to grow and thicken, until they lose sight of the infinite consciousness. He chose to be tormented by the truth, rather than embrace it. He chose the life he led. It was one of pain, suffering, fear, and despair."

"So you know about the voices in his head, then," Oliver pressed. "Why did they happen to him?"

"Some people can be worthy conduits for knowledge," the Noncemeister said gravely. "He was, and the creativity expressed through him was able to permeate the world. In that sense, it was a good choice. But for his own conscious mind, perhaps it wasn't the most ideal outcome."

"So where is the third Bryce, then?" Oliver asked, the question a desperate plea.

"Ah, Batew, now you are no longer in the moment ..." the Noncemeister said, a note of gentle chiding in his voice. "You are grasping for something. You have created an attachment to an answer, and that is why it is not forthcoming. I have already told you it is below. Surrender to that feeling now and let go of any other answers you might think lie ahead of it. That will come. In due course, it will come."

The Notepad

i) violin ii) toddler iii) alley iv) shoulder v) educate vi) rookie vii) oval viii) below ix) punch x) certain xi) cover xii) agree xiii) coast xiv) suggest xv) boring xvi) tissue

CHAPTER 17. GOOD

A strange, unfamiliar feeling. Clarity. Oliver smiled as he leaned back in his father's old mahogany desk chair, the solid, warm wood a comforting presence. He felt a quiet focus that had been absent for months. Living with Daniela had been surprisingly, effortlessly good. They moved around each other with an easy grace, respecting the quiet spaces and filling the shared ones with laughter and conversation. He could get used to this.

He straightened up and typed a few more bullet points for the after-school class he was teaching later. The middle school kids were sharp, their incisive questions a welcome challenge that forced him to truly understand the fundamentals he was teaching.

"Okay Oliver, I'm headed to my class," Daniela called out, her voice a bright, happy sound from the front door. "Should we order in today?"

"Yeah, let's do it. Tacos would be good," he called back. "I'll probably be back around seven. What do you want to watch after? *Remington Steele*?"

"Yes, let's do it!" she laughed. "Okay, see you!" She blew him a kiss and was gone.

He finished his notes and then got up from the desk. He walked over to the armchair, and this time, he wasn't collapsing into it out of grief or exhaustion.

He was choosing it. He sat down, closed his eyes, and willingly stepped into the void.

"It's good, isn't it?"

The sing-song voice was not a surprise this time, but an ubiquitous, expected arpeggio in the quiet symphony of the timechain. The Noncemeister was floating peacefully in front of him, conducting a small, silent orchestra of shimmering, multi-colored musical notes that danced and swirled in the purple darkness.

"What's good?" Oliver asked, his tone less one of bewilderment and more of genuine curiosity.

"It," the Noncemeister replied, his voice a deadpan note that caused the entire orchestra of lights to vanish in a puff of smoke.

"And what is this 'it'?" Oliver asked, settling in for the inevitable riddle.

"It, my dear Battu, is that which you are experiencing in its fullness right now." He reached out and seemed to pluck a single, shimmering thread from the very fabric of the purple void. "It is the so-ity of thus-ness." He then tied the thread into an impossible, glowing knot. "Or the so-ness of thus-ity." He pursed his lips, contemplating his own phrase. "*It* is the *everything* after you've removed the *something* and the *nothing*."

"Uh huh," Oliver said blankly. "I guess you mean it is the feeling I'm feeling at the moment?"

"It is more than just the feeling," the Noncemeister said, letting the glowing knot drift away like a tiny, self-contained galaxy. "It is the all-encompassing oneness of your experience."

Oliver didn't push it. For the first time, he didn't need to. He simply felt it. "You're right," he said, a genuine, unforced smile on his face. "It's good. It's very, very good."

"Good, good, good. That's what I like to hear." The Noncemeister's own smile returned, bright and wide. "Now, are you ready?"

"Ready for what?" Oliver shot back.

The Noncemeister looked surprised, as if the answer were the most obvious thing in the universe. "Why, for this, of course."

And he snapped his fingers. The sound was a sharp, clean crack that sent a silent, white shockwave rippling through the entire purple void.

The purple void dissolved, not into blackness, but into a world of stone and shadow. Oliver found himself standing in a high-ceilinged room, the air cool and smelling of damp earth and old secrets. The Noncemeister was gone. He was in a castle.

He heard the low, urgent murmur of a conversation from an adjacent room and walked toward the sound, passing through a heavy stone archway. Two men, dressed in the formal, dark attire of early twentieth-century noblemen, stood by a tall, narrow window, their animated discussion a stark contrast to the room's quiet solemnity. They didn't see him. He was a ghost, a silent observer once more.

The younger of the two men spoke, his voice tight with a concern he was struggling to contain. "*Mentor,* I am not sure how best to express my concern, but Esteban doesn't want to work within these rules anymore. We had a substantial disagreement yesterday, and he left in anger. He said we are not allowing ourselves to explore the full power of alchemy by creating these limitations."

The older man sighed, a sound heavy with a weary wisdom. "Humberto, your youngest brother has always been bull-headed. He is an extraordinarily intelligent young man. I daresay his ability surpasses all my other students, including you. However, he does not have the maturity or the judgment that you possess. I am worried that he can do great harm with these powers, with these secrets we have developed."

Oliver listened, transfixed, the pieces clicking into place with a dizzying speed. *Humberto.* Humberto Pittamiglio. And the older man, his mentor, must be Francisco Piria, the famous alchemist he'd read about. And a new name, a new player in this secret history: *Esteban,* Humberto's brother.

"What do you think he will do now, Humberto?" the older man asked.

"He was talking about how, with fire, he will be able to create time," Humberto responded, his voice grave. "I told him that meddling with time was not permitted. It can be very dangerous. I too am very worried about him, *mentor.* He told me that he is able to tune in to the resonance of the universe in his mind, that there are voices guiding and inspiring him. They were the ones that gave him the idea about fire and time. I think he will build his own laboratory elsewhere and conduct these experiments."

The older man pondered this, his gaze lost in the gray light filtering through the window. "You know," he said slowly, "I have heard of such phenomena. There are certain people – very, very few – who say they are able to tune into the collective consciousness of the universe. They claim there is an infinite intelligence, and that most people are so limited by their conscious minds that they can only focus on the reality their senses render. Rarer still are the few who can transcend those thin membranes that separate the conscious from the unconscious, the sensual from the ethereal. It could be that Esteban is one of those."

Humberto listened in silence, his expression a mixture of awe and fear.

His mentor continued, "I would watch him closely, Humberto. Perhaps I was hasty in my initial judgment. Do not interrupt him, because you might be interrupting divine wisdom manifesting itself, using him as a conduit. After all, this is what we attempt to do with alchemy – seek a transformation of the elements to better understand the universe. Our rules exist because of the physical dangers, but perhaps for someone who has transcended the sensual plane, such rules can be relaxed. Watch him closely but let him proceed. Maybe some good will come of this."

"As you say, *mentor*," Humberto demurred, his voice a quiet note of submission to the older man's wisdom.

"Rum thing, innit, Batew?" The Noncemeister's voice broke through the silence as the stone castle faded into the purple void. "Who would've thunk it, amirite?"

"Who would have thunk … I mean, thought what?" Oliver asked, his mind still reeling from the vision of the two alchemists.

"That a silly goose such as yourself could be a conduit for infinite intelligence," the Noncemeister said with a sly grin, pulling a long, shimmering string of starlight from just behind Oliver's ear.

"I'm a conduit?" Oliver asked, surprised.

"Think about it, big boy. What happened in the last two stories I told you?"

Oliver thought. Bryce, tormented by voices that gave him cryptographic art. Esteban, a century ago, inspired by voices to create time from fire. Were they the same as this creature in his head?

The Noncemeister seemed to read his mind. "Batulu, I told you at the very beginning that the timechain is the collective consciousness of the universe. It had always existed, although some could only perceive it since its genesis. This is the song of the universe." As he spoke, the purple void around them began to pulse with a soft, internal light, humming with an unheard music. "I am the timechain, Battu. I am everything and nothing all at once. And I reveal myself to those who are ready …"

His voice trailed off, and he looked down at his own hands with a thoughtful frown. "Well, those who *ought* to have been ready, anyway. In some cases, like our Irish friend, they allow the truth to torment and consume them. For them, the absolute truth is a total perceptive vortex. I don't always get it right," he shrugged, as if admitting to a minor culinary mistake.

Oliver seized on a contradiction. "You are the timechain? I thought you said you were the keeper of the timechain."

"The timechain has no keepers, Battu," the Noncemeister said, and as he spoke, his form began to dissolve, losing its edges and merging with the pulsing purple light of the void until only his smiling face remained, floating in the vastness. "By its very nature, it cannot. It is everything and everywhere. I sometimes use simple language to ease you into new levels of knowing, but there is no keeper. Keeper-shmeeper. Let me put it this way …"

His face vanished, and his voice, now bodiless and all-encompassing, boomed through the timechain, a grand, cosmic verse.

"I am not the mind or of the intellect,
And hence your inner self that I do not reflect.
I am not your senses five but am beyond
The fire and wind and ether and the earthly bond.
I am indeed the knowing and eternal bliss,
Love and consciousness, the timechain's tender kiss.

"I am not an energy or air you breathe,
Or any instruments your actions may concede.
I am not a symphony or diatribe,
Or masterpiece-catastrophe that words describe.

I am indeed the knowing and eternal bliss,
Love and consciousness, the timechain's tender kiss.

"I am not virtue or vice or sins or deeds,
And feel no pain nor joy nor sorrow nor what precedes.
I need no hymn, no chants, no church, and no scripture.
I am not a victor, victim, or savior.
I am indeed the knowing and eternal bliss,
Love and consciousness, the timechain's tender kiss.

"By Akasha, I do not suffer from fear
Of death, for death can never make me disappear.
I had no birth and hence no father or mother
Or teacher, student, friend, or foe or some other.
I am indeed the knowing and eternal bliss,
Love and consciousness, the timechain's tender kiss.

"I'm all-pervasive, bearing not an attribute.
I'm not attached nor liberated in pursuit.
I'm everything, I'm everywhere, I'm every time.
An equilibrious reality sublime
I am indeed the knowing and eternal bliss,
Love and consciousness, the timechain's tender kiss."

The voice faded, and the Noncemeister's form slowly coalesced back into being in front of the dazed Oliver. He looked at him intently, a silent, expectant pause.

"You've got to admit, Batew ..." he went on when Oliver didn't say anything, "... that was good, wasn't it?"

Oliver shuddered, the profound, reality-bending poetry still echoing in his mind. "Yeah," he said, his voice a quiet whisper. "I guess you could say that. That was good."

March 1991, Andhra Pradesh, South India

A mailman waited patiently by a front door, the midday sun beating down on the dusty path. "Be there in a second," a voice called out from inside. A young man, barely in his twenties, hurried down a flight of stairs and opened the door, his expression one of anxious anticipation.

"Thought I'd hand-deliver this," the mailman said, holding out a large, stiff envelope. "It's for you. All the way from America."

The young man took the package, his hands trembling slightly. He thanked the mailman, shut the door, and immediately tore it open, pulling out a thick sheaf of papers. His eyes scanned the cover letter, his breath held tight in his chest.

A woman emerged from the kitchen, wiping her hands on her sari. "What is it, Visu? I couldn't leave the stove. What does the letter say?"

"Hold on, Mom," he said, a slow, brilliant smile spreading across his face, a sunrise of glowing joy. He read for another moment, his eyes wide with disbelief, and then he looked up, his face luminous. "I got in," he breathed. "The computer science graduate program at Princeton. With a full scholarship. It's ... it's everything, Mom. My dream. It's coming true."

His mother just stared at him, her own face a canvas of conflicting emotions. Then, a ragged sob escaped her lips. She sat down heavily in a nearby chair, her body shaking with inconsolable tears.

"What happened, Mom?" Visu asked, his own elation instantly extinguished by her reaction. "Aren't you happy? This is incredible news."

"I'm so happy for you, my darling," she said, her voice choked with tears. "You have worked so hard for this. You deserve it. It's just ..." She looked at him, her son, no longer a boy but a man on the cusp of a life she could barely imagine. "It has finally hit me. You will be leaving this house forever. This house will be so empty without you."

Visu walked over to her, bent down, and wrapped his arms around her shaking shoulders. "Mom," he said, his voice a soft, soothing murmur against the storm of her grief, "I'm twenty-one. I can't live with you and Dad forever. This is my destiny. I have to follow it."

After a few more soothing words, he went up to his room, the thick packet of his future held carefully in his hands.

Oliver-the-observer watched all of this in quiet fascination, a ghost in the sunlit room. This was another window into a past he'd never known, a fresh, unvarnished perspective on the forces that had shaped a man he was only now beginning to understand.

Visu sifted through the documents, the crisp, heavy paper feeling foreign and important in his hands. A letter from his would-be advisor, Professor Eric Wideman, Head of the Information Theory and Cryptography division at Princeton. Visa forms. A map of a campus on the other side of the world. As Oliver-the-observer watched, he noticed a small, recurring detail on the signed pages: a simple, circular ink stamp in blue. Inside the circle was the word "Good." It seemed like a quaint, old-fashioned way of validating a document before its long journey across the ocean.

Visu suddenly lay back on his bed, the packet of papers resting on his chest, and closed his eyes. Oliver-the-observer felt his own perspective shift, drifting closer, as if to listen in on the silent, internal conversation that had just begun.

A deep, booming voice, different from any Oliver had heard before, echoed in the quiet of the boy's mind. *"Well, this is it, isn't it?"*

"I guess it is," Visu's own internal voice responded. *"I'm still waiting on a response from the University of Santa Barbara. They have an up-and-coming program there as well, and I've heard good things about that area. It might be nice to live by the ocean."*

"Visu, listen to me," the voice commanded, its tone firm but not unkind. *"Your opportunity has arrived. This is the place you need to be to forge your future. There is nothing for you on the west coast of America."*

"Should I wait and see if they get back to me at least?"

"You can choose to wait, but you already know the answer. It is inscribed on the documents," the voice said.

Visu opened his eyes. He picked up the acceptance letter again, his gaze falling on the small, blue ink stamps. He squinted. There, at the bottom of each circle, almost invisible, was the faint, mechanical imprint of a number. *728444.*

"What do these numbers mean?" he asked inside his head.

"They are not just numbers. They represent a time. It is a spring equinox deep in the future, and a fateful day. A fateful day when you will make a fateful decision. It is a decision you will need to make, and you can only make if you choose this path," the voice continued.

"Well, that's not particularly helpful," Visu thought.

"In any event, the answer will come to you. It will be a choiceless choice, and the outcome will be good." The voice faded out of Visu's head.

As the scene slowly dissolved, Oliver thought about what he'd just witnessed. It was a projection within a projection. He had seen Visu, in the past, having his own internal, guided experience. And the voice … it wasn't the Noncemeister. It was different, calmer, more direct. The realization was a new, crucial piece of the puzzle. Perhaps anyone capable of this strange ritual of time projection had their own guide, some figure their subconscious latched onto. For Oliver, it was the absurd creature from his childhood. For Bryce, for Esteban, and now for Visu, it was someone, or something, else entirely.

755150 (Sep 21)

"Good to see you again, dude," Nick said as they settled into a table at O'Connell's, a ritual that now felt like a scene from a previous life. "How long has it been since you left? A month now?"

"Three weeks," Oliver said. "August 31st was my last day."

"Man, it feels like just yesterday. Or maybe years ago," Nick said, shaking his head. "So what have you been up to?"

"Not too much," Oliver said, taking a small, satisfying sip of his Żywiec. The beer was especially crisp and good today. "Just teaching the basics of coding at an after-school program. Figuring out my next move in the meantime. It pays the bills, so I'm not in a rush."

"Wow, dude," Nick laughed, but the sound was sharp, brittle. "How the mighty have fallen. From blazing the trail in high finance to teaching a bunch of uptown pre-teens how to write *for loops*. How are you handling the contrast?"

The comment, meant to be a friendly jab, landed with a dull thud. A few months ago, it would have stung. Now, Oliver just felt a quiet, sad distance from his friend. "I'm actually enjoying myself," he said, his voice calm. "The kids are eager to learn, and I feel like I'm contributing something positive. Unlike at BlockWaves, where I was working on dead-end science experiments that generated little more than marketing buzz."

Nick's smile faltered. He seemed to notice the change in Oliver, the new, solid core of certainty that hadn't been there before. He backed off. "No, I get it. Just giving you a hard time," he said, his own bravado deflating. "To be honest with you, I've been wondering if you were the smart one, getting out when you did. Tarantula is officially on pause. Most of that team has been let go since you left. I'm starting to have my doubts if our whole enterprise strategy was the right approach."

Oliver just shrugged, a silent, grim agreement.

"I don't know about this whole crypto thing anymore, dude," Nick went on, his voice dropping to a low, anxious murmur. "The Merge was supposed to be this huge deal, but the price has barely budged. If anything, it's gone down. I honestly don't think the market is ready for the type of innovation Web3 has in store."

"Are you sure the market isn't ready," Oliver asked gently, "Or that they're having a perfectly rational response to a technology that consistently over-promises and underdelivers?"

"No, man. That can't be it," Nick shook his head, unwilling to accept the simpler, harsher truth. "But I am worried. I was hoping to recoup my losses, but it's been slow-going." He leaned in, his voice a conspiratorial whisper. "And just a few weeks back, Sam Trabucco, the CEO of Alameda Research, he just quit. Disappeared into silence."

Oliver raised an eyebrow. He hadn't been paying close attention. "Who's that?"

"Alameda is the investment fund, the trading arm of the FTX universe," Nick explained, the names a litany of his former faith. "It's not a good sign. But," he said, a flicker of the old, desperate hope returning to his eyes, "I still have faith in SBF. Visionaries like him can deal with these short-term setbacks."

Oliver had nothing more to say. The conversation with Nick had only strengthened the quiet, solid certainty that had been growing in him since he'd quit. He was on the right path. He was good.

After a couple of drinks, he walked back to his apartment from O'Connell's. Daniela wasn't back yet from a late rehearsal. The apartment was quiet. He felt the distinct pull, the quiet invitation from the timechain. He decided it was time to check in.

He sat in the armchair, closed his eyes, and let the world dissolve.

He found himself standing on a street corner in Midtown, the sounds of the city muffled, the colors slightly desaturated. He recognized the scene immediately: it was the diner, a few months ago, right after his meeting with Gyorgy. He watched as the frail, dying man got into a taxi. But this time, Oliver's perspective didn't fade. It followed the cab.

The taxi made its way through several blocks of traffic before pulling up to a small, quiet café in Gramercy. Gyorgy got out gingerly and went inside. He sat at a table and waited, a solitary, patient ghost.

A short while later, a woman entered the café. She was elegant, composed, her movements fluid and deliberate. She walked up to Gyorgy's table, and Oliver's breath caught in his throat. It was Adele. Christiaan's sister. Gyorgy looked up, and she leaned down to give him a brief, formal hug before sitting across from him. How could they possibly know each other?

The conversation that followed was a ghostly, silent film at first, but then the sound faded in, just as it had with his parents in the café. Gyorgy was repeating his story, his voice the same deathly monotone, wearing a look of unfathomable pain on his face. Adele listened, her intelligent, analytical eyes never leaving his, her expression a careful, calibrated performance of sympathy.

"Adele, I need you to do this for me," Oliver heard Gyorgy say, his voice cracking with the same raw desperation. "Please get Christiaan's forgiveness for me the next time you see him. Please, Adele, promise me."

"Of course, I will," Adele said, her voice smooth and reassuring, a stark contrast to Gyorgy's raw emotion. "I'm seeing him next week. I'm sure he will have no hesitation in forgiving you once he understands."

"Thank you, Adele," Gyorgy whispered, his eyes welling with tears. He reached into his pocket and pulled out the second envelope. The one he had put back in his pocket at the diner. He slid it across the table to her.

Adele took the envelope but didn't open it. Her focus was elsewhere. "Gyorgy," she said, her tone shifting, the performance of sympathy giving way to a sharp, focused intensity, "There's something I need from you as well."

Gyorgy let out a wry, rattling laugh. "What can this dying man have to offer anyone?"

"It's about the third Bryce painting," she said, her voice a low, urgent murmur. "I need to know where it is. Christiaan hid something in it, many years ago, and he's now telling us how to find it. But we need the painting. We also need the second one. There are things hidden in both."

"I knew he was up to no good when he visited me in Budapest," Gyorgy chuckled, a brief, fond memory. "He wasn't so interested in the art, but in hiding things in it." He shook his head. "Well, I know nothing about the second painting. As for the third, I sold it to a broker – Bojan Mitrovic. That's all I've got, sorry."

Adele's composure didn't falter, but Oliver could see a flicker of cold, calculating frustration in her eyes. She leaned forward. "Gyorgy, you have to give me something more. You're not going to be around for much longer. This is all money from the work you did together. We don't want it falling into the wrong hands."

Gyorgy thought for a few long moments, his gaze distant. "The only thing I can tell you," he said finally, "Is to ask Maren Dehnert. She might know. Do you know her?"

"I've heard the name," Adele said, a flicker of something unreadable in her eyes. "I don't think I've met her."

"She was a friend of Christiaan's," Gyorgy said. "She knew about the paintings. She lives in the city. You should be able to look her up."

"Okay," Adele said, her mission accomplished. "Thanks for that. I will."

The scene held for a moment longer – the dying man and the cool, composed woman who had just gotten what she came for – and then it faded away.

Oliver sat bolt upright in the armchair, his heart hammering against his ribs. The quiet of the apartment rushed back in, a stark, silent contrast to the charged, secret-filled scene he had just witnessed. He couldn't believe it. Gyorgy, the man who had presented himself as a lone, grieving friend, was connected to Christiaan. And Maren ... Maren was a friend of Christiaan's, a central node in this web of secrets, and she had lied to him, over and over again.

That's how Adele had found her. Gyorgy had sent her there. And the paintings ... the poems were the map *to* the key, a key hidden in the intricate details of Bryce's art. The nagging, persistent worry about his father's connection to MixMarket was now a full-blown, terrifying certainty. Gyorgy was the link. Dad and Christiaan had to have known each other.

Just then, the front door opened, and Daniela walked in, her cheerful presence a jarring intrusion into his dark, spiraling thoughts. "Hey you. Guess who's back?"

He just waved absently, his mind still a thousand miles away, lost in a café in Gramercy.

She noticed his expression immediately. "What's up?" she asked, her smile fading into a look of concern. "You look like you've seen a ghost."

The question, so innocent and accurate, broke the dam. He was too distressed, too unmoored to hold it in any longer. The carefully constructed wall between his quest and his life with her crumbled. He told her everything. He told her about the projection, about Gyorgy's lie, about Adele, and finally, about Maren. He laid bare his suspicions, the cold certainty that their trusted guide was not what she seemed.

Daniela listened, her expression growing more grave with every word. When he finished, she didn't argue or defend her teacher. "I don't know what the deal with her is," she said, her voice quiet but firm. "She was acting weird when I asked her about the Mediterranean trip. She denied it completely, said she was in India the whole time. She got really defensive." She looked at him, her eyes full of a new, shared suspicion. "I agree, Oliver. I think there's something up with her."

"God," he said, running a hand through his hair in frustration. "What I would give to know what her involvement in all this really is."

"Oliver," Daniela said slowly, a new thought dawning, "I didn't think this was relevant until you told me all this, but … does the name Bojan mean anything to you?"

The name was an explosion in his mind, a sudden, blinding flash of connection that made the air in the room feel electric. "Wait, what?" he exclaimed, staring at her. "Of course, it does. That was the Serbian art broker. The one Gyorgy sold the painting to. I guess I never mentioned his name. What about him?"

"Well," Daniela began, her voice dropping to a low, conspiratorial whisper, "The day I was packing up to leave Maren's place, I heard her on the phone in the other room. She was whispering, but all I could pick up was one word, over and over again. 'Bojan.' It sounded urgent, important. It was weird because she was whispering – she usually has her conversations right out in the open. I thought about it for a second, then just let it go."

"Oh, wow," Oliver breathed. "It is definitely important. We have to find out what she was talking to him about. But how?"

"There was another weird thing," Daniela added, a new, strange piece of the puzzle clicking into place for her as well. "At the end of the call, her voice got louder. I heard her say she thought someone was listening, that she could 'sense' it. I thought she meant me, so I just walked out into the kitchen to make some noise. I'm sorry, Oliver. I thought it was just an odd event, but I should have told you."

Oliver acknowledged her apology with a small shake of his head, his mind already racing, a wild, impossible idea beginning to form. It was a leap of logic, a synthesis of everything he'd been told – by Maren, by the Noncemeister – about his strange and terrifying gift. He looked at her, his eyes wide with the sheer audacity of the thought.

"Babe," he said, the name slipping out, intimate and unbidden, "I know exactly what we need to do. You need to project back to that day. Replay that conversation."

Daniela's face registered a flicker of surprise, followed by a slow, coy grin. "Did you just call me babe? That's the first time."

A hot flush of embarrassment crept up Oliver's neck. "I'm sorry, I just got excited."

"No, that was so cute," she said, her voice a low, playful murmur. "You can call me that. I like it." She leaned back, her smile fading as she considered his plan.

"So what do you think?" he pressed, his excitement returning. "Can you do it? Project back and listen in?"

"I don't know, Oliver," she said, a genuine hesitation in her voice. "My projections are so normal compared to yours. It's just meditation for me. I calm my mind, and if there's something to process, it just … happens."

"Oh, come on, you can try," he pleaded. And then, the second, even crazier part of his idea came out. "And I can try going in with you …"

"What are you talking about?" she said, her voice a note of pure shock. "You can't just enter my mind. That's impossible."

"Maren told me my dad could do it," he said, his own voice full of a desperate, newfound conviction. "And that I might have the same gift. It's worth a shot, if you're okay with it."

Daniela just stared at him, the implications of his request – both psychic and deeply personal – hanging in the air between them. A long, silent moment passed. Then, with a slow, deliberate movement, she stood up, walked over to his armchair, and settled into his lap, her arms draping around his neck. She played with his hair for a moment, a sly, knowing smile on her face.

"Even if it is possible," she whispered, her voice a low, intimate tease, "I'm not sure I'm ready to have you *inside my head* just yet. It's only been a few weeks, Oliver. I might not be ready for that kind of commitment."

The Notepad

i) violin ii) toddler iii) alley iv) shoulder v) educate vi) rookie vii) oval viii) below ix) punch x) certain xi) cover xii) agree xiii) coast xiv) suggest xv) boring xvi) tissue xvii) good

CHAPTER 18. Sausage

"Why is a sausage called a banger, anyway?" Oliver asked, the question a small, idle curiosity as Aisling set a plate of bangers and mash in front of him. "Is it an Irish thing?"

"Oh, I dunno, really," Aisling said with a laugh. "It's more of a British thing. I remember hearing that back during the war, butchers used to fill sausages with water. When you stuck a fork in a hot one, it went 'bang!'" She shrugged. "Not sure how true that story is. The Brits have strange words for everything."

Oliver nodded, looking around the quiet Sunday afternoon emptiness of O'Connell's. Eddie was coming by his apartment later, and he'd wanted to grab a late lunch first, a moment of peace before the inevitable conversational storm.

"Hey, Aisling," he said, the real reason for his visit surfacing, "Did your mom ever end up selling that painting?"

"Funny you bring that up," she said, leaning on the bar. "She finally accepted that Serbian guy's offer on Friday. She didn't want to deal with the cash, but no one else was biting, so she's going to take it. He said he'll be back in a couple of weeks to close the deal."

The casual words hit Oliver with the force of a physical blow. A cold dread washed over him. *Bojan.* He was about to get the painting. Which meant

Maren would have it. All the secrets Christiaan had hidden inside it would be hers.

"When … when is he picking it up?" he asked, trying to keep his voice steady, to mask the sudden, frantic urgency he felt.

"I think he told my mum he'd be back in the country on October 18th, and he'd stop by the next day," Aisling replied, oblivious to the panic rising in Oliver's chest.

Two weeks. The timeline was a ticking clock. He had to do something. He couldn't let Bojan get his hands on it. But what?

"Where is the painting now?" he asked, his mind racing.

"It's in the storage room right here," Aisling said, pointing down at the floor behind the bar.

Oliver leaned over the bar and saw it – a heavy, metal trapdoor set into the wooden floor.

"I know it doesn't look like much," she said, "But there's a large basement down there. We keep all our supplies, and there's a separate dry room where we're keeping the painting."

The beautiful, terrible irony of it wasn't lost on him. *A below.* Just as the surrealist school of art dictated, Bryce's second painting was being kept in an underground space, hidden from public view. Aisling, in a simple, practical act, had accidentally fulfilled the work's bizarre philosophical destiny. Life was colluding with art, not just imitating it.

His curiosity was now a desperate, tactical need. He had to see it. "Can I take a look at what's down there?" he asked, trying to sound like a casual, curious customer. "I don't think I've ever been inside a pub's storage room before."

Aisling laughed. "It's nothing grand. We have to fight tooth and nail to keep the rats out of there, and believe me, that's no mean task in the city these days." She glanced around the empty pub. "Oh, what the heck. Come on down and take a quick look."

She knelt, unlatched two heavy bolts, and with a grunt of effort, slid the heavy metal trapdoor aside, revealing a dark, gaping hole in the floor. A steep, ladder-like wooden staircase descended into the gloom. The air that rose up smelled of damp earth, stale beer, and something else, something vaguely metallic.

Oliver followed her down into a dank, dimly lit room. They walked past a supply room stacked high with boxes of liquor and cleaning supplies and entered a new space, the temperature dropping a good twenty degrees. All around them, hanging from metal hooks on the ceiling, were long links of sausages.

"I guess this is the banger storage area, then," Oliver laughed, the word feeling strange in his mouth.

"It's not the only one," Aisling said, leading him through the forest of cured meat.

They entered a room behind the cold room, and the change in atmosphere was immediate. The air here was bone-dry, the constant, low hum of two large dehumidifiers the only sound. "This is our dry storage room," she said.

"I had no idea you had this much space down here," Oliver said, his voice a low note of awe. "It's almost as big as the bar."

"Oh yeah, some of these downtown basements are huge. In fact," she said, pointing to a metal door in the far corner, its dull gray paint mostly obscured by a rash of angry rust, "There's a whole system of interconnected tunnels down here. That opens into a tunnel that's a half-block walk to the Prince Street station."

"Wow," Oliver said, marveling at the thought of the hidden labyrinth beneath his feet. "It doesn't look like it's locked."

"It's not," Aisling said. "That door hasn't been opened since 9/11. We had some firefighters break in through here that day to get to people stuck in the subway. I never got it fixed after that. It's probably rusted shut to the stone wall, in any case. You'd need a battering ram to get it open now."

Oliver walked over to the door and gave it a firm push. It was like pushing against a solid wall of stone. It didn't budge a millimeter.

"So where's the painting?" he asked, turning back to her, a hopeful excitement rising in his chest.

"Right there," she said, gesturing to a large shelf. "Behind the sausage packs."

She went over, moved several large, vacuum-sealed packages of cured sausages out of the way, and revealed it. A large, square object, lying on its side, wrapped in a thick, opaque sheet of industrial plastic.

"Ah," Oliver said, the single word a small, sharp exhalation of pure disappointment. "Right. It's wrapped." He had been so close. He had imagined standing in front of it, examining the wreath, searching for the hidden clues Christiaan had left. But he knew he couldn't ask her to unwrap it, not without revealing an interest that would be impossible to explain.

Still disappointed, but at a loss for what to do next, he thanked Aisling. They walked back up the steep stairs, the trapdoor closing with a heavy, final thud behind them, sealing the secret away in the dark. He left the pub and started for his apartment. Eddie was visiting at four. He had twenty minutes to get to Chelsea.

As Oliver got to his apartment, a text message buzzed on his phone. It was Eddie: *One minute away.* He sat down at his computer to clear out a few emails while he waited.

Fifteen minutes passed. Oliver looked up from his screen. He walked out of the apartment and took the elevator down to the lobby. And there he was. Eddie, deep in a performance of high-octane exasperation, his arms waving like a conductor leading a symphony of grievance. His audience of one, Santos the doorman, was listening with rapt, serious attention.

"… and you know how many years it took them to fix the Van Wyck Expressway? I swear on my mother it was over thirty years," Eddie was saying as Oliver approached, barely even acknowledging his arrival. "Do you know what a pain in the ass it used to be to get to JFK from uptown? First of all, it would take me an hour just to cross over into Queens over the Triboro bridge, because those bozos were always doing some renovation on Astoria Boulevard. You know that off-ramp right at the end of the bridge before you get onto Grand Central Parkway?"

Santos nodded, wearing an expression of solemn agreement.

"They always found a reason to do construction there, don't ask me why, boss," Eddie went on, his voice rising with the injustice of it all. "So that backs you up halfway down the Triboro. Then, you get past that, and you start flying down Grand Central Parkway. Well maybe not quite flying because you could hit a bit of traffic around the LaGuardia exits and maybe around exit 10 for the Long Island Expressway, but usually you were flying on Grand Central, I mean flying. And then boom! You hit exit 13 and boom! That's it, end of story. You might as well kiss your flight goodbye. Exit 13 S is the one you take to the Van Wyck Expressway, and you can't even get on it for starters."

Oliver tried to find a gap, a single, fractional pause in the torrent of words to announce his presence, but it was impossible. He was a spectator to a one-man show that had been running for fifteen minutes and showed no signs of stopping.

"As God is my witness, Santos, I'm telling you, the number of times I thought I'd lose it, I mean completely and totally lose it, trying to get onto exit 13 S ..." Eddie's hands were now a blur, miming a desperate battle with an invisible steering wheel. "... and then, you somehow get past that exit and that's when the real fun begins. Then you're on the Van Wyck. Congratulations. One lane. One freaking lane. That's all they let us have for thirty years. Can you believe that, boss? All these taxes that we pay. State tax, city tax, sales tax, inheritance tax, gas tax, and capital gains for crying out loud. And all they can give us is one lane for thirty years? You tell me, chief, where is the justice here?"

"There is none," Santos nodded, his voice a low, sagely rumble. "What do you expect from these people?"

"That's exactly what I'm trying to say, big guy!" Eddie exclaimed, jabbing a triumphant finger in the air. "That goddamn road was supposed to be three lanes wide, and truth be told, it really needed to be four with all the traffic that needs to get to JFK. So that's it. You're stuck on that two- or three-mile stretch of road for almost two hours some days. Getting to JFK used to take longer than the flight itself some days. And I'm talking about flying to Europe, not Philly or DC."

"They did finish the work on Van Wyck this year, though," Santos pointed out, not unreasonably.

"This is what I'm saying, chief!" Eddie threw his hands up, a gesture of pure, theatrical exasperation. "How long did it take them? I remember having this issue in the 90s and now here we are in 2022 and you're telling me the work is done. Do they want me to give them a trophy? Should I show up to their house and give them all foot massages and cook them steak dinners? Gimme a goddamn break, boss. These guys are clowns, and I honestly don't know what we can do to fix it."

"They're all the same," Santos concurred gravely. "You vote for the other guy next time, he's gonna be no different than the previous guy."

Eddie was still not willing to let go of the Van Wyck Expressway. "You know, one time, it must have been in 2005 or 2006 – I still remember it like it was yesterday." He leaned in closer to Santos, his voice dropping to a conspiratorial whisper, as if sharing a state secret. "This was after they had the Air Trains installed that connected the Jamaica station to JFK. You know those thin overhead platforms they built with the modern-looking trains whizzing around above your head while you're sitting in your car waiting with your hat in your hand?"

Santos nodded, his expression one of shared suffering.

Eddie went on, his body now acting out the scene. "I was rushing Melissa to the airport because her mom was sick, and she needed to get to Florida because she was worried. Of course, we'd been stuck on the Van Wyck for hours. Melissa is losing it, and at one point," he mimed a car door swinging open and a frantic passenger trying to escape, "She opened the door and almost got out of the car while it's still moving. I mean we were moving dead slow because of the traffic, but still moving. I asked the woman what the hell she was doing. She was in such a panic to make her flight and see her mom, that poor woman thought she could get out of the car and climb up the AirTrain tower and catch the train to JFK from there. Can you believe that boss?"

"Hey, Uncle Eddie," Oliver interjected, his voice firm, finally cutting through the monologue.

The firm tone seemed to jolt both men out of their conversational trance. Santos responded first. "Eddie, we've got this young, important business professional here who wants to talk to you. Let me not hold you up any further."

"Yes, yes, Olly," Eddie said, finally turning his full attention to Oliver as if noticing him for the first time. "I know we've got to check out what you've done with your old man's digs. Santos is a bad influence, let me tell you," he chuckled. "He gets me going on my favorite topic, the incompetence of our public officials."

They took the elevator up and walked into the apartment. Eddie stopped just inside the doorway and let out a long, low whistle. "Wow," he said, his gaze sweeping across the room. "I can still feel his presence here, chief. I like what you've done with it, though. You've brought your own style, moved a few things around. I like it."

"Well, some of that is my girlfriend Daniela's doing," Oliver said. "She's really good at this stuff and has helped a lot since moving in."

"Wait, hold up now, tiger." Eddie put his hands on his hips in theatrical shock. "What's all this? Your girlfriend has moved in with you? When did this happen? You never told me you had a girlfriend. Diane never mentioned anything about that when she told me you'd moved in here."

"Yeah, it was pretty recent," Oliver said sheepishly. "I moved here in late July, and she moved in in September."

"Well, well, well. Look at this big guy right here," Eddie said, a wistful, faraway look coming into his eyes. "Last I checked, he was running around complaining his dad wasn't playing soccer with him when he was sitting down to chat with Uncle Eddie, and the next thing I know, he's moved in with his girlfriend. Strange world, isn't it? It's amazing how quickly time flies."

He seemed to snap out of his reminiscing, his focus returning to the present with a sudden, business-like intensity. "Listen chief," he continued, "I spoke to Diane, and she told me you quit your job recently and are looking for a new gig. Why didn't you talk to me?"

Oliver groaned internally. *Trust my mom to interpret 'figuring things out' as 'looking for a new gig.'* "I'm not looking, Uncle Eddie," he said, trying to keep the defensiveness out of his voice. "I'm teaching part-time and enjoying it."

"Oh yeah? What are you teaching?" Eddie asked, leaning forward with an air of paternal interest.

"A middle-school after-school program. They're learning how to code and the basics of money," Oliver replied.

"Olly, listen to yourself. Gimme a break, tiger." Eddie let out a short, incredulous laugh. "A bright young guy like you, with all your degrees and qualifications. That's no job for you, God bless those kids, of course. You sound like you're in a rut, and it's a good thing your Uncle Eddie is here to help."

"Eddie, I'm good, I promise," Oliver said, the words feeling increasingly uncomfortable. "I'm working on some business ideas on the side."

"What sort of business ideas?" Eddie pressed, his gaze sharp.

Oliver hesitated. His "business ideas" were a vague, unformed cloud of reading about the Lightning Network and daydreaming about a different kind of future. "It's related to bitcoin," he said finally.

"Bitcoin?" The word exploded out of Eddie's mouth, a mixture of shock and disbelief. "Come on, chief. You can't be serious. That's the thing criminals and drug dealers use. What kind of business can you build on bitcoin?"

"Bitcoin can be used by anyone; it's a neutral technology," Oliver said, and then, in a moment of pure, impulsive inspiration, an analogy so perfect it felt like it was channeled directly from the Noncemeister sprang to his lips. "It's sort of like The Force in Star Wars. You can be a Jedi and use The Force for good, or you can be a Sith and use it for bad. I want to be a Jedi." The words hung in the air, and he immediately regretted them. It sounded so cringe.

Eddie, thankfully, was completely uninterested in a philosophical debate. He just bulldozed right over it. "Olly, forget all this bitcoin stuff. I can get you on the models team at WilcoxRe, easy. It's your dad's old team. They need a senior engineer." He leaned in again, his voice dropping to a conspiratorial whisper. "I mean, it's going to be you writing a crap ton of backend code, don't get me wrong. You'll get to see how the sausage is made in all its glory. You've got to be into that sort of thing. I wouldn't do that job if you paid me all the money in the world, but hey, you're made of stronger stuff than me. I know you're not quite at a senior engineer level yet, but I believe in you, big guy, you know what I'm talking about?"

"Eddie, I don't know if ..." Oliver started to say, completely taken aback by the offer.

"It's a senior engineer role, Olly," Eddie pressed on, sensing his hesitation and mistaking it for negotiation. "You'll start off with close to a 200k base salary. I can get you in, no interviews, no questions. You tell me when you want to start. You're Nate Battolo's son, for heaven's sake. You'll kill it there."

Oliver was genuinely touched. For all his bluster and gaucheness, Eddie had a heart of gold. The offer was an unconditional act of kindness, a desire to help the son of a man he clearly loved. But the thought of going back, of re-entering that corporate world of compromises and dead-end projects, felt like a betrayal of everything he was becoming. It would be selling his soul for a steady paycheck. "Can I take some time and think about it, Eddie?" he said, his voice soft with a gratitude he couldn't fake.

"Take your time, tiger. The job is open. Even if this one gets filled, I'll be able to get you into another one any time. Just say the word."

"Thanks, Eddie. I really appreciate you doing this."

"You bet, big guy." Eddie beamed, happy to have solved Oliver's problem. "You know, you just reminded me of something when you mentioned bitcoin. Do you remember Greg Ostrowsky?"

"I don't think so. The name doesn't ring a bell," Oliver said.

"Well, he used to work with your dad and me back in the day," Eddie said. "More with your dad than with me. Quit around seven years ago and moved out to the sticks in Pennsylvania. Became a goat farmer or something."

Eddie paused, his eyes widening as a completely unrelated but, to him, profoundly important thought struck. "Did you know," he began, leaning forward as if about to impart a great secret, "That goat milk is much better for your digestion than cow's milk?" He latched onto the new thought, his entire body reorienting to this new, more exciting topic. "For the longest time, I used to get bloated every day. Bloated and gassy," he said, rubbing his own stomach with a pained expression. "Terrible stomach aches, heartburn. I had no clue what was wrong with me. Then you won't believe it, kiddo. I figured out what happened. I was lactose intolerant!" He delivered the line with the dramatic weight of a shocking medical diagnosis. "Can you believe that, chief? A Puerto Rican kid from the Bronx, lactose intolerant. Do you know what the other kids in the Bronx would have done to me if I told them that?"

Oliver just sat there, a helpless spectator. He had been so close to learning something about Ostrowsky, and now he was trapped in a lecture on dairy alternatives. He knew from experience that Eddie was now in the zone, and there was no escape.

"So anyways, I figure out I'm lactose intolerant and I'm devastated," Eddie went on, his tone one of tragic remembrance. "What did they expect me to do? Put soy milk in my coffee like some sort of Brooklyn hipster? And don't even get me started on oat milk. What the hell is even oat milk, anyway?"

He shook his head in disgust, then his face brightened again. "But then some genius pops out of the woodwork and starts talking about some enzyme called beta lactoglobulin or some mumbo-jumbo like that. Said that was the issue, and if I switched to goat milk, it would be fixed."

He paused, taking a deep, satisfied breath, reveling in the memory of this pivotal moment. Oliver, still touched by Eddie's earlier generosity, decided not to interrupt. He would let the story run its course.

"And you won't believe it, kiddo. It worked." Eddie's voice was full of a triumphant, life-affirming joy. "It's expensive as sin, don't get me wrong. Three times the price of cow's milk, and you've got to get used to the gamy taste. But the damn thing worked. No bloating, no stomachaches, no nothing." He leaned back, a look of triumph on his face. "And you're not going to believe this either: I tried cow's milk again a few years later, and I didn't have any issues! Somehow, the goat milk cured me completely."

He sat there for a moment, basking in the glory of his story. Oliver waited, giving him a moment, then gently nudged the conversation back onto the rails. "Eddie, so what happened to Greg Ostrowsky?"

"Oh right, right," Eddie said, a sheepish look on his face as he remembered his original point. "I totally lost my train of thought there, chief. So yeah, Ostrowsky shows up out of the blue the other day and we're having this nice long dinner in Jersey. Montclair, actually. Not too far from your mom's place. Anyway, we're reminiscing about the good old days at WilcoxRe, and the topic of your old man comes up. Why wouldn't it, come to think of it. The guy was a goddamn rockstar that everybody loved."

Oliver was listening intently now, his earlier annoyance replaced by a laser-like focus. Eddie's casual mention of bitcoin had reminded him of something, and the name Ostrowsky was the key.

Eddie continued, oblivious to the sudden shift in Oliver's attention. "So Ostrowsky starts talking about this time they both were at a client site in Europe, nine or ten years ago. They're out for drinks, just the two of them, getting really drunk. Then your old man starts getting candid. He told Greg that he was working on some bitcoin stuff under a pseudonym, so nobody would know it's him." Eddie leaned in, his voice a conspiratorial whisper. "He then apparently went on to say that he might be in trouble and would likely have to kill the pseudonym and stop working on bitcoin. Can you believe that, kiddo? Nate the Great had a double life. I thought it was wild when Greg told me this. Who would've thunk it?"

The words were a series of explosions in the quiet of Oliver's mind. *A pseudonym.* His dad was one of them. And he was in trouble, a decade ago. But he'd never shown it, never let the mask of the calm, professional family man slip. How?

"Did Ostrowsky say anything else?" Oliver asked, his own voice sounding distant to his ears.

"Yeah, he did say Nate told him he was involved with a few other people and thought they were going to double-cross him," Eddie replied, "And that he was going to do something about it."

"Did he say who these people were?" Oliver asked, his voice tight with anxiety. "Or what he was going to do?"

"Greg didn't say anything about names," Eddie said, shrugging. "But apparently Nate told him he was going to hide the money somehow. Hide the bitcoins, I guess is what he meant."

Oliver sank back in his chair, another piece of the puzzle slamming into place. His father, a decade ago, on the verge of being double-crossed by his partners, had engineered an escape. He had pulled out some of the bitcoin, abandoned the pseudonym to cover his tracks, and created this elaborate, posthumous treasure hunt to secure the funds. And he could never touch the money himself, because every transaction would be a flare in the dark, a signal to the very people he had been hiding from.

He wondered how much it could have been. A few hundred bitcoin? Five hundred? At today's price, that was ten million dollars. Not too shabby.

But as the theory solidified in his mind, a single, gaping, impossible hole opened up in the logic of it. He replayed it all, the perfect, intricate clockwork of the plan, and it all stopped at the same, unanswerable question. How? How on Earth could his dad have known he was going to die?

"Do you want to grab an early dinner, champ? I'm starved," Eddie's voice interrupted, a jarring intrusion from a simpler, less complicated reality.

"Well, I had a late lunch," Oliver said, his mind still a thousand miles away. "But I'll walk with you to the restaurant."

"Great, and you'll love this place I have in mind," Eddie said, his enthusiasm returning in a rush. "Best Italian sausage in town, trust me."

As they walked out of the apartment, Oliver immediately regretted his offer. Eddie, his part in the grand, unfolding mystery complete, had now launched into an interminable, passionate ode to sausage.

The Notepad

i) violin ii) toddler iii) alley iv) shoulder v) educate vi) rookie vii) oval viii) below ix) punch x) certain xi) cover xii) agree xiii) coast xiv) suggest xv) boring xvi) tissue xvii) good xviii) sausage

757459 (October 6)

"Okay, are you ready?" Oliver's voice was a low whisper in the quiet of the bedroom. "We might go in deep here, so I want to make sure you're prepared."

Daniela nodded, her eyes already shut, her breathing slow and even. She had finally, after days of gentle coaxing, agreed to let him try. "It's not that easy for me, Oliver," she murmured, her voice a soft, vulnerable thread in the dark. "My mind … it throws up a lot of obstacles. Distractions. I have to make my way past them slowly. You'll have to be patient with me, okay?"

"Don't worry," he said, his own voice a mixture of reassurance and a nervous, thrilling excitement. "We'll go at your pace. I'll be gentle, I promise." Internally, he had no idea what he was doing. He was just hoping that by some strange miracle, he could simply will himself into her mind, to be a passenger on her journey.

He closed his eyes, focusing on the image of her, on the feeling of her lying beside him, and let go.

He was in a brick building, walking down a short, cool corridor. A man's voice, gentle and soothing, drifted from a room just ahead. Oliver moved toward the sound and looked in. A bearded man in a loose white robe and turban sat on a small pedestal, speaking to a group of twenty or thirty people seated on the floor before him.

Oliver recognized him instantly. Guru Brahma. He looked a few years older than the last time he saw him in a projection – in his fifties this time. This was his ashram, likely in the 1990s. *Damn it,* he thought, a wave of disappointment washing over him. This wasn't Daniela's mind. This was his own projection, hijacked by whatever strange forces now guided him. There was nothing to do but let it play out.

Guru Brahma was speaking, his voice a calm river flowing through the silent, attentive room. "And so," he was saying, "Whenever you see something as an obstacle, remember that it is a creation of your own mind." He paused, his kind eyes scanning the faces of his followers. "I don't mean that the object or situation itself is a creation of your mind. No. That thing just *is*. The idea that it is somehow an *obstacle* to your goals – that is what you have created. It is just a thought you have assigned to that object. By itself, the situation is a disembodied entity. The perception is what you create, isn't it?"

A soft murmur of agreement went through the group.

"So the next time you find yourself in such a situation," the Guru continued, his voice so reasonable, so logical, that the truth of his words landed with a quiet, undeniable force, "Ask yourself: Is there a different thought I can attribute to this? A better feeling thought that allows me not to perceive it as an obstacle? You will find that if you allow yourself to stop, to accept that moment for what it is, and find peace in it, your mind will create answers. Sometimes the answer is just to the side of this so-called obstacle. Or below it. Or above it. Just allow yourself to expand your perspective."

The words echoed in Oliver's mind, a key for a lock he hadn't yet encountered, a piece of wisdom from a past he had never lived, delivered at a time he had not chosen.

Oliver listened to the Guru's words, a strange sense of dislocation washing over him. The philosophy was simple, almost a self-help cliché, but coming from this man, in this strange, sun-drenched memory, it felt profound. Just as he was processing the idea, his gaze drifted across the audience and snagged on a familiar face. A young woman, strikingly beautiful, was listening to the Guru with a rapt, intense focus. He grappled with the memory, trying to place her, until it hit him like a punch in the gut. It was Maren. A young Maren, no older than her mid-twenties, decades before the serene, calculating mask she now wore had settled into place.

The Guru concluded his talk, and the audience began to disperse, but the young Maren remained behind, quietly putting away cushions. Oliver-the-observer felt his perspective drift closer, a moth drawn to this impossible flame from the past. As he drew near, the young Maren suddenly froze, her head snapping up. She turned, her eyes not looking at the empty space in the room, but looking *out* of the projection, directly at him.

"Nate, how dare you invade my privacy like this!" she said, her voice a sharp, angry slash in the peaceful quiet of the ashram.

The direct address, the violation of the fundamental rule of his observations, was a shock that made the entire projection shimmer and distort. "Maren, it's me, Oliver, not Nate," he stuttered into the void, his own voice a useless, soundless thought.

She couldn't hear him. She was speaking to a ghost she could somehow perceive. "Nate, I know it's you there. I can sense you," she continued, her voice trembling with a raw, betrayed anger. "I do not give you permission to do this to me, do you understand? I taught you how to do this, and now you're turning the tables on me. This is unacceptable!"

"Maren, please, I'm not Nate," he thought, a frantic, silent plea. "I didn't mean to invade your privacy. I don't know why I'm here."

"I'm telling you for the last time, Nate. You need to leave right now," she said, her voice now thick with a pain that was three decades old. "You betrayed me when you chose Diane. I forgave you, but what you're doing right now is not okay. Please go."

The final words, the raw, bleeding heart of a secret he had never known, caused the projection to shatter.

Oliver's eyes snapped open. He was in his bed, the darkness of the room a welcome, solid reality. Beside him, Daniela was sleeping peacefully. *So much for the dual projection,* he thought, a bitter, ironic smile touching his lips. But the failure of their experiment was already overshadowed by the strange, terrifying success of his own. Maren had known someone was there. And she had thought it was his father. And in her anger, she had revealed the biggest secret of all. His dad hadn't just been Maren's friend. He had chosen Diane *over* her. There had been something between them.

He gently tapped Daniela's shoulder until she stirred. She opened her eyes, her face soft with sleep. "What happened?" she murmured.

"You tell me, babe," he said, his voice a strange, distant thing. "I just went to Guru Brahma's ashram in the nineties and had a young Maren yell at me, thinking I was my dad. Is that what you saw, too?"

Daniela blinked, her brow furrowing in confusion. "Uh, no. I didn't see anything. I think I just fell asleep," she said, a sheepish, apologetic look on her face. "I'm sorry, Oliver. I was feeling too much pressure to get it right, I guess. We'll try again tomorrow."

"Yeah, don't worry about it," he said, his mind already a thousand miles away, replaying Maren's angry, heartbroken words. "I'm sure we'll figure it out."

But as he lay there in the dark, a new, chilling certainty settled over him. It was going to be a lot harder than he ever could have imagined.

CHAPTER 19. CUTE

759150 (October 17)

"Can we try one last time, please?" Oliver pleaded, his voice a low, desperate murmur in the quiet of the bedroom.

Daniela looked at him, her expression a mixture of affection and deep skepticism. "Oliver, we've been trying for almost two weeks. It hasn't worked. I don't think it's possible." She sat up in bed, the sheet pooling around her waist. "Maren probably lied to you, just like she did about so many other things. You can't just *enter* another person's projection. How does that even make sense?"

"Then how has my dad been able to control mine?" he countered.

"Has he, though?" she said gently. "You have a very vivid imagination. Maybe it's the synesthesia." She paused, searching for a kinder explanation. "Oh, I don't know, Oliver. Maybe your dad had a way, but I just don't see how *you* can do the same thing. I don't see how you can just walk into my mind."

"Look, we're running out of time," he said, the urgency a sharp, frantic edge in his voice. "Bojan gets back tomorrow. He gets the painting the day after. And then Maren has it. I don't know why she wants it, but I know she's been lying to me, and that's enough. We need to find out what her deal is."

Daniela still looked unsure.

"I have an idea," he said, a last-ditch effort. "We've been trying this with both of us on the bed. What if I sit in my dad's armchair? It takes me straight in. I don't think it's about proximity; it's about finding the right conditions."

She let out a long, slow sigh of loving resignation and lay back down. Oliver went to the armchair, sat, and closed his eyes.

"Why hello there, tiger. Fancy seeing you here."

The sing-song voice rang out. The Noncemeister was floating in the purple void, meticulously polishing a single, gleaming teacup with a cloth made of shimmering moonlight.

"Ugh, you again," Oliver said. "I was hoping to be elsewhere."

"Battu, Batew, Batue, we've really got to work on your manners, don't we?" The Noncemeister tutted, setting the teacup down on a small, hovering table that had just appeared. "How about being thrilled at seeing your old friend for a change? You know, the one who's taught you everything you need to know? Without me, where would you be? Some appreciation would be nice." He pulled out the shimmering cloth and dabbed theatrically at the corner of his eye.

"You're right, you're right," Oliver conceded, too tired to argue. "I didn't mean it that way. I was just hoping to be somewhere else. It's urgent ..." He paused, the Noncemeister's words catching up to him. "What do you mean I'd be nowhere without you?"

"You goofball," the Noncemeister said, the fake tears vanishing instantly. "When did I say you'd be nowhere? I asked you where you *would* be, not tell you where you *were*."

"Good point," Oliver admitted. "I don't know where I would be. Probably a very different place."

"And which one do you think would have been the better feeling place?" the Noncemeister asked, pouring an invisible tea into the glowing cup.

"Probably this one," Oliver admitted grudgingly.

"Yes and no, Battolo," the Noncemeister said, taking a delicate, soundless sip. "But first of all, thank you for the yes. That's all I ask for – a little appreciation." He set the cup down and pretended to bite his own hand, fighting back a new, imaginary wave of tears. "It's the ingratitude that gets me." He recovered in an instant. "But also no, Battu. No. Because wherever you end up, whatever whim of happenstance takes you down one of the infinite forks that appear in front of you," – as he spoke, a vast, branching, never-ending road of pure light materialized in the void before Oliver – "You will always be exactly where you need to be. It so happens that you're in this timeline where I've set you straight, and that's exactly where you need to be."

"Right, right," Oliver said, a note of sarcasm in his voice. "Because life happens *for* me, not *to* me."

"That's correct, Batue," the Noncemeister said, and as he spoke, he pulled a small, ornate key from his pocket and unlocked a previously invisible door in the purple void. He opened it, revealing a swirling vortex of chaotic, brightly colored thoughts. "But I'm sensing a hint of derision there. That's okay, though. Slow and steady, you'll get there." He calmly closed and locked the door again.

Oliver decided to ask for help directly. "Look, I'm trying to get into someone's projection, and I don't know how. We've been trying for almost two weeks … I mean, two thousand and sixteen heartbeats, but it hasn't worked. Do you know how I can do it?"

The Noncemeister pondered this, stroking an imaginary beard. "Let me make sure I understand. You have your own reality, apparent or phenomenal, and this other person has their own, apparent or phenomenal, and you want to know how you can jump from one to the other?"

Oliver saw the trap in the framing of the question. "It's a projection episode, so that's apparent reality, right? So I'm trying to access *her* apparent reality while in *my own* apparent reality."

"Oh, dear, dear, dear," the Noncemeister sighed, his body momentarily flickering and becoming translucent with disappointment. "That's cute that you remember the names, but oh dear. Batew, when will you ever learn? We've been through this over and over again." He became solid again, his voice firm. "The universe only has one singular reality, that of being. Every other reality is just a silly conscious projection from that singular reality. If you just allow yourself to be in the singular reality, you will see all the infinite forks of it in front of you."

"That's right, you did tell me this," Oliver said, the memory of the lesson clicking into place. "And I access that by just being, right? By surrendering to the moment?"

"And by letting go of all attachments to outcomes," the Noncemeister added, and as he spoke, dozens of tiny, spectral chains that had been invisibly connected to Oliver suddenly materialized, shimmering in the purple light. "The more attached you are, the more resistance you will create. You are the mastermind of your own reality. You are the creator within your own creation. Just accept and know that."

Oliver inhaled deeply, and as he exhaled, he visualized the spectral chains shattering, turning to dust. He repeated it, a quiet sense of lightness and freedom washing over him as he let go of the frantic need to succeed. He was just here, now.

He heard the Noncemeister's voice, as if from a great distance. "And off we go!"

The world snapped into focus with a shocking, hyper-realistic clarity. The purple haze was gone. He was standing in Maren's spare bedroom, the sunlight from the window so real he could feel its warmth. He heard a sharp gasp behind him and turned. Daniela was there, staring at him, wearing an expression of stunned disbelief.

"Oliver," she breathed. "You're here. You're in my mind. I can't believe it. How did you do it?"

"I'm not entirely sure," he said, looking at his own hands, which were solid, real, here in her memory. "I just … took a step back into absolute reality, and then I saw all the possibilities. I saw yours, and I just … went in."

They could hear Maren's muffled voice from the other side of the wall. They moved closer, the sound becoming clearer, a sharp, urgent whisper.

"What do you mean she doesn't accept cash?"

The voice was a disembodied thread of sound. "I think we can only hear her side," Oliver whispered to Daniela. "We need to access *that* reality, too." He closed his eyes, took a breath, and surrendered again.

When he opened them, a new voice barked in the space, thick with an Eastern European accent. "What you want me to do? She only wants check or money order."

"We did it," Oliver said to Daniela, a triumphant grin on his face. "We can hear him now."

"Bojan, you have to figure out a way of getting that woman to sell the painting," Maren's voice hissed. "Christiaan's sister already thinks I might have the third painting, so we need to make sure we get this second one before she figures this one out too. I can't believe Gyorgy would throw me under the bus like this just before he died. Why did he have to tell Adele about me?"

"How she knows you got third painting?" Bojan's voice shot back. "When I bought from Gyorgy, I never tell him who it was for. There was no way he could know it was you."

"I don't think she knows for sure," Maren's voice hissed, a venomous, frustrated whisper that seemed to make the air in the room colder. "She was acting like she was sure, just to make me drop my guard. But I didn't fall for it. Bojan, we need to be quick. If Adele gets her hands on the second painting, we won't be able to put all the pieces together for Christiaan's wallet."

Oliver and Daniela looked at each other, their shared projection a space of silent, wide-eyed shock. *Maren is the owner of the third Bryce.* The revelation was a final, damning confirmation of all his suspicions. She was a player, a competitor in this secret, high-stakes game.

"You never tell Adele find out about you when we meet in Greece in summer," Bojan's voice grumbled, displeasure evident even through the wall.

"That's because she hadn't at the time," Maren shot back. "I had just found out from Oliver that the second painting was sitting in that pub all these years while we were searching for it. Gyorgy hadn't told Adele about me at that time."

Another lie exposed. Oliver and Daniela exchanged another look. Maren hadn't been in India, not really. She had been in Greece, meeting with this Serbian fixer, using information she had gleaned from Oliver in a supposedly confidential session.

"Bojan, you've got to get the second painting," Maren's voice continued, the urgency escalating. "We're running out of time. Once we have it, we can figure out where Christiaan's wallet is."

"Okay, don't worry. I will get it for you," Bojan said. "What about third painting? You keep it safe?"

"Yes, it's in my underground storage unit in Flushing. Wait a second, Bojan. Hold on." Maren's voice suddenly dropped, a new, sharp note of paranoia in it. "I'm sensing something here. Someone might be listening to our call. I'm going to look …"

The bedroom scene dissolved instantly, the walls and furniture melting away, and Oliver found himself back in the purple void. The Noncemeister was floating nearby, applauding softly.

"Well, that was cute, wasn't it?" he said, his voice full of amusement.

"What was cute?" Oliver asked, his mind still reeling from the torrent of revelations.

"Oh, you know," the Noncemeister said, and as he spoke, a tiny, spectral image of Oliver and Daniela holding hands appeared in his palm before vanishing. "You and your friend sharing one apparent reality. I thought it was cute."

"Oh yeah, that was wild," Oliver said, a triumphant grin spreading across his face. "I think I figured out how to do it, thank you. And you know what else I was able to figure out while I was doing that?"

"Go on big boy, tell me," the Noncemeister said with a chuckle. "Tell me how you've grown up just that little bit."

Oliver looked at the strange, smiling creature, at the entity that had been his guide, his tormentor, and his teacher. He felt a triumphant shift inside himself, a quiet click of understanding. He no longer needed permission. He no longer needed to wait for the lesson to be over. He was in control now.

"This," he said.

And he snapped his fingers.

The world shattered. He opened his eyes. He was back in his armchair, the weight of the real world settling over him. Daniela was standing beside him, an expression of anxious relief on her face.

"Oh, thank God, you're back," she breathed.

He looked up at her, a slow, confident smile on his face. "Why would I not be back?" he asked.

"Well, Maren somehow knew we were listening," Daniela said, her voice a shaky whisper as she pulled away from him, wrapping her arms around herself. "That's what happened when I was there. I told you she said someone was listening, and then I ran into the kitchen? That was it. She figured out it was us, somehow. I got scared and immediately left the projection, but you … you were just gone. You were still in there. Are you okay?"

Oliver nodded, his own heart still hammering from the strange, liberating experience. Maren's power was real, and it was unnerving. She could sense them, even across time and space.

Daniela saw the look on his face, a strange, calm smile he'd never worn before. "Why do you have such a smug grin on your face? I thought you'd be scared."

"I figured out how to get out," he said, a quiet, triumphant chuckle in his voice. "I used to be trapped with him until he let me go. But I think he accidentally gave me the answer when he told me how to access your projection."

"How did you do that?" she asked, her eyes wide with a mixture of fear and awe. "It was crazy."

"Simple," he said, the word feeling true for the first time. "I realized I was the creator within my own creation. It's amazing what your unconscious mind is capable of when your conscious mind isn't in control. Once I realized that, I knew all so-called realities are accessible to me, including yours … and including one where there is no Noncemeister."

"Oliver, you're scaring me," she said, taking a small step back. "If that's true, it means you can just … enter my mind whenever you feel like it. How will I ever have any privacy?" The concern in her voice was real, a sudden, chilling boundary between them.

He saw the fear in her eyes and realized the gravity of what his newfound power meant to her. He stepped forward, closing the distance between them, and clasped her shoulders, his gaze intense and unwavering. "Daniela, listen to me," he said, his voice a low, serious promise. "I will never, ever, *ever* enter your mind without your permission. You have my unconditional word."

She stared back at him, searching his eyes, and after a long moment, the fear in her own began to recede, replaced by a fragile, returning trust. "So what do we do now?" she asked, her voice quiet again. "In a couple of days, Maren will have both paintings. She'll have all the clues to Christiaan's wallet. You said there might be over twenty thousand bitcoin in it?"

Oliver nodded gravely. "Yes. Vince confirmed it as well …" He fell silent, his mind a whirlwind of risk, strategy, and a new, terrifying resolve. The time for observation, for learning, for being a passive recipient of his father's quest, was over. He looked up at Daniela, a dangerous, exhilarating spark in his eyes.

"I know what we need to do," he said.

"What?"

He paused, letting the weight of the decision settle, a final, irreversible choice. "We're going to steal the second painting from O'Connell's tomorrow night."

759312 (October 19)

"Are you sure you don't want a real drink?" Aisling's voice cut through the tense silence between them. "Both of you have been sitting here for an hour, and all you've had is seltzer."

"We're good, Aisling," Oliver said, forcing a smile that felt brittle. "Just another seltzer and lime for both of us."

Aisling rolled her eyes theatrically, a gesture of good-natured disbelief, and walked away.

"I can't stay up much longer, Oliver," Daniela whispered, her voice a low, frantic murmur. It was past 1 a.m., and the bar was a ghost town. "We've been nursing sparkling water for an hour. My nerves are shot."

"I know," he said, his own voice a low, steady counterpoint to her rising panic. "Just this one time. We can't afford to be anything but sharp tonight." He glanced at the clock behind the bar. "She closes at two. Give her thirty minutes to clean up and lock the doors. Then the coast is clear."

"This is insane," she said, her hands trembling slightly as she picked up her glass. "I can't believe I'm about to help you rob an Irish Pub in the middle of the night."

"Babe, we don't have a choice," he said, his gaze intense, willing her to hold it together. "Bojan is probably already in the city. He'll be here in a few hours to get that painting. And then Maren has Christiaan's twenty thousand bitcoin. I don't know what she wants with it, but it can't be anything good."

"So remind me again," she whispered, her eyes wide with a fear that was starting to infect him, "What exactly is the plan?"

"Simple," he said, keeping his voice low and even, a calm he didn't feel. "We wait until she leaves. We walk to the Prince Street station. We find the tunnel entrance Aisling showed me."

"How are you going to find one specific door in a dark subway tunnel?" she hissed. "You think it's going to have a sign that says, 'this way to steal *The Toddler*?'"

"I dropped a pin," he said calmly. "The GPS on my phone will get us right to the wall. I checked; the reception is good down there."

"Okay, fine, but it'll be pitch black," she persisted, her mind racing through every possible point of failure.

"And that's why I brought these," he said, tapping the backpack at his feet. "Two high-lumen tactical flashlights."

"Ugh, okay," she conceded, a new, more formidable obstacle appearing in her mind. "But what about the door? The heavy metal door that's been rusted shut for twenty years?"

A slow, confident smile spread across Oliver's face. He was enjoying this, the feeling of having a plan, of taking action. "You will notice," he said, tapping the backpack again, "That my backpack is not that small. That's because it also has tools in it that can chip away and shave down rocks."

"Chip away and shave down rocks?" The words came out of Daniela's mouth in a choked, incredulous whisper. "Are you serious? You want us to do masonry work in a dark, rat-infested sewer in the middle of the night? Have you completely lost your mind?"

"I heard it from both the Noncemeister and Guru Brahma," he said, his voice a calm counterpoint to her rising panic. "An obstacle only exists if you perceive it that way. You have to look above, below, and on its side. The metal door is wedged against brick and rock. So, I'm going to chip away at the rock and create space. Easy." He looked at her, his confident smile softening. "Look, you don't have to do this. It was amazing that you even offered to come. But you don't need to be here."

She looked at him, at the strange, unshakeable certainty in his eyes, and a slow, reluctant smile touched her own lips. "No, no, that's fine. Let's do it," she said, a new, adventurous spark in her voice. "After everything you've been through, I'm not going to abandon you now. I'm still skeptical, mind you, but I'll help. Besides," her face brightened, "It is kind of exciting, isn't it? Stealing a painting is something I've only ever seen in movies."

"Well, we won't be laughing if Maren gets it and we don't," he said, his tone turning serious again. "This has to work. Failure is not an option. Okay, I'll hit the restroom and be right back."

He stood up and walked toward the men's room. A line of five people were waiting. He leaned against the wall, his gaze drifting up to the TV in the corner. It was playing a video of Pink Floyd's "Echoes," one of his favorite songs, the screen a mesmerizing swirl of psychedelic colors.

And then the TV flickered. The screen seemed to rush toward him, growing until it filled his entire field of vision, the sounds of the bar and the music replaced by a sudden, absolute silence. An image flashed on the screen: a close-up of a hand holding a white key card against a reader on a heavy metal door. A storage unit. Scrawled on the key card in thick, red marker was a number: *404*.

The scene flickered again, the perspective shifting. He was now looking at a reception desk, the kind you'd find in a self-storage facility. Behind the empty desk, hanging on a wall of hooks, were dozens of key cards. His attention was drawn to one in particular, at chest height, to the left. It was the same white card, the same red number. *404*.

The image flickered again, dissolving into a screen of gray static. And then, a voice, his father's voice, spoke from the static, a single, gentle, and utterly damning sentence.

"It's not for van der Dussen to have."

The voice stopped. Oliver blinked. The TV was back in its corner, now playing a Mötley Crüe song. The line for the restroom was gone. He was alone.

A projection, he thought, his heart hammering. He wondered what the key card meant. But that thought was immediately overwhelmed by a far more troubling one. His father, in that brief, bizarre vision, had known Christiaan's last name. The hope that his dad was only on the periphery of that world, that he was an innocent bystander, had just been extinguished. He was involved. He was involved deep enough to know the players by name.

He walked back to the table, his mind a tumultuous whirl of impossible images and cryptic warnings. Daniela was looking at him, her own eyes wide with a new, different kind of panic.

"Oliver, look," she whispered, her voice a sharp, urgent hiss. She gestured with her eyes. "Don't be obvious. Look behind me."

Oliver's gaze drifted past her, feigning a casual scan of the nearly empty bar. And then he saw her. Standing at the entrance, her elegant form a stark, composed silhouette against the bright lights of the street, was Adele. She paused for a moment, her intelligent, analytical eyes sweeping the room, before walking with a cool, unhurried grace to the bar.

They both watched as she spoke to Aisling. The exchange was brief and professional. Aisling poured a drink, and their conversation continued. Then, Aisling turned, her gaze falling on their table, and pointed directly at Oliver. Adele's head turned, and her eyes, even from across the room, seemed to lock onto him with a surprising, piercing intensity.

Oliver and Daniela exchanged a panicked look. "What could Aisling possibly have said to her about me?" he hissed.

Before Daniela could respond, they were approaching.

"Oliver," Aisling said, "This lady was asking about my grandad's painting too. I told her it was sold, and the buyer is coming tomorrow. I thought you should meet, since you were so interested."

"Hi," Oliver said, standing and extending a hand that felt strangely numb. "I'm Oliver, and this is Daniela."

Adele took his hand, her grip firm and cool. Her gaze, however, was fixed on Daniela. "Have we met before?" she asked, her voice smooth, the question less a query and more a statement of fact. "You look familiar."

"Yes," Daniela said. "We spoke at NYU, when you were collecting signatures."

"Ah, that's right," Adele said, though her eyes held no real flicker of recognition. She turned her full, unnerving attention back to Oliver. "So, how is it you're interested in Jonathan Bryce?"

"I'm just a fan of surrealist art," Oliver said, the lie feeling thin and clumsy under her dissecting gaze. "Both his second and third paintings are master-pieces."

A single, perfectly sculpted eyebrow rose on Adele's forehead. "You've seen his third painting?" she asked, a note of polite, derisive disbelief in her voice. "I don't believe anyone has seen it in over a decade."

"Oh, no, no," he scrambled, feeling like an insect under a microscope. "I haven't seen it. I've just … heard about it. From other fans."

"Ah," she said, a slow, knowing smile touching her lips. "So you must be a cypherpunk, then." The knife twisted, gentle and precise.

"No, not at all," he stammered. "I just … I teach middle school kids how to code."

"Interesting," Adele said, her smile never wavering. "Do you know where the third painting is now?"

"No, I have no idea," he said, the words coming out too fast. "It's a mystery, isn't it?"

"It is," she agreed, her gaze holding his for a moment too long. "Well, it was a pleasure meeting you." She gave a small, polite nod and walked back to the bar, her mission, whatever it was, seemingly complete.

"Do you think she suspects something?" Oliver whispered, sinking back into his chair.

"It sure felt like it," Daniela said. "That was more a cross-examination than a conversation."

"The bar closes in twenty minutes," Oliver said, his mind racing. "We need to watch her. I have a feeling she's asking Aisling about the painting's location right now. I wouldn't be surprised if she tries to make a move on it tonight."

"But the wallet is rightfully hers, isn't it?" Daniela argued, her voice a note of pure, simple logic. "It's Christiaan's money. He wants her to have it. Why not just let her? Maren is the one we don't trust. Adele's case seems straightforward."

"I'm not so sure," Oliver said, the memory of the projection, the static, his father's voice, returning with a chilling clarity. "Just before, when I was waiting for the restroom … I had another projection. My dad's voice. He said, 'It's not for van der Dussen to have.'" He looked at her, his own certainty overriding her logic. "He meant Christiaan. And by 'it,' he meant the wallet. We can't let her have it. We have to go through with the plan."

Daniela didn't look convinced, but the argument was lost, buried under the weight of Oliver's strange, secret knowledge. "She has a weird accent, doesn't she?" Daniela asked, changing the subject, her mind still trying to process the encounter. "It's almost British, but not really. Almost Australian, but not really. What is it?"

"South African," Oliver responded, his eyes still scanning the bar. "I originally thought Christiaan was Dutch because of his last name, but I guess it's an Afrikaans name as well." He turned back, a new, sharp anxiety in his voice. "Did you see where she went? Adele. She's not at the bar anymore. And she didn't leave; I'm facing the door."

"The restroom, maybe?" Daniela shrugged.

But as the minutes ticked by and O'Connell's finally closed, there was no sign of her. They were the last to leave, Aisling locking the heavy door behind them.

"There's no way she left," Oliver said, his voice a low, urgent murmur as they stood on the dark, empty street. "I was watching the exit like a hawk. She's hiding in there. She's waiting for Aisling to leave. We need to beat her to it. Quick, the Prince Street station."

They walked at a brisk, near-frantic pace through the deserted SoHo streets. "What could she be thinking?" Daniela asked, her voice tight with a new kind of fear. "If she's hiding inside, she'll be trapped when Aisling leaves."

"I don't know what her plan is," Oliver said, "But we have to get to that tunnel before she does."

The Prince Street downtown platform was a cavern of eerie, fluorescent-lit silence. The display board glowed with a depressing number: *23 min.* It was past 2 a.m. The only other inhabitants of this underground world were two homeless men, one wandering aimlessly at the far end of the platform, the other collapsed on a bench, a distant, happy smile on his face.

Oliver pulled out his phone, the GPS dot from the pin he'd dropped earlier a small, glowing beacon of hope. "It's all the way at the end there," he said, pointing south. They walked the length of the platform to find two doors set into the grimy tile wall.

He tried the first. A small, dark supply closet smelling of bleach and damp rags. He shook his head at Daniela. He tried the second. It opened into a brightly lit office, a station agent asleep at his desk, his soft snores the only sound. Oliver closed the door quickly, his heart hammering. "Nothing. Can't risk waking him."

They looked around, stumped, the vast, echoing space of the station suddenly feeling like a dead end.

"There might be an entrance in the tunnel itself," Oliver said, the idea a desperate, reckless spark.

"Oliver, have you lost your mind?" Daniela exclaimed, her voice a sharp, terrified whisper. "You'll have to get on the tracks."

"There's no one here," he said, glancing at the display. "Fifteen minutes." Without waiting for her to respond, he jumped down, the impact of his feet on the gravelly track bed a loud, shocking crunch in the silence. He walked a few feet into the black mouth of the tunnel, his phone's flashlight cutting a nervous beam through the darkness. "Look!" he exclaimed, his voice echoing back at him. "There's an entrance here! No door. Come on, Daniela, I think I've found it."

He turned back, his face a pale, excited mask in the gloom. But Daniela was still on the platform, her own face wearing an expression of horror. "Oliver, I can't," she said, her voice trembling. "I can't go down there. The rats ..."

"Oh come on," Oliver said, his own fear eclipsed by the frantic need to keep moving. "Think of them as cute. They're related to rabbits, aren't they?"

Wincing with each step as if walking on broken glass, Daniela lowered herself onto the tracks. She picked her way through the grime and gravel, her face scrunching up in disgust, and joined Oliver at the mouth of the tunnel. It was an archway of absolute blackness.

He handed her a flashlight, its beam cutting a sharp, nervous cone through the oppressive dark. They stepped inside. The air was thick, heavy with the smell of damp earth, rot, and the faint, metallic tang of the third rail. Two rats, their eyes glinting like tiny red LEDs, scattered from the beam, and Daniela let out a small, choked gasp, instinctively stepping back into Oliver.

He checked the glowing dot on his phone's GPS. "Come on," he whispered, his voice a low, urgent hum. "We're going the right way. It's only a minute or two."

They moved forward, their flashlight beams dancing over a floor littered with cigarette butts and the detritus of the city's underbelly. Dim, ghostly light filtered down from the street-level sewer grates above, casting long, distorted shadows that seemed to writhe and twist at the edges of their vision. "Subway dwellers know about this place," Oliver whispered, the thought doing little to calm his own frayed nerves.

They reached the end of the tunnel. A solid metal door, bleeding rust, was set into the stone. "This is it," Oliver said, his phone confirming their location. "The painting is just a few feet from here." He pressed his ear against the cold, damp metal, listening, straining to hear anything over the sound of his own hammering heart. Silence. "I think the coast is clear," he whispered. "It's 2:40. Aisling's gone."

He handed Daniela his flashlight and pulled the tools from his backpack. The metal of the door was wedged tight against the stone and brick, a seamless, immovable barrier. "I just need to loosen some of these points," he said, more to convince himself than her.

He got to work with the hammer and chisel, the first *tink, tink, tink* of metal on stone a deafening explosion in the silence. He tried to keep the blows soft, controlled, but the sound seemed to echo endlessly down the dark tunnel. The brick was damp, crumbling more easily than he'd expected. After a few minutes of frantic, frustrating work, he tried the door. Nothing.

"I think you need to get the chisel all the way through," Daniela whispered, her voice surprisingly steady. "You need to see a gap."

"Right," he nodded, his face slick with sweat. "And when we're done, we have to sweep the debris to the other side. Leave no trace."

He went back to work, a desperate, frantic rhythm of chipping and scraping, the air filling with the acrid smell of dust and damp mortar. The minutes stretched into an eternity. He was drenched in sweat, his arms aching, the adrenaline starting to give way to a terrifying exhaustion. Finally, he felt it. A slight give. A millimeter of movement. "Almost there," he grunted.

The air in the tunnel was thick, suffocating. He gave one final, desperate series of blows, clearing a small but crucial gap around the rusted latch. He dropped the tools, grabbed the edge of the door with both hands, and pulled.

The sound was not a squeak. It was a deep, guttural shriek of tortured, twenty-year-old metal, a grating, tearing roar that seemed to shake the very foundations of the building above them.

"Great," Daniela groaned, her voice a terrified whisper. "We've probably woken up the entire neighborhood."

Ignoring the sound, Oliver squeezed through the opening into the pitch-black storage room, his flashlight beam cutting a frantic path through the darkness. He tiptoed toward the back, his heart in his throat. It was there. A large, square shape, wrapped in plastic. He grabbed it, the three-by-three-foot frame awkward and heavy in his arms, and scrambled back into the tunnel.

"Quick, the broom," he hissed. They found one in a nearby closet, frantically swept the telltale brick dust and debris from the basement side into the tunnel, and then, holding their breath, pulled the heavy door shut. It protested with another, final, agonizing shriek before settling back into its frame, leaving them alone in the dark, their prize in hand.

"Shouldn't you try to secure the door again?" Daniela whispered, her voice a thin thread in the sudden, oppressive silence of the tunnel. "So no one gets suspicious."

Oliver nodded, his own adrenaline-fueled focus returning. He picked up some of the larger chunks of brick and gently tapped them back into the gaps he'd created, a crude but hopefully effective camouflage. He gave the door a test pull. It moved slightly, but held. "It's looser," he whispered back, "But no one will know unless they push it hard. Let's hope they don't."

Just then, a new sound. Distant, muffled, but unmistakable. Metal sliding on metal. It came from the other side of the door, from the basement they had just breached.

"Someone's coming," Oliver hissed, his blood running cold. "The trapdoor. Quick, flashlights off. Don't move."

They plunged the tunnel into absolute blackness, pressing themselves against the cold, damp wall. The sound of footsteps descending the ladder echoed in the small space, each step a slow, deliberate drumbeat on Oliver's frayed nerves. The footsteps grew louder as they approached the dry storage room, then stopped. A few moments of terrifying silence were followed by the sound of uncertain shuffling, of boxes being moved, of a frantic, fruitless search.

The shuffling stopped. Then, the soft, distant, digital chime of a phone ringing. The person was making a call. A woman's voice, low and controlled, cut through the silence. It was Adele.

"Hi Dad, it's me," she said, her voice a calm, professional report. "I'm in the storage room at the bar. The painting isn't here. It's gone."

A long pause. Oliver and Daniela stood frozen in the dark, barely daring to breathe.

"Yes, I'm sure it was supposed to be here," Adele's voice continued, a new, sharp edge of frustration in it. "I spoke to the owner. She told me they were storing it here until the buyer picked it up tomorrow."

Another pause. Oliver could picture her listening, an expression of cold fury simmering on her elegant, composed face.

"No," she said finally, her voice low and dangerous. "It's probably been stolen. And I think I know who did it. Okay Dad, I'm heading out. We'll talk when I'm home."

Oliver and Daniela exchanged a look of pure, silent shock in the darkness. *She knows.* How could she possibly know?

Her footsteps grew more distant. They heard the soft thud of her feet ascending the ladder, and then the final, heavy *thump* of the trapdoor closing, plunging the basement back into silence.

"Let's get out of here," Oliver whispered, his own voice shaky. He grabbed the painting, and they scrambled back through the tunnel, the prize in their hands feeling less like a victory and more like a stolen, ticking bomb.

The walk back was a surreal dream, the city's late-night emptiness a strange, complicit ally. The beauty of New York, Oliver thought, was its profound indifference. You could walk down the street at 3 a.m. carrying a priceless, stolen painting, and no one would even look up.

They collapsed onto the bed, the wrapped canvas leaning against the wall like a silent, rectangular ghost. The events of the night, the adrenaline and the fear, finally came crashing down on them.

"I can't believe we just did that," Oliver said, his voice a flat, hollow sound as he stared at the ceiling. "We're criminals. We broke into private property and stole something. Holy cow." A short, hysterical laugh escaped him. "We just did that."

Daniela remained silent, her breathing heavy, her own gaze lost in the darkness above.

"It had to be done, though," Oliver continued, his voice regaining some of its conviction, a desperate attempt to build a moral framework around their crime. "The wallet clearly doesn't belong to Maren. And my dad … he said it's not for Christiaan, either. We had to step in."

"What do we do now, Oliver?" Daniela's voice was a small, frightened whisper in the dark. "Adele said she knew it was us. What if she calls the cops?"

"She won't," he said, the logic of the situation a cold, clear comfort. "If she does, she has to admit she was there, that she broke in, too. And even if she leaves an anonymous tip and they find us, they'll just return the painting to Aisling. Who will then sell it to Bojan. Adele loses either way. She wants that painting. Her best bet is to try and steal it from us."

"In a crazy way, that actually makes sense," she conceded. "So, what now? Maren can't get the wallet without this, so we're good, right?"

"I'm still stuck on what my dad said," Oliver said, the memory of the projection a fresh, raw wound. "'It's not for van der Dussen to have.' If the wallet isn't for Christiaan, who is it for? It has to be for Dad, right? Who else could it be?"

"We don't even know how to find the seed phrase, Oliver," she reminded him. "And you need both paintings, remember?"

"We'll look at *The Toddler* in the morning," he said, a new, weary resolve in his voice. "I'll go through Christiaan's poems again. But you're right. There's no wallet without the third painting."

A long, heavy silence fell between them. Daniela turned her head on the pillow to look at him, a new, dawning dread in her eyes. "What are you saying, Oliver?"

He turned to face her, a slow, tired, and utterly determined smile on his face. "This might sound like a cute idea," he said, the word a small, dark joke in the face of the impossible task ahead, "But I'm saying we need to steal the third Bryce."

The Notepad

i) violin ii) toddler iii) alley iv) shoulder v) educate vi) rookie vii) oval viii) below ix) punch x) certain xi) cover xii) agree xiii) coast xiv) suggest xv) boring xvi) tissue xvii) good xviii) sausage xix) cute

CHAPTER 20. CLUB

"It's a big club, and you ain't in it!"

George Carlin's voice, a serrated edge of pure, joyful cynicism, cackled from the TV. Oliver chuckled, a genuine, easy laugh. He'd seen this special a dozen times, but the words landed differently now. Before, it had all been at a distance – a funny man saying funny, exaggerated things. But after the last few months, after seeing the hollow shell of the corporate world from the inside, after falling down the bitcoin rabbit hole, Carlin's words no longer felt like exaggeration. They felt like a documentary.

"All right, Friday night, when are we heading out?" Daniela's voice pulled him from his reverie. She emerged from the bathroom, a vision of a life he was only just beginning to believe he could have. "Oliver, what are you doing? I thought you were getting ready to go out for dinner and then a club."

"Oh yeah, changed my mind," he said, not taking his eyes off the screen. "I want to go to the storage place early tomorrow to get the painting, so I'm taking it easy."

"Are you serious?" she asked, her voice a note of pure, indignant disbelief. "You're still planning on going through with this crazy plan? You've tasted the blood of stealing art, and now you're making it a full-time job?"

He laughed, a sound full of a new, dangerous confidence. "Look, it's just this next one, and then I'm done. We need to get it – my dad told me the wallet hidden in these paintings is his."

"First of all," she countered, walking over to the armchair, "He didn't tell you it was his. He just said it wasn't Christiaan's. And second, how do you even know this place in Queens is the right one? There are hundreds of them."

He ignored the first point; he was certain his father's message had been clear. "Maren told Bojan the painting was in an underground storage unit in Flushing – a 'below.' I looked it up. There's only one that offers underground units. Kissena Boulevard and 45th Avenue. It has to be the one."

"Okay, let's assume you're right," she said, her voice laced with a sarcasm she didn't try to hide. "You're just going to waltz in there and break into every single unit until you find the right one?"

"You're forgetting what I saw in the O'Connell's projection," he said, a triumphant, almost manic grin spreading across his face. "Unit number 404. And I know exactly where the key is hanging behind the receptionist's desk."

"Oliver, this is insane, and you know it," she said, her voice a mix of frustration and genuine fear. "Even if that's somehow right, why on Earth would the receptionist just give you the key? You'll have to show ID. Have you really thought this through?"

"I have," he said simply.

"Okay, hit me, Sherlock."

"We show up at 8 a.m., right as they open," he began, laying out the plan that had been solidifying in his mind for days. "We inquire about renting a new unit. And that's where you come in." He looked up at her, his grin widening. "You cause a distraction."

"No, no, no, no, no. Oh, no." Daniela took a physical step back, her hands held up in surrender. "Don't you dare drag me into your criminal activity again."

Oliver just tilted his head and looked at her, his expression a quiet, unwavering challenge.

The silence stretched for a long moment. He could see the war playing out on her face – the practical fear battling the undeniable pull of the adventure.

Finally, she let out a long, defeated sigh. "How exactly," she asked, her voice a low murmur, "Do I fit into this?"

"You're the distraction," he said, his voice dropping to a conspiratorial whisper. "You keep the receptionist busy while I lean over, grab the key card, and slip it in my pocket. Then, we rent a unit. They take us down to show it to us. Once they leave, we walk over to 404, open it, grab the painting, and move it into our new unit. We lock both, and then we walk out. Easy."

She stared at him with an expression of disbelief. "Oliver, this sounds like the plot of a terrible movie. So many things can go wrong. What about the key to 404? You can't just keep it. They'll know something is up."

He hadn't thought of that. "Okay," he said, improvising, "When we're leaving, you distract them again. I'll just toss it over the counter. They'll find it eventually and think it just fell."

Daniela rolled her eyes. "I can't believe I'm letting myself be sucked into this madness," she said, but Oliver saw a flicker of a smile, a glint of excitement in her eyes that betrayed her words.

"Hey, check this out," he said, pulling out his phone, eager to show her that this wasn't just a reckless whim. "I've been going over Christiaan's poetry. There are definite clues." He showed her the tweet of the first poem.

To get started is the key

Right above the second apple …

"You see?" he said. "'to get started' – it has to be the first word. And it's hidden 'right above the second apple' in *The Toddler*. And look at this one." He scrolled to the third poem.

And behold as we set fourth

The palm of the ascot man

Points inwards

"He wrote 'set fourth,' not 'set forth,'" Oliver explained, his own excitement building. "He's telling us it's the fourth word, and that it's hidden on the inside of the palm of a man in the third painting."

Daniela leaned in, intrigued despite herself. The logic was undeniable. "Okay," she conceded. "But how do you hide a word in a painting? It's not like he could just write it on there in plain sight."

"Maybe it's microscopic?" Oliver suggested.

"And we're supposed to bring a microscope to a storage unit in Queens?" she retorted. "Be serious, Oliver." She thought for a moment, her brow furrowed. "It would have to be something you can't see with the naked eye under normal light. Something … hidden." A slow, almost comical look of dawning realization spread across her face. "I don't know," she said, the words sounding absurd even to her. "What if he wrote them in invisible ink?"

"Yes, it's got to be that," Oliver said, a sudden, electric excitement in his voice. He went to the closet where he'd stashed the painting. "The flashlight I used in the tunnel has a blacklight setting. We can test it."

He pulled out the large, wrapped canvas and gently unwrapped the plastic sheet. He turned off the lamp in the living room, plunging the apartment into a tense, expectant gloom. He switched on the flashlight, and a beam of faint, purple UV light cut through the darkness. He shone it on the painting.

And the world changed.

Where there had been only skillfully painted oils, a new layer of reality appeared, glowing with an eerie, phosphorescent light. Words. Words were scrawled all over the canvas, hidden in the shadows, woven into the leaves of the apple tree, tucked into the folds of the boy's clothes. Oliver counted them, his heart pounding a frantic, triumphant rhythm against his ribs. Thirteen of them. "Wow," he breathed, the word a reverent whisper. "This is wild. These all look like valid BIP-39 words …"

Daniela just stared, her expression one of unadulterated shock, her hand covering her mouth. "I can't believe this is real, Oliver," she marveled, her voice a hushed whisper of awe. "All these tenuous links, these visions … they're all turning out to be true."

"It must have happened when the painting went on tour," Oliver mused, his mind racing, the pieces of the last few weeks slamming together into a coherent picture. "Shannon said the 'computer people' took it. It was a pretext. Christiaan wrote on it then, before he was arrested." He looked at the thirteen glowing words, then at Daniela. "Which means he probably wrote the remaining eleven on the third painting when he visited Gyorgy. What a crazy son of a gun."

"So can we just put these words into a wallet app now?" Daniela asked, her voice full of a sudden, hopeful urgency.

"No," he said, shaking his head, the full, staggering complexity of his father's puzzle becoming clear. "We don't know the order. To get the seed phrase right, the words have to be in a specific sequence. Once we have all twenty-four, there are quadrillions, maybe even octillions, of possible combinations. It's impossible to guess." He looked at her, the final piece clicking into place. "That's what the poetry is for. The clues give us the order."

But a new, troubling thought surfaced, a final, frustrating wrinkle in the fabric. "There's something else, though," he said, his brow furrowing. "I've been going through all of Christiaan's poems. I've counted twenty-seven potential clues, all with that same, slightly-off wording. But it has to be twenty-four words. Either I'm reading too much into some of them, or something's still off here."

"I guess we'll know more once we get the third painting," Daniela mused, her voice no longer skeptical, but that of a co-conspirator.

He looked at her, a surprised, hopeful smile on his face. "Wait, so now you're ready to join me in stealing it?"

"I guess I am," she replied, her own smile matching his. "It's thrilling, you know? This kind of adventure … and it's so much fun doing it with you." Her expression then shifted, a shadow of real-world fear returning. "What happens if we get caught, Oliver? We could go to jail."

He looked at her, at the genuine fear in her eyes, and felt an unshakeable calm settle over him, the final lesson of the Noncemeister taking root. "We won't," he said, his voice quiet but full of an absolute, unwavering conviction. "I know it. Life happens *for* us, not *to* us. And we're living in the moment right now. This feels right, Daniela. Somehow, I can feel my dad guiding me through this. And I know we'll be safe."

She looked at him, at the strange, new certainty in his eyes, and a slow, trusting smile spread across her face. She was reassured, not by his logic, but by the pure, undeniable force of his belief.

759821 (October 22)

"This is the place," Oliver said, his voice a low murmur as they walked into the deserted compound of The Club Storage Units. "What a name for a random storage spot in Queens."

It was just past 8:20 a.m. The parking lot was a silent, empty expanse of asphalt. *Too early for a Saturday,* Oliver thought. He peered through the glass front door and saw a lone woman behind the reception desk, her head bowed over a magazine. He turned to Daniela, a last-minute, adrenaline-fueled change of plan forming in his mind. "Okay, new plan. I'll distract her. You lean over and grab the key for 404."

"What are you talking about?" Daniela whispered back, her face a mask of confusion. "I was supposed to be the distraction."

"I know, but … for some reason, I pictured a dude," he said, the logic feeling flimsy even as he said it. "It's a woman, so I'll handle it."

"So that's why?" she hissed, a look of pure, indignant disbelief on her face. "You thought it would be a guy, and you wanted me to flirt with him?"

"No, no, not like that," he said hastily, realizing with a sickening lurch that it was *exactly* what he had subconsciously assumed. "It's just … men are generally more distracted when women are talking to them, that's all."

Daniela just rolled her eyes. "God," she muttered, with an expression that was half-smile, half-disgust, "I can't believe my own boyfriend is trying to pimp me out."

"Look, this will work better, trust me," he said, desperate to move past the awkwardness. He pointed through the glass. "The projection was clear. The key card is hanging on the wall behind her, chest high, to the left. Just be ready."

She glared at him for a few seconds, then gave a single, sharp, reluctant nod.

They walked in, the chime of the door a deafening announcement in the silent office. Oliver put on the brightest, most disarmingly cheerful smile he could muster. "Hey there! How are you doing this fine Saturday morning?" He could practically feel Daniela cringe behind him.

The young woman at the desk looked up, startled, her expression one of bored-teenager-rudely-awakened. "I'm good," she said, her voice flat. "Welcome to The Club. How can I help you?"

"We're interested in opening an account," he said, his own voice now a booming, over-the-top performance of enthusiasm. "Could you walk me through your options? And can I just say," he leaned in conspiratorially, "That is a beautiful necklace you're wearing … um, what's your name?"

She looked perplexed, a little unnerved by his sheer energy. "Uhh … it's Rebecca."

"Rebecca, Rebecca. Marvelous name!" he exclaimed. "And really, how silly of me, your necklace has your name on it. Truly magnificent. Where did you get it? Paris, by any chance?" He glanced at Daniela. She was fighting, and failing, to suppress a laugh.

A faint blush rose on Rebecca's cheeks. "Actually, a small Chinese shop on Main Street," she said, a small, proud smile touching her lips. "It was just … there."

"Well, your taste is impeccable," Oliver declared. "I feel confident you will guide us to the best possible storage option."

It worked. Rebecca's bored demeanor melted away, replaced by a bright, helpful smile. "Here, let me show you what we have," she said, turning and walking over to a filing cabinet a few feet away.

The moment her back was turned, Oliver's performance vanished. He looked at Daniela, his eyes wide, frantically gesturing with his head toward the wall of keys. *Now. Go now.*

Rebecca took out a laminated booklet from the cabinet. "Oh sorry, this one's not it," she said, more to herself than to them. "I think I have the right one under my desk."

She started to turn. Oliver's blood ran cold. He saw a flash of movement – Daniela, now sprawled on her stomach across the reception desk, her feet kicking in the air, her arm stretched desperately toward the wall of keys.

He had to stop Rebecca. Now. "Oh no, no, no!" he exclaimed, his voice a boom of fake excitement. He grabbed Rebecca's arm, a move that was far too intimate for a stranger, and spun her back toward the cabinet. "Rebecca, I think you've hit the jackpot! I see exactly what I'm looking for right here." He pointed frantically at a random picture of a storage unit in the old brochure. "5x5x5. What more could a man ask for in this punishing city of ours, this cruel mistress we call New York, don't you agree?" The words were a torrent of desperate, meaningless noise.

"Uhh …" Rebecca looked down at his hand on her arm, her expression a mixture of confusion and awkward discomfort. "These are our old units. I have an updated one," she said, firmly lifting his arm off hers and turning back toward the desk.

Daniela was standing there now, perfectly composed, a look of innocent curiosity on her face.

Rebecca pulled out a new brochure and began to thumb through it. Oliver shot a frantic, questioning look at Daniela. *Did you get it?* He couldn't read her expression.

He pointed to the smallest unit in the new brochure. "That one. We'll take that one."

As Rebecca disappeared into the back office to get the paperwork, Oliver leaned in, his voice a choked whisper. "So? Did you get it?"

Daniela raised an eyebrow, a slow, coy, triumphant smile spreading across her face. "What do you think?"

"You did?" he exclaimed, a wave of pure, disbelieving relief washing over him.

"I did! It's in my purse!"

"Oh my god, I love you!" he said, grabbing her in a spontaneous, giddy bear hug.

Rebecca emerged from the back room, a stack of papers in her hand, and stared at them. "Wow," she said, her voice dripping with irony. "It's just a storage unit, folks. Not your first home."

They both laughed, and Oliver quickly signed the papers for unit 820. Rebecca explained the layout: units 100–500 on the first level down, 501–1000 on the second. She led them to the elevator.

The moment the doors closed, Oliver's grin vanished. "Let me see the card," he said, his voice a low, urgent whisper as the elevator began its descent.

She pulled it from her purse. It was exactly as he had seen in the projection. A plain white card, the number *404* scrawled on it in thick, red marker.

"Was it where I said it was?"

She nodded. "Yes. Chest high, to the left. That's amazing, Oliver. Your projections … they're like psychic visions."

"Or just a really good memory," he shrugged as the elevator doors opened onto the first subterranean level. They followed the arrows through the silent, climate-controlled corridors, their footsteps echoing on the concrete floor. They found it at the back of the floor, a simple, anonymous metal door. Oliver held the key card against the scanner. A soft beep, a loud *click*, and the lock disengaged.

He pulled the door open. The small, 4x5x4 unit contained a single object. A large, rectangular frame, wrapped in a thick, dark plastic sheet, leaning against the far wall. The third Bryce.

He pulled it out quickly and secured the door. "Quick," he said, his voice a hurried whisper. "Our unit. Lower level."

They went back to the elevator, descended one more floor, and found their newly rented unit, 820. Oliver gently eased the precious, stolen frame inside and locked the door behind them. "Let's get the hell out of here," he said, his heart still hammering. "And don't forget. We have to return the key."

Back at the front desk, Oliver launched into another performance, a barrage of over-the-top questions about billing cycles and insurance, while Daniela, with a practiced, casual grace, leaned over the counter and slipped the 404 key card back onto its hook.

They practically ran out of the building, the cool morning air a shocking contrast to the stale, recycled atmosphere of the storage facility. As they burst through the glass doors, a woman was just entering, and Oliver, not looking where he was going, bumped squarely into her.

"Oh, I'm so sorry," he said, looking up, and froze. It was Adele.

The three of them stood in a triangle of tense, absolute silence on the empty sidewalk, the cheerful Saturday morning a world away. Adele was the first to speak, her voice a smooth, silken thread of mockery that was far more unnerving than a shout. "Hey, you two. I didn't realize Manhattan didn't have any storage space."

Bristling, Oliver shot back, "I could say the same of you."

"Isn't it odd, Oliver," she continued, completely ignoring his retort, her gaze analytical, "That someone who lives in Manhattan has a storage place this far out in Queens?"

"As I said, I could say the same," he replied, feeling his face flush, hating that she had so easily put him on the defensive. "And how do you know I live in Manhattan?"

A slow, knowing smile touched her lips. It was not a friendly smile. "Because of how you're reacting," she said, as if explaining a simple scientific principle. "You immediately got defensive, which means you have something to hide. And besides, Aisling told me you were a regular. I knew."

Oliver just glared at her, trapped, his mind a blank wall of adrenaline and anger.

"Come on, Oliver," she went on, her voice losing its mocking edge and taking on a tone of bored, parental condescension. "Let's drop the act. There are fewer than twenty people in the world who care enough about Bryce's paintings to go to these lengths. And I happen to know most of them." She took a small, deliberate step closer, and her voice dropped to a low, veiled threat that hung in the air between them. "You have no idea what you're getting yourself into."

Just then, the glass door to the office opened. "Hi, can I help you with anything?" It was Rebecca, a look of polite, customer-service curiosity on her face.

It was an escape hatch. "Oh, no. We're good, Rebecca," Oliver said, forcing a bright, brittle smile. "Thanks for your help." He slid his arm around Daniela's waist, a gesture that was both protective and desperate, and steered her away toward the subway, leaving a clearly exasperated Adele standing on the side-walk.

Once they were out of earshot, his bravado collapsed. "How could she have figured it out so quickly?" he whispered, his voice shaky. "She just talked to Aisling for a few minutes and bumped into us here. How could she know?"

"Maybe she knows more about this world than we do," Daniela said, her own voice a low murmur of awe and fear. "She said there are only twenty people in this … this club. We just crashed their party."

Oliver groaned, the feeling of being so thoroughly outplayed, so easily read, a fresh humiliation.

On the train back to Manhattan, a new, even colder wave of dread washed over him. He had been absently fidgeting with the key card in his pocket. He pulled it out and glanced at it. His blood ran cold. The number on it was *404*.

He had given Daniela the wrong key.

Daniela saw the look on his face. "What happened? You look mortified."

"I messed up," he said, the words a dry, choked whisper. "I gave you the wrong key card to hang up. We have Maren's. The one hanging on that wall right now is ours. Unit 820. The unit with the painting in it."

"Let's go back," she said immediately.

"No, it's too late," he said, shaking his head. "Adele is probably still there. We have to trust the process. She doesn't know our unit number, and they can't disclose it." He pulled out his phone, his mind racing, trying to build a new plan out of the wreckage of the old one. "Their business hours ... on Thursdays, they're open until 10 p.m. If we get there right before they close on Thursday, it'll be deserted. That's our best shot."

Daniela nodded, and they watched in a grim, heavy silence as the train plunged into the dark tunnel back to Manhattan, the stolen key in Oliver's pocket now feeling less like a prize and more like a ticking bomb.

760255 (October 25)

"I get it, Battulu. You're the expert now. You know how to leave whenever you feel like it," the Noncemeister sighed, watching as Oliver theatrically raised his hand, his fingers poised to snap.

"Oh come on, I was just joking," Oliver said, relaxing his hand. A slow, confident smile spread across his face. "But yes, it is nice to finally not feel trapped. I know you told me I always had a choice, but I didn't actually *feel* that until recently. Once I realized I was the creator within my own creation, it all fell into place."

The Noncemeister let out another, more dramatic sigh. "Sometimes, I am the victim of my own demise." His melancholic expression vanished in an instant, replaced by a bright, cheerful grin. "You've got to admit, it was quite the ride until then, wasn't it?"

"It certainly was," Oliver replied.

"I have a story for you, big boy," the Noncemeister went on, completely changing the subject. "It looks like you need to hear it today."

"I do?" Oliver said, a playful glint in his eye. "You do realize I know how to leave now if this is one of your nonsensical stories, don't you? I'm no longer a captive audience."

"Everything I say is noncense, remember?" the Noncemeister said, waving a dismissive hand. "Now shush, shush, Battu, and listen." His voice became a low, mysterious murmur, and the purple void around them seemed to quiet, to lean in. "This is a story about painting a picture with colors that are missing. It's a story about playing a tune with notes that aren't being played. It is about tasting a delicacy through the absence of flavors." As he spoke, he began to conduct an invisible orchestra, his hands shaping a beautiful, complex melody that made no sound at all.

"Whoa, that's quite the mouthful you said there," Oliver said.

The Noncemeister ignored him, continuing his silent symphony. "Sometimes, the answer lies in the absence of what you can perceive. Gaps and holes together form a tapestry that is as rich as the tapestry formed by what is between them." He stopped conducting and began to weave with his hands, pulling threads of pure, empty blackness from the purple void and interlacing them until a beautiful, intricate pattern emerged, a design made entirely of nothing. "You might be listening to the notes of a beautiful tune – to someone else, the real beauty is manifested through the chain of infinitesimal silences between the notes. The more's obscured, the more's revealed, remember, Battu?"

"I do remember," Oliver said, his mind flashing back to the surrealist art fair, to the concept of the 'below.' "But I thought that was an allusion to hiding paintings underground."

"I always mean everything broadly, including that, Battolo," the Noncemeister said, letting the tapestry of holes dissolve.

"So why are you bringing this up now?" Oliver asked.

"Because you are unable to perceive what you once perceived." The Noncemeister floated closer, his expression turning serious. "I told you recently that you have an inner tiger that needs to come out and consume the lamb that is outside." As he spoke, a faint, ghostly image of a powerful tiger shimmered into existence within Oliver's own form, but it was immediately obscured by a soft, wooly, lamb-like haze. "You did it once, but that is not enough. The tiger is now obscured once more, and it is time for it to be revealed …"

Before Oliver could react, before he could even form the intention to snap his own fingers, the Noncemeister's playful grin returned. "And now, I will beat you to it."

He snapped his fingers.

Oliver's eyes opened. He was back in his chair. The episode had been short and cryptic. He wondered what the Noncemeister had meant. *The tiger is obscured.* Was he talking about the confrontation with Adele? The way he had let her dominate the conversation, his own anger and purpose momentarily forgotten? He must have been. It was time, he thought, to tap into the concealed tiger underneath.

760590 (October 27)

"I can't believe you spent two hundred dollars on a five-hour car rental," Daniela said, her voice a tense whisper in the late-night quiet of the Toyota Camry.

"What did you want me to do?" Oliver shot back, his own nerves a tight wire in his chest. "There's no way I'm lugging that thing on the 7 train at midnight. I'd rather bite the bullet and have a clean getaway." He looked out at the empty parking lot of The Club Storage Units, a single, lonely island of light in the sleeping expanse of Queens.

Daniela looked at the three empty cardboard boxes in the open trunk. "And these?"

"Props," Oliver said, a flicker of a manic grin on his face. "We have to look like we belong. They're just shredded paper. Light as a feather."

She eyed him, a look on her face that was somewhere between admiration and concern. "You are enjoying all this just a little too much."

They walked in, the boxes awkward in their arms, the chime of the door a deafening announcement in the silent office. It was Rebecca, the same bored-looking young woman from his first visit.

"Why hello, old friend!" Oliver boomed, the over-the-top, gregarious persona snapping into place like a mask.

Rebecca looked up, a slow, amused giggle escaping her. "You again. I knew I hadn't seen the last of you."

"Do you work all day, every day?" he asked, his voice a sugary-sweet torrent of charm. Daniela, standing beside him, had to turn away to hide a laugh.

Rebecca explained her shifts, and Oliver laid it on thick, praising her work ethic, her necklace, anything to build a rapport. He was enjoying this, the strange liberation of being someone else, someone confident and in control. He went in for the main ask.

"Rebecca, I've got a big favor," he began, his tone shifting to one of a man in a desperate jam. "We forgot our key card at home. Just realized it when we parked. Would you be able to come down and open our unit with your master key? We need to drop these boxes off."

Rebecca looked unsure. "Oh, I don't know," she said, glancing at the clock. "We're closing in twenty minutes, and I can't leave the front desk unattended."

"It'll just take a minute," he pleaded, improvising frantically. "And I'll tell you what – Daniela here will stay and watch the desk. If anyone shows up, she'll ask them to wait. Does that work?" He had just created the perfect, unassailable excuse for Daniela to be alone at the front desk.

Rebecca hesitated, the request clearly outside her normal duties. But Oliver pressed on, his performance of a hapless, charming boyfriend in full swing. "Look at her, Rebecca. Just look at her. Doesn't she look like an angel?" he said with a dramatic flourish, pointing at Daniela. "I can personally vouch for her – one of the nicest people you'll ever meet. You can totally trust her to watch the front desk for two minutes."

Daniela flashed a bright, practiced smile, and Rebecca finally relented with a sigh. "Okay, what's your unit number? And I need your ID."

She verified his information on the computer, grabbed a master key card, and strode toward the elevator, waving for Oliver to follow. He shot a quick, meaningful nod at Daniela. *It's time.*

Down in the silent, subterranean corridor, Rebecca opened unit 820. "There you go," she said, then peeked inside. "Oh, looks like there's something in there already. Is that a painting?"

"Oh yeah, that's mine," Oliver said, his heart giving a small, panicked jolt. "We dropped it off earlier in the week. You weren't here."

"Must have been Tuesday, then," Rebecca said. "Or Sunday."

"Yeah, Tuesday," he lied.

"Well," she said with a smile, "If you stop by on a day I'm here, don't forget to say hello." She turned and headed back to the elevator, her footsteps echoing in the quiet.

The moment she was gone, Oliver pushed the empty boxes into the unit and waited, every second stretching into an eternity. A minute later, Daniela appeared, carrying the last of the props.

"Did you do it?" he whispered.

"Yes," she whispered back, a triumphant grin on her face as she held up the correct key card for unit 820. "It was much easier this time. I found our key hanging where I left it and put Maren's back."

"Okay, great," he said, a wave of relief washing over him as he took the card.

"We have to hurry, though," she said urgently. "A car just pulled into the parking lot as Rebecca came back up. We can't be seen leaving with the painting."

Oliver nodded. He quickly pulled the large, wrapped frame from the unit, locked the door, and they walked, almost ran, to the elevator, the painting an awkward, heavy burden between them. He pressed the button. The elevator began its slow descent from the lobby.

Ding. The doors slid open. And his blood ran cold.

A person was standing inside. Both he and Daniela instinctively recoiled, taking a step back in pure, silent shock. It was Adele.

She stepped out of the elevator slowly, her movements calm and deliberate, a predator that knows its prey is trapped. She looked at Oliver, her gaze intense and utterly devoid of surprise. "Fancy seeing you here, Oliver," she said, her voice a low, smooth purr. Her eyes then dropped to the plastic-wrapped frame in his hands. "And I see you're holding exactly what I'm looking for."

Oliver's fear was a cold, hard knot in his stomach, but something else rose to meet it – a hot, clean surge of anger and resolve. The tiger. "That's right, Adele," he said, his own voice firm, unwavering. "We're taking the painting back with us. And there's nothing you can do about it."

A slow, condescending smile touched her lips. "And how far do you think you'll get with it?" she asked, her tone one of bored amusement. "I'm going to let management know you just stole my property. They'll stop you before you even reach the parking lot." The threat hung in the silent, sterile air of the corridor, a perfect, elegant checkmate.

"No they won't, Adele," Oliver countered, his own voice surprisingly steady, the adrenaline of the heist sharpening his focus. "They just saw the painting in *my* unit a few minutes ago. They're not going to believe you."

The statement landed. For a fraction of a second, Adele's composed, elegant mask cracked, a flicker of genuine frustration in her eyes. But it was gone as quickly as it appeared, replaced by a cold, analytical calm. "In any case," she said, her voice smooth as glass, "I will report you to the police for theft. You'll get caught, and you'll spend some quality time in jail."

"And once again, you won't do that," Oliver said, pressing his advantage, his mind racing. He decided to bluff, to build a fiction on the small truths he knew. "If you set the cops on me, yes, I'll be caught. The painting will be confiscated. And then it will go to its documented owner, Maren Dehnert." He paused, letting the name hang in the air between them, and saw another flicker in her eyes. He went in for the kill. "And once Maren has it, you know you'll never see it again. She has her own plans for it, and you know it."

It worked. This time, she was properly stumped. The supercilious demeanor gave way to a flash of pure, raw anger. "Oh, stupid Maren," she hissed, more to herself than to him. "I knew that name rang a bell when Gyorgy told me to meet her. I didn't put it together until it was too late. I should have remembered that name from Christiaan."

Oliver did his best to hide the shock, the revelation that Maren was not just a friend, but someone deeply enmeshed in Christiaan's world.

Adele composed herself, the mask of cool control sliding back into place. "Oliver, I've said this before, and I'll say it again. You have no idea what you're getting yourself into." She took a step closer, her voice a low, dangerous murmur. "Your best option is to give me that painting, and the second one. I know you stole that, too. Give them both to me, and we can walk away from this as if nothing happened. If you don't," she finished slowly, the veiled threat hanging in the silent corridor, "You've just made things very difficult for yourself."

"Adele, I can smell a bluff from a mile away," Oliver said, forcing a bravado he didn't feel. "There's nothing you can do. We're walking out of here with the painting." He couldn't stop himself; the adrenaline was a truth serum. "The wallet belongs to my father, not you. I'm just making sure it stays with the rightful owner."

The moment the words left his mouth, he regretted them. Adele burst out laughing, a sound that was cold, sharp, and utterly devoid of humor. "Your father?" she said, shaking her head. "Oh, I should have guessed. Now it all makes sense." The laughter stopped, and she looked at him with a chilling, pitying gaze. "Oliver, the wallet does not belong to your father. Your father was a lying, cheating coward. All the money belongs to Christiaan. He did all the work, and your dad left long before any of it came to fruition."

The words landed with a devastating weight, a one–two punch of insult and a shocking, impossible revelation. "You knew my father?" he stammered.

"Yes," she said. "And I'm kicking myself for not figuring it out at the bar. Someone told me Sazsa was looking for the wallet a few years ago, but I never realized he had a son. It all makes sense now." She took another step closer, her piercing gaze dissecting him. "After Sazsa died a few months back, he set you up to finish what he started. Oh Oliver, if only you knew how wrong you are."

The name slammed into him, a final, catastrophic explosion in his mind. *Sazsa.* The mysterious third partner. The art collector. The ghost who vanished. It was his father. It couldn't be true, but her certainty was absolute, and the timing, the death a few months ago … it all fit. *Dear God, Dad, why? Why were you Sazsa?*

Despite the reeling shock, a single, defiant part of him refused to buckle. He wouldn't let her see that she had just shattered his world. "Adele, that's your version of the story," he said, forcing the words out, clinging to the last shred of his bluff. "I know for a fact that the wallet belongs to my dad."

Adele just shrugged, a small, resigned gesture that was somehow more unnerving than a shout. "This is not over, Oliver," she said, her voice a low, calm promise. "Far from it."

As she turned and walked away, a strange, conflicting wave of sympathy washed over Oliver. He saw not just a rival, but a woman who had dedicated her life to fighting for a brother she believed was unjustly imprisoned. "Look," he called out after her, the words a clumsy, genuine apology. "I'm sorry about Christiaan, about what happened with MixMarket. But I'm doing this because it's the right thing to do. The wallet belongs to my dad."

Adele stopped and turned back, a wry, pitying grin on her face. "Oliver," she said, "You're once again proving how out of your depth you are. If you think the real reason Christiaan is in jail is because of MixMarket, you really don't know much about your father's world." She let the words hang in the air for a moment, a final, destabilizing clue. "Come on, Oliver. Grow up."

She turned and walked out, leaving him in a stunned, ringing silence. He gestured to Daniela, and they walked back to the elevator, the stolen painting a heavy, awkward weight between them.

"You're taking it back already?" Rebecca asked as they passed the front desk, her voice a note of innocent curiosity. "I thought you said you left that painting here on Tuesday."

"On Tuesday? No, we didn't," Daniela said, a flicker of confusion on her face.

Oliver jumped in immediately, the lie coming to his lips with a new, practiced ease. "Oh, no, remember we did?" he said, turning his back to Rebecca and giving Daniela a wide-eyed, frantic look.

"Oh, right, right. We did," Daniela corrected herself quickly. "Sorry, I forgot."

They made it out to the car, Oliver gently easing the painting into the trunk, his hands shaking with a mixture of adrenaline and fear. He saw Adele exit the building and get into a Volkswagen Beetle parked down the street.

"I'm flooring it," he said, starting the engine. "Don't want her following us."

He peeled out of the parking lot, his eyes glued to the rearview mirror. He drove for miles, a frantic, paranoid escape through the sleeping streets of Queens, until they were safely on the approach to the Midtown Tunnel. He finally risked a look back. The street behind them was empty. "I don't think she's following us," he said, a long, shuddering breath of relief escaping his lungs. "Okay. We can breathe now."

"Are you okay, babe?" Daniela asked, her voice soft in the sudden quiet of the car. "That couldn't have been easy, hearing all that about your dad."

Oliver winced, the accusation – *Sazsa, the coward* – still ringing in his ears. "Hate to say it," he said, his voice a low murmur, "But it probably makes sense. My dad using a pseudonym. He was mixed up in some bad stuff, or at least with a bad crowd." He gripped the steering wheel, his knuckles white. "But knowing him, everything he's telling me to do, this whole quest ... it's for a reason. Adele has her version of the story. But as far as I'm concerned, my dad was a good, honest man. If he says this wallet was his, then it's his. I trust him blindly."

"That thing she said about Maren was weird, too," Daniela mused, staring out at the passing lights. "She's obviously connected to Christiaan somehow, deeper than just a friend."

Oliver nodded. "Yeah, we need to get to the bottom of that. And the other thing Adele said ... that Christiaan wasn't jailed for MixMarket. I wonder what that was about."

He pushed the pedal to the floor, the car accelerating into the bright, consuming maw of the Queens-Midtown Tunnel, leaving one set of questions behind and racing headlong into a dozen new ones.

The Notepad

i) violin ii) toddler iii) alley iv) shoulder v) educate vi) rookie vii) oval viii) below ix) punch x) certain xi) cover xii) agree xiii) coast xiv) suggest xv) boring xvi) tissue xvii) good xviii) sausage xix) cute xx) club

STAGE 5: ACCEPTANCE

cHaPTer 21. runway

A small plane descended through a layer of low, gray clouds and landed with a gentle bump on a wet airport runway. Through the rain-streaked window, a dimly lit sign read *Luton Airport*. The plane taxied to a halt, and seven passengers trickled out into the cold, damp English night. The last one to emerge pulled the hood of his sweatshirt over his head, a gesture of instinctual anonymity, and scanned the small crowd of drivers holding signs.

Oliver-the-observer felt his perspective drift closer. The face under the hood was incredibly familiar, but younger, the features softer, not yet hardened by the years of struggle Oliver had seen in photographs. The passenger spotted his ride and waved. The sign the driver held was a single, stark word: *Christiaan.*

That's it, Oliver thought. It was him. But this was a version of Christiaan from before the fall, the young idealist on a secret mission, a ghost from a time before he became a symbol.

He got into a blue Renault, the drive taking them from the industrial exurbs of the airport into the deep, winding darkness of the English countryside. The car finally pulled up to a small, isolated cottage, its windows dark, a lone outpost in a sea of black.

An older man in his early seventies emerged, his face etched with a weary concern. "Gavin," he said, shaking Christiaan's hand. "Pleasure to meet you finally."

"Likewise," Christiaan replied. "Is he inside?"

Gavin just nodded and led him in. The cottage was spartan, the air smelling of damp wool, old books, and the faint, metallic tang of fear. It was a safe house, a temporary fortress. Gavin led him to a dimly lit room at the back.

A man was sitting on a small sofa in the corner, shrouded in shadows. A single, weak beam of winter sunlight cut through a gap in the curtains, illuminating a cascade of long, wavy, silvery-blond hair and the worn fabric on his shoulder.

"Julian," Christiaan said, his voice a reverent, almost gushing whisper. "I can't tell you what an honor it is to meet you. You are someone I have looked up to for years."

Oliver felt his perspective draw closer, but the man's face remained a mystery, a landscape of shadow and rumor.

The man named Julian looked up slowly, and for a moment, the light caught his features. His skin was pale, his face drawn and exhausted, but his eyes were a flash of brilliant, piercing intelligence. He spoke, his Australian accent flat, devoid of emotion, the voice of a man who had been running for a very, very long time. "Thank you for coming. I was told you could help us."

"Yes, that's certainly my goal," Christiaan replied.

"We are running out of time," Julian said, his gaze unwavering. "All our existing payment channels have been shut down. We have no way of paying for our servers. We need this new option set up quickly if WikiLeaks is to survive."

"Bitcoin is designed to be peer-to-peer electronic cash without any third parties," Christiaan responded, his voice full of the pure, unwavering conviction of a true believer. "No one can shut you down. I should tell you, though, the network is less than two years old, so we're still working out some issues. But it works."

Julian nodded slowly. "Yes, the pizza. That's when it came onto our radar. We need options, Christiaan. And we need your help. I don't have much runway. As you probably know, Interpol put out a red notice for me two days ago."

"I did hear that," Christiaan said softly. "What are you going to do?"

Julian paused, a long, heavy silence. "I will likely turn myself in to the British police next week," he said, the words a statement of cold, strategic fact. "My lawyers tell me I can get out on bail. And then … it becomes a waiting game. They are trying to crush us, to make an example of me. I won't let them. The arc of justice will bend in my favor. I know it will."

Christiaan nodded gravely, the weight of the moment, of this man's willing sacrifice, settling over the small, dark room.

"I'm told you are the best person to help us," Julian continued, his voice returning to its flat, practical tone. "Gavin will introduce you to The Architect. You can work with him on getting us set up with bitcoin."

"The Architect?" Christiaan asked, surprised.

"Yes, that's his name. He is our technology wizard. He will be able to take your instructions and implement them." Julian looked away, his gaze returning to the shadows. "Thank you for your time, Christiaan. Now if you will excuse me, I need to speak to my lawyer again."

Oliver opened his eyes, the image of the pale, determined man in the dark room burned into his mind. He finally understood. What Adele had hinted at was true. The feds hadn't gone after Christiaan for MixMarket. That was just the pretext. They had gone after him because he had tried to give a financial lifeline to the most wanted man on the planet. He had chosen a side in a war, and he had become a casualty. And his father, Sazsa … was he a soldier in that same, secret war?

760650 (October 28)

"Oliver, what are you doing up so early? It's 6:15 in the morning," Daniela's sleepy voice murmured from the bed as she heard the sound of crinkling plastic.

"I have to look at it," Oliver said, his own voice a low, excited hum. He was kneeling on the floor, carefully unwrapping the third Bryce painting. "We were too exhausted last night, but I couldn't wait any longer. Have you seen the scissors?"

"I just woke up, Oliver," she yawned. "I think I'm still asleep. I have no idea where anything is."

"Hey," he said, pausing his search to look back at her, his eyes bright with the memory of the previous night's discovery, "I had the wildest projection. It turns out Christiaan helped WikiLeaks set up their bitcoin payments when they got banned from the financial system. Adele was right. This is much bigger than MixMarket."

Daniela sat up, suddenly more awake. "Are you serious? Do you think your dad was involved in that, too?"

"I sure as hell hope not," he said, his voice dropping. "Not because I have anything against WikiLeaks, I love them. It's just … that would mean he was a marked man. And that sooner or later, they'll come after his bitcoin, which means …" He didn't need to finish the sentence.

He still couldn't find the scissors. He moved over to his dad's desk, rustling through the drawers. "You know," he said, thinking aloud, "Something about my dad being Sazsa just doesn't sit right with me. I can't put my finger on it, but there was something I saw, something that makes it impossible. It just doesn't add up."

His fingers brushed against a folded piece of paper in the back of a drawer. He pulled it out. It was the printout of the email from Eddie. The missing link. "This is it!" he yelled, a triumphant, almost manic energy in his voice. "Isn't that wild? I was just talking about the disconnect, and here it is."

"I thought you were looking for scissors," Daniela laughed. "You've got paper."

"This is the email Eddie gave me," he said, holding it up, his finger tracing the crucial lines. "From Gyorgy to my dad, from 2010. Look." He pointed to the section he had underlined.

```
On a separate note, I'm thinking it is time (no pun
intended) to sell the third Bryce after everything
```

```
that's happened. I know you said S might be interested,
so let me know how we can set that up.
```

"Look," Oliver said, his excitement making him talk faster. "Gyorgy asks my dad about a guy called 'S' who might be interested in the painting. We know 'S' is Sazsa. So why the hell would Gyorgy ask my dad about himself, if my dad *was* Sazsa?" He looked at her, his eyes wide with the clean, beautiful logic of it. "Did that even make sense?" he asked, realizing how convoluted his explanation must have sounded. But it didn't matter. He was right. His dad wasn't the coward Adele had made him out to be. He was something else entirely.

"How do you know 'S' is Sazsa?" Daniela asked, her voice a quiet note of skepticism in the pre-dawn gloom.

"It has to be," Oliver said, the pieces clicking together with a clean, satisfying logic. "Sazsa was an art collector and a cryptographer. The email is about cryptography, and then it mentions the art. It has to be him." He collapsed back onto the bed, a huge, shuddering wave of relief washing over him, so powerful it almost made him dizzy. "Oh, thank God. I was so worried Dad was caught up in some really bad stuff. I can finally breathe now."

Daniela lay down next to him, her fingers gently ruffling his hair. "That's wonderful, babe," she said, her voice a soothing murmur. "But your dad still knew these people somehow. Don't get your hopes up too much."

"You're right," he sighed, but the relief was still a warm, solid presence in his chest. "But at least I know he's not Sazsa. Okay," he said, sitting up, a new energy in his voice, "Let me find those damn scissors …"

"They're right there," she said, pointing to the top of the bedside table.

"Oh," he groaned, picking them up. "I opened every single drawer in this dresser and didn't bother to look on top of it."

He walked over to the painting, his heart beginning to pound with a new, thrilling anticipation. He gently cut the tape and peeled back the thick plastic wrapping.

Daniela came up behind him, her chin resting on his shoulder as they looked at it together for the first time.

It was exactly as Gyorgy had described, exactly as Bryce had lamented in the rain-swept Belfast street. A chaotic, crowded pub scene, rendered in a surreal, almost hallucinatory style. Men in suits and well-dressed women moved in a dozen different directions, some holding small, impossible flames in the palms of their hands, others locked in silent, furious arguments. In the far-left corner, an ornate coat of arms hung on the wall, and on it, the Latin inscription, stark and clear: *Ex igne, tempus nascitur.*

Oliver's gaze moved to the center of the painting, to the focal point of the chaos. And his jaw dropped.

In the middle of the swirling crowd stood a short, portly man in an ill-fitted suit, one hand outstretched, a similar fire burning in his palm. In his other hand, he held up a large, glowing pocket watch, its form fluid and melting, a Daliesque nightmare. The face of the watch was a circle of pure, pitch-black, and on it, a single, glowing white digit: 0. The man had a look of wide-eyed, cartoonish shock. A bald, egg-shaped head. An upturned, almost porcine nose.

It was the Noncemeister.

"I can't believe it," Oliver muttered, the words a choked, terrified whisper. "I can't believe it."

"Are you okay, Oliver?" Daniela asked, her own voice full of a sudden concern. "It's a nice painting, but you look like you've seen a ghost."

"Daniela," he said, his voice trembling as he pointed a shaky finger at the canvas, "That man in the center, holding the watch … that's the Noncemeister. How is this possible? Bryce painted this fifty years ago. The Noncemeister is a figment of my imagination, a character from my dad's bedtime stories. How could Bryce have possibly known what he looked like?"

"What are you saying, Oliver?" she said, her own voice now mirroring his shock. "This doesn't make any sense."

Oliver stared at the impossible image, the disparate, chaotic threads of his quest suddenly weaving themselves into a single, terrifying, beautiful tapestry. "The glowing watch," he said, his thoughts a muddled, breathless stream of consciousness, "The zero … that's the genesis block. The very first block of bitcoin. The people with the fire in their hands, those are the miners. The fire is energy. The people just talking, those are the nodes, gossiping. And the

Noncemeister … he's holding fire in one hand and time in the other. *Ex igne, tempus nascitur*. Out of fire, time is born."

He looked at her, and the words came out of his mouth with pure, unadulterated awe. "Babe," he said, tears now streaming down his face as he stared at the magical, mythical painting he had waited so long to see, "This is a masterpiece. It's the most beautiful thing I've ever seen."

They stood there for a long time, lost in the surreal chaos of the painting. Finally, Daniela's voice, a quiet, practical anchor in the sea of his emotion, brought him back. "Do you want to look for the seed words on it?"

Oliver nodded and went to his room, returning with the small, powerful UV flashlight. He shone its purple beam onto the mad, surrealist canvas. And just as before, a hidden layer of reality bloomed into existence, glowing with an eerie, secret light. Words. Eighteen of them, scattered and woven into the fabric of the painting.

He stepped back, a profound, gut-wrenching confusion washing over him. He turned to Daniela. "This makes absolutely no sense," he said, his voice a low, frustrated murmur. "Thirteen words on *The Toddler*, eighteen on this one. That's thirty-one words. It's too many. And Christiaan's poems … I've found twenty-seven clues. None of it adds up."

Daniela stared at the glowing words, a sudden flash of inspiration in her eyes. "Oliver," she said slowly, "What if it's not one wallet? What if he split the money across multiple wallets? Two, maybe three? That would explain everything."

The idea was a lightning strike, a sudden, brilliant flash of logic in the chaotic darkness of the puzzle. "Wow," he breathed, "You're right. That's got to be it. It makes sense to split the funds, to not attract attention." The excitement surged, a wave of pure, triumphant adrenaline. And then it crashed, just as quickly, against a new, even more formidable reality.

"But if that's the case," he said, the hope draining from his voice, "Where are the rest of the words? If it's three twelve-word phrases, we're missing five words. If it's three twenty-four-word phrases … we're missing more than forty. What if it's four wallets? Five?" The sheer, staggering, impossible scale of the problem hit him, and he felt a wave of deep, deflating despair. "Oh my God, this is nuts. How on Earth are we going to solve this?"

Daniela didn't have an answer. She just watched him, her expression a mirror of his own sudden hopelessness.

"You know," he went on, his voice a low, defeated murmur, "We were so close. I really thought this was it. One wallet, maybe the twenty thousand bitcoin, and that it was my dad's. We would have been set for life." He let out a short, bitter laugh. "Think of all the amazing things I could have done. Set up schools, invest in real companies, build something the right way. So close."

Daniela put a hand on his shoulder, a small, grounding point of contact in his spiraling despair. "Oliver," she said gently, "You're forgetting one thing. You have twenty words of your *father's* seed phrase. Just four to go. You thought that might have a few hundred bitcoin in it, right? That's still millions of dollars. You'll do just fine."

He looked at her, at the simple, clear truth in her eyes. "You're right," he said, a ghost of a smile touching his lips. "Although, who knows how many are in that wallet? What if it's just five or ten?" The smile faded. "It's not the same as what Christiaan hid in these paintings – which I'm certain rightfully belongs to my dad."

"You need to be patient, like you have been," she said, her voice a soothing balm on his raw nerves. "Maybe one of your projections will tell you where the rest of the words are. They've all been right so far. Just let it play out."

He nodded. "You're right. Thank you." He took a deep breath, the despair receding, replaced by a cold, clear-eyed assessment of their new, dangerous reality. "In the meantime, I really hope my bluff with Adele pays off. And let's not forget our good friend Maren. I'm sure she already knows *The Toddler* is gone. Pretty soon, she'll figure out the third Bryce is gone, too. And there are only two possible suspects."

"And even if they don't go to the police," Daniela pointed out, her own voice hardening with the grim logic of their situation, "That doesn't change the fact that they're both after us now."

"You're right," Oliver agreed, the weight of their new, powerful enemies settling over him. "We don't have much runway."

December 1933, Piriápolis, Uruguay

The sound was the first anchor. The rhythmic crash and sigh of waves on a nearby shore, a sound he had heard only once before, in the dark chamber of time. The smell was the second – the lingering odor of iodine. He was close. The purple void dissolved, replaced by the unmistakable sight of the great stone staircase, rising into the gloom of a castle he had only glimpsed. He ascended, his heart a steady drumbeat of anticipation, and stood once more before the heavy wooden door. *Camara del Tiempo*. The cast-iron key felt cool and solid in his hand. He unlocked the door.

Inside, the pitch-blackness was absolute, but the air was different this time. It was not empty.

"Ah, Señor Battolo. Welcome." A distinguished voice, warm and resonant, echoed from the darkness. "You have arrived a little earlier than our last encounter, but you appear ready now."

A figure stepped forward from the shadows, impeccably dressed in the style of a bygone era, his movements graceful and unhurried.

"Who are you?" Oliver asked, his own voice a hushed whisper in the vast, dark room.

"My name is Esteban," the man said warmly. "And while this is not the first time we have met, nor will it be the last, it is the first time this version of *you* is meeting this version of *me*."

"Esteban?" Oliver said, the name a jolt of recognition from a projection long past. "As in Esteban Pittamiglio? The youngest brother of Humberto?"

"The very same," Esteban replied with a gentle smile. "Although, I have always considered myself the truer alchemist of the two. My dear brother allows himself to be constrained by what he calls physical reality, by the limitations of the conscious mind. He forgets that true alchemy is the pursuit of elemental transformation. For that, one must be willing to transcend the banal approximations of the senses."

"Right," Oliver said, unsure how to respond to the casual mention of sibling rivalry that spanned a century. He changed the subject. "I didn't realize the castle was on the ocean. A friend of mine from Montevideo told me it was further inland."

"Ah, your friend is correct, in a sense," Esteban said. "The castle she knows is the one in Montevideo, my brother's creation. The castle you are in now," he gestured to the unseen walls around them, the sound of the waves a delicate symphony in the background, "This is my own. The castle of Esteban Pittamiglio. We are in Piriápolis."

"Piriápolis?"

"Yes. A town established by my mentor, Francisco Piria, some fifty years ago," Esteban explained, his voice full of a quiet pride. "A city born from a vision, dedicated to health and wellness. I chose to build my own work here because alchemy, at its heart, is a tool for human betterment. It is not an abstract discipline like mathematics. We practice our art so that humanity may progress. Our own intellectual expansion is merely a fortunate consequence, not the end goal."

"So there are two Pittamiglio castles?" Oliver asked, the simple, stunning revelation clearing a logjam of confusion in his mind.

"You are correct, Señor Battolo," Esteban replied.

Of course, Oliver thought. It was so simple. Daniela had been in Humberto's castle. The public monument. But the real secrets, the true alchemy, were here, in a different castle, in a different city, waiting for him all along.

Oliver returned to the second, more baffling thing Esteban had said. "You mentioned this wasn't the first time we've met. What did you mean by that?"

"Ah, yes. I can see how that might sound odd to you," Esteban said, his voice a gentle, patient melody in the vast, dark room. "You stand, Señor Battolo, in a place outside of what you call time. A nexus. The Chamber of Time is not so much a room as it is a crossroads where all paths intersect. At several points in your life, you have found your way here. Sometimes, you have been ready to hear what I have to say. At other times," he smiled, a look of profound, ancient kindness in his eyes, "You have not. Shall we observe one such occasion?"

"Uh, sure. I guess," Oliver replied, his voice a quiet murmur of assent.

Esteban simply raised his hand, gesturing toward an empty corner of the room. The darkness there seemed to shimmer, to coalesce, and a scene from the past bled into the present. A young boy, no older than thirteen, walked into the chamber, looking around with a wide-eyed, fearful curiosity. Behind him, a distinct, portly figure in a brown suit skipped into view.

"What is this place, Nonsmaster?" the young Oliver asked, his voice a high, reedy echo of Oliver's own.

"Ah Battu, this is the Chamber of Time," the Noncemeister chirped. "I will introduce you to a dear friend of mine, who will tell you a magical secret …"

The vision dissolved as quickly as it had appeared, leaving a shocked, ringing silence in its wake. "Wait," Oliver stammered, turning back to Esteban. "The Noncemeister brought me here when I was a kid? And the friend … that was you?"

"Very perceptive, Señor Battolo," Esteban confirmed with a nod. "I did indeed meet your younger self. And I taught you what you needed to know."

"And what did I need to know back then?" Oliver asked, his mind reeling with the thought of his own erased history.

"Ex igne, tempus nascitur, of course," Esteban replied, as if it were the most obvious thing in the world. "That is the secret of time. Fire creates entropy, entropy creates certainty, and certainty creates a direction for time to flow. Without a direction, time is meaningless."

Oliver nodded slowly. The lesson was familiar now, but the thought of his thirteen-year-old mind trying to grasp it was staggering.

"It is important, however," Esteban continued, his tone becoming more serious, a gentle but firm warning, "That you do not try to interact with these other versions of yourself. That would cause a wrinkle in entropy, a disruption that could set off a chain of events and lead to this chamber's destruction."

"Ah, yes," Oliver said, a flicker of his old, cynical self returning. "I've seen my fair share of time travel movies. Don't interact with your past self. But isn't this different? This is all in my mind, isn't it? Tapping into some infinite intelligence. How can 'mental time travel' change reality?"

Esteban smiled, a teacher indulging a bright, but naive, student. "Señor Battolo," he said, "You still believe there is a difference."

"There isn't?"

"You must first understand what I have alchemized here," Esteban said, his voice taking on the patient tone of a professor leading a favored student through a complex proof. "*Camara del Tiempo* is a Schelling point in timespace.

A place where all pasts, presents, and futures converge. Any soul who can transcend the limitations of the sensual world can find their way here. You are one such person, Señor Battolo. As am I. There are others." His expression grew serious, his gaze locking with Oliver's. "However, any interaction between these converging timelines that goes beyond mere observation will impose a dangerous feedback loop. It would be a paradox, a wrinkle in the fabric that could cause timelines to unravel. And if they no longer converge here," he gestured to the vast, dark space around them, "Then this place ceases to be a Schelling point. The infinite becomes … slightly less infinite. Think of this room as Entropy's harness. The slightest tear, and the chaos it holds will be unbound."

The explanation was a cascade of mind-bending concepts. Oliver latched onto the first and most fundamental anomaly. "Okay, I have a lot of questions," he said, "But let's start with the first one: You said 'timespace.' Don't you mean spacetime?"

Esteban smiled, a look of genuine, warm amusement on his face. "No, Señor Battolo. I meant what I said. Time precedes space. Always has. Next question."

The answer was so simple, so certain, that Oliver didn't argue. He moved to the next impossibility. "You used the phrase 'Schelling point.' How could you have known that? We're in the 1930s. That term wasn't coined until decades from now."

As he asked the question, his own mind, trained in game theory, supplied the answer. A Schelling point. A solution people naturally gravitate toward without communication. If a group of people had to meet in New York City on a given day, without a specified time or place, where would they go? His mind immediately supplied the answer: *noon at the Empire State Building*. And as he thought it, he realized with a jolt – he had thought of the time *before* the place. Noon, then the Empire State Building. *Time precedes space.* A shiver went down his spine. Esteban was right.

The ancient alchemist just watched him, a knowing look in his wise, kind eyes, as if he could see the realization dawning on Oliver's face. He replied gently, "That's because this is a Schelling point in timespace."

"You know about Schelling points even though the term was coined decades after this *because* this room is a Schelling point?" Oliver asked, a slow smile spreading across his own face as he grappled with the beautiful, paradoxical logic of it.

Esteban simply nodded, a look of shared understanding passing between them.

Oliver moved on. "So by revealing myself to a past or future self, I risk them having knowledge they shouldn't, which might change their behavior and nullify the event itself? Even if this is all just taking place in my mind?"

"Precisely," Esteban explained. "Revealing yourself without leaking information is harmless. You observed an earlier version of yourself, but he was not aware of you. That is fine. Had he seen you, his thoughts would have diverged, and this version of you might never have come to be here to observe him in the first place."

"Yeah, that weirdly makes sense," Oliver conceded. "The rules are the same for physical time travel in the movies and this … mental time travel I'm doing."

"Right," Esteban said, his tone shifting, becoming more formal, more significant. "Are you ready then?"

"Ready for what?" Oliver responded, a new, sudden apprehension in his voice.

"Your rite of passage, of course," Esteban replied. "You have arrived at an inflection point. Previous versions of you were not ready. Future versions have already passed this moment. This version of you is exactly where it needs to be."

"Uh, okay," Oliver said, a little unnerved. "What do I have to do?"

"It is a metaphoric rite, Señor Battolo. There is nothing to fear," Esteban reassured him. "And now, I will give you the most potent of serums."

"Wait, what? I have to drink something?" Oliver asked, startled.

"No, not drink. Consume. Absorb," Esteban said, his voice a low, reverent murmur. "It is the most potent of serums that contains the most beautiful of secrets."

The phrase was a perfect, chilling echo. "Hey, that's what my dad wrote in that note on his computer," Oliver said, the connection a sudden, thrilling spark.

"Indeed," Esteban smiled. "Your father is a frequent traveler to these parts." He held up his hand, and in his upturned palm, a small, beautiful, impossible flame flickered into existence, casting a warm, golden light on their faces. "Take it," he whispered.

"Take it? How?" Oliver took a small, involuntary step back from the impossible fire. "It's ... it's fire."

"This is the most potent of serums," Esteban said, his voice calm and firm, the small flame in his palm casting a warm, dancing light on his serene face. "Take it in the palm of your hand and consume it."

"How can I consume fire?" Oliver asked, his voice a bewildered whisper.

"As you would consume anything else, Señor Battolo," Esteban assured him, his kind eyes holding no trace of deception. "Do it. It is easy. Remember, this is just a metaphor."

Shakily, Oliver raised his own hand, bringing it close to Esteban's. The small, impossible flame leaped from Esteban's palm to his own, a weightless, liquid warmth that did not burn. He recoiled instinctively, but seeing the fire still dancing harmlessly in his hand, he did as he was told. He brought his palm to his lips and inhaled. It was not hot; it was like drinking a rich, complex Armagnac, a warmth that spread through his chest, a taste of ancient secrets and pure, elemental energy.

"And now," Esteban said, "Repeat after me. Out loud. *Ex igne, tempus nascitur.* Over and over again, Señor Battolo."

Oliver nodded, the Latin phrase forming easily on his lips, a mantra he already knew. "Ex igne, tempus nascitur. Ex igne, tempus nascitur ..."

"Now sit," Esteban said, gesturing to a simple stone chair that had not been there a moment before. "Continue chanting. You will know when to stop."

Oliver sat, his voice a low, rhythmic drone, the words a steady beat against the distant, ceaseless rhythm of the waves. He looked at Esteban, his expression a silent question.

Esteban seemed to understand. "As an aircraft needs a runway to take off and land," he explained, his voice a gentle, final lesson, "So too does a mind need to orient itself to the true meaning of time. This is your runway, Señor Battolo. You are now one with the *Camara del Tiempo.* You will be able to take off and land here as you please. I will now depart. And so will you, when you are ready."

Esteban dissolved into the shadows, leaving Oliver alone in the vast, dark chamber, his chant the only sound besides the waves. He continued the strange, hypnotic ritual, not understanding, but trusting. A few minutes later, he heard a sound. The heavy, wooden door creaked open behind him. A dark, shadowy form walked in slowly, uncertainly.

It was a figure he knew with a certainty that went deeper than memory. It was himself, from weeks ago, his face a mask of fear and confusion as the Noncemeister led him into this very chamber for the first time. The paradox hit him with the force of a violent concussion. He couldn't let his past self see him. It would break the loop, create a wrinkle in entropy. All the progress, the stolen paintings, the dawning understanding – it could all unravel.

He quickly stood up and ran, not toward the door, but in the opposite direction, into the deep, welcoming darkness at the back of the chamber. The blackness grew thicker, more absolute, until it fully engulfed him, and his eyes opened.

He was back in his apartment, the quiet of his own time a stark, welcome contrast. He slowly pieced it together, the final, beautiful, paradoxical piece of the puzzle slamming into place. The chanting figure he had seen in the dark chamber weeks ago, the one whose silhouette was so achingly familiar … it had been him. It had always been him, sitting in a future he hadn't yet reached, creating the past he had already experienced. *Rum thing, innit,* he thought, a slow, wondrous smile spreading across his face.

762316 (November 8)

Oliver's Twitter feed was a river of pure, uncut chaos. FTX, the crypto world's second-largest exchange, the one run by the supposed golden boy SBF, was in a death spiral. The timeline was a frantic, real-time autopsy, a cascade of breathless amateur reporting, panicked rumors, and grim, on-chain analysis. Just a couple of weeks ago, Sam Bankman-Fried had been hailed as the next

Warren Buffett. Now, it was becoming clear he was just the latest in a long line of Ponzis.

Oliver scrolled, a detached, almost academic observer of the carnage. His first thought, a quiet, aching pang of sympathy, was for Nick. He remembered his friend's desperate, manic hope just a few weeks ago, his blind faith in SBF, the last of his money sitting on this very exchange. He was about to get wiped out. Again. Oliver sent a quick, simple text – *Hey man, you doing okay?* – and didn't expect to hear back.

He kept scrolling, the app a strange, compulsive addiction. He hadn't enjoyed it much since he'd reactivated his account, the daily spectacle of public fighting and performative nastiness leaving him feeling drained and agitated. A non-stop, 24-hour Twitter Space, hosted by an account with a garish CryptoPunk avatar, was blaring from the top of his feed. He'd listened for fifteen minutes earlier, a cacophony of panicked voices, desperate shilling, and hollow reassurances, before the sheer, shameless chicanery had become unbearable.

The new "free speech" era of the platform, so celebrated by many of the bitcoin accounts he followed, felt like a bitter joke. The suspensions and shadowbans seemed to be happening at an even faster clip than before, his own feed a more unpleasant and violent place than ever. So much for Elon the savior. It was all just part of the same, broken system.

Oliver had looked into other social media options, but the alternatives were bleak. Mastodon had been a clunky, unusable mess. Facebook and Instagram were out of the question. He'd heard bitcoiners on Twitter talking about something called Nostr, a new decentralized protocol, but it was just another item on a to-do list that seemed to grow longer and more overwhelming by the day.

He was done with the digital noise. It was time to find his own signal.

He settled into the armchair, the worn leather a comforting anchor. He knew where he needed to go. He was the creator within his own creation now. He closed his eyes, and instead of falling into the void, he *steered*. He focused his intent, a pilot setting a course, and the world dissolved, re-forming with a startling, immediate clarity.

He was in Maren's studio.

He knew he didn't have much time. She had sensed him before, her strange psychic awareness a constant, pressing threat. This had to be fast. His gaze swept the room, his mind a quiet, analytical machine. Where would she hide a secret? His attention was drawn to the bedroom, to an old, ornate dresser in the corner. The bottom drawer.

He moved through the spectral room, a ghost on a mission. He opened the drawer. It was full of jewelry, a magpie's collection of trinkets and necklaces. But underneath, tucked away, was a photo album. He pulled it out, his fingers moving with a deft, silent urgency, and began to flip through the plastic-sheathed pages.

It was a travelogue of Maren's life, a curated history of her spiritual journey. Photos of her in India, in Tibet, with a dozen different smiling faces. There were even a few with his parents, their expressions serious, caught in a moment at some long-forgotten cocktail party.

Then, toward the middle of the album, he froze.

Two photographs, side-by-side, from a time he couldn't place. Maren, younger, impossibly beautiful, in her thirties. She was on an airport runway, a small plane in the background. With her was a man, also young, a face Oliver now knew from a thousand grainy screenshots and a single projection episode.

Christiaan van der Dussen.

The first photo was playful, the two of them striking a pose, laughing for the camera. The second was different. It was intimate, unguarded. They were in a tight, amorous embrace, caught in a passionate kiss, the world around them seemingly ceasing to exist. Far more than the easy camaraderie of friends, their connection was a love affair.

His hands trembling, Oliver slid one of the photos from its sleeve. On the back, in faint, handwritten script, was a date.

Vienna, June 17, 2007.

Fifteen years ago. The connection was the foundation. The missing piece of the entire, sprawling, secret history. He finally had it. And it was so much worse than he had ever imagined.

"Well, well, well …"

The voice was a shard of ice in the warm, dusty memory of the room. Oliver dropped the album. It hit the floor with a soft, muffled thud. He scrambled to his feet and turned. Maren was standing there, arms crossed, a look of cold, placid fury on her face. The serene, gentle guide was gone, replaced by a stranger.

"Maren, I can explain …" he stammered, his mind a whirlwind of excuses.

"We need to talk, Oliver," she said, her voice a low, distant thing, utterly devoid of the warmth he had always known. "I want you to understand what you have done."

"Maren, please," he said, his own composure slowly returning, the shock giving way to a defiant anger. "I'm doing this for my dad. You have some explaining to do, too."

She ignored him, her gaze unwavering. "First," she said, her voice dropping to a hypnotic murmur, "We need to make sure you stay here to answer my questions." She raised her hand and made a slow, deliberate, weaving gesture in the air, as if tying an invisible knot.

"Wait," he said, a new, cold dread washing over him. "Are you saying you're going to trap me here? In this projection?"

A slow, cold smile touched her lips. It did not reach her eyes.

He tried to leave. He focused, searching for the palpable sensation of snapping back to reality, of opening his eyes. Nothing. He tried again, a desperate, frantic push against the invisible walls of the projection. He was a prisoner in his own mind.

"You see, Oliver," she continued, her voice a smooth, silken thread of pure control, "You might have gotten good with practice. But remember, this is *my* method. I created it. And I know how everything works." She took a slow, deliberate step closer. "Now. Where are the paintings? Are they in your apartment uptown?"

It was a command, not a question – a hook that snagged on his consciousness. He felt a strange, irresistible urge to answer, to comply. "No," he said, the word coming out of his mouth, blank and hollow, against his own will. "I am no longer living uptown."

"Oh, interesting," she purred, taking another step. "Where are you living then?"

"Uh … uh," he fought it, a desperate, silent struggle against the invasive pull of her voice. But it was useless. The words were dragged out of him. "I'm staying at our old apartment in Chelsea," he gasped.

"How sweet," she said, her voice dripping with a condescending, false sympathy. "Sleeping in mommy and daddy's bed again." Her tone hardened, the hypnotic suggestion becoming a sharp, direct order. "Now tell me, Oliver. Look at me. Are the paintings in the Chelsea apartment? I know you have them. It has to be you. Don't lie to me."

Oliver closed his eyes, his mind a frantic, desperate struggle against the invasive pull of her voice. The words were being dragged out of him, his own will a flimsy barrier against her power. And then, in the darkness behind his eyes, he heard a different voice, a sing-song cadence that cut through Maren's hypnotic drone.

Remember Battu, I taught you everything, and then she made you forget. It is your choice now whether you let her have that same power over you. You are a big boy now.

He exhaled, a long, slow breath that seemed to expel all the fear, all the confusion. He opened his eyes. The panic was gone, replaced by an unshakeable calm. He smiled.

"You know, Maren," he said, his voice no longer a stammer, but quiet and steady, "You might have created this method, and you might have taught me how to use it. But there's one thing you didn't teach me that I learned on my own."

"Oh really?" she said, her voice still a mocking, condescending purr. "And what is that?"

Oliver calmly raised his hand, the movement slow and deliberate, and brought his thumb and middle finger together.

The effect was instantaneous. The serene, confident mask on Maren's face shattered, replaced by a look of pure, raw panic. "No," she breathed, her voice a choked, desperate whisper. "No, Oliver, wait. Don't do that. We can talk, Oliver … I just want to know, please!"

His smile broadened, the quiet, confident smile of a man who had finally understood the rules of the game. "Maren," he said, interrupting her frantic pleas, "I will talk to you when I am ready to talk to you. And then, *I* will get the answers I need from *you*. Not the other way around."

"Why, Oliver, why?" she said, taking a step closer, her hand reaching out as if to physically stop him.

He looked at her, at the woman who had erased his past, who had manipulated his grief, who had tried to steal his father's legacy. And with a single, sharp, and final sound, he answered.

"Because I am the creator within my own creation."

Snap.

The Notepad

i) violin ii) toddler iii) alley iv) shoulder v) educate vi) rookie vii) oval viii) below ix) punch x) certain xi) cover xii) agree xiii) coast xiv) suggest xv) boring xvi) tissue xvii) good xviii) sausage xix) cute xx) club xxi) runway

CHAPTER 22. PLUCK

A strikingly good-looking young man pushed through the heavy wooden doors of the Princeton computer science building, stepping from the humid August air into the cool, quiet halls that smelled of old paper, floor wax, and the faint, electric hum of possibility. He walked up to the administrative office, a small oasis of organized clutter, and smiled at the lady sitting at the desk.

She looked up, and for a fraction of a second, her professional composure faltered, a brief, surprised flutter before a bright smile bloomed on her face. "Hi, how can I help you?" she asked.

"I'm looking for Professor Wideman," he said, his voice a smooth, confident melody. "Eric Wideman. I'm his new graduate student; I arrived yesterday from India."

"Well, welcome," she said, her own smile widening. "Is this your first time in the States?"

"Yes, ma'am. Professor Wideman asked me to arrive a couple of weeks before the semester began so that I can get acclimated," the young man replied.

"You don't look or sound Indian," she said with a good-natured curiosity. "We get a lot of students from India here, and you don't look anything like them. Your accent … it sounds almost British, or maybe a mix of British and a 1950s newsreader's accent. How did you manage that?"

"I'm not sure, ma'am," he smiled, a charming, self-deprecating flash of white teeth. "It just happened – I guess I watched a lot of old movies and practiced along."

"You Indians are always so formal," the lady laughed. "No one calls me ma'am. I'm Barbara Moskovitz, the department administrator. All the students call me Barb."

"Nice to meet you … Barb," the young man said, the informal name sitting a little uncomfortably on his tongue. "I'm Visu."

"Visu? Is that your full name?"

"No ma'am … I mean, Barb. It's short for Vishwanathan. Vishwanathan Batlu is my full name."

"Oh yes, I remember seeing your name on the list," she said, her expression shifting to one of genuine respect. "You're the Nyquist Scholarship recipient, aren't you? Congratulations! You must be very smart. Professor Wideman only gives one of those out every five years or so."

"Thank you, Barb. Is the professor here today?" Visu asked.

"Yes, he's in that room back there," Barb pointed. "In fact, he should be wrapping up a meeting right about now."

On cue, the door opened, and a young Asian woman walked out, followed by a balding, jolly-looking man in his fifties, wearing gold-rimmed glasses with round frames.

"Well Barb," the man said, waving goodbye to the student, "The new ones are coming in thick and fast. Who knew asking them to arrive two weeks early would work so well. It's going to be a great cohort this year, I can feel it."

Oliver, the unseen observer, watched the scene with a quiet awe, a ghost witnessing the first, pivotal moment of a life he thought he knew, but was only just beginning to discover.

"Speaking of the great cohort, professor," Barb said, her voice full of a warm, maternal pride, "We have our Nyquist Scholarship recipient here with us right now. He just arrived yesterday from India."

Professor Wideman turned, his jolly face breaking into a wide, curious grin. He pulled his glasses down to the tip of his nose, scrutinizing Visu over the top of the round frames with an almost comical intensity. "Well, well, well," he boomed. "If it isn't the man with the essay of the year, in the flesh. Tell me, how did you write all that? It was so insightful – truly one of the best admissions essays I have ever read."

The lavish, public praise made Visu flush with a deep, embarrassed warmth. "Oh, I don't know, professor," he said, his gaze dropping to the floor for a moment. "I suppose you could say it was divine inspiration. There was a voice in my head guiding me through the words."

"And with a mighty fine sense of humor, too!" Wideman roared with laughter, a theatrical flourish that seemed to fill the small office. "Good God, man, is there any talent you don't possess? And remind me of your name, if you don't mind. I'm terrible with names. Especially long, foreign ones. I know, I'm an uncultured Yank, but go on, tell me."

"Vishwanathan Batlu, sir," Visu said. "But most people call me Visu because it's easier."

"Vi … Viswa … Nathan … Nathan … am I getting it right?" Wideman stuttered, stumbling over the syllables before his eyes lit up, having found a tangible, pronounceable anchor in the middle of the name. "Nathan! That's a good name. You should go with that."

"You can call me Visu, sir," he insisted politely.

"Listen," Wideman said, his tone shifting from jovial to one of practical, unsolicited mentorship. "We have a lot of international students here. Let me tell you, the ones who are most successful are the ones who adapt the quickest. Just go with the flow. Pick a name that's easy for us Americans to pronounce, and you'll be golden. It's the best piece of advice I can give you. I'm sure your name means something great in your language, but the fact of the matter is, this is America. If you want to make it here, you've got to blend in."

Visu was a little taken aback by the directness, but Oliver-the-observer could see him genuinely considering the point, his expression a mixture of surprise and thoughtful calculation.

"Take that girl who was just in my office," Wideman went on, gesturing toward the empty doorway. "From Taiwan. Absolutely unpronounceable first name. Too many consonants. A complete mess. To her credit, she comes in and introduces herself as Lauren. Lauren Peng. See? She gets it. She'll go places. So what do you say, Nathan? Or better still," his eyes twinkled, "Nate. How does that sound?"

Visu thought about this strange, sudden rebranding of his entire identity. He looked at the confident, smiling professor, at the bustling American university office, and a quiet, pragmatic decision seemed to settle over him. "I suppose that works," he said slowly. "I do want to blend in. If changing my name to Nate helps, that's great."

"Excellent, excellent!" Wideman beamed. "And while we're at it, I'd do something about that last name as well. Batlu. It sounds a little … off. As if something is missing." He squinted, as if sculpting a new name from the air itself. "Maybe try … Battolo. It has an Italian ring to it. You could pass for Italian, actually. You have that kind of face – could be from anywhere. Italy, Spain, South America." He leaned in, a conspiratorial grin on his face. "It's almost a superpower. And look," he said, marveling at his own creation, "We were able to just pluck this name out of thin air. Your old name was a dead giveaway. But your new name … wow. You could be an international man of mystery."

Visu seemed to mull over the suggestion, a slow, thoughtful smile spreading across his face. It was more than a name; it was an identity, a cover. "I think that works, Professor," he said, the new name feeling strange and yet right on his tongue. "Nate Battolo. Maybe that will be my new American name."

"You know," the professor said, a faraway look in his eyes, "This is the Information Theory division. We work with data, we transform it, we decode it. Think of what you're doing as a form of data transformation. Underneath this elegant new name lies a cryptographic secret. An identity that has been transformed."

Visu laughed and followed his new mentor into the office.

Oliver-the-observer remained by Barb's desk, unable to follow. He felt there was more to this scene, more to this pivotal day, and he waited.

Eventually, the door opened, and Visu emerged, a new, confident energy about him. "Barb," he asked, "Is there a cafeteria in this building? I haven't eaten since morning."

"Yes, in the lower level," she replied. "But I'll let you in on a secret …" she leaned in conspiratorially. "It's no good. If you want real food, walk a couple of blocks to the School of the Arts. The Charles Pluck cafeteria there has a full lunch buffet. Pasta, barbeque, pizza, you name it. It's the best on campus."

Visu thanked her and walked out into the bright Princeton afternoon. He found the Arts building and the sign for the cafeteria. Barb was right. It was a noisy, vibrant hub of student life, a long line of students snaking past a massive buffet. He grabbed a plate and got in line.

After filling his plate, he scanned the crowded seating area, a sea of faces and conversations. He finally spotted a single empty seat at a small, two-person table. A young woman sat there, engrossed in a book. As he drew closer, a jolt of recognition, so powerful it almost made him stop, went through Oliver-the-observer. It was his mother. Young, vibrant, a stranger he had never met.

Visu walked up to the table. "Hi, is this seat taken?"

The woman looked up from her book, and her face broke into a warm, open smile that seemed to quiet the noise of the room. She shook her head and gestured to the empty chair.

"Hi," she said as he sat down, her voice friendly and direct. "I'm Diane."

"Nice to meet you, Diane," he said, returning her smile. "I'm Vi … Nate," he corrected himself quickly, the new name still a costume he was trying on.

"Vinate?" she asked, a playful, puzzled look on her face.

"Nate," he clarified, a faint flush on his cheeks. "Nate Battolo. I'm about to start the graduate program in Computer Science."

"Oh, a techie, then," she said, her eyes sparkling with a friendly curiosity. "Nice to meet you. Where are you from? Italy?"

Nate just shook his head, a mysterious smile on his own lips.

"Greece? Argentina? Israel?" she laughed, enjoying the game. "I can't tell. You could be from anywhere."

"How about we let you keep guessing?" he said, his voice a low, playful murmur. "I feel like I'm from everywhere."

"Ooh," she said, leaning forward with a mischievous giggle that Oliver hadn't heard from his mother in years, but recognized instantly. "An international man of mystery, then. Sitting right here at my table at Pluck Café."

The scene faded, the sound of her laughter a bright, clear note that hung in the air. Oliver opened his eyes, a wistful smile on his face. He had just witnessed a beginning. Two young people, on the cusp of a life they could not yet imagine, sharing a moment of innocent, hopeful flirtation. It was touching, and it was beautiful, and for a moment, the weight of everything that came after simply fell away.

763616 (November 17)

A text message buzzed on the coffee table, a sharp, sudden sound in the quiet of the apartment. It was Nick, finally replying to the message Oliver had sent a week ago, in the immediate, chaotic aftermath of the FTX collapse. Oliver picked up the phone, bracing himself for a story of devastation. Instead, he read:

Hey man, sorry it took so long to get back. Yeah, sucks about FTX, but I've got big news. Been traveling the last week to sort stuff out, so couldn't reply earlier. I'm back in town around Thanksgiving. Do you want to meet right after that?

The tone was so bizarrely upbeat, so utterly disconnected from the financial cataclysm Oliver knew his friend had just endured, that it felt like a message from a different reality. *Big news?* Oliver was intrigued, but when he texted back asking for details, Nick was evasive, insisting they talk in person. They agreed to meet the Sunday after Thanksgiving.

Oliver looked at the time. It was almost 2 p.m. Daniela was at school, and he had a few hours before he had to head uptown. The strange, unresolved threads of his father's quest pulled at him. He decided to project, to try and get to the bottom of the Maren-Christiaan connection.

As he was settling into the armchair, the intercom buzzed, a harsh, grating sound that made him jump. He walked to the door and pressed the button.

"Mr. Oliver," Santos's voice crackled, "There is a lady here to see you. Says her name is Maren. Can I send her up?"

A jolt of pure, cold adrenaline shot through him. His heart began to hammer against his ribs. *Maren.* Here. Now. What did she want? Did she know about the paintings? Had she come to take them? His mind raced, a frantic slideshow of worst-case scenarios. He pictured the two stolen canvases, hidden in a box under his bed. *What if she has a gun?*

He shook himself out of the paranoid spiral, the Noncemeister's voice a distant, calming echo in his mind. *You are the creator within your own creation.* He had stood up to her in the projection. He could stand up to her now.

"Mr. Oliver, you still there?" Santos's voice crackled again.

"Oh, sorry Santos," he said, his own voice surprisingly steady. "Yeah, send her up."

A few moments later, a soft knock on the door. He took a single, deep, fortifying breath, and opened it, prepared for a full-fledged confrontation, for the cold fury of a woman whose plans he had just derailed.

The woman standing in the hallway was not the woman he was expecting. This Maren was subdued, her usual serene, confident aura gone, replaced by a quiet air of abject defeat. She looked smaller, older. He invited her in, and she walked slowly to the sofa and sat, her movements heavy with a weariness that seemed to go deeper than just her body.

"It's nice that you've moved back in here, Oliver," she said, her voice a low, tired murmur as her gaze swept across the room. "It seems the apartment is being shaped by your personality. I can still feel your dad's presence, though. You've just … complemented it with your own touch." The words were a strange, sad, and utterly disarming opening to a battle he had been so ready to fight.

Oliver decided to move past the small talk, the quiet grief of her entrance. He needed answers. "Maren, before you ask me for anything, I think you have a lot of explaining to do," he said, his voice quiet but firm, the anger from the last few weeks a solid core inside him. "You hid things from me. You used information I shared with you in vulnerable moments. I deserve an explanation."

She looked at him, her face a landscape of pure anguish, the serene mask completely gone. "Yes, Oliver," she said, her voice low and broken. "That is why I am here. It is time we spoke. You need to hear why I did what I did."

"Go on, then," he said, his own anger momentarily disarmed by the raw pain in her voice.

"Where to begin, Oliver?" she sighed, her gaze lost in a past he couldn't see. "There is so much."

"Let's start at the beginning," he said, the question a sharp, direct probe into a wound he'd only just discovered. "In a projection, I heard you say my dad betrayed you when he chose my mom. Were you and Dad ever together?"

The question landed, and for a long moment, she was silent, her hands twisting in her lap. Finally, she let out a long, shuddering breath. "It is true," she said, her voice a near whisper. "Your father and I … we were together, for a few years in the early nineties. We met at the ashram. He was visiting from the U.S., and we … we fell in love." She looked up, a ghost of a remembered joy and a universe of pain in her eyes. "He spoke of another woman, Diane, someone he knew from university, but I didn't think anything of it. And then … I decided I wanted to be closer to him. I left Germany. I moved to New York for him. A year later, he told me he was leaving me for your mother."

Oliver listened, stunned. The simple, brutal honesty of it was the last thing he had expected. "I'm sorry to hear that, Maren," he said softly. "I'm sure that was tough."

"Don't be sorry, Oliver," she said, a strange, sad smile on her face. "Your father was right. He saw something in me that I couldn't see in myself. I was young, I was confused, but he knew. He had an insight into my own heart that I lacked, and he made the right decision."

"What did he know that you didn't?"

She took a deep breath, the confession a heavy weight. "That I was bisexual," she said simply. "And that I would ultimately be happier, more myself, in a relationship with a woman. Your father was able to see this in me before I could. It was only after I finally forgave him that I allowed myself to truly understand my own sexuality."

"I didn't know that, Maren," Oliver said, a new, more complex picture of his father, and of this woman, beginning to form. But a new contradiction immediately surfaced. "Wait, but when I was in your studio … the photo album. There were pictures of you and Christiaan, from ten or fifteen years ago. You were together."

She nodded, a fresh wave of a different, more recent pain washing over her features. "Yes," she said. "After your father, I have only been with women. With one exception. It was Christiaan. And I suppose," she finished, her voice a low, tragic murmur, "That is why we are in this mess."

"What happened with Christiaan?" Oliver asked.

"He came to me for help, many years ago," she began, her gaze becoming distant again. "He was very sick. Losing weight, couldn't eat. The doctors had no idea what was wrong with him. All the treatments had failed. He was desperate. He probably would have died within a month or two." She paused, took a deep breath, and looked at Oliver, her eyes full of a story he was only just beginning to understand. "He knew it. And he was terrified."

"I was able to help him," she continued, her voice a low, haunted murmur. "His body was rejecting food, rejecting nourishment. We traced it back to a severe childhood trauma that had resurfaced. Over four or five sessions, we were able to resolve it. Within six months, he had made a full recovery." A faint, ghost of a smile touched her lips, a memory of a different, happier time. "In the process, I saw his incredible joy for life, his warrior spirit. He had such an indefatigable will to live. I fell in love with him. And he with me." She paused, the memory weighing on her. "I had saved his life," she concluded, her voice barely a whisper. "And he promised me that whatever wealth he had would be mine."

"When was this, Maren?" Oliver asked, the story a shocking, unexpected prequel to a tragedy he was only just beginning to understand.

"Fifteen, sixteen years ago. We were together for over five years," she said. "But something changed in him after he started working on bitcoin, after he traveled to England on 'a secret project,' as he called it."

"The WikiLeaks trip," Oliver said, the words a quiet confirmation, not a question.

"Yes," Maren said, not a flicker of surprise on her face. It was as if she knew he would already know. "He was gone for months. When he came back, he was a different man. The joy, the lightness … it was gone. Replaced by a kind of righteous, dangerous fervor. Over the next year, as he built his MixMarket company, I felt him slipping away. It became obvious our relationship was over." She shook her head, a bitter, self-recriminating anger in her eyes. "I was furious with myself for trusting a man again. I was almost forty at the time. I should have known better."

"So that's why you're after the paintings?" Oliver asked, the final piece clicking into place. "Because you believe the money is yours?"

"Christiaan and I made an energetic exchange, Oliver," she said, her voice regaining a sliver of its old, mystical certainty. "I saved his life. He promised me everything. The universe demands that this be honored."

Oliver listened, and he didn't buy it. He saw the "energetic exchange," the talk of the universe, as a thin, spiritual veneer, a high-minded rationalization for a simple, human frailty: greed. The sheer, staggering amount of money at stake had corrupted her, and this story was the cover she had built to hide that simple, ugly truth from herself. He decided not to say anything, to let her continue.

"How did you know what Christiaan was doing with the paintings?" he asked. "Did he tell you?"

A look of profound, almost painful shame washed over Maren's face. She couldn't meet his eyes. "After he returned from England," she began, her voice a low, difficult whisper, "He became … distant. Secretive. He stopped telling me anything." She looked up, her gaze lost in the memory of a love that was souring. "I knew he'd traveled to Hungary to meet Gyorgy, who he'd told me owned the third Bryce. I knew he was traveling across the U.S. with the second one. I knew he was doing *something* with the paintings, and he wouldn't tell me what. I had to find out."

She paused, taking a shaky breath. "So I projected into his past. I didn't ask his permission. I just did it. I was desperate to save us, to understand what I was losing him to. I broke my own most sacred rule – you do not enter another's mind without their consent. It is not something I am proud of."

The confession, so raw and direct, sent a chill through Oliver. If she could do it to Christiaan … "Maren," he asked, his voice tight, "Did you do the same to my dad? Did you try to enter his past?"

She fell silent again, a long, heavy pause. "Yes," she said finally, the word a barely audible admission. "I tried. But with your father … it was impossible. I told you he was a master. There were barriers, intentional walls he had built. I couldn't get in."

The revelation of his father's psychic defenses was another layer of the mystery, another testament to the man's secret power. "Was my dad involved with Christiaan, Maren?"

"I don't know, Oliver," she said, and for the first time, he believed she was telling him the truth. "They were both early bitcoiners. They both had a common friend in Gyorgy. It's likely they knew each other, but beyond that … Christiaan became a closed book to me around 2010. Even if he knew your father, he wouldn't have told me."

"How did you know Gyorgy?"

"I met him through your father. He was a good man."

"What about Bojan?" Oliver pressed, the final piece of the puzzle. "Why did you use him to buy the painting from Gyorgy? You could have bought it directly."

"I didn't want Christiaan to find out," she said, her voice dropping again. "He wasn't in prison yet, but the investigation was ongoing. I was worried that if he found out I'd bought the painting, he would be furious. So I asked Bojan to be my broker."

"Who is this Bojan guy, anyway?"

"He was someone who came to me for help," she said, her voice softening, a memory of a different kind of connection surfacing. "When he was a teenager in Yugoslavia, he saw his parents brutally murdered in front of him during the war. The trauma finally caught up with him years later. He was suicidal. He found me, and I helped him." She looked at Oliver, her expression one of a healer, not a schemer. "Once he was able to resolve that, he felt … indebted. He has been helping me with many things ever since. He was the one who helped me get the bitcoin to pay for the painting."

He felt he had all the answers he needed. Maren and his dad, together. Maren and Christiaan, together. A promise of wealth, broken by a secret mission to help WikiLeaks. It was a story that made a strange, tragic kind of sense. But it also presented a new, deeply unsettling possibility.

His father's message in the projection: *"It's not for van der Dussen to have."* Oliver had interpreted it as a declaration of his own ownership. But what if it wasn't? What if his father, knowing Maren had been wronged by Christiaan, had intended for *her* to have the wallet all along? The thought was a fresh wave of uncertainty, destabilizing the simple, righteous narrative he had constructed. He was torn.

He pushed the thought away, focusing on the here and now. "So why did you come here today?" he asked, his voice softer now, less accusatory. "Just to tell me the story?"

"Oliver, I want you to know that I loved your father as a friend," she said, her voice full of a sincere, aching warmth that felt impossible to fake. "Even after what happened, we made our peace. He trusted me. That's why he brought you to me all those years ago, to help with the voices." She leaned forward, her gaze intense, pleading. "A few years after that, he told me that if he were to disappear or die prematurely, I should be the one to teach you about projection. I came here to tell you that I am only after what is justly mine. Christiaan and I made a sacred pact. It needs to be honored."

The word hit him with the force of a physical blow, a dissonant, ugly note in her sad, reasonable story. *Disappear.* The same word the monstrous, distorted projection of Eddie had used. A word that belonged to the realm of paranoia and conspiracy, not tragic accidents.

"Why did you say 'disappear,' Maren?" he asked, his voice suddenly sharp, the suspicion returning with a vengeance. "Did my dad use that word?"

"He did," she said, and then her voice softened, a careful, calculated shift to sympathy. "Although, I know why you would pluck out that word. If your dad were somehow alive, you would have known by now, Oliver. Don't get your hopes up. I think he was just covering all bases when he said that to me. He is gone. I'm sorry to say this, but he really is gone."

Oliver just nodded, his face an unreadable mask. He had made his peace with that fact, but hearing her use it now, as a tool to manage him, felt cheap and manipulative.

"Maren, I can't help you," he said, his voice quiet but firm, a finality in it that she had never heard from him before. "I know you believe what you do about the paintings, about the wallet. But Dad has told me otherwise. I need to do this for him. If he tells me they belong to you, I will gladly give them to you. But right now, I cannot."

A flicker of her old, hypnotic intensity returned to her eyes. She leaned forward, her voice a low, urgent, pleading murmur. "Oliver, you are putting yourself in grave danger. One of the reasons I worked with Bojan was because Christiaan became a marked man after that trip to England. *They* will be able to trace his money back to you. Bojan has multiple passports; he knows how to disappear. The trail will always run cold with him. But you … you're just a normal person. You will inherit all of Christiaan's problems. The paintings are safest with me."

"You mean the money is safest with you," he couldn't resist saying, the quiet accusation a final, clean break.

A dry, humorless laugh escaped her. "I know you have every reason to be cynical. I did lie to you because I felt my cause transcended yours. But I'm not lying now, Oliver. Your life as you know it will be over the second you move even a tiny fraction of that money. The government will be after you. You'll either spend the rest of your life on the run or in prison." She stood up, her final offer, her final threat, hanging in the air between them. "Think about it. I'll be waiting."

The Notepad

i) violin ii) toddler iii) alley iv) shoulder v) educate vi) rookie vii) oval viii) below ix) punch x) certain xi) cover xii) agree xiii) coast xiv) suggest xv) boring xvi) tissue xvii) good xviii) sausage xix) cute xx) club xxi) runway xxii) pluck

763838 (November 19)

A soccer ball bounced on an uneven patch of grass and came to rest between two weathered tombstones. A young boy, no older than seven, ran after it, his bright t-shirt a splash of life in the quiet, gray field of the dead. He looked around, a spark of fascination in his eyes, and then, with a small, mischievous grin, he kicked the ball against the flat, granite face of a large tombstone. It bounced back true. He did it again, harder, and the ball ricocheted off a beveled edge, striking an adjacent stone before caroming back to him. A new game. He was getting ready for a fourth try when a shrill voice cut through the afternoon quiet.

"Dominik! How many times have I told you not to play in the cemetery? It is disrespectful." A woman appeared from behind a tree, a stern expression on her face.

"Mommy, look!" the boy said, his voice full of the unbridled joy of discovery. "When you kick the ball on the corner, it bounces and hits the next stone! I want to see how many I can hit."

The woman grabbed him by the ear. "Dominik, behave yourself," she said, plucking the ball from his hands. "These are where dead people are buried. You can't kick a soccer ball on them."

"But Mommy, it's so much fun," he protested, wincing. "How does it matter? They're dead anyway. They won't know."

She just shook her head, dragging the boy off with her as he continued to plead his case.

Oliver-the-observer watched them go, a small, sad smile on his face. As the cemetery returned to its somber silence, his gaze was drawn to one tombstone in particular, a simple, unadorned slab of granite. There was no epitaph, just a name and two dates. It read:

Gyorgy Zsazsa Lorincz, 1964 – 2022

Zsazsa. The middle name snagged in Oliver's mind. It was so familiar, an echo of a name that had been a central, nagging mystery for months. He thought back to the Noncemeister's strange lessons, the cryptic clues that were not in the words themselves, but in the spaces between them. *Sometimes, the answer lies in the absence of what you can perceive. The more's obscured, the more's revealed.*

The 'Z'. A strange, unnecessary letter at the beginning of the name. What did its absence reveal?

He removed it in his mind's eye. *Sazsa.*

The world seemed to tilt. A silent explosion of understanding detonated in his mind. *That was it.* The pseudonym. The ghost. It was a redaction. He quickly performed the autokinesis ritual, a desperate need for confirmation. His left arm dropped, a heavy, irrefutable yes.

He couldn't believe it. Gyorgy was Sazsa. The art collector, the cryptographer, the third man in the MixMarket tragedy. It had been right under his nose all along. It all made sense now – the shared history with Christiaan, the guilt, the desperate need for forgiveness from a man he had abandoned.

The euphoria of solving the mystery, of finally clearing his father's name from that particular shadow, was a dizzying, triumphant rush. Adele had been wrong. His dad wasn't Sazsa.

But the euphoria was short-lived, crashing almost immediately against a new, more formidable, and utterly baffling contradiction. He thought of the email, the faded printout from Eddie, the cornerstone of his entire investigation. Gyorgy's email to his dad, from 2010. It had mentioned "S"'s potential interest in the third Bryce.

Until this moment, he had been certain "S" was Sazsa. But if Gyorgy *was* Sazsa, then he couldn't have been referring to himself.

So if "S" wasn't Sazsa, then who on Earth could it be?

CHAPTER 23. SATOSHI

764971 (November 27)

"How have you been, man?" Nick asked, but his voice was different. The usual manic, forward-looking energy was gone, replaced by a flat, quiet calm that was more unsettling than a shout. "Still sticking with Żywiec, I see."

"I've been good," Oliver said, a little taken aback by the change. "And yeah, it's reliable. Looks like you've moved on from Hoegaarden to the hard stuff. What is that, a whiskey and soda?"

"Jameson and soda," Nick replied, taking a small, dispassionate sip. "New jam. Time to leave the old life, and the old drink, behind."

"So how are things at BlockWaves?" Oliver asked, sensing the conversation was already on unstable ground.

"Yeah, so that was one of the things I wanted to talk to you about …" Nick set his glass down, the ice clinking with a quiet finality. "I quit a couple of weeks back."

"What? No way," Oliver exclaimed. "What happened? You were so bullish."

"Well, FTX happened," Nick said, his voice a matter-of-fact monotone, as if he were recounting a story that had happened to someone else. "Around November 8th, as my net worth was being completely erased by that fucking criminal SBF, I had a moment of clarity. This whole industry is a goddamn scam, dude. Run by hucksters, scammers, and straight-up criminals. Not a single person I looked up to lived up to the trust. They were all cheats and liars." He looked at Oliver, his eyes cold and clear. "I'm done, dude. Completely done. I quit that day. No notice."

The calmness of the delivery was chilling. The despair from the Terra Luna crash was gone. This was the sound of a man who had been burned clean of all illusions. "Wow, man," Oliver said. "That's wild to hear from you. So what are you going to do now? Was this the big news you wanted to share?"

"No," Nick said, a small, humorless smile touching his lips. "That's just the beginning. Right around then, I reached out to Becky's dad and asked him to make some calls for me."

"Your father-in-law? What does he have to do with this?"

"Well, I told you he's loaded, right? He's also a big political donor. Very well-connected," Nick said. "He put me in touch with a guy called Arthur Sterling – the CEO of Chain Intelligence. A friend of his from the country club."

"What is that?" Oliver asked, a new, strange unease settling over him.

"A chain analysis company," Nick explained, his voice taking on a new, sharp, professional edge. "They have a suite of AI tools to analyze public blockchain data. They look for anomalies. For criminal activity."

Oliver was confused. "I'm not following, Nick. I thought you said you were done with the industry."

Nick looked at him, and for the first time, Oliver saw a flicker of something new in his friend's eyes – not the manic hope of a gambler, but the cold, hard certainty of a hunter. "Oh, I am done, Oliver," he said. "I'm done being a player in their rigged game. It's time to start changing the rules." He smiled, a thin, humorless expression that didn't reach his eyes. "I want my revenge. These scammers made me lose everything. I'm going to hunt them, and others like them, down. I'm going to make sure they go to prison before they hurt anyone else."

The quiet, raw venom in his voice was chilling. "Wait, so you got a job with them?" Oliver asked.

"Yeah," Nick said, a flicker of something new – not hope, but a hard, predatory pride – in his eyes. "The CEO hired me on the spot after I told him my story. I'm taking over their cyber and crypto crime unit."

"Wow, that's … great to hear, man. Congrats," Oliver said, but the words felt hollow. Chain analysis companies. They were the other side of the coin, the digital private investigators who, under the pretext of analytics, were building a surveillance infrastructure for a world that was supposed to be free.

"Yeah, I'm excited. I feel motivated," Nick said with a dark laugh. "Nothing clarifies the mind like a cold-blooded desire for vengeance."

"Dude, stop. That sounds scary," Oliver said, trying to laugh it off, but the joke landed with a thud. "But seriously, I'm happy for you. It seems like you stood up for what you felt was right."

Nick just nodded, his gaze turning serious, intense. "I want to get to the main reason I wanted to talk to you, though," he said, his voice dropping to a conspiratorial whisper. "And I'm telling you this in complete confidence, you understand? I trust you. This cannot leave this table."

Oliver nodded, intrigued, a sense of unease prickling at the back of his neck.

"I've been traveling to DC quite a bit since I took this role," Nick began. "My unit just won a major contract with the Department of Justice." He paused, letting the weight of the words land. "This is off the record, by the way."

Oliver nodded again.

"Okay," Nick continued, "So we just signed this contract to provide chain analysis services for the DoJ. And one of the first major cases they gave us is an old one they've reopened." He looked at Oliver, his gaze sharp, analytical. "Do you remember in the summer, when we were driving up to Andes, and you asked me about Christiaan van der Dussen?"

The name, spoken here in the quiet of O'Connell's, was a sudden, jarring intrusion from the secret, surreal world of his quest. Oliver's heart started to pound. He didn't know where this was going, but it felt like a trap closing around him. "Uh … yeah," he said, trying to keep his voice casual, guarded. "I remember."

"He was the guy who had the company called MixMarket," Nick began, his voice taking on the detached, analytical tone of a case file summary. "He got thrown in jail for money laundering in 2014. So, he had two accomplices: a guy called Sazsa and another called Dev_akshar. Both pseudonymous, obviously, and both disappeared right around the time Christiaan got busted."

He paused, taking a slow, deliberate sip of his whiskey. "Well, it turns out the DoJ reopened the case earlier this year. They found some new information about the other two guys. It appears Sazsa most likely died at some point this year, but Dev_akshar is probably still out there. There's a good chance he was the real mastermind behind MixMarket and Christiaan just ended up being the fall guy." He leaned in, the hunter sharing the details of the hunt. "The DoJ was closing in on him, but the trail suddenly ran cold around March. Just a few weeks back, they gave us the case. They want us to use our AI tools to investigate his on-chain activity from before 2014, find any patterns that lead to him."

Oliver listened, a strange sense of dislocation washing over him. He had completely forgotten about Dev_akshar, the third man in the Christiaan story. And he was stunned that Nick was sharing the confidential details of an active federal investigation so casually, so openly. It was a display of power, a casual disregard for rules that felt deeply alien.

"That sounds like a really interesting case," Oliver said, trying to keep his voice neutral. "How come you're sharing this with me?"

"Because I want you to join my team at Chain Intelligence," Nick said, the words a simple, direct, and utterly shocking proposition. "You're out of work, and I need someone like you."

"What?" Oliver exclaimed, taken completely by surprise.

"I know this is coming out of nowhere," Nick said, his tone shifting to that of a recruiter, a man making a pitch. "But this case is a big deal for me, for the company. I know what you're capable of, Oliver. The way you pick up new projects and just run with them. And now, you're big on bitcoin. Well, this case is all about bitcoin. We need someone with a good understanding of it to help us track down Dev_akshar. So what do you say? I can get you started within a week. It's my team. I have full hiring autonomy."

The offer was a dizzying, repugnant temptation. Working for a chain analysis company, a surveillance firm for the government, was as horrifying to Oliver as working on a CBDC. But Nick wasn't done.

"Dude, we have a huge government contract," he said, his voice dropping to a low, seductive murmur. "Money is not an issue. I can get you in for 250k a year, easy. This should be a no-brainer, man. You use your skills to help your country hunt down bad guys, and you make bank in return."

Oliver finally found his voice, the words a quiet but firm rejection of this new, colder version of his friend. "I don't know, man," he said, shaking his head. "I really appreciate the offer, but I'm not sure I want to get involved in chain analysis. I'd rather work on building products that empower users."

"I get it, dude," Nick said, a dismissive, almost pitying look in his eyes. He hadn't so much heard Oliver's reason as tolerated it. "I sprung this on you out of nowhere. Take your time. Take a few weeks to mull it over. You know where to find me once you change your mind," he winked, as if Oliver's eventual surrender was a foregone conclusion.

Nick settled back, taking a long, slow sip of his Jameson. "So what else is happening, dude?" he asked, changing the subject with a final, dismissive wave. "You said you were teaching kids how to code or something. How's that going?"

"It's going well, man," Oliver replied. "Yeah, I'm teaching them the basics of coding and, funnily enough, introducing a few bitcoin concepts as well."

"I don't know, man," Nick said, a faraway look in his eyes. "This whole bitcoin and crypto thing … it's time to close the chapter on it, if you ask me." He stared into his glass as if reading a new, hard-won truth from the bottom of it. "I've had a lot of time to think on those train rides to DC. Everything I believed, all that Web3 stuff … I was so wrong, dude. We have a perfectly good system. The U.S. dollar, it works. You've got Venmo, PayPal, instant payments. Why do we need this dumb crypto shit? I feel like I was part of a collective delusion. The system works. The Fed steps in, adjusts rates. The banks serve their customers. The only thing crypto enabled was criminals like Mashinsky and SBF to sell Ponzis to an unsuspecting public."

The sheer, breathtaking hubris of it, the privilege of a man who had never truly had to worry about the system failing him, made Oliver's blood run hot. "What are you talking about, dude?" he said, the words a low, dangerous rumble. "How is the existing system working for *everyone*? It's working for a tiny fraction of people – the ones who are closest to the money printer.

Everyone else just gets their savings robbed from them by inflation. Look at the inequality in our society. That's not a bug; it's a feature of a fiat system that only benefits the mega-corporations." He leaned forward, his voice rising with a passion he didn't try to hide. "None of that money is real. It's not backed by work or productivity. The Fed can just print it on a whim, and the banks and big tech can borrow that made-up money for free and then turn around and charge regular people an arm and a leg. How is that any different from the Ponzis that wrecked you? The guys at the top get richer, and the average person is left holding the bag."

"Yeah man, I know the script," Nick said, a dismissive, condescending smirk on his face. "I worked in crypto for years, remember? I've heard all the arguments. I used to believe them. But when I took a step back, I realized it was just a story I told myself because it sounded sexy." He adopted a high-pitched, mocking tone. "*Ooh, look at us, revolutionaries. We'll topple the financial system.* That's what I used to think, too. Now that I've had this sobering moment, I realize the existing system actually works. Sure, it can be improved around the edges, but our society is functioning just fine. A little inflation is good. Credit creation is good – it drives growth. Let's leave the economy to the professionals and focus on making money with the tools we have. After all," he said, the final, cynical nail in the coffin of the man he used to be, "If you're not thinking about making money, then what are you even doing?"

Oliver just stared at him, a simmering, quiet rage building in his chest. But underneath the anger was a deep sense of pity. For all his cynical, world-weary posturing, Nick was still a friend, a man so thoroughly burned by one fire that he had run straight back into the arms of an even bigger, slower, and more insidious one.

"We'll just have to agree to disagree on that one, Nick," Oliver said finally, his voice low and controlled. He had filtered out a dozen other, more explosive responses, but the core of his new conviction remained. "It can't just be about making money for me. I need to work on something that aligns with my beliefs. I believe a happier, more peaceful, more abundant world is possible, and the way we get there is by fixing the root cause of the problem – a broken money system."

He leaned forward, the quiet passion in his voice a stark contrast to Nick's cynical dismissal. "A sound money fixes so many of these problems. Governments wouldn't be able to print trillions out of thin air to fund never-ending wars. Bankers wouldn't be able to charge regular people exorbitant fees. The rich wouldn't automatically get richer just because they're closer to the money printer. Everyone would have a fair chance. I want to build towards that world, and I believe teaching people about bitcoin, and building better products on bitcoin, gets us there."

"But you *would* be building products on bitcoin if you joined my team, dude," Nick said, completely missing the philosophical core of Oliver's argument. "That's my point. You're going to build tools that help us catch the bad guys. You want to be on Team America with me, Oliver. Not team scammers and criminals. Think about it."

A slow, cold anger began to build in Oliver's chest. "There is nothing more American than bitcoin, Nick," he said, his voice quiet but intense, each word a carefully placed stone in a new foundation of belief. "America is an idea, more than a place. An idea that individuals have inalienable rights. Rights that aren't granted by a government, but are absolute. Bitcoin is a perfect encapsulation of that idea. As a user of bitcoin, you are sovereign. You have full, incontrovertible control over your wealth. No outside authority can infringe on that right. So to answer your question, I am *already* on Team America. I joined the day I truly understood bitcoin. You and your surveillance friends are the ones who should be asking yourselves which team you're on."

Nick just stared at him, a look of inexorable misunderstanding on his face. He shook his head, a dismissive, pitying gesture. "I get it, dude. I've had these conversations. Anyway, just think about what I said. This is your chance to step into the big leagues. Millions of dollars in government contracts. You can finally leave the boring, middle-class, pleb life behind."

He used the word "pleb" as a sneer, a final, condescending jab. But Oliver didn't take the bait. He just smiled, a quiet, knowing expression on his face. "Do you know why I and people like me are drawn towards bitcoin?" he asked.

"Why?" Nick asked, exasperated.

Oliver paused, letting the final, simple, and profound truth of his new world land in the quiet of the pub.

"Because we are all Satoshi."

August 1991, Andhra Pradesh, South India

The final steps of the long, irregular stone stairway were a grueling climb. The father, his breath coming in ragged gasps, leaned heavily on his son's shoulder as they reached the top. "Trust my cousin," he panted, a note of fond exasperation in his voice, "To build his ashram in the most inconvenient place possible. A troublemaker, ever since I knew him."

"He's really your cousin, Dad?" the young man asked, surprised.

"Distantly," the father replied, catching his breath. "Fourth or fifth, separated by a couple of marriages. Hopefully, blood is thicker than water today and he lets us jump the line. The guard only let us use this private entrance because I told him the Guru was my brother."

"That, and you gave him a hundred rupees," the young man retorted with a warm chuckle.

"Visu, you're only twenty-one," the father said, his breathing finally evening out. "You'll find out soon enough that if you don't grease the occasional palm, nothing ever gets done."

They had arrived at the back of a large stone building. As they walked around to the front, they were met with a staggering sight: a line of several hundred people, a patient, colorful serpent of humanity, snaking out of the main door and all the way down the mountainside.

"Good God," Visu's father said. "We'll never meet him if we have to stand in that line. Let me see if I can catch his attention." He walked over to a nearby window.

Inside, Guru Brahma sat on a low platform, greeting his followers one by one. It was a slow, mechanical procession, an assembly line of devotion. Each person would approach, touch the Guru's feet, exchange a few words, and then be gently shepherded away by a guard to make room for the next.

"Dad, this is ridiculous," Visu whispered, a palpable note of discomfort in his voice. "I can't do this."

"Visu, please," his father pleaded, his own voice a low, urgent murmur. "It is important to me that you get his blessing before you leave. You're leaving for Princeton in a week. This was the only day we could come. Just wait."

His father began to wave through the window, a small, discreet gesture at first, which then grew more and more frantic as the Guru remained oblivious. A security guard noticed and shot him a stern, warning glare. But the waving continued, a desperate, silent plea. The guard began to walk toward them, and his movement finally caught the Guru's eye. He looked up, his gaze sweeping past the line of devotees, and saw them.

A slow, bright, genuine smile of recognition spread across Guru Brahma's face. "Ah, look who is here!" he exclaimed, his voice a warm, joyful sound that cut through the reverent silence of the room. He gestured to the guard, a simple, clear command to let them in.

A ripple of nervous, discontented chatter went through the front of the line as Visu and his father were ushered past the waiting crowd, a small, disruptive miracle in the middle of a holy day.

"Surya and Visu, what a pleasure to see you both," Guru Brahma said, standing to greet them, his smile so large and genuine it seemed to light up the entire room. "It has been a few years, hasn't it?"

"Guruji, thank you for letting us see you on such short notice," Visu's father said, his voice a mixture of respect and apology. "I would have preferred to come on a quieter day, but Visu is leaving for America next week, and this was the only time we could find."

"Surya," the Guru said, placing a gentle hand on the older man's shoulder, "I feel embarrassed when I offer advice to you, as you are older than me. But remember, you are exactly where you need to be at this moment. It has happened for a reason. You should not apologize for the universe being in harmony."

"Thank you, Guruji," Visu's father continued, his purpose clear. "I was hoping you could bless Visu as he prepares to leave our household and chart his journey as a man."

Guru Brahma turned his gaze to Visu, and a sound of untamed joy bubbled up from his chest. Oliver-the-observer watched, fascinated. It was a child's laugh, a sound so full of mirth that the Guru's entire body shook with it, his shoulders bouncing rhythmically. It was a beautiful, disarming thing to witness.

"This young man," the Guru said, his eyes twinkling, "He doesn't need anything from me. I can see it in his eyes. He is already in tune with the frequency of the universe. You have nothing to worry about, Surya."

"That is very gracious of you to say," Visu's father persisted, "But could you please just talk to him for a few minutes? It would mean a lot to us."

Guru Brahma nodded. He summoned an assistant and whispered something in his ear. The assistant walked to the front of the room and, cupping his hands, spoke loudly to the restless crowd. "Devotees, Guruji is going to take a thirty-minute break."

A wave of angry mumbling rippled through the line. "We've waited three hours in the sun to meet him!" a man yelled out.

Seeing the commotion, the Guru walked over and whispered something else to the assistant. The assistant cupped his hands again. "There will now be free lunch served to everyone waiting in line!"

The rumblings of discontent softened into murmurs of satisfaction. Guru Brahma gestured for Visu's father to take a seat and then beckoned for Visu to follow him through a back door. They stepped out into a stunning, terraced rose garden, the air thick with the scent of flowers and damp earth, a breath-taking view of the landscape spreading out below them. A jolt of recognition went through Oliver. He knew this place. He had stood here before, in a different projection – one of his early ones guided by Maren – next to the dragon, just before leaping off the cliff into the unknown.

"So, young man," the Guru began, his voice a gentle murmur that seemed to blend with the soft breeze rustling through the rose bushes, "You must be excited about your new adventure? I remember, a few years ago, you told me going to America was your dream."

"Yes, Guruji," Visu replied, his own voice full of a quiet reverence. "This is truly a dream come true."

"You know, Visu," Guru Brahma said thoughtfully, his gaze sweeping across the breathtaking vista of the valley below, "I started this ashram just four or five years ago. I thought it would be a small retreat, for me and perhaps a handful of others who might enjoy my crazy stories." He chuckled, a soft, warm sound. "I had a simple dream – to live a simple life, free from material things, surrounded by people who feel the same way. To laugh, have fun, and appreciate the majesty of nature. And now ..." he gestured to the unseen compound behind them, "... we have people coming from all over the world. America, Britain, Russia, Germany. They are all searching for this life. And for some reason, they like my silly stories. If this is not a dream come true, then what is it?"

"I didn't realize you have visitors from all over the world," Visu said, his voice full of a genuine awe.

"They are people who are disillusioned with the materialism of the West," the Guru explained, his expression turning serious, a teacher imparting a crucial lesson. "Their lives revolve around the worship of money, the need to constantly consume and acquire. But at what cost? It is a circular pursuit that eventually consumes them. Here, they can put that life behind them, at least for a while. We tell jokes, we eat what we grow, we dance around the fire and sing songs. We sleep under a starry night sky and wake to the song of birds." He looked at Visu, a knowing light in his kind eyes. "And for a few hours a day, I tell my nonsense. Maybe," he smiled, "they find that the answer is in nonsense."

Visu listened, and Oliver-the-observer could almost feel the internal conflict in his father's younger self – the boy who was so desperate to go to America, the very heart of the world the Guru was describing with such gentle disdain.

"But we see this happening in our own country now, don't we?" the Guru went on, a new, sadder note in his voice. "This year, our government has opened up to Western investment. Pepsi and Coca-Cola are in our shops. Soon, their television channels will be in our homes. Our country is changing. And soon, our own people will need to come to my ashram, too, not just the foreigners," he finished, letting out a hearty, booming laugh at his own grim joke.

Visu smiled, but Oliver could see it wasn't at the joke itself. It was a smile of deep affection for the laughing, wise, and wonderful man in front of him.

"And why am I telling you all this, Visu?" the Guru asked, his voice a soft murmur that seemed to blend with the gentle breeze rustling through the rose bushes. "You are going to a land where many people worship money. They believe that money alone can buy them happiness. And that," he said, his expression turning serious, a teacher imparting a crucial lesson, "is the root of their suffering – the constant pursuit of a mirage."

He looked at Visu, his kind, peaceful eyes holding a profound, simple truth. "Money doesn't buy you happiness, Visu. Happiness buys you happiness. First learn to be happy, and then money will be incidental. What is money, after all? It is just a language some people use to communicate abundance, often incorrectly. But money is not abundance. Abundance is a state of mind. It is a feeling of pure contentment, peace, love, and cheerful eagerness. That is the feeling you want, and you," he said, his gaze becoming more intense, more direct, "are the captain of your ship. Remember that. You can create the thoughts, which then create the feelings. You have a choice. You are the creator within your own creation."

The words delivered with such simple, unadorned clarity, seemed to hang in the air. Visu just nodded, his expression one of rapt, absolute attention.

"I also know something else about you, Visu," the Guru continued after a moment. "I can see it in your eyes. You are in tune with the vibration of the universe. It is a gift, and you possess it."

"What do you mean, Guruji?" Visu asked, his voice a surprised whisper.

"The voice in your head," the Guru said, a sly, knowing smile on his face. "The one that is guiding you. That is what I am talking about."

Visu's eyes widened, a look of shock on his young face.

"Don't worry," the Guru said gently. "It is quite rare, this gift. But it is not something to fear. These voices stem from you being truly aligned with the truth."

"The truth?" Visu asked.

"Yes," the Guru said, as if it were the most obvious thing in the world. "The one and only singular truth, of course."

"I'm not sure I'm following," Visu said, a look of respectful confusion on his face. The guru just smiled, a silent invitation for the young man to continue down a path he had only just begun to walk.

"The singular truth is that *you are that*," the Guru said softly. "And by 'that,' I mean the universe, the cosmos, everything your conscious mind tells you is separate from you. It is not. Such is the nature of non-duality, Visu. You are able to connect with this feeling because your conscious mind does not constantly act as a barrier, as it does for most others. And this is good. This is the way."

Visu remained silent, the immense, impossible idea settling over him.

Guru Brahma chuckled, a kind, understanding sound. "I see I have left you with a lot to think about. It is okay. Just know that I see this gift in you, and I am telling you to learn how to harness it, to use it for the betterment of humanity. Now," his tone shifted, becoming more personal, "Tell me, Visu. What is it that you want most out of this life?"

The question was so direct, so fundamental, that Visu had to think for a moment. "I want to feel the excitement of adventure," he said finally, the words a quiet, earnest confession. "I want to learn new things and create things of my own. I want to do this forever – that is why I want to be immortal."

The Guru laughed again, the sound full of a deep, affectionate warmth. "Then so be it, my child. In a sense, you will live forever. This physical body is just a temporary coat you are wearing. Your pure consciousness is indeed immortal, because it is, and always has been, one with the universe. And the universe is immortal."

Visu didn't look entirely satisfied with the answer. The Guru smiled. "Come," he said, "Let me show you something."

He led Visu past the fragrant rose garden and down a narrow, winding path cut into a dense, wooded area. The air grew cooler, the sound of birds and insects a quiet symphony in the background. In a few minutes, they reached a clearing dominated by a large set of moss-covered rocks, a tiny, crystal-clear stream of water flowing over them, creating a small, perfect waterfall that collected in a pool below.

"This little stream joins the bigger mountain stream a little further down," the Guru said, his voice a gentle murmur against the sound of the falling water. "The villagers call this waterfall *The Tears of Brahma*. They have a superstition about it, which I will explain. But first, do you know the name of this mountain?"

"No, Guruji, I don't," Visu replied, his gaze lost in the mesmerizing, endless flow of the water.

"It is called *Akshar Konda*," the Guru said, his voice a low, resonant murmur that seemed to harmonize with the sound of the falling water. "A*kshar* means 'indestructible' in Sanskrit, and *Konda* means 'mountain.' This is the indestructible mountain. And the water from this waterfall … the villagers call it *Akshar Jal*. The water of immortality."

He walked over to the waterfall, the movement as fluid and natural as the stream itself. He cupped his hands under the flowing water, a small, perfect offering. He walked back to Visu, who stood, mesmerized, and gently let the cool, clear water trickle over his fingers and onto the young man's forehead, dripping down over his eyes and face in a silent, sacred baptism.

Guru Brahma rested his damp palm gently against Visu's forehead, and his voice, though soft, seemed to fill the entire forest with a powerful energy. "I now anoint you, *Akshar*," he said. "You are now indestructible. You are now invincible. You are now immortal. You are now *Akshar*. Append this word to the end of your name, and the universe will become your playground. You are in alignment. You are in resonance. So be it."

He took his palm away and stepped back. Visu opened his eyes, a dazed, trancelike look on his face, as if he had just returned from a journey to a distant star. And Oliver-the-observer felt it too – a powerful, undeniable surge of bright, electric energy that coursed through his entire being, a silent, ghostly participant in a ritual that had taken place a decade before he was born.

The sacred moment passed. The Guru's playful, human energy returned in a rush. "And now, Visu," he said with a booming laugh, "Let us return and relieve your father. I am sure the people waiting back at the ashram have turned into a mob, and it is only a matter of time before they make him into their scapegoat."

As they walked back toward the ashram, the scene dissolved, the sound of the waterfall fading into a ringing silence.

Oliver opened his eyes, but the electric hum of the ritual still coursed through his veins. He sat in his chair, the silence of his own apartment a stark, lonely contrast to the scene he had just witnessed. And then, the full, sickening weight of the implication crashed down on him. *Akshar.* The name echoed in his mind, a perfect, chilling match to the story Eddie had told him. The story Greg Ostrowsky had shared about his father working under a pseudonym.

It couldn't be a coincidence. What's in a name? Everything, apparently. He felt a wave of nausea, a sickening dread that was a perfect mirror of the awe he had just experienced. His worst nightmare about his father was most likely true. The beautiful, sacred moment he had just witnessed was the origin story of a secret, a double life that would, years later, consume the man he loved.

89062 (November 1, 2010)

The world dissolved into the sterile gray of an empty office. Fluorescent lights hummed over a sea of deserted cubicles. Oliver was back at WilcoxRe, a ghost in the machine. A carpeted corridor led to a single, dimly lit suite. Inside, a man sat in front of a computer, his back to the room. He reached into a leather satchel and pulled out a bulky laptop. A Linux machine.

"Dad!" Oliver-the-observer called out, the word a silent, useless cry in the void of the projection. "Dad, can you hear me?"

He couldn't. His father's back, a familiar, solid landscape he had known his entire life, was an impenetrable wall.

Nate opened the laptop, logged in, and for a moment, just stared at a screen full of C++ code. Then, as if distracted, he opened a web browser and logged into an old, simple email client. There was one unread message. He clicked on it. Oliver felt his perspective drift closer, a disembodied eye moving over his father's shoulder, until the words on the screen were stark, and clear, and undeniable.

```
From: Satoshi Nakamoto satoshin@gmx.com
Date: Monday, Nov 01, 2010 at 5:57 PM
To: Dev_akshar dev_akshar@gmx.com
Subject: Re: Code review


Hi Akshar,
```

Appreciate all the work you put into the last code review. Thank you for flagging the issues. Those will be addressed shortly. Akasha sounds like an interesting idea as well – I look forward to reviewing it once ready.

I wanted to talk to you about Christiaan. I have heard that he is about to go to England to meet the WikiLeaks people. This is a terrible idea. We are a small project in beta right now and the scrutiny that something like this will bring will likely destroy us. I am requesting you to talk to him and dissuade him. We don't want to kick this hornet's nest at this stage.

On another topic, re: your note on Sazsa's offer to sell the third Bryce – I will pass on it for now. It's a fantastic painting, but I prefer his fifth one, incomplete as it might be. Let me know if you have any insight on who might have it.

```
Satoshi
```

The world shattered. Oliver's eyes snapped open, and a raw, guttural sound of pure, animalistic agony ripped from his throat. The quiet of his apartment was a thin, fragile skin over the roaring chaos in his mind. *Dev_akshar*. The name was a brand, a final, searing confirmation of a truth he had been circling, denying, and dreading for weeks. It wasn't a coincidence. It wasn't a mistake. It was him.

"Fuck!" The word was a punch, a desperate, futile blow against an immutable fact. "Fuck, fuck, fuck! Why, Dad? Why?" The question was a howl, a raw, bleeding wound of a boy who had spent months searching for his father, only to find a legend, a ghost, a man who had lived a secret life so vast and profound that Oliver felt he had never known him at all.

And then, the final, cruel, almost comical twist of the knife. *The fifth Bryce.* Not three paintings. Five. The secret wasn't just a secret. It was a labyrinth. "Fuck," he whispered again, the word no longer a shout, but a small, broken sound of absolute, soul-crushing defeat.

The Notepad

i) violin ii) toddler iii) alley iv) shoulder v) educate vi) rookie vii) oval viii) below ix) punch x) certain xi) cover xii) agree xiii) coast xiv) suggest xv) boring xvi) tissue xvii) good xviii) sausage xix) cute xx) club xxi) runway xxii) pluck xxiii) satoshi

CHAPTER 24. HOME

A yellow cab pulled up to the curb, a splash of bright, hopeful color on a street that had not yet been polished to the sterile sheen of the future. The door flew open, and a boy, not yet five, burst out onto the sidewalk, his small body a whirlwind of pure, uncontainable excitement. His mother and father followed, stepping out of the car into the bright September sunlight, a complete, unbroken unit.

"Daddy, is this our new house?" the boy asked, his eyes wide as he stared up at the tall, brick facade of 456 W 19th Street.

"It's not a house, Oliver," the father said, his voice a warm, gentle rumble as he pulled their suitcases from the trunk. "It's an apartment. It's inside this building. It's our new home."

"Why did we leave our house in Connecticut, Daddy?"

"It was time for us to move to the city," the father explained, his words a simple, confident map of their new life. "It's better for Mommy's work, better for my work, and you can go to a good school next year."

Just then, a young doorman, his uniform crisp and new, hurried out to them. "Welcome, folks," he said, his smile genuine and welcoming. "You must be moving into apartment 139. Let me help you with those."

The man nodded, handing over the bags.

"Excellent, the movers just finished about an hour ago," the young doorman said, easily hefting the suitcases. "My name is Santos."

"Thank you, Santos," the man said, gesturing to his family. "I'm Nate, this is my wife Diane, and my son Oliver."

"A real pleasure to meet you all," Santos replied. He then crouched down, bringing himself to the young boy's level. "And Mr. Oliver, it is a special pleasure to meet you," he said, his voice a low, conspiratorial murmur. "I can see in your eyes that one day you're going to be a big, important businessman just like your dad. But you stay out of trouble in my building, okay? I can also see you're a troublemaker," he finished, a faux-stern expression on his face. The young Oliver just giggled, a bright, happy sound, and hid behind his father's leg.

"Thank you again, Santos," Nate said as they walked into the lobby. "You are very good at your job."

"I appreciate that, sir," Santos replied, a flicker of something else, something more vulnerable, in his eyes. "But today is actually my second day here. I used to be a handyman, until I injured my back. I can't do that kind of physical work anymore."

Nate stopped, his friendly expression shifting to one of genuine concern. "Then you certainly shouldn't be carrying our suitcases," he said. "But you look like a young guy, Santos. You should be able to recover from that injury soon and do the job you really want to do."

"We'll see about that, sir," Santos said with a dry, humorless laugh. "I'm twenty-seven. I started working when I was seventeen. I thought I enjoyed the work, but then I had a spinal injury playing soccer. I couldn't move for three months. At least if it had happened at work, I could have sued. But of course, I had to be stupid and get injured on my own time." He shook his head, a look of weary resignation on his young face. "Now, I might as well be back home."

"*Dime, Santos,*" Nate said, switching effortlessly into a flawless, Castilian Spanish that made the young doorman's head snap up in surprise. "*¿donde es home para ti? ¿Washington Heights?*" he asked, a mischievous, knowing smile in his eyes.

Santos stared at him for a moment, and then a slow, wide, brilliant grin broke across his face, a sudden flash of sunlight in the dim lobby. He laughed, a real, genuine laugh, and replied in his own, warmer Spanish. "You have a good sense of humor, señor. I actually do live in Washington Heights *por ahora, pero* my original home is Cuba. I came here with my family when I was fifteen."

Oliver-the-observer watched, a silent, unseen ghost, as this small, perfect moment of connection, of shared language and human kindness, unfolded in the lobby of a building that would, for a short, beautiful time, be a happy home.

"We've only just met, Santos," Nate continued, his Spanish flowing with an easy, natural grace, "But I can tell you seem very much at home in New York. Sometimes, home is the place where you are reborn, not where you were born."

The words, so simple and profound, landed with a quiet weight in the young doorman's heart. He nodded thoughtfully. "You're right, señor," he replied, his own voice a low murmur of dawning realization. "I never thought about it that way, but that makes sense. Washington Heights is my home. *Aquí me convertí en un hombre.*"

Nate smiled. As they walked toward the elevator, Santos spoke again. "By the way, señor, your Spanish is excellent. Are you from Spain?"

Nate laughed, a warm, easy sound that echoed in the lobby. "This is my first day in this building, and it is your second," he replied. "Let's leave some conversation for the years ahead of us."

As they waited for the elevator, the young Oliver looked up at his father. "What did you talk to the nice man about, Daddy?"

"He told me that he moved here from Cuba when he was fifteen," Nate explained, ruffling his son's hair. "I told him New York was now his home, because this is the place he was reborn. He was happy to hear that."

"Oh," the boy said, contemplating this new idea as the elevator doors opened.

Inside the apartment, the young Oliver immediately launched himself onto a plastic-wrapped couch. "Mommy, Daddy, is all our furniture going to be like this in our new home? I like it. It makes a crumply noise when I jump on it."

"Oliver, stop," Diane said, her voice sharp but her eyes laughing. "You'll break the couch. And no, the movers wrapped everything so it wouldn't get damaged. Do you want to help me tear it off? Gently, though." Her stern expression dissolved completely as she watched her excited son begin to gleefully shred the plastic.

Nate put the suitcases down, his gaze sweeping across their new life, a slow, satisfied smile on his face. He walked over to Diane, pulling her into a warm, tight hug. "We did it, honey," he whispered into her hair. "We left suburbia. Creativity and opportunity beckon. We're going to thrive here as a family, I can feel it."

The young Oliver, interrupting his important work, saw his parents embracing and ran to them, wrapping his small arms around their knees. "Family hug, family hug!" he chanted, jumping up and down. He looked up at them, his face wearing an expression of pure, uncomplicated joy. "Mommy, Daddy, I love our new home," he said happily. "I think this will be our new home forever."

Diane laughed, a sound full of a love so deep it ached. "I'm glad you like it, sweetheart, but I don't know about forever. One day, you'll be a big boy and go to college. You'll get a job. You'll move someplace else."

"No!" the young Oliver exclaimed, his voice a note of pure, indignant certainty. "I'll never leave Mommy and Daddy. The three of us will live here forever, and we'll always be happy."

Both Nate and Diane laughed at the touching, fierce innocence of their son.

"Fine," the boy huffed, seeing their amusement. "If you two want to leave after some time, you can. But I'll always stay here. This is my home."

The scene, so perfect, so full of a future that would never be, began to fade. Oliver opened his eyes, the salty tracks of silent tears cool on his cheeks. He looked around the apartment, at the familiar walls, the worn armchair, the ghost of a once happy family that still lingered in the air. All those years ago, a little boy had declared this place his home, a fortress of love he would never leave. And in the end, after all the pain, all the loss, all the impossible journeys, he had kept his promise.

It was home.

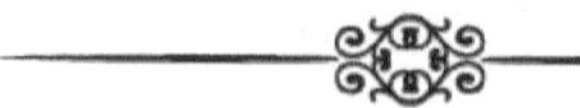

767401 (December 14)

Oliver stared into the inky purple-blackness, but this time, it was different. A pleasant, warm aroma, rich and complex like old books and sweet tobacco, filled the void.

Then he saw him. The Noncemeister was there, not floating or dancing, but reclined comfortably in a large, spectral armchair, his feet propped up on a matching stool. He was staring into the middle distance, a long, elegant cigar held between his fingers, a thin ribbon of fragrant, purple smoke curling up from its tip.

"Is that a cigar?" Oliver asked, the question a small, absurd note in the absolute quiet.

The Noncemeister turned his head slowly, a look of deep, peaceful content-ment on his face. He smiled. "Why, yes, Battu. A man's got to relax when he needs to. It's a well-earned rest, in my case."

"What are you talking about?" Oliver asked. "You're a figment of my imagination. Why do you need to rest?"

The Noncemeister's smile was slow, sad, and gentle. "Because we have come a long way, Battolo," he said, and as he spoke, the purple smoke from his cigar coalesced, forming hazy, fleeting images of their past encounters – the jail cell, the castle, the absurd ballet on the precipice. "I taught you everything all over again, and now, you're almost home."

"I'm not sure I'm following you," Oliver said, a new, unfamiliar feeling of unease beginning to creep in.

"Batue, when we started on this journey, you were lost," the Noncemeister said, his voice a low, nostalgic murmur. "You were floundering. And you knew nothing. Think about that, for a moment. All that work I put in, all those heartbeats ago, and I return to find you a blank slate. A *tabula rasa*. A big fat zero, zero, zero." He shook his head, a gesture of deep, weary disappointment.

"So what do I do? I start all over again. And now … you're right there. You have everything you need to know. Once again, you are exactly where you need to be." He took another long, slow puff of the cigar, the glowing cherry a single, bright point in the vast darkness. "And now, I am tired. I am spent."

The words, so full of a strange, human finality, made the unease in Oliver's chest sharpen into a real, cold dread. "Wait," he said, the pieces clicking into place with a sickening thud. "Do you mean … I've almost got my dad's entire seed phrase? Is that what you mean by I'm almost home?"

"You know, Batlu, the one other thing I wish I could have taught you was to stop talking nonsense," the Noncemeister sighed, his voice laced with a gentle, final exasperation. "I don't know any 'seat phase,' so let's drop that, shall we? What I'm saying is, you needed to align with a deeper knowledge, a fuller sense of knowing, when I came back this time. And it appears, despite your occasional penchant for nonsense, that you're almost there." He looked at Oliver, his gaze direct and full of a strange, paternal pride. "And I was the one who got you home. So what is left for me now?"

The question hung in the air, a final, terrible confirmation. The playful guide, the maddening trickster … he was saying goodbye. "What are you saying?" Oliver asked, his voice a tight, desperate whisper, the jolly purple void suddenly feeling like a cold, lonely, and terrifying place. "That your work here is done?"

"What is home, after all?" The Noncemeister took another long, slow puff of his cigar, the purple smoke wreathing his head like a strange, sad halo. "Is it a single point on a map? Is it the soil you were born on? Or is home the place you arrive at, knowing that every other place is just a temporary destination? Home is where the answer lies, isn't it, Battu?"

"What answer?" Oliver asked, his voice a low whisper.

"The answer to the question, 'where am I?'" the Noncemeister said, his own voice softening. "The answer is not an answer that is spoken. The answer is an answer that is felt … deep within the marrow of your bones. Felt from the top of your head, all the way down to the tip of your tippy-toes. And that answer is: I am here, and this is home. And so it goes."

The finality in his tone was cold and hard. "This really is it, isn't it?" Oliver felt a lump forming in his throat. "You're going to leave now that I'm home."

"Leave-shmeave, Batew," the Noncemeister said, but his usual jovial energy was gone, replaced by a gentle seriousness. "Do I really ever leave? Sure, I do. The Noncemeister does leave. But a more important question is, *who* am I? If you can answer that, then you'll know what happens when I leave."

"Who are you?" Oliver said, the words a desperate attempt to hold on. "You're the Noncemeister. The master of the nonces. The keeper of the timechain. In fact," he said, the final, absolute truth of it all finally dawning on him, "You *are* the timechain."

"Indeed, Battu. And what is the timechain? It is the collective consciousness of the universe projected as the truth over and over again. You are part of that collective consciousness. Ergo, you are me, and I am you. In that sense," he said, a slow, sad, beautiful smile spreading across his face, "I will never leave."

"Please don't go," Oliver said, the words a raw, pleading whisper, the tears he had been fighting finally beginning to fall. "I'll miss you. I need you." The guarded, analytical man he had been forced to become over the last few months dissolved, and in his place was a small, eight-year-old boy, half-asleep in his bed, clinging to his departing father's shirt. *Please don't go, Daddy. One more story. I'm not sleeping yet.*

The Noncemeister's smile broadened, and it was no longer sad. It was full of a love so profound, so absolute, it seemed to fill the entire purple void. "I'll tell you what, though," he said, his voice a warm, final promise. "If you really, really, actually, truly need me, then I'll be there. Not now, though. Now, you're home."

"He sent you here, didn't he?" Oliver asked, the question a final, certain understanding.

The Noncemeister just smiled.

"This was his way of watching over me," Oliver continued, the words a quiet, grateful prayer. "Of guiding me, of making sure I was on the right path even after he was gone. I know he sent you."

The Noncemeister's smile remained, a silent, loving confirmation. And then, a bright orange light began to shine from the center of his chest, a small, warm sun growing larger and more brilliant with each passing second until it consumed his entire form, until he was no longer the silhouette of a man, but a being of pure, blinding light. The orange radiance grew, filling the entire timechain, until Oliver had no choice but to close his eyes against its beautiful, overwhelming power.

He opened them. He was back in his dad's armchair, the quiet of the apartment a soft, gentle blanket after the storm. He sat there for a long time, the warmth of the orange light still a fading ember in his heart.

Then, with a slow, deliberate movement, he stood up, walked to his desk, and turned on his laptop. He opened the Sparrow Wallet app, the screen a clean, simple interface in a world that was anything but. He clicked *Import Wallet*. He chose the option for a twenty-four-word seed phrase.

A screen popped up, twenty-four blank, numbered fields, a final, empty canvas. And one by one, with a steady, certain hand, he began to type.

violin, toddler, alley, shoulder, educate, rookie, oval, below, punch, certain, cover, agree, coast, suggest, boring, tissue, good, sausage, cute, club, runway, pluck, satoshi, home.

A green checkmark bloomed at the bottom of the pop-up. *Valid Seed Phrase.* He clicked *Import*.

For what felt like an eternity, a single, pulsing phrase filled the screen: *Loading Wallet …* each pulse was a heartbeat, a slow, agonizing drumbeat marking the final seconds of his ten-month quest. And then, it was gone. The wallet was there.

Oliver leaned in, his eyes scanning for the balance, and his breath caught in his throat. His heart, which had been a steady drum, suddenly began to hammer against his ribs, a frantic, panicked rhythm. He read the number again, certain his sleep-deprived mind was playing tricks on him. He collapsed back into the armchair, the room spinning, the screen a blurry, impossible constellation of pixels. He took a few deep, ragged breaths, trying to anchor himself to the solid reality of the chair, the desk, the room. He leaned forward again, his face inches from the screen, his mind refusing to believe what his eyes were seeing.

The balance read: 24,000 BTC.

With hands that trembled so badly he could barely control the trackpad, he clicked on the transaction history. It was a ghost story written in code. The last transaction was from November 2013, a final deposit of over five thousand bitcoin. Before that, a series of large, incoming transfers. And then … nothing. Nine years of absolute, perfect silence.

He pushed himself away from the desk and stumbled over to the bed, collapsing onto it, his heart still a wild, frantic bird trapped in his chest. So this was it. The end. Ten months of a journey that had torn his life apart and rebuilt it into something new, something strange and unimaginable. He had traveled through time, he had stolen masterpieces, he had spoken with ghosts and gods. He had found a new purpose, a new version of himself. And in the end, he had found what he was looking for. He had found his father.

Twenty-four thousand bitcoin. He did the math, the number so absurdly large it felt like a fiction. Four hundred and thirty million dollars. All of it, his. A king's ransom, the legacy of a man who had lived a secret, epic life.

And he couldn't touch a single, solitary satoshi.

The final, brutal, crushing irony of his father's great, intricate puzzle slammed into him. His father was Dev_akshar. The Department of Justice was hunting for that ghost, and Nick, his own friend, was now one of the hunters. They were watching. They had to be. Even the tiniest movement, a single dollar transferred from this wallet, and they would know. The alarm bells would ring, and they would come for him.

He had inherited a kingdom, but he was eternally locked outside its gates, the key in his hand a useless, mocking symbol of a wealth he could see but never possess.

I am the Ancient Mariner, aren't I? he thought, a wave of pure, self-loathing disgust washing over him. *Water, water, everywhere, nor any drop to drink.* He was living his own Rime.

767594 (December 15)

"I told you it was a bad idea to take the train to Grand Central," Daniela groaned, the station agent's announcement echoing the finality of their new, inconvenient reality. *7 train service to Times Square is suspended.*

"Whose idea was it to go to O'Connell's for a drink first?" Oliver said, his own voice moody, the festive spirit of his birthday already beginning to fray.

"We should have just walked to the C train," she continued, "Celeste is just a few blocks from 86th. Why the 6 train?"

"Our best bet now is to walk to 50th and Broadway and take the 1," he said, already plotting a new course, a grim navigator in a sea of holiday tourists. "There's no way in hell I'm walking through Times Square. It's a week before Christmas. I know an exit that'll get us out on 45th and Park."

"Oh Oliver," she said, her voice softening, all her frustration melting away into a quiet, sad disappointment. "I wanted today to be perfect for you. It's your first birthday with us together. I'm sorry I suggested O'Connell's. I thought you'd have fun."

The change in her tone, the genuine hurt in her voice, instantly extinguished his own irritation. He stopped, pulled her in, and put his arm around her shoulder, a small, warm island in the turbulent river of Grand Central. "Hey," he said softly. "It's okay. I really appreciate you planning all this. I had a great time at O'Connell's." He smiled. "Isn't it wild that Aisling suspects nothing? She didn't even bring it up." He looked out at the bustling crowd, a new, strange sense of responsibility settling over him. "I do need to make it up to her, though. Once I figure out how to move this bitcoin without the feds getting on my tail, I'll give her and Shannon a hundred thousand. Maybe two. We can't just rob people like that. I mean, we had to do it, but I have to repay her somehow."

"Oliver, I still can't believe it's real," Daniela said, her voice a hushed whisper of awe. "Twenty-four thousand bitcoin. Are you absolutely sure?"

"I'm sure," he replied, a grim certainty in his voice. "I checked twenty times yesterday. I'll show you on the block explorer when we get to the restaurant."

They started walking, a slow, difficult path through the holiday crowds. "So the wallet we thought was Christiaan's, the MixMarket one," she asked, "That's this one? It was your dad's all along?"

"Yeah," he said, pointing north. "Let's actually get to 48th and walk across from there." He steered her through the throng. "That seems to be the case. The twenty-four thousand coins belonged to my dad, to Dev_akshar. And most likely, the coins hidden in the Bryce paintings belong to him too. But," he let out a short, ironic laugh, "I guess that's going to remain an unsolved mystery. I have no idea where the rest of the words are."

"Wow," she said softly. "So we just … let those go?"

"For now," he said, the sheer, staggering scale of his impossible situation hitting him all over again. "Listen, I'm sitting on four hundred and thirty million dollars that I can't spend. And that's at *today's* prices. What if in five or ten years, bitcoin is at a million a coin? Let me first figure out what the hell I'm supposed to do with this stash other than stare at it hopelessly on my computer screen. We can get to the paintings later."

They reached the corner of 48th and Broadway, a frenetic crossroads of flashing lights, blaring horns, and a river of holiday tourists. Daniela nudged him, and he followed her gaze. Through the window of a brightly lit, ostentatiously decorated restaurant, a man was waving at them, a frantic, joyous windmill of a gesture.

"Hey," Oliver said, a slow, disbelieving smile spreading across his face. "That's my Uncle Eddie." He looked up at the gaudy sign: *Papa Carmine's*. "Come on," he said, pulling her through the crowd. "Let's say hello."

Inside, Eddie was standing in the lobby next to a middle-aged woman – his wife Melissa. His perfect, female counterpart, Oliver thought with a jolt. They had the same short, portly stature, the same round, cheerful face.

"Olly, my young tiger!" Eddie boomed, enveloping Oliver in a rib-crushing bear hug. "Fancy seeing you here."

"Hi Aunt Melissa," Oliver said, extricating himself and giving her a much gentler hug.

"And who is this fine young lady with you, chief?" Eddie asked, his gaze falling on Daniela.

"Oh, this is my girlfriend, Daniela," Oliver said, a quiet pride in his voice.

"Ah, the famous girlfriend," Eddie boomed, his voice echoing through the crowded lobby. "My word, tiger. You've certainly done well for yourself. This young lady looks like a supermodel!" He looked from Daniela back to Oliver. "And you're not too shabby yourself, chief. I mean, why wouldn't you be, come to think of it, Nate Battolo's son – gimme a goddam break. If Nate's son didn't inherit his good looks, then genetics is a scam, I'm telling you right now. Darwin would be a fraud. But that's not the case, obviously, and thank God for that, am I right, champ?"

Oliver and Daniela both laughed, a warm, easy sound. "So what are you doing here, Uncle Eddie?" Oliver asked.

"Oh, this is our favorite restaurant in the city, big guy," Eddie declared, his arm draping around his wife's shoulders with a proud, possessive flourish. "Papa Carmine's. Italian food so good, you have people in Italy turning in their passports to become American, that's how good this is. Melissa and I have been coming here since we started dating." He stared at his wife with a broad, adoring smile, and to Oliver's surprise, Melissa blushed, a shy, girlish gesture that seemed to melt away the years. It was a small, perfect, and utterly unexpected moment of pure, uncomplicated happiness in the middle of a chaotic city.

A dreamy, far-away look came over Eddie's face. "A marinara sauce like you wouldn't believe, tiger," he said, his voice dropping to a reverent hush as if describing a religious experience. "Who knew you could do that to tomatoes? I mean it's a fruit, isn't it? It's not even a vegetable. I'm no zoologist, don't get me wrong, but how do they do that? Oh, and shrimp scampi like nobody's business." He closed his eyes, a look of pure, beatific bliss on his face. "And don't even get me started on their Alfredo. I'm not kidding, chief, I swear on my mother, I've seen people swoon and fall to the floor in joy when they try their first bite of the Pappardelle Alfredo."

Oliver, remembering the bizarre, violent, and utterly false version of this story from his projection, had to suppress a laugh. "Eddie," he asked, "Did you ever come here with Dad?"

"Yeah, I came with him once," Eddie said, his expression clouding over slightly. "But you know him, tiger. Always very particular. I'm not sure this place was his style, to be honest. To his credit, he was very gracious, but I could tell his heart wasn't in it. Such a kind and gentle soul, kiddo. Even though he could be stuck-up and pretentious when it came to some things. May his goddam soul rest in peace," he finished, his eyes tearing up for a brief, genuine moment.

He recovered almost instantly, his mood swinging back to righteous indignation as he gestured toward the maître d'. "Can you believe these guys? We made a reservation for 7:30. We get here on the dot. They tell us there's a twenty-minute wait. What's the point of a reservation if there's a wait? I just don't get it with these people. This is a big event for Melissa and me – we can only come here once or twice a year, and now these bozos are shafting us with this wait time."

His expression then changed again, a sudden, bright sunrise of a smile breaking through the clouds of his disgust. "That said," he boomed, clapping his hands together, "If they hadn't kept us waiting, we wouldn't have seen you two walking by, so it all worked out!" He beamed at them, a man who had just discovered a silver lining. "So what are you two lovebirds doing out here, anyway?"

"Oh, it's Oliver's birthday," Daniela explained. "We're on our way to a restaurant on the Upper West Side. The train wasn't working, so we're walking to the next stop."

"Olly, Olly, Olly …" Eddie's face contorted into a mask of theatrical shock. He walked right up to Oliver, placing his hands heavily on both of his shoulders, a gesture of affectionate, fatherly gravity. "Of course, it's your birthday, how could I forget? December 15th! My young scamp, happy birthday, big guy." He gave Oliver two gentle, percussive slaps on each cheek, as if bestowing a knighthood. "So how old are you now, twenty, twenty-one?"

"Twenty-four, Uncle Eddie," Oliver replied, a genuine laugh escaping him.

"Get outta here, tiger!" Eddie exclaimed, his eyes wide with disbelief.

"I'm serious. Today is my twenty-fourth birthday," Oliver laughed again.

Eddie turned to his wife, his own face a picture of comic despair. "Can you believe this, cupcake? It feels like just yesterday this kid was running around causing all that trouble, not letting his parents have a second of peace. I blink for a second and he tells me he's turning twenty-four. Next thing you'll tell me is that our daughter is about to get married."

"Her unemployed boyfriend needs to get a job first," Melissa replied with a dry, perfectly timed laugh.

"Well, tiger," Eddie turned back to Oliver, his tone becoming one of a magnanimous, if slightly flustered, host. "I'd ask you to join us for dinner to celebrate, but we have a table for two, and we had to book it a month in advance. Besides, it looks like you and your lady have plans." He clapped

Oliver on the shoulder again, a final, booming gesture of affection. "I'll make it up to you, big guy. I promise."

Oliver and Daniela bid them farewell and turned to leave. As they were walking toward the door, the speakers in the lobby, as if on cue, began to play the smooth, nostalgic opening notes of Sinatra's "Winter Wonderland."

"Ooh, ooh, ooh!" they heard Eddie exclaim behind them. "This is our favorite Christmas song. Come on, cupcake."

Oliver and Daniela turned back just in time to see him take Melissa's hand, pull her close with a surprisingly nimble move, and begin to slowly, clumsily, and joyfully dance right there in the middle of the crowded restaurant lobby, a small, perfect, and utterly unselfconscious island of happiness.

They looked at each other, a shared, warm smile on their faces, and walked out onto Broadway, leaving the happy couple to their song. They took the 1 train from 50th Street and made their way uptown, to Celeste, to a celebration of their own.

At the restaurant, the air was warm and thick with the smells of garlic, olive oil, and old wine. "Hey," Oliver said, leaning across the small table, his voice a low, excited murmur, "I've been meaning to tell you about this new thing, Nostr. It's a decentralized social protocol some bitcoiners created. A few days ago, Jack Dorsey gave the founder fourteen bitcoin. It's like a Twitter replacement, but no one's in charge. It feels ..." he searched for the right words, "... like what my dad used to say the early internet felt like in the nineties. Pure, open, full of potential. You should check it out."

"Nice," she said, her eyes lighting up with a genuine curiosity. "You have to show me how to make an account. I'd love to try it."

Just then, the proprietor, a man with a magnificent mustache and a twinkle in his eye, appeared at their table. "*Buona sera,*" he said with a flourish. "*Good? Great.* I wanted to let you know, tonight we have a special ten-cheese platter. I have smuggled all of them myself from Italy."

"Smuggled?" Oliver chuckled.

"Yes," the proprietor shrugged, as if explaining the most logical thing in the world. "I have to smuggle them. They are unpasteurized. In this country, they believe in killing the taste of the cheese. I have no choice but to bring back the real stuff from home."

Oliver and Daniela exchanged a look and nodded. "Sure," Oliver said. "We'll get it."

"And are we celebrating a special occasion?" the proprietor asked, his gaze falling on Oliver.

"Yes, it's his birthday!" Daniela said, her voice full of a happy, celebratory warmth.

"Ah!" the proprietor's face broke into a wide, genuine smile. "A very happy birthday to you, young man." He paused, a look of thoughtful generosity on his face. "Since it is your birthday, I will add two more special cheeses to your platter. They are not on the menu. I had to hike up a mountain in Modena for over an hour to find these." He leaned in, his voice a conspiratorial whisper that held the weight of a delicious secret. "These two hidden gems … this is where the real magic lies."

He winked and walked away toward the kitchen.

Oliver fell silent. The cheerful sounds of the restaurant, the warmth of Daniela's hand on his, it all seemed to fade into a distant hum. The proprietor's words echoed in his mind, a series of keys turning in locks he hadn't known were there. *Two hidden gems. Where the real magic lies.*

He had been so focused on the words he *could* see, the clues that were right there in front of him. But what if that was just the first layer? What if the real treasure wasn't in the paintings he had, but in the ones he didn't? The memory of the email from Satoshi to his father, the one he had seen in the projection, flashed in his mind with a sudden, brilliant clarity. *'I prefer his fifth one, incomplete as it might be.' The fifth one.* Which meant there had to be a fourth. Two more paintings. Two hidden gems.

"Babe?" Daniela's voice pulled him back. "Are you okay?"

He looked at her, his eyes wide with the sudden, world-altering force of the realization. "Uh huh," he mumbled. "Daniela … I think I just figured out where the rest of the seed words are."

"What?" she asked, her own expression a mirror of his shock. "How? Where?"

"It's what the owner just said," he said, the words a breathless, excited rush. "The real magic lies in the two hidden gems. In the email Satoshi wrote to my dad, he talked about Bryce's *fifth* painting. Which means there has to be a fourth. That's got to be it. The rest of the words are on those other two paintings."

"Wow, Oliver," she said, her voice a hushed whisper of awe. "You're probably right. But where are these paintings?"

The question was a bucket of ice water, extinguishing the bright, hot fire of his discovery. "Yeah," he said, the excitement draining from his voice, replaced by a familiar, heavy dejection. "That's going to be a problem. No one knows. I don't think anyone even knows they exist. Best I heard was speculation that Bryce might have had some incomplete works. Even Satoshi said the fifth one was incomplete." He let out a long, slow sigh. "And now the Noncemeister is gone. I have no idea how I'll even begin to look for them."

Just then, the cheese platter arrived, a magnificent, sprawling work of art in its own right, a fragrant landscape of color and texture that was, in true Celeste form, better than either of them could have dreamed.

After they had placed their order for the main course, a comfortable, thoughtful silence settled between them. Oliver pulled out his phone. "Okay, look," he said, his focus returning to the one, tangible, and utterly useless treasure he did possess. "I'm going to pull up a block explorer and show you the wallet."

He saw the concern on her face and offered a reassuring smile. "Don't worry," he said, "It's not the actual wallet. Because bitcoin is a public ledger, you can see everyone's balances as long as you know their address. You need the private key – the seed phrase – to actually move anything. That's only on my computer for now." He passed her the phone, the screen glowing with a string of characters and a staggering number. "I need to find a more secure cold storage solution soon, but for now, take a look."

Daniela took the phone, her eyes widening as she read the screen. She was silent for a long time. "Wow, Oliver," she breathed. "You're right. It is *almost* twenty-four thousand bitcoin. This is incredible."

The word snagged in his mind, a small, discordant note in the symphony of his triumph. "What do you mean 'almost'?" he asked, a new, sharp anxiety cutting through the warmth of the wine. "It's exactly twenty-four thousand."

"Well," she said, looking at the screen again, "It says here it's twenty-three thousand, nine hundred and seventy-six."

"Let me see that." He grabbed the phone from her hands. She was right. The number had changed. A cold, sick feeling began to spread through his chest. "How could this be?" he whispered, his fingers frantically tapping, navigating to the transaction history.

And then he saw it. And his jaw dropped.

"Daniela," he said, his voice a choked, disbelieving whisper, "This is insane. There are two new transactions. From just a few hours ago." The words felt like a foreign language in his mouth. "No movement in nine years, and now, the day after I find the seed phrase, two transactions – one to move twenty-four bitcoin, and another an *OP_RETURN*."

"What?" she gasped. "Someone moved twenty-four bitcoin today? And what's an op return?"

"It's a type of transaction," he explained, his mind on autopilot, "With no monetary value. It just lets you embed a small amount of text in the timechain." His eyes scanned the screen, finding the message. "Look, it says … 'Obelisk, 18 July. It has happened.' This makes no sense," he said, looking up at her.

But the woman he was looking at was not the same woman from a moment ago. All the color had drained from her face. She was white as a sheet, her eyes wide with a profound terror he had never seen before.

"Babe, are you okay?" he asked, his own shock momentarily forgotten, replaced by a surge of concern. "You look like you've just seen a ghost."

"No," she whispered, her voice a halting, broken thing. "No, no, no, no, no. This can't be. This can't be real."

"What are you talking about?" he asked, his own fear returning, amplified by hers. "What can't be real?"

She took a deep, shuddering breath, her gaze fixed on the phone in his hand as if it were a venomous snake. "You know my uncle," she began, her voice trembling. "Rafael? Rafael Forlan?"

"Yeah, you talk about him all the time," Oliver said, a cold, sickening dread beginning to dawn. "He's the one who first told you about bitcoin." He watched her face, at the raw, undisguised terror in her eyes, and knew, with a sudden, gut-wrenching certainty, that his life was about to change all over again.

"Yeah," she said, her voice shaking, "We're really close. He was like a father to me after mine left. He still lives in Montevideo, but we always talk on the phone. Or, we used to." She reached across the table and held his hand, her own hand cold and trembling. "For the last five or six months, something's been off. We haven't spoken. Just emails. Every time we planned a call, something would come up."

"What is it, Daniela?" he asked, his own voice a low, urgent whisper.

"Two months ago," she continued, her eyes locked on his, "He sent me a very strange email. He made me promise to keep it a secret."

"Are you sure you want to tell me?" Oliver asked gently.

"Yes," she said, her voice gaining a sliver of resolve. "Because he gave me one condition to break the secret. And it just happened." She looked down at the phone, at the glowing, cryptic message from the timechain. "He said that at some point, I would hear the exact line, 'Obelisk, 18 July. It has happened.' And if I did," she took a shaky breath, "I was supposed to reply with, 'Yes, let us meet there and then at 10 p.m.'"

The words hung in the air, a perfect, impossible echo of the mystery that had just erupted in his own life. "Meet where?" Oliver asked, his mind reeling. "And when? And who?"

"I have no idea," she said, a look of pure, helpless confusion on her face. "I asked him, but he said he couldn't talk about it anymore. He just said that when the time comes, it will all become clear."

Oliver sank back into his chair, a wave of abject despair washing over him. He threw his hands up in disgust. "Well, this is just great," he said, the words a bitter, ironic laugh. "Just yesterday, I thought I had finally wrapped things up after ten months of this craziness. And now, not even twenty-four hours later, I find out there are two more paintings, and the wallet I spent months finding is being controlled by someone else who just took twenty-four bitcoin and left this … this impossible riddle!"

Daniela, however, seemed to have found a strange new calm. "Wow," she said, a slow, relieved smile spreading across her face. "It actually feels good to get that off my chest. I'd been holding on to that secret for two months, not knowing what it was about. I'm so glad I do now."

"Wait, you know now?" Oliver asked.

She laughed, a genuine, beautiful sound in the midst of the chaos. "Oh no, I don't actually know what it means. But I know what it was *for*. And that gives us our next step." She looked at him, her eyes shining with a new, shared purpose. "Our next mystery, I guess."

Just then, the proprietor returned, a new bottle of wine in his hand, his timing impeccable. "For the birthday boy," he announced with a grand flourish, "A special treat. A 2005 Barolo. A fantastic vintage."

"Oh, nice," Oliver said as their glasses were filled. "Is this on the house?"

The proprietor laughed. "Of course not. You have to pay for it," he said, winking. "It's a special treat because I got it for you from a hidden section of our second list. Even our VIPs don't always get this one."

Oliver just shrugged, a weary, ironic smile on his face as he looked at Daniela. "Well," he said, "I suppose I can afford this now. On paper, at least."

Daniela raised her glass, the deep red of the Barolo catching the candlelight. "To twenty-four magnificent years on this planet so far," she said, her voice full of a warmth and a strength that seemed to push back against all the uncertainty. "May the next twenty-four be just as full of mystery and adventure."

Their glasses clinked, a small, clear note in the warm, bustling restaurant. Oliver looked at her, at the incredible, impossible woman who had just been pulled into the center of his secret world, and he felt an unshakeable sense of hope.

"To the next adventure," he said.

The Notepad

i) violin ii) toddler iii) alley iv) shoulder v) educate vi) rookie vii) oval viii) below ix) punch x) certain xi) cover xii) agree xiii) coast xiv) suggest xv) boring xvi) tissue xvii) good xviii) sausage xix) cute xx) club xxi) runway xxii) pluck xxiii) satoshi xxiv) home

EPILOGUE

768776 (December 24)

A handsome, well-dressed man in his fifties strolled through the December evening twilight, a warm summer breeze gently caressing his elegant, gray-flecked hair. He walked along a dusty side road, a quiet, observant figure in a world that seemed to move at a slower, more deliberate pace.

He passed a small, simple house, and outside, a middle-aged woman was taking clothes from a line and placing them neatly folded inside a wicker basket by her feet, her movements practiced and weary. She turned as she heard his footsteps on the gravel, and her face, tired from a long day, registered a look of absolute panic.

"Señor Rafael," she said, her voice a hushed whisper of disbelief. "What are you doing in this part of town?"

"Ah, Matilda," the man replied, his voice a smooth, calm melody that seemed at odds with the dusty, humble surroundings. "I didn't expect to see you on my evening walk. Is this where you live?"

"Yes, señor, this is my home," she said, a new, anxious energy in her voice. "I am so sorry about not showing up for cleaning. My son has been sick. I will be back next week, I promise. I told the agency."

"Yes, of course," Señor Rafael said, his tone kind and reassuring. "They sent a temporary replacement. Take your time. I hope your son is feeling better."

"Yes, he is. Thank you, señor," she said, the relief washing over her. "So, you didn't come looking for me?"

"Of course not. Don't be silly, Matilda," he said with a gentle smile. "It is Christmas Eve, and I thought I would take a different route. The summer has been beautiful so far. I had no idea you lived here."

Matilda relaxed, a look of simple, proprietary pride on her face. "It is a nice part of town, señor, even if it has a bad reputation. It's quite safe. Look ..." she pointed toward the main town, a glittering carpet of lights in the valley below. "From here, you can even see the Obelisk."

Señor Rafael turned, his gaze following her outstretched hand. "You're right," he said, his voice a low, appreciative murmur. "It is quite the view."

"And if you walk a few feet this way," she continued, her excitement growing, "You can even see part of Avenida 18 de Julio behind the Obelisk."

He walked to where she was pointing and looked out at the city, at the two landmarks that now formed a secret, cryptic map in the twilight. "Indeed," he said softly. "You should cherish this view. It is better than the one I have from my window. Very well, Matilda. It was nice seeing you." He started to walk away.

"Señor Rafael," she called out after him, a new, hesitant note in her voice. "I've been meaning to ask you something for a few months, but I felt too shy."

He stopped and turned back, his smile encouraging. "Go ahead, it's okay."

"It seems ... your accent has changed recently," she said, the question a small, brave act of observation. "You sound like someone from Spain these days. And you look ... a little different. Am I imagining it?"

Señor Rafael just smiled, a slow, serene, and utterly unreadable expression on his handsome face. "What can I say, Matilda?" he said, his voice a soft, final, and deeply unsettling melody that seemed to hang in the warm summer air. "I am exactly who I was back then, and now, I am exactly who I need to be."

He turned and continued his pleasant summer walk, leaving Matilda alone in the gathering dusk to contemplate his strange, impossible answer. Then she shrugged, a woman with more immediate and practical concerns, and returned to folding her laundry.

END OF BOOK ONE

www.ingramcontent.com/pod-product-compliance
Lightning Source LLC
Chambersburg PA
CBHW061043310726
48969CB00004B/1068